CRITICAL ACCL
HAMISH

THE CASEBOOKS OF HAMISH MACBETH

DEATH OF A GOSSIP
DEATH OF A CAD

M. C. Beaton

BANTAM BOOKS
TORONTO · NEW YORK · LONDON · SYDNEY · AUCKLAND

DEATH OF A GOSSIP & DEATH OF A CAD
A BANTAM BOOK : 0 553 50664 1

First publication in Great Britain

PRINTING HISTORY
Bantam edition of *Death of a Gossip* published 1994
Bantam edition of *Death of a Cad* published 1995
Reissued as omnibus edition 1998

Bantam Books are published by Transworld Publishers Ltd,
61–63 Uxbridge Road, London W5 5SA,
in Australia by Transworld Publishers (Australia) Pty Ltd,
15–25 Helles Avenue, Moorebank, NSW 2170,
and in New Zealand by Transworld Publishers (NZ) Ltd,
3 William Pickering Drive, Albany, Auckland.

Printed and bound in Great Britain by
Cox & Wyman Ltd, Reading, Berkshire.

In memory of Fleet Street days –
for my very dear friend,
Rita Marshall,
with love

DEATH OF A GOSSIP

CAST OF CHARACTERS

(in order of appearance)

John Cartwright: Owner of the Lochdubh School of Casting: Salmon and Trout Fishing

Heather Cartwright: His wife, and joint owner of the school

Marvin Roth: American businessman and budding congressman

Amy Roth: His wife

Lady Jane Winters: Society widow

Jeremy Blythe: Barrister from London

Alice Wilson: Secretary from London

Charlie Baxter: Twelve-year-old child from Manchester

Major Peter Frame: Ex-army, expert angler

Daphne Gore: Debutante from Oxford

Hamish Macbeth: Village constable

Priscilla Halburton-Smythe: Local landowner's daughter

Detective Chief Inspector Blair: Head of Strathbane CID

Detectives Jimmy Anderson and Harry McNab: Blair's assistants

John Harrington: Courting Priscilla Halburton-Smythe

Colonel and Mrs Halburton-Smythe: Priscilla's parents

Mr Johnson: Hotel manager

Angus MacGregor: Poacher

You came and quacked beside me in the wood,
You said: 'The view from here is very good.'
You said: 'It's nice to be alone a bit.'
And: 'How the days are drawing out,' you said.
By God – I wish – I wish that you were dead.

– RUPERT BROOKE

DAY ONE

Angling: incessant expectation, and
perpetual disappointment.
– ARTHUR YOUNG

'I hate the start of the week,' said John Cartwright fretfully. 'Beginning with a new group. It's rather like going on stage. Then I always feel I have to apologize for being *English*. People who travel up here to the wilds of Scotland expect to be instructed by some great hairy Rob Roy, making jokes about saxpence and saying it's a braw bricht moonlicht nicht and lang may your lum reek and ghastly things like that.'

'Don't chatter,' said his wife, Heather, placidly. 'It always works out all right. We've been running this fishing school for three years and haven't had a dissatisfied customer yet.'

She looked at her husband with affection. John Cartwright was small, thin, wiry, and nervous. He had sandy, wispy hair and rather prominent pale blue eyes. Heather had been one of his first pupils at the Lochdubh School of Casting: Salmon and Trout Fishing.

He had been seduced by the sight of her deft back cast and had only got around to discovering the other pleasures of her anatomy after they were married.

Heather was believed to be the better angler, although she tactfully hid her greater skill behind a pleasant

11

motherly manner. Despite their vastly different temperaments, both Heather and John were dedicated, fanatical anglers.

Fishing was their hobby, their work, their obsession. Every week during the summer a new class would arrive at the Lochdubh Hotel. Rarely did they have a complete set of amateurs; experienced fishermen often joined the class, since they could fish excellent waters for reasonable rates. John would take care of the experts while Heather would mother the rank amateurs.

The class never consisted of more than ten. This week they had received two last-minute cancellations and so were expecting only eight.

'Now,' muttered John, picking up a piece of paper, 'I gather they all checked in at the hotel last night. There's an American couple from New York, Mr and Mrs Roth; a Lady Winters, widow of some Labour peer; Jeremy Blythe from London; Alice Wilson, also from London; Charlie Baxter, a twelve-year-old from Manchester – the kid's not living at the hotel, he's staying with an aunt in the village; Major Peter Frame. Oh dear, we had the galloping major before. These men who hang on to their army titles don't seem able to adapt to civilian life. Then there's Daphne Gore from Oxford. I'll send the major off on his own as soon as possible. Perhaps you'd better look after the kid.'

John Cartwright glanced out of the hotel window and scowled. 'Here comes our scrounging village constable. I told the hotel I needed coffee for eight people. But Hamish will just sit there like a dog until I give him some. Better phone down and tell them to set out an extra cup.

'What that policeman needs is a good, juicy murder. Keep him off our hands. All he's got to do all day is mooch around the village getting under everyone's feet.

12

Jimmy, the water bailiff, told me the other day he thinks Hamish Macbeth *poaches*.'

'I doubt it,' said Heather. 'He's too lazy. He ought to get married. He must be all of thirty-five at least. Most of the girls in the village have broken their hearts over him at one time or another. I can't see the attraction.'

She joined her husband at the window, and he put an arm around her plump shoulders. Hamish, Lochdubh's village constable, was strolling along the pier that lay outside the hotel, his hat pushed on the back of his head, and his hands in his pockets. He was very tall and thin and gawky. His uniform hung on his lanky frame, showing an expanse of bony wrist where the sleeves did not reach far enough and a length of woolly Argyll sock above large regulation boots. He removed his peaked hat and scratched his fiery red hair. Then he reached inside his tunic and thoughtfully scratched one armpit.

The smell of hot coffee wafted up from the hotel lounge below the Cartwrights' bedroom window. It obviously reached the nostrils of the policeman, for Hamish suddenly sniffed the air like a dog and then started to lope eagerly towards the hotel.

The Lochdubh Hotel had been built in the last century by the Duke of Anstey as one of his many country residences. It was battlemented and turreted like a castle. It had formal gardens at the back and the clear, limpid waters of Lochdubh at the front. It had stags' heads in the lounge, armoury in the hall, peat fires, and one of the best chefs in Scotland. Prices were astronomical, but the tourists came in droves, partly because the main road ended abruptly in front of the hotel, making it the only haven in a wilderness of barren moorland and towering mountains.

The village of Lochdubh nestled at the foot of two great peaks called the Two Sisters. It was a huddle of houses built in the eighteenth century to promote the fishing industry in the Highlands. The population had been declining steadily ever since.

There was a general store-cum-post office, a bakery, a craft shop, and four churches, each with a congregation of about five.

The police station was one of the few modern buildings. The old police station had been a sort of damp hut. Constable Hamish Macbeth had arrived to take up his duties a year before the fishing school was established. No-one knew quite how he had managed it, but, in no time at all, he had a trim new house built for himself with a modern office adjoining it with one cell. The former policeman had made his rounds on a bicycle. Constable Macbeth had prised a brand-new Morris out of the authorities. He kept chickens and geese and a large, slavering guard dog of indeterminate breed called Towser.

Lochdubh was situated in the far northwest of Scotland. In winter it went into a long hibernation. In summer, the tourists brought it alive. The tourists were mostly English and were treated by the locals with outward Highland courtesy and inner Highland hate.

John Cartwright had been struggling for a month to make the fishing school pay when he had met Heather. It was Heather who had taken over the bookkeeping and put advertisements in the glossy magazines. It was Heather who had trebled John's low fees, pointing out shrewdly that people would pay up if they thought they were getting something exclusive and the rates were still reasonable considering the excellent salmon rivers they were allowed to fish. It was Heather who had made the whole thing work. She was plump, grey-haired, and motherly. Her marriage to John Cartwright was her second. John often thought he would never know what went on under his wife's placid brow, but he loved her as much as he loved angling, and sometimes, even uneasily, thought that the school would not have survived without her, although most of the time he prided himself on his business acumen and his wife comfortably did all she could to foster this belief.

He tugged on his old fishing jacket with its many pockets, picked up his notes, and looked nervously at his wife.

'Don't you think we should . . . well, meet them together?'

'You run along, dear,' said Heather. 'Give me a shout when you're ready to show them the knots. Once you get started talking, you'll forget to be nervous.'

John gave her a swift kiss on the cheek and made his way along to the main staircase. He prayed they would be a jolly crowd. At least he knew the major, although that was more a case of being comfortable with the evil he knew.

He pushed open the lounge door and blinked nervously at the eight people who were standing around eyeing each other warily. A bad sign. Usually by the time he put in his appearance, they had all introduced themselves.

Constable Hamish Macbeth was sitting in an armchair at the window, studying the *Daily Telegraph* crossword and whistling through his teeth in an irritating way.

John took a deep breath. Lights, camera, action. He was on.

'I think the first thing to do is to get acquainted,' he said, smiling nervously at the silent group. 'My name is John Cartwright, and I am your instructor. We find things go easier if we all get on a first-name basis. Now, who would like to start?'

15

'Start what?' demanded a heavyset woman imperiously.

'Hah, hah. Well, start introducing themselves.'

'I'll be first,' said an American voice. 'My name is Marvin Roth, and this is my wife, Amy.'

'I'm Daphne Gore,' drawled a tall blonde, studying her fingernails.

'Jeremy Blythe.' A handsome, stocky young man with a cheerful face, fair curly hair, and bright blue eyes.

'Charlie Baxter.' The twelve-year-old. Chubby, beautiful skin, mop of black curls, remarkably cold and assessing eyes in one so young.

'Well, you know me. Major Peter Frame. Just call me Major. Everyone does.' Small grey moustache in a thin, lined face; weak, petulant mouth; brand-new fishing clothes.

'Alice Wilson.' Pretty, wholesome-looking girl; slight Liverpool accent; wrong clothes.

'I am Lady Jane Winters. You may call me Lady Jane. *Everyone* does.' The heavyset woman. Heavy bust encased in silk blouse, heavy thighs bulging in knee breeches, fat calves in lovat wool stockings. Heavy fat face with large, heavy-lidded blue eyes. Small, sharp beak of a nose. Disappointed mouth.

'Now we've all got to know each other's names, we'll have some coffee,' said John brightly.

Hamish uncoiled himself from the armchair and slouched forward.

Lady Jane eyed his approach with disfavour.

'Does the village constable take fishing lessons as well?' she demanded. Her voice was high and loud with a peculiarly grating edge to it.

'No, Mr Macbeth often joins us on the first day for coffee.'

'Why?' Lady Jane was standing with her hands on her

16

hips between Hamish and the coffee table. The police-man craned his neck and looked over her fat shoulder at the coffee pot.

'Well,' said John crossly, wishing Hamish would speak for himself. 'We all like a cup of coffee and . . .'

'I do not pay taxes to entertain public servants,' said Lady Jane. 'Go about your business, Constable.'

The policeman gazed down at her with a look of amiable stupidity in his hazel eyes. He made a move to step around her. Lady Jane blocked his path.

'Do you take your coffee regular, Officer?' asked Marvin Roth. He was a tall, pear-shaped man with a domed bald head and thick horn-rimmed glasses. He looked rather like the wealthy upper-eastside Ameri-cans portrayed in some *New Yorker* cartoons.

Hamish broke into speech for the first time. 'I mostly take tea,' he said in a soft Highland voice. 'But I aye take the coffee when I get the chance.'

'He means, do you take milk and sugar?' interposed John Cartwright, who had become used to translating Americanisms.

'Yes, thank you, sir,' said Hamish. Lady Jane began to puff with outrage as Marvin poured a cup of coffee and handed it over her shoulder to the constable. Alice Wilson let out a nervous giggle and put her hand over her mouth to stifle it. Lady Jane gave her shoulders a massive shrug and sent the cup of coffee flying.

There was an awkward silence. Hamish picked the cup from the floor and looked at it thoughtfully. He looked slowly and steadily at Lady Jane, who glared back at him triumphantly.

'Oh, *pullease* give the policeman his coffee,' sighed Amy Roth. She was a well-preserved blonde with large, cow-like eyes, a heavy soft bosom, and surprisingly tough and wiry tennis-playing wrists.

'No,' said Lady Jane stubbornly while John Cartwright flapped his notes and prayed for deliverance. Why wouldn't Hamish just *go*?

Lady Jane turned her back on Hamish and stared at Marvin as if defying him to pour any more coffee. Alice Wilson watched miserably. Why had she come on this awful holiday? It was costing so much, much more than she could afford.

But as she watched, she saw to her amazement the policeman had taken a sizeable chunk of Lady Jane's tightly clad bottom between thumb and forefinger and was giving it a hearty pinch.

'You pinched my bum!' screamed Lady Jane.

'Och, no,' said the policeman equably, moving past the outraged lady and pouring himself another cup of coffee. 'It will be them Hielan midges. Teeth on them like the pterodactyls.'

He ambled back to his armchair by the window and sat down, nursing his coffee cup.

'I shall write to that man's superior officer,' muttered Lady Jane. 'Is anyone going to pour?'

'I reckon we'll just help ourselves, honey,' said Amy Roth sweetly.

Seeing that there was going to be no pleasant chatter over the cups, John Cartwright decided to begin his lecture.

Warming to his subject as he always did, he told them of the waters they would fish, of the habits of the elusive salmon, of the dos and don'ts, and then he handed around small plastic packets of thin transparent nylon cord.

He was about to call Heather down to tell her it was time to show the class how to tie a leader, when he suddenly felt he could not bear to see his wife humiliated by the terrible Lady Jane. She had been remarkably

18

quiet during his lecture, but he felt sure she was only getting her second wind. He decided to go ahead on his own.

'I am now going to tell you how to tie a leader,' he began.

'What on earth's a leader?' snapped Lady Jane.

'A leader,' explained John, 'is the thin, tapering piece of nylon which you attach to your line. A properly tapered leader, properly cast, deposits the fly tightly on the surface. The butt section of the leader, which is attached to the line, is only a bit less in diameter than the line. The next section is a little lighter, and so on down to the tippet. Now you must learn to tie these sections of leader together to form the tapering whole. The knot we use for this is called a blood knot. If you haven't tied this thin nylon before, you'll find it very difficult. So I'll pass around lengths of string for you to practise on.'

'I saw some of these leader things already tapered in a fishing shop,' said Lady Jane crossly. 'So why do we have to waste a perfectly good morning sitting indoors tying knots like a lot of Boy Scouts?'

Heather's calm voice sounded from the doorway, and John heaved a sigh of relief.

'I am Heather Cartwright. Good morning, everybody. You were asking about leaders.

'Commercially tied leaders are obtainable in knotless forms,' said Heather, advancing into the room. 'You can buy them in lengths of seven and a half to twelve feet. But you will find the leader often gets broken above the tippet and so you will have to learn to tie it anyway. Now, watch closely and I'll show you how to do it. You can go off and fish the Marag if you want, Major,' added Heather. 'No need for you to sit through all this again.'

'No experts in fly fishing,' said the major heartily. 'Always something to learn. I'll stay for a bit.'

Alice Wilson wrestled with the knot. She would get one side of it right only to discover that the other side had miraculously unravelled itself.

The child, Charlie, was neatly tying knots as if he had fallen out of his cradle doing so. 'Can you help me?' she whispered. 'You're awfully good.'

'No, I think that's cheating,' said the child severely. 'If you don't do it yourself, you'll never learn.'

Alice blushed miserably. 'I'll show you,' said a pleasant voice on her other side. Alice found Jeremy Blythe surveying her sympathetically. He took the string from her and began to demonstrate.

After the class had been struggling for several minutes, Heather said, 'Have your leaders knotted by the time we set out tomorrow. Now if you will all go to your rooms and change, we'll meet back here in half an hour. John will take you up to the Marag and show you how to cast.'

'Well, see you in half an hour,' said Jeremy cheerfully. 'Your name's Alice, isn't it?'

Alice nodded shyly. 'And mine's Daphne,' said a mocking voice at Jeremy's elbow, 'or had you forgotten?'

'How could I?' said Jeremy. 'We travelled up together on the same awful train.'

They walked off arm in arm, and Alice felt even more miserable. For a moment she had hoped she would have a friend in Jeremy. But that fearfully sophisticated Daphne had quite obviously staked a claim on his attentions.

Lady Jane surveyed Alice's powder-blue Orlon trouser suit with pale, disapproving eyes. 'I hope you've brought something suitable to wear,' she said nastily. 'You'll frighten the fish in that outfit.'

Alice walked hurriedly away, not able to think of a suitable retort. Of course, she had thought of plenty by the time she reached the privacy of her bedroom, but then, that was always the way.

She looked at her reflection in the long glass in her hotel bedroom. The trouser suit had looked so bright and smart in London. Now it looked tawdry and cheap.

The stupid things one did for love, thought Alice miserably as she pulled out an old pair of corduroy trousers, an army sweater and Wellington boots and prepared to change her clothes.

For Alice was secretary to Mr Thomas Patterson-James. Mr Patterson-James was chief accountant of Baxter and Berry, exporters and importers. He was forty-four, dark, and handsome – and married. And Alice loved him passionately.

He would tease her and ruffle her hair and call her 'a little suburban miss,' and Alice would smile adoringly back and wish she could become smart and fashionable.

Mr Patterson-James often let fall hints that his marriage was not a happy one. He had sighed over taking his annual vacation in Scotland but explained it was the done thing.

Everyone who was anyone, Alice gathered, went to Scotland in August to kill things. If you weren't slaughtering grouse, you were gaffing salmon.

So Alice had read an article about the fishing school in *The Field* and had promptly decided to go. She imagined the startled admiration on her boss's face when she casually described landing a twenty-pounder after a brutal fight.

Alice was nineteen years of age. She had fluffy fine brown hair and wide-spaced brown eyes. Her slim, almost boyish figure was her private despair.

She had once seen Mr Patterson-James arm in arm with a busty blonde and wondered if the blonde was Mrs Patterson-James.

It was not like being in the British Isles at all, thought Alice, looking out at the sun sparkling on the loch. The village was so tiny and the tracts of heather-covered moorland and weird twisted mountains so savage and primitive and vast.

Perhaps she would give it one more day and then go home. Would she get a refund? Alice's timid soul quailed at the idea of asking for money back. Surely only very common people did that.

Mr Patterson-James was always describing people as common.

Suddenly she heard raised voices from the terrace below. Then loud and clear she heard Mr Marvin Roth say savagely, 'If she doesn't shut that goddam mouth of hers, I'll shut it for her.'

There was the sound of a slamming door and then silence.

Alice sat down on the bed, one leg in her trousers and one out. Her ideas of American men had been pretty much based on the works of P G Wodehouse. Men who looked like Marvin were supposed to be sweet and deferential to their wives, although they might belong to the class of Sing-Sing '45. Was everyone on this holiday going to be nasty? And whose mouth was going to be shut? Lady Jane's?

Jeremy Blythe seemed sweet. But the Daphnes of this world were always waiting around the corner to take away the nice men. Did Mrs Patterson-James look like Daphne?

Alice gloomily surveyed her appearance in the glass when she had finished dressing. The corduroys fitted her slim hips snugly, and the bulky army sweater hid the

deficiency of her bosom. Her Wellington boots were ...
well, just Wellington boots.

Carefully setting a brand-new fishing hat of brown
wool on top of her fluffy brown hair, Alice stuck her
tongue out at her reflection and went out of her room
and down the stairs, muttering, 'I won't stay if I can't
stand it.'

To her surprise, everyone was dressed much the same
as she was, with the exception of Lady Jane, who had
simply changed her brogues for Wellingtons and was
still wearing the breeches and blouse she had worn at
the morning lecture.

'We'll all walk up to the Marag,' said John Cartwright.
'Heather will go ahead in the station wagon with the
rods and packed lunches.'

Loch Marag, or the Marag as it was called by the
locals, was John's favorite training ground. It was a
circular loch surrounded by pretty sylvan woodland. At
one end it flowed out and down to the sea loch of
Lochdubh in a series of waterfalls. It was amply stocked
with trout and a fair number of salmon.

The major took himself cheerfully off to fish in the
pool above the waterfall while the rest of the class
gathered with their newly acquired rods at the shallow
side of the loch to await instruction. Instead of a hook,
a small piece of cotton wool was placed on the end of
each leader.

It was then that the class discovered that Lady Jane
was not only rude and aggressive, she was also incredibly
clumsy.

Although the loch was only a short walk from the
hotel, she had insisted on bringing her car and parking
it at the edge of the loch. She backed it off the road on
to the grass and right over the pile of packed lunches.

She refused to listen to John's careful instructions and

23

whipped her line savagely back and forth, finally winding it around Marvin Roth's neck and nearly strangling him. She then strode into the water, failing to see small Charlie Baxter and sending him flying face down in the mud.

Charlie burst into tears and kicked Lady Jane in the shins before Heather could scoop him up and drag him off.

'I'll kill her,' muttered John. 'She's ruining the holiday for everyone.'

'Now, now,' said Heather. 'I'll deal with her while you look after the others.'

Alice listened carefully as John Cartwright's now slightly shaking voice repeated the instructions.

'With the line in front of you, take a foot or so of the line from the reel with your left hand. Raise the rod, holding the wrist at a slight down slant. Bring the line off the water with a smooth motion but with enough power to send it behind you, stopping the rod at the twelve o'clock position. Your left hand holding the line pulls downwards. When the line has straightened out behind you, bring the rod forward smartly. As the line comes forward, follow through to the ten o'clock position, letting the line fall gently to the water. Oh, *very* good, Alice.'

Alice flushed with pleasure. Heather had said something to Lady Jane, and Lady Jane had stalked off. Without her overbearing presence, the day seemed to take on light and colour. Heather shouted she was returning to the hotel to bring back more packed lunches.

A buzzard sailed above in the light blue sky. Enormous clumps of purple heather studied their reflections in the mirror surface of the loch. The peaty water danced as Alice waded dreamily in the red and gold shallows, which sparkled and glittered like marcasite. She cast, and cast, and cast again until her arms ached. Heather came back with new lunches, and they all gathered around the station wagon, with the exception of Lady Jane and the major.

Suddenly, it *was* a holiday. A damp and scrubbed Charlie had been brought back by Heather. He sat with his back against the station-wagon wheel contentedly munching a sandwich.

All at once he said in his clear treble, 'That is quite a frightful woman, you know.'

No-one said, 'Who?'

Although no-one added his criticism to Charlie's, they were all bonded together in a common resentment against Lady Jane and an equally common determination that she was not going to spoil things.

'Oh, there's Constable Macbeth,' said Alice.

The lanky figure of the policeman had materialized behind the group.

'These sandwiches look very good,' he said, studying the sky.

'Help yourself,' said Heather, rather crossly. 'Packed lunches are not all that expensive, Mr Macbeth.'

'Is that a fact,' said the constable pleasantly. 'I'm right glad to hear it. I would not want to be taking away food that cost a lot.'

To Alice's amusement, he produced a small collapsible plastic cup from the inside of his tunic and held it out to Heather, who muttered something under her breath as she filled it up with tea.

'You obviously don't get much crime in this area, Officer,' said Daphne caustically.

'I wouldnae say that,' said Hamish between bites of ham sandwich. 'People are awfy wicked. The drunkenness on a Saturday night is a fair disgrace.'

25

'Have you made any major arrests?' pursued Daphne, catching Jeremy Blythe's eye and inviting him to share in the baiting of Hamish.

'No, I hivnae bagged any majors. A few sodjers sometimes.'

Amy Roth let out a trill of laughter, and Daphne said crossly to Hamish, 'Are you being deliberately stupid?'

Hamish looked horrified. 'I would no more dream of being deliberately stupid, miss, than you yourself would dream of being deliberately bitchy.'

'Fun's over,' whispered Jeremy to Alice. 'Back comes Lady Jane.'

She came crashing through the undergrowth. Her broad face was flushed, and she had a scratch down one cheek. But her eyes held a triumphant, satisfied gleam.

John Cartwright hurriedly began to make arrangements to move his school on to further fishing grounds for the afternoon. Boxes of hooks were distributed. More knots demonstrated – a towel knot and a figure of eight.

This time even Lady Jane struggled away in silence to master the slippery nylon. The fever of catching fish was upon the little party.

'Now,' said Heather, 'we'll issue you each with knotted leaders, but have your own leaders knotted and ready for tomorrow morning. We have the Anstey River for the afternoon. Carry this fishing permit – I'll give you each one – in your pockets in case you are stopped by the water bailiffs. Marvin and Amy, I believe you have done some fly fishing in the States. We'll start you off on the upper beats. We suggest you keep moving. Never fish in one spot for too long. If you come back to the hotel before we set out, then we'll issue you with waders. John and I will show each of you what to do as soon as we're on the river. We'll need to take the cars.

26

John and I will take Alice and Charlie. Daphne can go with Jeremy, and I believe the rest of you have your own cars. Has anyone seen the major?'

Lady Jane spoke up. 'He was fishing about on the other side of the loch, pretending to be an angler. At least it makes a change from pretending to be an officer and a gentleman.'

'The rest of you go on to the hotel,' said John hurriedly. 'I'll go and look for the major.'

'I wish you were coming with me,' said Jeremy to Alice.

She looked at him in surprise. She had been so obsessed with Mr Patterson-James that she had never really stopped to think any other man might find her attractive.

As Jeremy moved off with Daphne, Alice studied him covertly. He really was a very attractive man. His voice was pleasant and slightly husky. He did not seem to have to strangle and chew his words as Mr Patterson-James did. Her heart gave a little lift, and she unconsciously smiled at Jeremy's retreating back.

'No use,' said Lady Jane, appearing at Alice's elbow. 'He's one of the Somerset Blythes. Quite above your touch, wouldn't you say? Daphne's more his sort.'

Alice was consumed by such a wave of bitter hatred that she thought she would suffocate. 'Fook off!' she said, in a broad Liverpool accent.

'Attagirl!' remarked Marvin cheerfully.

Lady Jane muttered something. Alice thought she said, 'I'll make you sorry you said that,' but she must have been imagining things.

Alice was prepared to find herself cut off from Jeremy for the rest of the day. But when they reached the river Anstey, which broadened out at one part into a large loch, Heather arranged that Jeremy and Alice should

27

take out the rowing boat and fish from there while the rest were distributed up and down the banks several miles apart.

Before she allowed Alice to go out in the boat, Heather gave her a gruelling half-hour lesson in casting. Alice caught her hat, caught the bushes behind, wrapped her leader around the branches of a tree, and then quite suddenly found she had mastered the knack of it.

'Don't keep worrying about all that line racing out behind you,' said Heather. 'Just concentrate on what you've been told. Now you're ready to go. Jeremy, you've obviously done this before.'

'Yes, but very clumsily,' said Jeremy.

'Take the boat and row upstream and then drift slowly back down,' said Heather. 'You may not catch a salmon but you should get some trout.'

He rowed them swiftly up the stream while Alice nervously held her rod upright and wondered what on earth she would do if she caught a fish. The day was warm and sunny, and she felt laden down with equipment. Her long green waders were clumsy and heavy. She had a fishing knife in one pocket and mosquito repellent in the other, since clouds of Scottish midges were apt to descend towards dusk.

She had a fishing net hanging from a string around her neck, and from another string a pair of small sharp scissors.

On top of her wool fishing hat, kept back from her face by the thin brim, was a sort of beekeeper mosquito net which could be pulled down over her face if the flies got too bad.

Jeremy rested the oars. 'Pooh, it's hot. Let's take some clothes off.'

Alice blushed painfully. Of course he meant they should remove some of their outer woollens, but

28

Alice was at an age when everything seemed to sound sexy. She wondered feverishly whether she had a dirty mind.

Thank goodness she had had the foresight to put a thin cotton blouse under her army sweater. Alice took off her hat and then her sweater after unslinging the fishing net and laying it in the bottom of the boat. She kept her scissors around her neck. Heather had been most insistent that they keep a pair of scissors handy for cutting lines and snipping free hooks.

'Well,' said Jeremy, 'here goes!'

The water was very still and golden in the sun. A hot smell of pine drifted on the air mixed with the smell of wild thyme. Alice felt herself gripped by a desire to catch something – *anything*.

She cast and cast again until her arms ached. And then . . .

'I've got something,' she whispered. 'It's a salmon. It feels enormous.'

Jeremy quickly reeled in his line and picked up his net. 'Don't reel in too fast,' he said. He picked up the oars and moved the boat gently. Alice's rod began to bend.

'Reel in a bit more,' he said.

'Oh, Jeremy,' said Alice, pink with excitement, 'what am I going to do?'

'Take it easy . . . easy.'

Alice could not wait. She reeled in frantically. Suddenly the line came clear, and she jerked it out of the water.

On the end of her hook dangled a long piece of green weed.

'And I thought I had a twenty-pound salmon,' mourned Alice. 'Do you know, Jeremy, I'm still shaking with excitement. Do you think I'm very primitive, really?

I mean, I wouldn't normally hurt a fly, and there I was, ready to kill anything that came up on the end of that hook.'

'I don't think you're all that quiet and timid,' said Jeremy, casting again. 'Only look at the way you put down Lady Jane. I heard all about that.'

'I can't believe I did that,' said Alice thoughtfully. 'I've never used that sort of language to anyone in my life. But it was all so beautiful when we were having lunch, I wanted it to go on for ever. Then suddenly she was there, bitching and making trouble. She drops hints, you know. Almost as if she had checked up on us all before she came. She . . . she told me you belonged to the Somerset Blythes.' Alice bit her lip. She had been on the point of telling him the rest.

'She did, did she? Probably one of these women with little else to do with their time. I hope she doesn't make life too hard for the village constable. She probably will complain to his superiors.'

'Poor Hamish.'

'I think Hamish is well able to take care of himself. And what policeman, do you think, would rush in to take his place? Hardly the spot for an ambitious man.'

'What do you do for a living?' asked Alice.

'I'm a barrister.'

Alice felt a pang of disappointment. She had been secretly hoping he did something as undistinguished as she did.

'What do you do?' she heard Jeremy asking.

He was wearing a short-sleeved check shirt and a baggy pair of old flannels, but there was a polished air about him, an air of social ease and money. All at once Alice wanted to pretend she was someone different, someone more important.

'I'm chief accountant at Baxter and Berry in the City.' She gave a self-conscious laugh. 'An odd job for a woman.'

'Certainly for someone as young as yourself,' said Jeremy. 'I didn't think such a fuddy-duddy firm would be so go-ahead.'

'You know Baxter and Berry?' queried Alice nervously.

'I know old man Baxter,' said Jeremy easily. 'He's a friend of my father. I must tease him about his pretty chief accountant.'

Alice turned her face away. That's where telling lies got you. Futureless. Now she wouldn't dare ever see Jeremy again after this holiday.

'When I was your age, which was probably all of ten years ago,' said Jeremy gently, 'I told a perfectly smashing-looking girl that I was a jet pilot . . .'

'Oh, Jeremy,' said Alice miserably, 'I'm only the chief accountant's secretary.'

'Thank you for the compliment.' He grinned. 'It's a long time since anyone's tried to impress me.'

'You're not angry I lied to you?'

'No. Hey, I think you've caught something.'

'Probably weed.' Alice felt young and free and light-hearted. Mr Patterson-James's saturnine face swam around in her mind, faded and disappeared like Scotch mist.

She reeled in her line, amused at the tugs, thinking how like a fish floating weed felt.

There was a flash and sparkle in the peaty brown and gold water.

'A trout!' said Jeremy. He held out his net and brought the fish in.

'Too small,' he said, shaking his head. 'We've got to throw it back.'

'Don't hurt it!' cried Alice as he worked the fly free from the fish's mouth.

'No, it's gone back to Mum,' he said, throwing it in the water. 'What fly were you using?'

'A Kenny's Killer.'

He took out his box of fishing flies. 'Maybe I'll try one of those.'

A companionable silence settled between them. The light began to fade behind the jumbled, twisted crags of the Two Sisters. A little breeze sent ripples lazily fanning out over the loch.

And then out of the heather came the midges, those small Scottish mosquitoes. Alice's face was black with them. She screamed and clawed for her mosquito net while Jeremy rowed quickly for the shore.

'Quick – let's just bundle in the car and drive away from the beasts,' he said.

Alice scrambled into the bucket seat of something long and low. They shot off down the road, not stopping until they were well clear of the loch. Jeremy handed Alice a towel to wipe her face.

Alice smiled at him gratefully. 'What about Daphne? I'd forgotten all about her.'

'So had I.' Jeremy was shadowed by a stand of trees beside the car. He seemed to be watching her mouth. Alice's heart began to hammer.

'Did . . . did you buy this car in Scotland?' she asked. 'I mean, I thought you and Daphne came up by train.'

'We did. My father had been using the car. He knew I was coming up this way and so he left it in Inverness for me to collect.'

'You've known Daphne a long time?'

'No. Heather wrote to me to ask me if I would join up with Daphne. She had written to Heather saying she did not like to travel alone.'

He suddenly switched on the engine. Alice sat very quietly. Perhaps he might have kissed her if she hadn't kept on and on about stupid Daphne. Daphne was probably back at the hotel changing into some couture number for dinner. Damn Daphne.

'I never thought indecision was one of my failings,' said Jeremy, breaking the silence at last. 'I didn't want to spoil things by going too fast too soon.'

Alice was not quite sure if he meant he had wanted to kiss her and had changed his mind. She dared not ask him in case he should be embarrassed and say he was talking about fishing.

But he suddenly took one hand off the wheel and gave her own a quick squeeze.

Alice's heart soared. A huge owl sailed across the winding road. Down below them nestled the village of Lochdubh.

Busy little fishing boats chugged out to sea. The lights of the hotel dining room were reflected in the still waters of the loch. Down into the evening darkness of the valley they sped. Over the old humpbacked bridge which spanned the tumbling waterfalls of the river Marag. Along the waterfront, past the low white cottages of the village. Out in the loch, a pair of seals rolled and tumbled like two elderly Edwardian gentlemen.

Tears filled Alice's eyes, and she furtively dabbed them away. The beauty of the evening was too much. The beauty of money emanating from the leather smells of the long, low, expensive car and the faint tangy scent of Jeremy's aftershave seduced her senses. She wanted it all. She wanted to keep the evening for ever. Scenic beauty, male beauty, money beauty.

A picture of Lady Jane rose large in her mind's eye, blotting out the evening.

If she tries to spoil things for me, I'll kill her, thought Alice passionately.

And being very young and capable of violent mood swings, she then began to worry about what to wear for dinner.

When she entered the dining room an hour later, the rest of the fishing party, except for Lady Jane, Charlie, and the major, was already seated.

To her disappointment, the only available seat was at the other end of the table from Jeremy.

Jeremy was sitting next to Daphne and laughing at something she was saying.

Daphne was wearing a black chiffon cocktail gown slit to the waist so that it afforded the company tantalizing glimpses of two perfect breasts.

Long antique earrings hung in the shadow of the silky bell of her naturally blond hair. Her usually hard, high-cheek-boned face was softened by eye shadow and pink lipstick.

Jeremy was wearing a well-cut charcoal grey suit, a striped shirt, and a tie with one of those small hard knots. He wore a heavy, pale gold wrist watch.

Alice wished she had worn something different. All her clothes had looked cheap and squalid. At last she had settled for a pale pink cashmere sweater, a tailored skirt, and a row of Woolworth's pearls. She had persuaded herself in the privacy of her bedroom that she looked like a regular member of the county. Now she felt like a London typist trying ineffectually to look like a member of the county. The dining room was very warm.

Amy Roth was wearing a floating sort of chiffony thing in cool blues and greens. It left most of her back bare. At one point, Marvin slid his hand down his wife's back, and Amy wriggled her shoulders and giggled.

Heather was wearing a long gown that looked as if it had been made out of chintz upholstery, but she managed to look like a lady none the less, thought Alice gloomily. John Cartwright was cheerful and relaxed, obviously glad that the rigours of the first day were over.

The hotel had contributed several bottles of non-vintage Czechoslovakian champagne, their labels discreetly hidden by white napkins.

The food was delicious – poached salmon with a good hollandaise sauce. Everyone began to relax and become slightly tipsy.

Emboldened by the wine, Alice decided to forget about Jeremy and talk to the Roths. Marvin, it transpired, was a New Yorker born and bred, but Amy hailed from Augusta, Georgia. Marvin was her third husband, she told Alice, very much in the way a woman would describe an expensive gown that had been a good buy.

Marvin was quiet and polite and very deferential to his wife, the way Alice imagined American men should be. She began to wonder if she had really heard him shouting earlier in the day, but the Roths did seem to be the only Americans in the hotel.

The party grew noisier and jollier.

And then Major Peter Frame came stumbling in. His eyes were staring, and his hands were trembling. He clutched on to a chair back and looked wildly around the group.

'Where is that bitch?' he grated.

'If you mean Lady Jane,' said Heather, 'I really don't know. What on earth is the matter?'

'I'll tell you,' said the major with frightening intensity. 'I went back up to the Marag this evening, just above the falls. And I got one. A fifteen-pounder on the end of my line. It was a long battle, and I was resting my

35

fish and having a smoke when she comes blundering along like an ox. "Can I get past?" she says. "Your line's blocking the path." "I've got a big 'un on the end of that line," I says. "Don't be silly," says she. "I can't wait here all night. It's probably a rock," and before I could guess what she meant to do she whipped out her scissors *and cut my line.* She cut my line, the bloody bitch. The great, fat, stinking *cow.*

'I'll murder her. I'll kill that horrible woman. Kill! Kill! Kill!'

The major's voice had risen to a scream. Shocked silence fell on the dining room.

And into the middle of the silence sailed Lady Jane.

She was wearing a pink chiffon evening gown with a great many bows and tucks and flounces; the type of evening gown favoured by the Queen Mother, Barbara Cartland, and Danny La Rue.

'Well, we're all very glum,' she said, amused eyes glancing around the stricken group. 'Now, what can I do to brighten up the party?'

DAY TWO

Then as the earth's inner, narrow crooked lanes
Do purge salt waters' fretful tears away
– JOHN DONNE

Alice fumbled with a sleepy hand to silence the buzzing of her travel alarm and stretched and yawned. Her room was bathed in a grey light. She had forgotten to close the curtains before going to bed. Fat, greasy raindrops trickled down the window.

Somehow the horrible first dinner had miraculously turned out all right. Lady Jane had carried all before her. Before the major had had time to round on her, Lady Jane had apologized with such an overwhelming blast of sincerity and charm, with such subtle underlying appeals to his status as an officer and gentleman, that the major's angry colour had subsided, and, after that, people had begun to enjoy themselves. It was Lady Jane who had suggested that they should all get together in the lounge after dinner and help each other tie their leaders. It was Lady Jane who had kept the party laughing with a flow of faintly malicious anecdotes.

Alice remembered Jeremy's well-manicured hands brushing against her own and the smell of his aftershave as he had bent his head close to hers to help her tie knots. He had seemed to lose interest in Daphne.

There was to be another lecture that morning before

they went out fishing for the day. Alice got out of bed and went to the window and looked out. She could not even see the harbour. A thick mist blanketed everything and the rain thudded steadily down. Perhaps she would be lucky and would be teamed up with Jeremy again. Alice closed her eyes, imagining them both eating their packed lunches in the leather-smelling warmth of Jeremy's car with the steamed-up windows blocking out the rest of the world.

After a hasty shower, she took out her pink plastic rollers and tried to comb her hair into a more sophisticated style, but it fluffed out as usual.

To her dismay, they were not all to be seated at the same table for breakfast, and she was ushered to a table where the major was already eating sausages. Jeremy was with Daphne and Lady Jane at the other end of the dining room.

The major glanced at Alice and then rustled open a copy of *The Times* – last Friday's – and began to study the social column.

'Wet, isn't it?' volunteered Alice brightly, but the major only grunted in reply.

Probably doesn't think I'm worth talking to, thought Alice gloomily.

She rose and helped herself to cereal and rolls and juice, which were placed on a table in the centre of the room, and then shyly ordered the Fisherman's Breakfast from a massive waitress who was built like a Highland cow.

When the breakfast arrived, she poked at it tentatively with a fork. Bacon, eggs, and sausage, she recognized, but the rest seemed odd and strange.

'What are these?' she asked the major. He did not reply so she repeated her question in a rather shrill voice.

'Haggis and black pudding and a potato scone,' said the major. 'Very good. Scotch stuff, you know. Introduced to the stuff when I was first in the Highlands on military training.'

'Were you in the SAS?' asked Alice.

'No.' The major smiled indulgently. 'They hadn't been formed in my day. We called ourselves something else.'

'Oh, what was that?'

'Mustn't say. Hush-hush stuff, you know.'

'Oh.' Alice was impressed.

'Of course I was in the regular army for most of the big show.'

'Which was . . . ?'

'World War Two. Can still remember leading my men up the Normandy beaches. Yanks had taken the easy bits and left us with the cliffs. "Don't worry, chaps," I said. "We'll take Jerry this time." They believed me, bless their hearts. Would have died for me. 'Straordinary loyalty. Quite touching, 's matter of fact.'

Alice wished her mum could see her now. 'Quite one of the old school,' Mum would say.

'Tell me more,' urged Alice, eyes glowing.

'Well,' said the major happily. 'There was a time . . .'

His voice faded away as a bulky shadow fell across the table. Alice looked up. Lady Jane's pale eyes surveyed the major with amusement. 'Telling Miss Wilson all your tales of derring-do? All those pitched battles around the tea tent on Salisbury Plain?'

Now what could there be in those remarks to make the major sweat? Alice looked from one to the other. Lady Jane nodded her head and gave a little smile before walking away.

The major looked after her, mumbled something, and went off mopping his forehead with his handkerchief.

Charlie Baxter, the Roths, and all the rest were

already in the lounge. A cheerful fire was blazing on the hearth. The heavyset waitress lumbered in and threw a pile of old tea leaves, cabbage stalks, and old rolls on the fire, which subsided into a depressing, smoking mess.

Heather examined all their leaders and tugged at the knots. Several gave way. 'I wish you wouldn't say you can tie these things when you obviously can't,' said Lady Jane to the major.

'You are supposed to tie them yourselves,' pointed out Heather.

'Like a bloody schoolroom,' muttered Lady Jane. 'Oh, here's that wretched man again.'

Constable Macbeth lounged in, water dripping from his black cape. He removed it and squatted down by the fire, raking aside the sodding lumps of congealed goo and putting on fresh coal and sticks. Then, to Alice's amusement, he lay down on his stomach and began to blow furiously until the flames started leaping up the chimney.

'This hotel has central heating, hasn't it?' Amy Roth shivered. 'Why doesn't someone turn it on?'

'Now I want you all to try to tie your leaders properly this time,' came Heather's voice. Everyone groaned and began to wrestle with the thin, slippery nylon.

Constable Macbeth had ambled over to an armchair by the window. Suddenly Alice saw him stiffen. It was almost as if he had pointed like a dog. He got to his feet, his tall, thin frame silhouetted against the greyness of the day.

Overcome by curiosity, Alice rose quietly and walked to the window. Whatever, or whoever, Constable Macbeth was looking at was absorbing his whole attention.

Alice looked out.

A slim, blonde girl was getting out of a Land-Rover. She had a yellow oilskin coat and shooting breeches and green Wellington boots. Her beautiful face was a calm, well-bred oval. She was struggling to lift a heavy wicker basket out of the Land-Rover.

The policeman turned around so quickly he nearly fell over Alice. He seized his cape and darted from the room and reappeared a moment later below the window. He said something to the girl, who laughed up at him. He leaned across her and wrested the basket from the Land-Rover. The girl locked the car, and then they walked away, the constable carrying the basket.

I wonder who she is, thought Alice. Rich-looking with that cold sort of damn-you stare. Not a hope there, Lady Jane would no doubt say.

'This goddam thing has a life of its own,' came Marvin Roth's voice.

'What we need,' said Lady Jane, 'is some useful slave labour. Some *sweated* labour, wouldn't you say, Mr Roth?'

'Watch that mouth of yours, lady,' grated Marvin Roth.

There was a shocked silence. Oh dear, thought Heather, I should never have tried to cope with them alone. That dreadful woman. She keeps saying things which sound innocuous to me but which seem terribly barbed to the person they're directed against. She's got that mottled red about the neck which usually means high blood pressure. I wish she would drop dead.

'And now,' said Heather out loud, amazed to hear how shaky her own voice sounded, 'I will pass round some pieces of string and teach you how to tie a figure of eight.'

To Heather's relief, her husband came into the room. 'We're running a bit late,' he said. 'Better get them started. We'll issue them with rods again, that is, the ones who want to rent stuff – I think only the major has

41

brought his own – and then we'll get them off to the Upper Alsh and Loch Alsh.'

Alice pulled on her waders in her room and checked she had everything tucked away in the pockets of her green fowling coat – scissors, a needle (for poking out the eyes of flies – artificial ones, she had been glad to find out – and for undoing knots), and a penknife. She placed her fishing hat on her head and made her way back downstairs, hoping the other guests thought she was a seasoned fisherwoman.

In the car park, John was passing out maps, explaining that Loch Alsh was some distance away. Water dripped from his hat on to his nose. Rain thudded down on the car park. 'At least it will keep the flies away,' he said. 'Now, let me see – Jeremy, you'll take Daphne.' Alice had a sinking feeling in her stomach as John went on to say she was to come along with himself and Heather and young Charlie Baxter. Alice felt Lady Jane's eyes on her face and angrily jerked her already sodden hat down on her forehead.

The journey seemed endless. The mountains were blotted out by the mist. The windscreen wipers clicked monotonously back and forth. Alice looked at Charlie. He was hunched in the far corner. Alice did not know what one talked to children about. 'Enjoying yourself?' she asked at last.

The child's hard, assessing gaze was fixed on her face. 'No,' he said at last. 'I hate that ugly fat woman. She's cruel and mean and evil. Why doesn't she die? Lots of people die in the Highlands. They get lost and starve and die of exposure. They fall off cliffs. Why can't something happen to *her*?'

'Now, now,' said Alice reprovingly. 'Mustn't talk like that.'

There was a long silence, then, 'You've very silly, you

know,' said the child in a conversational tone of voice.

Alice coloured up. 'Don't be impertinent.'

'*You* were being impertinent,' said the maddening Charlie. 'Anyway, you hate her just as much as I do.'

'If you mean Lady Jane, she *is* very trying,' said Heather over one plump shoulder. 'But her faults seem worse because we're such a small group. You wouldn't notice her much in a crowd.'

'*I* would,' said Charlie, putting an effective end to that bit of conversation.

Alice began to feel carsick. The big estate car swayed on the slick macadam surface of the road and cruised up and down over the many rises and bumps.

At last the car veered sharply left and lurched even more over a dirt track where clumps of heather scraped the side of the car.

When Alice was just about ready to scream that she was about to be sick, they lurched to a halt.

She climbed out, feeling stiff and cold.

A rain-pocked loch stretched out in front of her and vanished into the mist. All was still and silent except for the constant drumming of the rain. Heather and John began to unload the rods as the others drove up.

'Now, who wants to row the boat?'

'Me!' cried Charlie, showing rare animation.

'Then you can be my ghillie,' said Lady Jane, a ghillie being a Highland servant. 'Too many bushes around here. I'd be better in the middle of the loch.'

'With a stone around your fat neck,' muttered Amy Roth. She caught Alice staring at her and blushed like a schoolgirl. 'She's such a lady,' thought Alice, amused. 'I bet she feels like fainting any time she says "damn." '

Heather hesitated. Charlie was looking horrified at the idea of rowing Lady Jane. On the other hand, Charlie seemed to be the one member of the party that

43

Lady Jane had so far not managed to intimidate. And he could be rescued after an hour.

'Very well,' said Heather. 'The Roths and the major can go with John further up the loch and fish the river. We should get good brown trout or small salmon so you will only need light rods.'

'What about me?' asked Alice.

'You come with me and I'll start you off,' said Heather. 'Jeremy, you go along to the left and Daphne to the right. Keep moving now. We'll only fish for a little bit and then we'll meet back here in two hours' time.'

Alice kept looking hopefully in Jeremy's direction while they assembled their rods. Daphne had caught her fly in her jacket, and Jeremy was laughing and joking as he wiggled it free for her.

Alice shivered. The rain had found its way inside her collar.

'Come along,' said Heather. 'No, don't carry your rod like that, Alice. You'll either spear someone or get it caught in a bush.'

Jeremy waded off into the loch, and Alice watched him go until he was swallowed up in the mist. Lady Jane's petulant voice sounded over the water, 'Can't you row a little harder?' Poor Charlie.

Alice waded along the shallows after Heather. 'Just here, I think,' said Heather. 'Try casting here.'

Wet and miserable, Alice jerked her rod back and caught the bush behind her. 'No, like this,' said Heather patiently, after she had extricated Alice's hook. She took Alice's arm in a firm grasp and cast the fly so neatly that it landed on the water without a ripple. 'Good,' murmured Heather. 'Now again. And again.'

Alice's arm began to ache. She cursed and stumbled and slipped on the slippery boulders in the water beneath her feet. 'I'll try a little bit further on,' said

Heather placidly. 'You're doing just grand. Remember to stop the rod at the twelve o'clock position. The loch's quite shallow for a good bit, so if you move slowly out from the shore, you might get a bite and then you don't have the risk of getting your hook caught in the bushes.'

Why don't I just say I'll never learn how to fish and I don't care, thought Alice wretchedly. Jeremy's not interested in me. I don't belong here. But somehow she found herself wading slowly out into the loch, casting as she went.

Then the line went taut.

Alice's heart leapt into her mouth.

It was probably a rock or a bit of weed. She began to reel in, feeling with growing excitement the tugs and shivers on the line. A trout leapt in the air at the end of the line and dived.

'Help!' screamed Alice, red with excitement. Would Heather never come? What if she lost it? She could not *bear* to lose it. Seized with a fever almost as old as the hills around her, Alice reeled in her line.

'That's it,' said Heather quietly, appearing suddenly at Alice's side. 'Get your net ready.'

'Net. Yes, net,' said Alice, scrabbling wildly about and dropping her rod in the water. Heather bent down and seized the rod.

'Get the net ready,' said Heather again. Alice wanted to snatch the rod back but was afraid of losing the fish. Forward it came, turning and glistening in the water. Alice scooped the net under it and lifted it up, watching the fish with a mixture of exultation and pity.

'Quite a big one,' said Heather. 'Three pounds, I should think. It'll make a good breakfast.' She led the way to the shore after removing the hook from the trout's mouth.

'Can't you kill it?' asked Alice, looking at the panting,

struggling fish. 'Oh yes,' said Heather, slowly picking up a rock. All her movements were slow and sure. 'We'll just put it out of its misery.'

How abhorrent the idea of killing things seemed in London, thought Alice, and how natural it seemed in this savage landscape. Heather slid the trout into a plastic bag. 'Put that in your fishing bag,' she said to Alice. 'It's about time for lunch. I think I hear the others returning.'

Alice was the only one who had caught anything and received lavish praise from everyone but Lady Jane and Charlie Baxter. The child looked exhausted, and Heather was fussing over him, helping him into the front seat of the car and pouring him hot tea.

'You're a marvel, Alice,' said Jeremy. 'Did you really catch that brute all by yourself?'

'Yes, did you *really*?' asked Lady Jane.

Alice hesitated only for a moment. Heather was a little bit away, hopefully out of earshot. 'Yes,' said Alice loudly. 'Yes, I did.'

'I'd better keep close to you this afternoon,' grinned Jeremy. 'Seems like you have all the luck.'

Alice's pleasure was a little dimmed by, first, the lie she had told, which she was now sure Heather had overheard, and, second, by the fact that Jeremy and Daphne were to share a cosy lunch in his car while she herself was relegated to the back of the Cartwrights' station wagon.

Lunch tasted rather nasty. Great slabs of pâté, cold and heavy, and dry yellow cake and boiled eggs. But the fishing fever had Alice in its grip, and she could hardly wait to try her luck again. Somehow, Alice felt, if she managed to catch another fish all on her own then the lie would be forgiven by the gods above. For the first few moments after they climbed from the cars again, it looked as if the day's fishing might have to be cancelled. A wind had risen and was driving great buffets of rain into their faces.

'It said on the forecast this morning it might dry up later,' yelled John above the noise of the rising wind. 'I say we ought to give it another half hour.'

Everyone agreed, since no-one wanted to return home without a fish. If Alice could catch one, then anyone could, was the general opinion.

'I'm all right now,' Charlie said, after Heather had towelled his curls dry. 'It was that woman. Row here. Row there. And then she said . . . she said . . . never mind.'

'Slide along behind the wheel, Charlie,' said Heather firmly. 'I really think you ought to tell me what Lady Jane said to upset you.'

But Charlie would only shake his drying curls and look stubborn.

Heather was determined to have a word with her husband about Lady Jane as soon as possible. But the roar of an engine told her that John was already setting out with the major for the upper beats of the river.

'Would you like me to run you back to the hotel?' she asked the boy.

He shook his head. 'As long as I can fish alone,' he said. 'I'll wait with the rest and see if the weather lifts.'

Alice was oblivious to the slashing rain as she waded out into the loch again with Jeremy at her side, deaf to the sounds of altercation from the shore as Heather told Lady Jane firmly that she was to leave Charlie alone and drive to the upper beats to join the major, the Roths, and John.

'Brrrr, it's cold,' said Jeremy. 'Where did you catch your trout?'

'Just here,' said Alice. 'I'll show you.' She cast wildly

47

and heard the fly plop in the water behind her, then clumsily whipped the line forward. 'I'm tired,' she said defiantly, 'and my arm aches. That's why I can't do it right.'

'Look, it's like this,' said Jeremy. 'Keep your legs apart' – Alice blushed – 'with the left foot slightly forward. Bring the rod smartly up towards your shoulder using the forearm and hold your upper arms close to your body. When you make the back flick, the line should stream out straight behind, and when you feel a tug at the top of the line, you'll know the back cast is completed, and then bring it into the forward cast.'

Alice's line cracked like a lion tamer's whip. 'Are you sure you caught that fish yourself?' laughed Jeremy.

'Of course I did,' said Alice with the steady, outraged gaze of the liar.

'I'll try further down,' said Jeremy, beginning to wade away. 'I wonder if Daphne's had any luck.'

Damn Daphne, thought Alice savagely. All her elation had fled, leaving her alone in the middle of a howling wilderness of wind and rain.

She simply *had* to get Jeremy back.

Remembering everything she had been taught, she balanced herself on the slippery pebbles under the water and cast carefully and neatly towards Jeremy's retreating back.

'Caught 'im,' thought Alice. Aloud, she called, 'Sorry, Jeremy darling. I'm afraid I've hooked *you*.' Now, in the romances that Alice read, Jeremy should have said something like, 'You caught me a long time ago,' and then walked slowly towards her and taken her in his powerful arms.

What he did say in fact was, 'Silly bitch. There's the whole loch to fish from. Come here and help me get this hook out.'

Blushing and stumbling, Alice edged miserably towards him. The hook was embedded in the back of his jacket. She twisted and pulled and finally it came free with a ripping sound.

Jeremy twisted an anguished face over his shoulder. 'Now look what you've done. Look, just keep well clear of me.' He waded off into the driving rain.

Tears of humiliation mixed with the rainwater on Alice's face. She felt hurt and lost and alone. Her face ached with trying to maintain a posh accent. Jeremy would never have behaved like that with someone of his own class.

She decided to turn about, give up, and go back and shelter in the car until this horrible day's fishing was all over.

Alice stumbled towards the shore. Suddenly the water turned gold. Sparkling gold with red light dancing in the peaty ripples. She turned and looked towards the west. Blue sky was spreading rapidly over the heavens. Mountains stood up, sharp and prehistoric with their twisted, deformed shapes. Heather blazed in great, glorious clumps, and the sun beat down on Alice's sopping hat.

'Alice! Alice!' Jeremy was churning towards her through the water, holding up a fairly small trout.

'Marvellous girl.' He beamed. 'Knew you would bring me luck.' He threw his arms around her, slapping her on the back of the head with his dead trout as he did so.

Transported from hell to heaven, Alice smiled back. 'Come along,' said Jeremy. 'I've got a flask of brandy in the car. Let's take a break and celebrate.'

While Jeremy got his flask, Alice took off her hat and her wet coat and put them both on the bushes to dry. Jeremy sat down on a rock beside her and handed her the flask and she choked over an enormous gulp of brandy.

The liqueur shot down to her stomach and up to her brain. She felt dizzy with happiness. They had had their first quarrel, she thought dreamily. How they would laugh about it after they were married!

Elated with brandy and sunshine, they cheerfully agreed to return to the loch and try their luck again. And Alice did try. Very hard. If only she could catch a fish all by herself then she could be easy in her conscience.

But by four in the afternoon, Heather appeared to call them to the cars. They were to return to the hotel for another fishing lecture.

Even Alice felt sulkily that it was all too much like being back at school. Why waste a perfectly good afternoon sitting indoors in a stuffy hotel lounge?

But none of them had quite realized how tired they were until John Cartwright began his lecture on fly tying. Despite the heat from the sun pouring in the long windows, a log fire was burning, its flames bleached pale by the sunlight. A bluebottle buzzed against the windows.

While Heather's nimble fingers demonstrated the art of fly tying, John discoursed on the merits of wet and dry flies. Names like Tup's Indispensable, Little Claret, Wickman's Fancy, Black Pennell, and Cardinal floated like dust motes on the hot, somnolent air. 'Sound like racehorses,' said Jeremy sleepily.

Alice felt her eyes beginning to close. The major was asleep, twitching in his armchair like an old dog; the Roths were leaning together, joined by fatigue into a fireside picture of a happily married couple. Lady Jane had her eyes half closed, like a basking lizard, and Daphne Gore was painting her nails vermilion.

Suddenly Alice jerked her eyes open. There was a feeling of fear in the room, fear mixed with malice.

While John droned on, Heather had stopped her demonstration to flip through the post. She was sitting very still, holding an airmail letter in her plump hands. She raised her eyes and looked at Lady Jane. Lady Jane raised her heavy lids and smiled. It was not a nice smile.

Heather's face had gone putty-coloured. She put a hand on her husband's sleeve and passed him the letter. He glanced at it and then began to read it closely, his lips folded into a grim line.

'Class dismissed,' he said at last, putting down the letter and assuming a rather ghastly air of levity.

'What was all that about?' murmured Jeremy to Alice. 'And why do I feel it has something to do with Lady Jane?'

'Care for a drink before dinner, Jeremy?' came Daphne's cool voice.

'Are you paying?' asked Jeremy, his face crinkling up in a smile.

'What's this? Men's lib?' Daphne slid her arm into his and they left the lounge together. Alice stood stock still, biting her lip.

'I told you you were wasting your time.' Lady Jane's large bulk hove up on Alice's portside.

Fury like bile nearly choked Alice. 'You are a horrible, unpleasant woman,' she grated.

This seemed to increase Lady Jane's good humour. 'Now, now,' she purred. 'Little girls in glass houses shouldn't throw stones. And I *do* trust our stone-throwing days are over.'

Alice gazed at her in terror. She *knew*. She would tell Jeremy. She would tell *everybody*.

She turned and ran and did not stop running until she reached her room. She threw herself face down on the bed and cried and cried until she could cry no more. And then she became conscious of all that barbaric wilderness of Highland moor and mountain outside. Accidents happened. Anything could happen. Alice pictured Lady Jane's heavy body plummeting down into a salmon pool, her fat face lifeless, turned upwards in the brown, peaty water. Abruptly, she fell asleep.

When she awoke, she thought it was still early because of the daylight outside, forgetting about the long light of a northern Scottish summer.

Then she saw it was ten o'clock. With a gasp, she hurried from the bed and washed and changed. But when she went down to the dining room, it was to find that dinner was over and she had to put up with sandwiches served in the bar. Everyone seemed to have gone to bed. The barman informed her that the fat FEB had gone out walking and perhaps the other was with her – that Lady Whatsername. Alice asked curiously what a FEB was but the bartender said hurriedly he 'shouldnae hae said that' and polished glasses furiously.

Charlie Baxter threw leaves into the river Anstey from the humpbacked bridge and watched them being churned into the boiling water and then tossed up again on their turbulent road to the sea. His aunt, Mrs Pargeter, thought he was safely in bed, but he had put on his clothes and climbed out of the window. His mother had written to say she would be arriving at the end of the week. Charlie looked forward to her visit and dreaded it at the same time. He still could not quite believe he would never see his father again. Mother had won custody of him in a violent divorce case and talked endlessly about defying the law and keeping Charlie away from his father for life. Charlie felt miserably that it was somehow all his fault; that if he had been a better child then his parents might have stayed together. He turned from the bridge and headed towards the hotel.

The sky and sea were pale grey, setting off the black, twisted shapes of the mountains crouched behind the village.

Charlie walked along the harbour, watching the men getting ready for their night's fishing. He was debating asking one of them if he could go along and was just rejecting the idea as hopeless – for surely they would demand permission from his aunt – when a soft voice said behind him, 'Isn't it time you were in bed, young man?'

Charlie glanced up. The tall figure of Constable Macbeth loomed up in the dusk. 'I was just going home,' muttered Charlie.

'Well, I'll just take a bit of a walk with you. It's a grand night.'

'As a matter of fact, my aunt doesn't know I'm out,' said Charlie.

'Then we would not want to be upsetting Mrs Pargeter,' said Hamish equably. 'But we'll take a wee dauner along the front.'

As Hamish Macbeth was turning away, a voice sounded from an open window of the hotel, 'Throw the damn thing away. It's like poison.' Mrs Cartwright, thought Charlie. Then came John Cartwright's voice, 'Oh, very well. But you're worrying overmuch. I'll throw this in the loch and then we can maybe get a night's sleep.'

A crumpled piece of blue paper sailed past Charlie's head and landed on the oily stones of the beach. The tide was out.

Charlie picked it up. It was a crumpled airmail. 'You shouldn't look at other people's correspondence,' said

Hamish Macbeth severely, 'even though they may have chucked it away.'

'I wasn't going to read it. It's got a lovely stamp. Austrian.'

They passed the Roths, who were walking some distance apart. Marvin's face was flushed and Amy's mouth was turned down at the corners. 'Hi!' said Marvin, forcing a smile.

'It's a grand night,' remarked the policeman. The American couple went on their way, and Charlie hurriedly thrust the airmail into his pocket.

When they reached his aunt's house, Charlie said shyly, 'Do you mind leaving me here? I know how to get in without waking her.'

Hamish Macbeth nodded, but waited at the garden gate until the boy disappeared around the side of the house.

Then he made his way home to his own house where his dog, Towser, gave him a slavering welcome. Hamish absentmindedly stroked the animal's rough coat. There was something about this particular fishing class that was making him uneasy.

DAY THREE

Thy tongue imagineth wickedness: and with lies
thou cuttest like a sharp razor.
— The Psalms

Alice had reasoned herself into an optimistic frame of
mind, although anxiety had first roused her at six in the
morning. She had dressed and had taken herself out on
a walk up the hill behind the hotel.

A light, gauzy mist lay on everything, pearling the
long grass and wild thyme, lying on the rippling silk of
the loch, and drifting around the gnarled trunks of old
twisted pines, last remnants of the Caledonian forest.
Harebells shivered as Alice moved slowly through the
grass, and a squirrel looked at her curiously before
darting up a tree.

Alice sat on a rock and talked severely to herself. The
youthful peccadillo that had landed her briefly in the
juvenile court was something buried in the mists of time.
Why, her mother's neighbours in Liverpool hardly
remembered it! It was certainly something that Lady
Jane could *not* know about. It had appeared in the local
paper, circulation eight thousand, in a little paragraph
at the bottom of page two. At the time, it had seemed
as if the eyes and the ears of the world's press had been
on her when she had read that little paragraph. But now
she was older and wiser and knew that she had been of

no interest whatsoever to the media. That was the hell of being so hypersensitive. You began to think people meant all sorts of things because of their lightest remarks. Who was Lady Jane anyway? Just some silly, bitchy, discontented housewife. Jeremy had said she had been married to Lord John Winters, a choleric backbencher in Wilson's government, who had died of a heart attack only two months after he had received his peerage for nameless services.

Then there was Daphne Gore. Alice envied Daphne's obvious money and cool poise. Lady Jane hadn't been able to get at *her*. But she, Alice, must not let her own silly snobbery stand in the way of luring Jeremy away from Daphne. Come to think of it, Lady Jane had not riled Jeremy either. Perhaps that was what money and a public school gave you – armour plating.

John Cartwright awoke with an unaccustomed feeling of dread. Certainly, he was used to enduring a bit of stage fright before the beginning of each new fishing class, but that soon disappeared, leaving him with only the heady pleasure of being paid for communicating to others his hobby and his passion . . . fishing.

Now Lady Jane loomed like a fat thundercloud on the horizon.

Perhaps he was taking the whole thing too seriously. But neither he nor Heather had really performed their duties very well this week. Usually, they meticulously took their class through more intensive instruction on casting, leader tying, fly tying, and the habits of the wily salmon. But so far both of them had been only too glad to get their charges out on the water, as if spreading them as far apart as possible could diffuse the threatening atmosphere. There was nothing they could do – legally – to protect themselves from Lady Jane. There were two alternatives. They could pray – or they could murder Lady Jane. But John did not believe in God, and he shrank from the idea of violence. Lady Jane had been charming at dinner last night and seemed to be enjoying herself. Perhaps he could appeal to her better nature . . . if she had one.

The mist was burning off the loch when the class assembled in the lounge. It promised to be a scorching day. Alice was wearing a blue-and-white gingham blouse with a pair of brief white cotton shorts that showed her long, slim legs to advantage. She was wearing a cheap, oversweet perfume that delighted Jeremy's nostrils. Women who wore cheap scent always seemed so much more approachable, conjuring up memories of tumbled flannel sheets in bedsitting rooms. She was concentrating on practising to tie knots, her fine, fluffy brown hair falling over her forehead. He went to sit beside her on the sofa, edging close to her so that his thigh touched her bare legs. Alice flushed, and her hands trembled a little. 'You look delicious this morning,' murmured Jeremy and put a hand lightly on her knee. Alice realized, all in that delightful moment, that her knees could blush.

'I am so glad to meet a young man who actually pursues single girls,' commented Lady Jane to the world at large. 'I'm one of those old-fashioned women who believe adultery to be a sin, the next worst thing to seducing servants.'

This remark, which sounded like something from *Upstairs Downstairs*, went largely unnoticed, but it had an odd effect on both Jeremy and Daphne Gore. Jeremy slowly removed his hand from Alice's knee and sat very still. Daphne dropped her coffee cup and swore. 'No good comes of it,' pursued Lady Jane. 'I've known girls run off and make fools of themselves with Spanish

57

waiters and young men who seduce married barmaids. Disgusting!'

There was a long silence. Daphne's distress was all too evident, and Jeremy looked sick.

'Of course,' came Constable Macbeth's soft Highland voice, 'some of us are protected from the sins of the flesh by our very age and appearance. Would not you say so, Lady Jane?'

'Are you trying to insult me, Officer?'

'Not I. I would be in the way of thinking that it would be an almost impossible thing to do.'

Lady Jane's massive bosom swelled under the thin puce silk of her blouse. She's like the Hulk, thought Alice. Any moment now she's going to turn green and explode.

'Were I not aware of the impoverished circumstances of your family,' said Lady Jane, 'I would stop you from scrounging coffee. Six little brothers and sisters to support, eh? And your aged parents in Ross and Cromarty? So improvident to have children when one is middle-aged. They can turn out retarded, you know.'

'Better they turn out retarded – although they're not – than grow up into a silly, fat, middle-aged, barren bitch like yourself,' said Hamish with a sweet smile.

'You will suffer for this,' howled Lady Jane. 'Don't you know who I really am? Don't you know the power I have?'

'No,' said Amy Roth flatly. 'We don't.'

Lady Jane opened and shut her mouth like a landed trout.

'That's right, honey,' said Marvin Roth. 'You can huff and you can puff, but you ain't gonna blow any houses down here. You can make other folks' lives a misery with your snide remarks, but I'm a New Yorker, born and bred, and Amy here's a Blanchard of the Augusta,

58

Georgia, Blanchards and you won't find a tougher combination than that.'

A strange change came over Lady Jane. One minute she looked about to suffer the same fate as her late husband; the next, her angry colour had died and she looked almost lovingly at Amy.

'Dear me,' she said sweetly, 'a Blanchard born and bred?'

'Yes, ma'am,' said Marvin Roth proudly. 'Amy's *old* money, just like the Rockefellers.'

'Please!' called John Cartwright. 'Let me begin or we'll never get the day started.'

They shuffled their chairs into a semicircle. Heather unrolled a screen and then started setting up a small projector. 'Lantern slides,' groaned Lady Jane.

A tic appeared in John's left cheek, but he gamely went on with his lecture, showing slides of what salmon looked like when they headed up river from the sea, when they were spawning, and when they were returning to the sea.

'Our prices at this school are very reasonable,' said John. '*Very* reasonable,' he repeated firmly after Lady Jane snorted. 'The better-class salmon beats are all strictly preserved and can only usually be fished at enormous cost. Salmon are fly-caught, particularly the ones of small size, on ordinary reservoir-strength trout rods. Regular salmon anglers, however, also include in their tackle longer rods, some designed for two-handed casting, larger reels, heavier lines, stouter leaders, and flies much bigger on average than those used for trout.'

'If we had a decent government in power,' interrupted Lady Jane, 'instead of that Thatcher woman's dictatorship, then *everyone* would be able to fish for salmon, even the common people.'

John sighed and signalled to Heather to pack up

the projector. He and Heather loved the Sutherland countryside, and he usually ended his talk by showing beautiful colour slides of rivers and mountains and lochs. But he felt beauty would be wasted on the present gathering. 'We will fish the Upper Sutherland today. Heather will pass around maps. The pools on the upper river are small, easy to fish, closely grouped together and within easy distance of the road. During the summer, the fish cannot get over the Sutherland falls and so that's why they concentrate in the upper beats. On your map, you will see the Slow Pool marked. This is a very good holding pool, but it is particularly good in high water when it is best fished from the right bank. Heather and I will take Alice and Charlie and the rest of you can follow as before.'

The day was gloriously hot, and even Charlie Baxter lost his customary reserve and whistled cheerfully as the large estate car swung around the hairpin bends of the Highland roads. At one point a military plane roared overhead, flying so low the noise of its jets was deafening. 'A Jaguar!' said Charlie.

John fiddled with the knobs of the car radio. A blast of Gaelic keening split the air. He tried again. Gaelic. 'Isn't there anything in English?' asked Alice, feeling the more cut off from civilization by the sound of that incomprehensible tongue coming from the radio. 'She's got a ticket to ride' roared the Beatles, and everyone laughed and joined in. There was something about the scorching sun and clear air that reduced the likes of Lady Jane to a dot on the horizon. Alice could now well understand why people once thought the night hideous with evil creatures.

Alice was only sorry the estate car was big enough to take their rods lying down flat in the back. It would have been jolly to have them poking upright out of the open window, advertising to the world at large that she was a professional fisher of salmon.

They parked in a disused quarry and climbed out to meet the others. Lady Jane was wearing a Greek fisherman's hat that gave her fleshy face with its curved beak of a nose an oddly hermaphroditic appearance.

John spread out the map on the bonnet of the car and sorted them out into pairs. Daphne and Lady Jane were to fish the Calm Pool, a good holding pool, and were told that the streamy water at the top was best. The major and Jeremy were to try their chances at the Slow Pool; the Roths at the Silver Bank; and Alice and Charlie at the Sheiling. Heather would go with Alice and John with the major and Jeremy.

Alice fished diligently until Heather announced they should break for lunch. Fishing fever had her in its grip and she had not thought of Jeremy once.

At lunch it transpired that Lady Jane and the major were missing. Jeremy said the local ghillie from Lochdubh had taken him aside and had begun talking to him, and the major had packed up and left with him. Daphne said crossly that Lady Jane had thrashed her line about the water enough to scare away a whale and then had mercifully disappeared.

The absence of Lady Jane acted on the spirits of the party like champagne. Heather had augmented the hotel lunch with homemade sausage rolls, potato scones, and fruit bread covered in lashings of butter and strawberry jam. Alice was dreamily happy to see that Daphne's skin was turning an ugly red in the sun while her own was turning to pale gold. A little breeze fanned their hot cheeks and Jeremy made Alice's day perfect by opting to fish with her for the rest of the afternoon.

After some time, Jeremy suggested they should take a rest. Alice lay back on the springy heather by the water's edge and stared dreamily up into the blue sky.

'What do you think of Lady Jane?' asked Jeremy abruptly. Alice propped herself up on one elbow. 'I dunno,' she said cautiously. 'I think she's learned the knack of fishing of a different sort. I think she knows everyone's got some sort of skeleton in the cupboard and she throws out remarks at random and watches until she sees she's caught someone. Like with you and Daphne this morning. Whatever she meant by that servant and Spanish waiter remark, it upset you and Daphne no end.'

'Nonsense,' said Jeremy quickly. 'I was upset for Daphne's sake. I could see the remark had got home.' But you were upset *before*, thought Alice. 'I think the woman's plain mad. All that talk about her having power is pure rot. She's nothing but the widow of some obscure Labour peer. She's not even good class. I phoned my father about her the other night. He says she's the daughter of old Marie Phipps, who was secretary to and mistress of Lord Chalcont, and Marie forced his lordship into sending Jane to a finishing school in Switzerland. There never was a Mr Phipps, you know.'

'You mean she's *illegitimate*,' gasped Alice. 'How splendid. I'd like to throw that in her face.'

'Don't, for God's sake,' said Jeremy harshly. 'She'd bite back like a viper.'

'But you said she's got no power.'

'Hasn't any power,' corrected Jeremy automatically, and Alice hated him for that brief moment. 'It's just that I'm thinking of standing for Parliament and I'm very careful about avoiding enemies.'

'You'd be marvellous,' breathed Alice. Why, he could be Prime Minister! Maggie Thatcher couldn't live for ever.

'You're a funny, intense little thing,' said Jeremy. He

leaned forward and kissed her on the lips, a firm but schoolboyish embrace. 'Now, let's go fish.' He grinned.

Alice waded dizzily into the Sheiling, her legs trembling, a sick feeling of excitement churning in her stomach. The future Prime Minister of Britain had just kissed her! 'No comment,' she said to the clamouring press as she swept into Number Ten. Where did Princess Di get her hats? She must find out.

Sunshine, physical exercise, and dreams of glory. Alice was often to look back on that afternoon as the last golden period of her existence.

The sun burned down behind the mountains, making them two-dimensional cardboard mountains from a stage set. The clear air was scented with thyme and sage and pine.

To Alice's joy, Daphne had been suffering from mild sunstroke and had been taken back to the hotel by Heather. So she was allowed to ride home with Jeremy.

There is nothing more sensuous than a rich fast car driven by a rich slow man through a Highland evening.

Alice felt languorous and sexy. The setting sun flashed between the trees and bushes as they drove along with the pale gold brilliance of the far north.

The grass was so very green in this evening light, this gloaming. Green as the fairy stories, green and gold as Never-Never Land. Alice could well understand now why the Highlanders believed in fairies. Jeremy slowed the car outside the village as the tall blonde Alice had seen with Constable Macbeth came striding along the side of the road with two Irish wolfhounds on the leash.

'That's the love of Constable Macbeth's life,' said Alice, delighted to have a piece of gossip.

'No hope there,' said Jeremy, cheerfully and unconsciously quoting Lady Jane. 'That's Priscilla Halburton-Smythe, daughter of Colonel James Halburton-Smythe.

Her photograph was in *Country Life* the other week. The Halburton-Smythes own most of the land around here.'

'Oh,' said Alice, feeling a certain kinship with the village constable. 'Perhaps she loves him too.'

'She wouldn't be so silly,' said Jeremy. '*I* wouldn't even have a chance there.'

'Do people's backgrounds matter a great deal to you?' asked Alice in a low voice.

Jeremy reminded himself of his future as a politician. 'No,' he said stoutly. 'I think all that sort of thing is rot. A lady is a lady no matter what her background.'

Alice gave him a brilliant smile, and he smiled back, thinking she really was a very pretty little thing.

The sun disappeared as they plunged down to Lochdubh. Alice prayed that Jeremy would stop the car and kiss her again, but he seemed to have become immersed in his own thoughts.

When they arrived at the hotel, it was to find the rest of the fishing party surrounding Major Peter Frame. He was proudly holding up a large salmon while Heather took his photograph. Two more giants lay in plastic bags on the ground at his feet.

'How on earth did you do it?' said Jeremy, slapping the major on the back. 'Hey, that fellow's got a chunk out the side.'

' 'Fraid that's where I wrenched the hook out, old man,' said the major. 'Got too excited.'

'Gosh, I wish I had stayed with you,' said Jeremy. 'But I thought you went off somewhere else. Did you?'

The major laid his finger alongside his nose. 'Mum's the word, and talking about mum, the filthy Iron Curtain champers is on me tonight.'

'Let's take them to the scales and log your catch in the book,' said John, his face radiant. The photograph would go to the local papers and the fishing magazines. He loved it when one of his pupils made a good catch. And no-one had ever had such luck as this before.

They all were now looking forward to the evening, reminding themselves that that was the time when Lady Jane could be guaranteed to be at her best. They were to meet in the bar at eight to toast the major's catch.

Alice slaved over her appearance. She had bought one good dinner gown at an elegant Help the Aged shop in Mayfair. Although the clothes were secondhand, most of them had barely been worn and the dinner gown was as good as new. It was made of black silk velvet, very severe, cut low in the front and slit up to mid-thigh on either side of the narrow skirt.

She was ready at last, half an hour too early. This was one time Alice was determined to make an appearance. Her high-heeled black sandals with thin straps gave her extra height and extra confidence. In the shaded light of the hotel room, her reflection looked poised and sophisticated.

Alice was just turning away from the mirror when all the barbed remarks Lady Jane had made seemed to clamour in her brain. It was no use pretending otherwise; Lady Jane had set out to find out something about each one of them. Jeremy must never know. The future Prime Minister of Britain could not have a wife with a criminal record. But then, Lady Jane knew something about Jeremy. Had he seduced a servant? But that was an upper-class sin and therefore forgivable, thought Alice miserably. She sat down on the edge of the bed and looked about her with bleak eyes.

How perfectly splendid it would be to go back to Mr Patterson-James and hand in her notice, and say she was going to be married to Jeremy Blythe – 'one of the Somerset Blythes, you know.' There was Mum and Dad in Liverpool to cope with. Alice thought of her small, poky, shabby, comfortable home. Jeremy must never be allowed to go there. Mum and Dad would just have to travel to London for the wedding.

But between Alice and all those dreams stood Lady Jane. A wave of hate for Jane Winters engulfed Alice; primitive, naked hate.

Ten past eight! Alice leapt to her feet with an anguished look at her travel alarm.

The bar was crowded when she made her entrance. 'Dear me, the Merry Widow,' remarked Lady Jane, casting a pale look over Alice's black velvet gown. The fishing party had taken a table by the window where the major was cheerfully dispensing champagne. Alice's entrance had fallen flat because the major was describing how he had landed his first salmon, and everyone was hanging on his every word. 'It's almost a good enough story to be true,' said Lady Jane.

'Well, obviously it's true,' said the major, his good humour unimpaired. 'Here I am and there are my fish, all waiting in the hotel freezer to be smoked. By the way, Alice, your trout's still there. You forgot to have it for breakfast.'

'You and Alice have a lot in common,' said Lady Jane sweetly. 'I can see that by the end of the week that hotel freezer will be *packed* with fish that neither of you caught.'

The rest of the group tried to ignore Lady Jane's remark. 'Tell us where exactly you caught those salmon, Major,' asked Jeremy.

'Yes, do tell,' echoed Daphne. 'It isn't fair to keep such a prize place to yourself.'

The major laughed and shook his head.

'Oh, *I'll* tell you,' said Lady Jane. She was wearing a sort of flowered pyjama suit of the type that used to be in vogue in the thirties. Vermilion lipstick accentuated the petulant droop of her mouth. 'I was talking to Ian Morrison, the ghillie, a little while ago and the dear man was in his cups and told me *exactly* how you caught them.'

An awful silence fell on the group. The major stood with a bottle of champagne in one hand and a glass in the other and a silly smile pasted on his face.

'I think we should all go in to dinner,' said Heather loudly and clearly.

'I say, yes, let's,' said the major eagerly.

They all rose to their feet. Lady Jane remained seated, a gilt sandal swinging from one plump foot as she looked up at them.

'Major Frame didn't catch those fish at all,' she said with hideous clarity. 'Ian Morrison took him up to the high pools on the Anstey. In one of those pools, three salmon had been trapped because of the river dwindling suddenly in the heat. They were dying from lack of oxygen. One was half out of the water and a seagull had torn a gash in its side, *not* the dear major's fictitious hook!'

One by one they filed into the dining room, not looking at each other, not looking at the major. Alice couldn't bear it any longer. She took a seat by the major. 'I don't believe a word of it,' she said, patting his hand. 'That terrible woman made it all up.'

The major smiled at her in a rigid sort of way and drank steadily from his champagne glass.

Charlie Baxter had been invited to join them for dinner. He had not been in the bar and therefore did not know about the major's humiliation. But he looked from face to face and then settled down to eat his food so that he could escape as quickly as possible.

Lady Jane launched into her usual evening flow of

anecdotes while the rest stared at her with hate-filled eyes.

What the major had done was not so bad. Alice thought he had been very clever. She herself, she was sure, would have sworn blind she had caught them.

Heather Cartwright was miserable. She had already posted off the photographs, developed quickly by John in their own darkroom, to the local papers and fishing magazines. Heather didn't know which one she wanted to kill – Lady Jane or the major. When it had seemed as if the major had landed that splendid catch, Heather and John had heaved a sigh of relief. Surely nothing Lady Jane said could touch them now. It was the most marvellous piece of publicity for the fishing school. But the silly, vain major had now played right into Lady Jane's hands. Well, *I* can just about bear it, thought Heather, but if anything happens to this fishing school, it will kill John.

'I always think those silly beanpole women who model clothes are a hoot,' Lady Jane was saying. 'I remember going to Hartnell's collection and there were the usual pan-faced lot of mannequins modelling clothes for the Season and the salon was so hot and stuffy and we were all half asleep. They were marching on saying in those awful sort of Putney deb voices, "For Goodwood, For Ascot," and things like that, and then this one marches on and says, "For Cowes," and we all laughed fit to burst.' Lady Jane herself laughed in a fat, jolly way.

Marvin Roth was gloomily longing for the appearance of that village constable with the red hair. No-one else seemed to have the courage to be rude to Lady Jane. If she did know something about him, Marvin Roth, then good luck to her. But that remark of hers to the constable about 'having power' was worrying. What sort of power?

Blackmail, thought Marvin Roth suddenly. That's it.

And there was nothing he could do about it. Had they been in New York, then things might have been different. There was always someone who could be hired to clear away people like Lady Jane . . . although he had heard that even in old New York things were not what they were in the early seventies, say, when a thousand dollars to the local Mafia could get someone wasted. If only he could do it himself. Maybe he should just try to pay her off before she approached him. Amy must never know. Amy was the prize. In order to get divorced from that little whore of a first wife, he had paid an arm and a leg, but gaining Amy Blanchard had been worth it. He knew Amy hoped he would make it big on the political scene. Of course, Amy either knew or had guessed about his unsavoury past, but any approach to Lady Jane must be kept secret. There was a vein of steel running through Amy, and he was sure she would despise him for trying to conciliate Lady Jane.

Marvin polished his bald head with his hand and looked sideways at Lady Jane. No, ma'am, he thought, the day I let a broad like you screw up my act, well, you can kiss my ass in Macy's window.

At last the horrible dinner was over. Alice smoothed down the velvet of her gown with a nervous hand and smiled hopefully at Jeremy. He looked at her vaguely and turned abruptly to Daphne Gore. 'Come on,' he said to Daphne. 'We've got to talk.'

Alice's eyes filmed over with tears. She was dreadfully tired. She felt alien, foreign, alone. When she passed the bar, it was full of people drinking and laughing, the other guests who did not belong to the fishing school. She hesitated, longing for the courage to go in and join them, longing for just one compliment on her gown to make some of her misery go away.

*　　*　　*

Constable Hamish Macbeth leaned on his garden gate and gazed across the loch to the lights of the hotel. He had fed the chickens and geese; his dog lay at his feet, stretched across his boots like a carriage rug, snoring peacefully.

Hamish lit a cigarette and pushed his cap back on his head. He was not happy, which was a fairly unusual state of mind for him. This was usually the time of the day he liked best.

He had to admit to himself he had let Lady Jane get under his skin. He did not like the idea of that fat woman ferreting out details of his family life, even if there was nothing shameful to ferret out.

It was true that Hamish Macbeth had six brothers and sisters to support. He had been born one year after his parents had been married. After that there had been a long gap and then Mr and Mrs Macbeth had produced three boys and three girls in as quick a succession as was physically possible. As in many Celtic families, it was taken for granted that the eldest son would remain a bachelor until such time as the next in line were able to support themselves. Hamish had deliberately chosen the unambitious career of village constable because it enabled him to send most of his pay home. He was a skilful poacher and presents of venison and salmon found their way regularly to his parents' croft in Ross and Cromarty. The little egg money he got from his poultry was sent home as well. Then there was the annual prize money for best hill runner at the Strathbane Highland games. Hamish had taken the prize five years in a row.

His father was a crofter but could not make nearly enough to support all six younger children. Hamish had accepted his lot as he accepted most things, with easy-going good nature.

But of late, he had found himself wishing he had a little bit more money in his pocket and yet he would not admit to himself the reason for this.

What he *could* admit to himself was that he was very worried about the fishing class. Crime in Hamish's parish usually ran to things like bigamy or the occasional drunk on a Saturday night. Most village wrangles were settled out of court, so to speak, by the diplomatic Hamish. He was not plagued with the savage violence of poaching gangs, although he felt sure that would come. A new housing estate was being built outside the village; one of those mad schemes where the worst of the welfare cases were wrenched out of the cosy clamour of the city slums and transported to the awesome bleakness of the Highlands. To Hamish, these housing estates were the breeding grounds of poaching gangs who dynamited the salmon to the surface and fought each other with razors and sharpened bicycle chains.

Something in his bones seemed to tell him that trouble was going to come from this fishing class. He decided it was time to find out a little more about Lady Jane.

He sifted through the filing cabinet of his mind, which was filled with the names and addresses and telephone numbers of various friends and relatives. Like most Highlanders, Hamish had relatives scattered all over the world.

Then he remembered his second cousin, Rory Grant, who worked for the *Daily Recorder* in Fleet Street. Hamish ambled indoors and put through a collect call. 'This is Constable Macbeth of Lochdubh with a verra important story for Rory Grant,' said Hamish when the newspaper switchboard showed signs of being reluctant to pay for the call. When he was at last put through to Rory, Hamish gave a description of Lady Jane Winters and asked for details about her.

71

'I'll need to go through to the library and look at her cuttings,' said Rory. 'It might take a bit of time. I'll call you back.'

'Och, no,' said Hamish comfortably. 'I am not paying for the call, so I will just hold on and have a beer while you are looking.'

'Suit yourself,' said Rory. Hamish tucked the phone under one ear and fished a bottle of beer out of his bottom drawer. He did not like cold beer and, in any case, Hamish had grown up on American movies where the hero had fished a bottle out of his desk drawer, and had never got over the thrill of being able to do the same thing, even though it was warm beer and not bourbon.

He had left the police office door open, and a curious hen came hopping in, flew up on top of the typewriter, and stared at him with curious, beady eyes.

Priscilla Halburton-Smythe suddenly appeared in the doorway, a brace of grouse dangling from one hand, and smiled at the sight of Hamish with his huge boots on the desk, bottle of beer in one hand, phone in the other and hen in front.

'I see you're interviewing one of the village criminals,' said Priscilla.

'Not I,' said Hamish. 'I am waiting for my cousin in London to come back to the telephone with some vital information.'

'I mean the hen, silly. Joke. I've brought you some grouse.'

'Have they been hung?'

'No. I shot them today. Why do you ask?'

'Oh, nothing, nothing. It is verra kind of you, Miss Halburton-Smythe.'

Since Hamish's family did not like grouse, the policeman was calculating how soon he could manage to get into Ullapool, where he would no doubt get a good price for the brace from one of the butchers. If they were fresh, that would give him a few days. Hamish did not possess a freezer except the small compartment of his refrigerator, which was full of TV dinners.

Hamish stood up, startling the hen, who flew off with a squawk, and pulled out a chair for Priscilla. He studied her as she sat down. She was wearing a beige silk blouse tucked into cord breeches. Her waist was small and her breasts high and firm. The pale oval of her face, framed by the pale gold of her hair, was saved from being insipid by a pair of bright blue eyes fringed with sooty lashes. He cleared his throat. 'I cannot leave the telephone. But you will find a bottle of beer in the refrigerator in the kitchen.'

'I thought you didn't like cold beer,' called Priscilla over her shoulder as she made her way across the tiny hall to the kitchen. 'I aye keep one for the guests,' called Hamish, thinking wistfully that he had kept a cold bottle of beer especially for her since that golden day she had first dropped in to see him about a minor poaching matter four whole months ago.

'No more trouble, I hope,' added Hamish as Priscilla returned with a foaming glass. 'I hope it is not the crime that brings you here.'

'No, I thought you might like some birds for the pot.' Priscilla leaned back and crossed her legs, tightening the material along her thighs by the movement. Hamish half closed his eyes.

'Actually, I'm escaping,' said Priscilla. 'Daddy's brought the most awful twit up from London. He wants me to marry him.'

'And will you?'

'No, you silly constable. Didn't I say he was a twit? I say, there's a picture show on at the village hall tonight.

73

Second showing, ten o'clock. Wouldn't it be a shriek if we went to it?'

Hamish smiled. 'My dear lassie, it is Bill Haley and his Comets in *Rock Around the Clock*, which was showing a wee bit before you were born, I'm thinking.'

'Lovely. Let's go after whoever you're speaking to speaks.'

'I cannot think Colonel Halburton-Smythe would like his daughter to go to the pictures with the local bobby.'

'He won't know.'

'You have not been long in the Highlands. Give it a day, give it a week, everyone around here knows everything.'

'But Daddy doesn't *speak* to anyone in the village.'

'Your housemaid, Maisie, is picture daft. She'll be there. She'll tell the other servants and that po-faced butler, Jenkins, will see it as his duty to inform the master.'

'Do you care?'

'Not much,' grinned Hamish. 'Oh, Rory, it is yourself.'

He listened intently. Priscilla watched Hamish's face, noticing for the first time how cat-like his hazel eyes looked with their Celtic narrowness at the outer edges.

'Thank you, Rory,' said Hamish finally. 'That is verra interesting. I am surprised that fact about her is not better known.'

The voice quacked again.

'Thank you,' said Hamish gloomily. 'I may be in the way of having to report a wee murder to you in the next few days. No, it is chust my joke, Rory.' Hamish's accent became more sibilant and Highland when he was seriously upset.

He put down the phone and stared into space.

'What was all that about?' asked Priscilla curiously.

'Gossip about a gossip,' said Hamish, getting to his feet. 'Wait and I'll just lock up, Miss Halburton-Smythe, and we'll be on our way. I'll tell you about it one of these days.'

DAY FOUR

Above all, when playing a big fish, stay calm.
– PETER WHEAT,
The Observer's Book of Fly Fishing

It was a very subdued party that met in the lounge in the morning. Heather Cartwright was visibly losing her usual phlegmatic calm. Her plump face was creased with worry, and her voice shook as she asked them to be seated.

Lady Jane was absent, but everyone seemed to jump a little when anyone entered the room. John Cartwright, in a weary voice, said he felt they had not all learnt the art of casting properly and so he would take them out to the lawn at the back to give a demonstration. His eyes turned to the major to make his usual remark, that those with experience could go ahead, but somehow he could not bring himself to say anything.

They stood about him, shivering in the chill, misty morning air as he demonstrated how to make the perfect cast. He warmed to his subject but his little audience fidgeted restlessly and moved from foot to foot.

Finally, their unease reached him, and he stopped his lecture with a little sigh. 'Enough from me,' he said. 'We will go to the upper reaches of the river Anstey. I'll leave word at the desk for Lady Jane. There is no point in disturbing her if she's sleeping late.'

Like the day before, the warmth of the sun began to penetrate the mist. 'Bad day for fishing,' said the major knowledgeably, and Alice could only envy the quick way in which he had recovered from his humiliation.

'I like the sunshine,' she said, and then could not resist adding, 'and I hope Lady Jane doesn't turn up to spoil it.'

'Got a feeling we won't be seeing her,' said the major cheerfully.

And then it was as if they all had the same feeling. Everyone's spirits began to lift. John Cartwright smiled at his wife and pressed her hand as he drove up the twists and winds to the river. 'I've a feeling we've been worrying too much about that woman,' he murmured to Heather. 'Don't worry. I'll see to it she doesn't plague us any more.'

Alice gave a little sigh of relief. Obviously the Cartwrights were going to tell Lady Jane to leave. She grinned at Charlie, but Charlie was looking white and sick and turned his head away.

She shrugged. Again, the sunshine was bleaching away the worries of the night. She was prepared to accept that she did not stand a chance with Jeremy. Let him have Daphne. There was no use fighting it. She would enjoy the exercise and scenery as much as she could. Once more her thoughts returned to Mr Patterson-James. She was sure he would be impressed when she described her holiday.

But when she climbed out of the car and waited for Heather to hand her her rod, she could not help wishing Jeremy would join her as he had done on the other days.

But John Cartwright, with the continued absence of Lady Jane, was once more on form. He was determined his little class should get the proper schooling. He said he was going to give them a demonstration of how to catch a salmon. When they all had their gear on he led the way up a twisting path beside the river at a smart trot. Alice felt the sweat beginning to trickle down her face as she stumbled along after him. Below them, at the bottom of the steep bank, the river Anstey foamed and frothed. At times, delicate strands of silver birch and alder and hazel screened the river from their view, and then, around another turn it would appear again, tumbling headlong on its road to the sea. To the right, the tangled forest climbed up the mountainside.

Marvin Roth put an arm around his wife's shoulders to help her. 'Didn't mean to take you on a survival course,' he said. Amy shook his arm away and strode ahead of him up the path with long, athletic strides. Marvin hesitated, took off his cap, and passed a hand over the dome of his bald head. Then he replaced his cap and plunged after her.

'What's up with you this morning, Miss Alice?' came Jeremy's voice behind Alice. 'Don't I get a smile?'

Remember, it's no use, Alice chided herself fiercely. Aloud she said, 'I haven't any energy to do anything other than try to keep up. It's so *hot*. I didn't think the Scottish Highlands would be so hot.'

'It's like this sometimes,' said Jeremy, falling into step beside her. He was wearing a blue cotton shirt open at the neck, as blue as the sky above. He smelled of clean linen, aftershave, and masculine sweat. The heavy gold band of his wrist watch lay against the brand-new tan of his arm. Alice's good resolutions began to fade.

'What did you think about our major's little trick?' Jeremy went on. 'Not quite the manner of the officer or the gentleman, as our Lady Jane would point out.'

'I think it was understandable,' said Alice. 'It must have been a terrible temptation to lie. Only think the way people go on about cars and horses and . . . boats.

It's surely more in the nature of a gentleman to *lie* when it comes to sports.'

She gave Jeremy a rather hard-eyed stare. Alice's better nature was trying to drive him away, but Jeremy only felt she had gone off him and was a little piqued.

'Didn't *you* lie yourself?' he jeered. 'Our gossip accused you of lying about the fish you were *supposed* to have caught.'

Easy tears rushed to Alice's eyes. 'I think you're horrid. How can you accuse me of such a thing?'

'Hey, steady on!' Jeremy caught her arm. 'There's no need to fly off the handle like that.'

'I don't know what's up with me,' said Alice, scrubbing her eyes with the back of her hand. 'I think it's that Jane female. She's always hinting things in a spiteful sort of way.'

'You know,' said Jeremy, taking Alice's hand in a warm clasp, 'I don't think we'll ever see her again. I feel she's taken the hint and left. No-one can be that thick-skinned – it surely got through to her that not one of us can stand her.'

He gave her hand a squeeze. Alice's mercurial spirits soared, and her resolution to forget about Jeremy whirled up to the summer sky and disappeared. After they had been climbing about a mile, and Amy Roth was loudly and clearly threatening to call it a day and turn back, John finally came to a stop. 'Down here to the Keeper's Pool,' he called, 'and be very quiet.' The tangled undergrowth gave way at their side of the pool where a ledge of flat rocks hung over the water. The pool swirled and boiled like a witch's cauldron.

It was a joy to watch John casting. He did a roll cast across the pool, landing the fly delicately on the surface. All at once, fishing fever gripped John and he forgot about his class. Suddenly, with a flash of silver scales, a salmon leapt high in the air. Alice clapped her hands in excitement, and everyone said, 'Shhhhh.'

Now the whole class was as intense as their teacher. Then, just as John was casting, Charlie slipped and nearly fell into the pool. Heather shouted, 'Look out!' and caught his arm. John turned to make sure the boy was safe, leaving his line tumbling and turning in the water.

He turned back once he had assured himself that Charlie was all right. He flicked at his line and his rod began to bend. 'You've got one,' breathed the major.

'I don't know . . . I think it's a rock,' muttered John. He moved to another angle and tried to reel in his line. He had something heavy on the end of it, something that was twisting and turning.

His heart began to beat hard. Of course, if it wasn't a rock, it could be a sunken branch, twisting and turning in the churning of the water. He moved back round to where the group was standing on the beach of rocks. Underneath the rock shelf the water was clear and still, a little island of calm just outside the churning of the pool.

He reeled in again, feeling his excitement fade as whatever it was that he had hooked moved from the turbulent water into the still shallows. A log, he thought.

And then Daphne Gore, the usually cool and unflappable Daphne, began to scream and scream, harsh, terror-stricken screams tearing apart the sylvan picture of pretty woods, singing birds, and tumbling water.

Alice stared down into the golden water directly below her feet as she stood on the ledge. And Lady Jane stared back.

Slowly rising to the surface came the bloated, distorted features of Lady Jane Winters. Her tongue was sticking out, and her blue eyes bulged and glared straight up into the ring of faces.

'She must have hit her head and fallen in,' whispered Alice, clinging to Jeremy.

John waded into the water, heaved the body up, and then let it fall with a splash. He turned a chalk-white face up to Heather. 'Get Macbeth,' he said. 'Get the police.'

'But didn't she just fall?' asked Heather, as white as her husband.

John prodded at Lady Jane's fat neck. 'There's a leader round her neck. She's been strangled. And look.' He pointed to Lady Jane's legs.

'Oh, God,' said Alice, 'there's chains wrapped round them.'

'She could have done it herself,' said Amy Roth through white lips. 'Marvin. Help me. I feel sick.'

'Get the police, dammit,' shouted John. 'And get that child out of here. The rest, stay where you are.'

'If it's murder, we'd better all stay,' said Marvin, holding Amy tightly against him.

'Don't be silly,' said Heather. 'It took someone powerful to overcome a woman like Lady Jane and strangle her with a leader. Come along, Charlie. I'll take you to your aunt's and then I'll bring Constable Macbeth.'

'Take me to your leader,' said Daphne and began to giggle.

'Can't anyone stop her?' pleaded Amy.

'Pull yourself together, Daphne,' snapped John Cartwright.

'Steady the buffs,' urged the major.

Daphne sat down abruptly, pulled out a gold cigarette case, and extracted a cigarette with hands that trembled so much the cigarettes spilled out on the rock. Jeremy stooped to help her. Their eyes met and held in a long stare.

'Go up the hill and wait at the top,' commanded John. 'I'll stay with the body.'

Alice, Jeremy, Daphne, the major, and Marvin and Amy Roth made their way up the path. They moved, bunched together, along the upper path until it opened out into a small glade. They sat down in silence. Major Peter Frame pulled out a packet of cigarettes and offered them around.

Marvin was the first to speak. 'I always knew that dame was a party pooper,' he said gloomily. 'She's worse dead than alive. She was murdered, of course.'

'Well, it wasn't any of us,' said Alice. She tried to speak bravely, but her voice trembled and she rubbed at the gooseflesh on her arms.

'Yeah, she was the sort of woman *anyone* would have murdered, I reckon,' said Amy Roth shakily. 'Was she rich? Maybe one of her relatives followed her up here and bumped her off.'

'By Jove, I think you're right,' the major chimed in eagerly. 'I mean, *de mortuis* and all that, but she was a really repulsive, nasty woman. Look at the way she kept getting at each of us. Stands to reason she'd been doing the same thing to other people for years.'

'I suppose the holiday's over,' said Daphne, looking once more her calm self. 'I mean, what's going to happen to us?'

'It won't be left to Macbeth, not a murder,' said Jeremy. 'They'll be sending in some of the big brass. I s'pose they'll take statements from us, take a note of our home addresses, and let us go.'

'It's so unfair,' drawled Daphne. 'Just as I was getting the hang of this fishing thing. You know, I felt so sure that today would be the day I would catch something.'

Everyone looked at Daphne with approval. They were not only joined by the tragedy of the murder but bound in fellowship by that old-as-time obsession, the lure of the kill.

'Well, I've paid for this week and I jolly well expect to get full value,' said the major, 'or they'll need to give me my money back. As soon as that oaf of a village copper gets our statements, I'm off to spend the rest of the day fishing, and if John Cartwright isn't up to it, I'll take any of you as pupils if you'll have me.'

'I'll go with you for a start,' said Jeremy, and the others nodded. The major might have lied about his magnificent salmon bag, but he was undoubtedly an expert angler. His line never became tangled in bushes, and he made his own flies, several of which flaunted their garish colours on his hat.

'I thought of killing her,' said Alice suddenly. 'I'm *glad* she's dead, and I feel guilty at the same time. I feel I *wished* her to death.'

There was a shocked silence.

'Well,' said Jeremy uncomfortably, 'may as well be honest. I think we all felt like that.'

'Not me,' said Amy Roth. The skin at the corners of her eyelids had a stretched, almost oriental look. 'We Blanchards are made of pretty strong stuff.'

'Tell us about it,' said Daphne harshly. 'Tell us about the bloody ol' plantation and massah's in de col', col' ground. Tell us anything in the world, but don't talk about the murder.'

'Not if you're going to be rude,' said Amy, leaning against her husband's shoulder and seeking his hand for comfort.

'I didn't mean to be rude. I really would like to hear about it. All I can think of is a sort of *Gone With the Wind* setting, all crinolines and mint juleps.'

Amy laughed. 'Believe it or not, it was a little bit like that. Of course, that life all went when I was still a child. Pa was a gambler in the true Southern tradition. Well, lemme see. It was a big barn of a place, the Blanchard mansion, like you see in the movies. Pillared colonial front, wide verandahs all round. Green shutters, cool rooms smelling of beeswax and lavender. Flowers evvy-wheah,' said Amy, becoming Southern in accent as she warmed to her subject. Amy's normal voice was a light, almost Bostonian accent. 'And antiques! I decleah, there were more Chippendales and whatyoucallums there than you'd get in one of your English stately homes. We hud been importing them for *yeahs*.'

'Listen!' The major put a hand to his ear in a sort of list-who-approacheth way. Most of his gestures were stagey.

Heather appeared with Constable Macbeth behind her. The policeman was wearing his usual black uniform, shiny with wear. He pulled off his cap, and his red hair blazed in the sun like fire. It was that true Highland red that sometimes looks as if it has purple lights.

'I will chust go down and look at the body,' he said placidly. 'There will be detectives coming up from Strathbane by this afternoon, but I must make sure nothing is touched. If you will wait where you are, I will return in a wee moment and take the statements.'

They waited now in silence. A little knot of dread was beginning to form in the pit of each stomach. It had just been becoming comfortably unreal. Now reality was with them in the shape of the village constable who was down at the pool bent over the body.

A small, fussy man erupted into the glade and glared about him. 'Dr MacArthur,' said Heather, 'I'll take you down. Mr Macbeth is with the body now.'

'The procurator fiscal is on his way from Strathbane,'

said the doctor. 'But I may as well make a preliminary examination. Macbeth's talking about murder. But the man's havering. She could have got her own leader wrapped around her neck and fallen into the pool.'

'And wrapped chains around her legs to sink her?' said Marvin Roth dryly.

'Eh, what? Better go and see.'

He disappeared with Heather.

Again, the group waited.

'I'm hungry,' said Alice at last. 'I know I shouldn't feel hungry, but I am. Would it be too awful if we went back to the cars and had something to eat?'

'Better wait,' said the major. 'Can't be very long now.'

But it seemed ages. They could hear people coming and going. The sun was very high in the sky, and flies droned and danced in the green quiet of the glade.

At last, Hamish Macbeth appeared looking hot and grim.

'We'll all just be going back to the hotel,' he said. 'I'm getting this path closed off until the big brass arrives. The water bailiffs have said they will stand guard.'

A moment before, each one of them had felt he would give anything to be able to move. Now they were overcome by a strange reluctance. There was one large fact each of them had to face up to sooner or later, and each one was putting off the moment.

They all gathered in the hotel lounge. Constable Macbeth surveyed them solemnly.

'The manager has given me the use of a wee room off the reception, so I'll take you one at a time. You first, Mr Cartwright.'

'I'll come too,' said Heather quickly.

'No need for that,' said the constable easily. 'This way, Mr Cartwright.'

Heather sat down, flushed with distress. She looked

like a mother seeing her youngest off to boarding school for the first time.

John followed Hamish Macbeth into a small, dark room furnished simply with a scarred wood desk, some old filing cabinets, and two hard chairs. Hamish sat down beside the desk, and John took the chair opposite.

'Now,' said the policeman, producing a large notebook, 'we'll make a start. It is the doctor's guess that Lady Jane was in the water all night. When did you last see her?'

'At dinner last night,' said John. 'We were celebrating the major's catch.'

'Or rather, the major's find,' murmured Hamish. 'And was she wearing then what she was wearing when she was found dead?'

'Yes, I mean no. No, she was wearing a flowery trouser suit thing last night with evening sandals. She seemed to be wearing her usual fishing outfit when . . . when we saw her in the pool.'

Hamish made a note and then looked up. 'Did you know Lady Jane's job?'

'Job?' said John. 'I didn't know she worked.'

'Well, we'll leave that until later. Did your wife know the nature of Lady Jane's job, I wonder?'

A faint line of sweat glistened on John's upper lip. There was a silence. Hamish patiently repeated the question.

'No,' said John, suddenly and savagely. 'Look here, Macbeth, what is this? You know us both. Do you think either of us would kill her?'

'That is not for me to say,' said Hamish. 'But I willnae get to the person who did it if I don't start to eliminate those that did not. Now what were you doing late last night?'

'How late?'

'She was last seen going up to her room at ten-thirty, according to the hotel servants.'

'I went to bed,' said John, 'and Heather too. We'd had a fairly exhausting day.'

'Did anyone in the group seem to hate Lady Jane?'

'No, we all loved her,' said John sarcastically. 'Good God, man, use your wits. Nobody liked her, not even you.'

'Mphmm. Lady Jane had a nasty habit of making remarks. Did she say anything to you?'

'Nothing in particular. Just general carping.'

'Aye, well, that will do for now. If you'll just send Mrs Cartwright in.'

As John entered the room, Alice was saying with a nervous giggle, 'Just think. One of us must have killed her. I mean, it stands to reason . . .'

It was out in the open now, put into words; that thought they had been keeping resolutely at bay since Lady Jane's body was discovered.

'He wants to see you,' said John to Heather. He added in a low voice as he held open the door for her, 'I told him we didn't know what she did.'

The door to the lounge opened, and a small, anxious-looking woman dressed in a lumpy, powder-blue dress fussed in, dragging Charlie with her. 'I'm Mrs Baxter, Tina Baxter,' she announced, staring around the room with rather bulging blue eyes. 'I only arrived today. My poor boy.' She tried to hug Charlie, but he flinched away from this public demonstration of maternal affection.

'You should keep the boy away from this,' said John. 'There was no need to bring him along.'

'There was every need,' said Tina Baxter. 'I was told the police wanted to interrogate the whole fishing class and nobody is going to frighten my little boy with a lot of questions.'

She proceeded to tell the bemused company about her divorce and the difficulties of rearing a boy single-handed, and that Charlie had written to her saying this Lady Jane was a cruel and evil woman. Her words began to tumble out one over the other in an increasingly unintelligible stream.

Then she stopped suddenly and stared at the door with her mouth open. Hamish's big brass had arrived from Strathbane.

A big, heavyset man draped in a grey double-breasted suit introduced himself as Detective Chief Inspector Blair. He was flanked by two other detectives, Jimmy Anderson and Harry MacNab. Jimmy Anderson was thin and wiry with suspicious blue eyes, and MacNab was short and dumpy with thick black hair and wet-looking black eyes.

'Which one of you runs this school?' demanded Mr Blair. He spoke with a thick Glaswegian accent.

'I do,' said John. 'Constable Macbeth is talking to my wife at the moment.'

'Where?'

'In there,' said John. 'I'll show you the way.'

'No need,' said Blair. 'We'll introduce ourselves.'

Hamish got to his feet as the three men entered the small office. Heather gratefully escaped.

'Macbeth, is it?' said Blair, sitting down in the chair Hamish had just vacated. 'We've got a real juicy one here. Bit out of your league, Constable. The boys and the forensic team are combing the ground. Good bit of work on your part to get the water bailiffs to stand guard.'

He smiled at Hamish and waited for a look of gratitude to appear on the constable's face at the compliment. Hamish looked stolidly back, and Blair scowled with irritation.

'Yes, well, I suppose they all know they're supposed

to stay put until I'm satisfied that no-one in this school did it. School, indeed. All that money and fuss just to catch a fish.'

'I think it would be better if I told them they are not to leave Lochdubh at the moment,' said Hamish. 'Them not having the ESP.'

'Enough of that,' snapped Blair. 'Before I have the rest in, what do you think the motive was for this murder?'

'I think it had something to do with Lady Jane's job,' said Hamish slowly.

'Job? What job?'

'Lady Jane Winters was, in fact, Jane Maxwell, columnist for the London *Evening Star*.'

'That rag! Well, what's so bad about being a columnist?'

'I understand she specialized in taking holidays where there were going to be small groups of British people. She would find out something nasty about each one, since she liked to prove that everyone has a skeleton in the closet. There have been complaints to the press council, but her column's been too popular. Folks chust lap it up and think it will never happen to them. Maybe someone in this group knew about her column, although the fact that she was Jane Maxwell was kept a closely guarded secret.'

'And how did *you* find out if it's that much of a secret?' asked Blair, his eyes raking over the lanky length of the village constable.

'I haff my methods, Watson,' grinned Hamish.

'I am not putting up with any cheek from a Highlander,' snarled Blair. 'How did you find out?'

'I have a relative that works in Fleet Street.'

'And which of these fishing lot knew about her being Jane Maxwell?'

89

'I do not know,' said Hamish patiently. 'I was just beginning to find out when you arrived. I have talked with John Cartwright and you interrupted me when I was in the process of talking to Mrs Heather Cartwright.'

'Before I start with the rest, I'd better fix up accommodation for me and my men. I'll stay here myself, but it's a bit pricey for the lot of us. We've got five officers combing the bushes along with the forensic team at the moment. I saw that police station of yours. You do yourself very well. Any chance of a spare bed or two?'

'I have not the room. I have the one bed for myself and the other bedroom has not the bed but the gardening stuff and the poultry feed and the bags of fertilizer . . .'

'OK, OK, spare me the rural details.' Blair looked piercingly at Hamish, who gave him a sweet smile.

Simple, thought Blair. Would have to be to live here all year round.

He placed his beefy hands on the desk and looked at Hamish in a kindly way. 'I'm thinking you're a wee bit too inexperienced for this sort of high-class crime,' he said. 'We'll use your office at the station because I'm damned if I'll pay hotel phone prices. I have to fight hard enough to get my expenses as it is. Just you attend to your usual rounds and leave the detective work to us. We're all experienced men.'

Hamish looked at the detective chief inspector blankly. Only a few minutes before he had been wondering how to keep out of the case. He had taken a dislike to the chief detective and his sidekicks and did not want to tag around after them. But now he had been told to keep clear, well, all that did was give him a burning desire to find out who had killed Lady Jane.

'I'll be off then,' said Hamish. Blair watched him go and shook his head softly. 'Poor fellow,' he said. 'Never had to do any real work in his life before, and, like all these Highlanders, fights shy of it as much as possible. Send in that American couple, MacNab. Typical pair of tourists. May as well get rid of them first.'

Hamish ambled along the front, gazing dreamily out over the loch. The early evening sun was flooding the bay with gold. The pair of seals were rolling and turning lazily, sending golden ripples washing about the white hulls of the yachts and the green and black hulls of the fishing boats.

He saw the slim, elegant figure of Priscilla Halburton-Smythe walking towards him, and, suddenly overcome with a mixture of shyness and longing, he stopped and leaned his elbows on the mossy stone wall above the beach.

She stopped and stood beside him. 'What's all this I hear?' said Priscilla. 'The hillside's crawling with bobbies, putting things in plastic bags.'

'Lady Jane Winters has been murdered.'

'I heard something to that effect. Big, fat, nasty woman, wasn't she?'

'Aye, you could say that.'

'And who did it, Holmes?'

'I chust don't know, and I've been more or less told to go home and feed my chickens by the detectives from Strathbane.'

'Well, you must be pleased about that. I mean, you never were exactly one of the world's greatest workers.'

'How would you know that, Miss Halburton-Smythe? It is not as if I have the murder on my hands every day of the week.'

'You must admit when Daddy wants to talk to you about poaching or something, you're never where you should be. I told Daddy not to worry you about poachers since you're one yourself.'

'That is not a very nice thing to say.'

'I was only joking. Do you really want to find the murderer? Do you need a Watson? I shall follow you about saying, "By Jove, you're a wonder. How on earth did you think of that?" '

'Oh, I suppose I'll do as I'm told and keep out of the way,' said Hamish equably.

'Funny, I thought you'd have been dying to find out for yourself. All that Highland curiosity.' Priscilla sounded disappointed.

'Aye, well . . .' began Hamish, and then his gaze suddenly sharpened. Mrs Baxter and Charlie could be seen leaving the hotel.

'Are you going to ask them questions?' asked Priscilla, following his gaze. 'Can I listen?'

'Och, no. The wee lad has a very interesting stamp and I wanted to have another look at it.'

'Hamish Macbeth, I give you up!'

He gave her a crooked grin. 'I did not know you had ever taken me on, Miss Halburton-Smythe.'

He pushed his hat up on his forehead, thrust his hands in his pockets, and strolled off to meet the Baxters.

Highly irritated, Priscilla watched him go.

DAY FIVE

A counsel of perfection is very easy advice to give,
but is usually quite impracticable.
– MAXWELL KNIGHT, *Bird Gardening*

Alice started to dress hurriedly, although it was only
seven in the morning. She wanted to escape from the
hotel before they were besieged by the press again. They
had started to filter in gradually, and by late evening
they had grown to an army: an army of questioning
faces. Alice's juvenile crime loomed large in her
mind. If Lady Jane could have found out about *that*,
then they could too. Normally Alice would have been
thrilled to bits at the idea of getting her photograph
in the papers. But her murky past tortured her. Jeremy
had been particularly warm and friendly to her the
evening before. She felt sure he would not even look at
her again if he found out. The major had howled
at the hotel manager over the problem of the press,
and the manager had at last reluctantly banned them.
He was thoroughly fed up with the notoriety the murder
had brought to his hotel and had hoped to ease the
pain with the large amount of money the gentlemen
of the press were spending in the bar. But guests
other than the major had complained, guests who came
every year. And so the reporters and the photographers
were now billeted out in the village, most of them at a

boarding house at the other end of the bay.

Alice was just on the point of leaving the room when the telephone began to ring. She stared at it and then suddenly rushed and picked it up. Her mother's voice, sharp with agitation, sounded over the line. 'What's all this, luv? Your name's in the morning papers. You didn't even tell us you was going to such a place. We're that worried.'

'It's all right, Mum,' said Alice. 'It's got nothing to do with me.'

'I know that, luv, but that woman that was murdered, her photo's in the papers and she was around here last week, asking questions. Said she was writing a piece on young girls who had made the move to London and their reasons for doing it.'

She must have got all our addresses from Heather, thought Alice with a sudden sickening lurch of the heart. Heather even sent me the names of the other guests, sort of to make it sound social.

Her voice shrill with anxiety, Alice asked, 'Did she find out anything about me being in court?'

'You was never in court, luv.'

'Yes. 'Member? It was when I broke Mr Jenkins' window and he took me to the juvenile court.'

'Oh, *that*. She didn't ask me and I don't suppose anyone around here remembers a silly little thing like that. She talked to Maggie Harrison, mind.'

Alice held tightly on to the phone. Maggie Harrison had been her rival for years. If Maggie could have remembered anything nasty about her, Alice, then Maggie would have undoubtedly told everything.

'Are you there?' Her mother's voice sounded like a squawk. 'I'm in a call box and the money's running out. Can you call me back?'

'No, Mum, I've got to go. I'll be all right.'

'Take care of yourself, will you? I don't like you getting mixed up with those sort of people.'

The line went dead.

Alice slowly replaced the receiver and wiped her damp palm on her sweater. Well, Lady Jane couldn't write anything now.

She turned quickly and ran from the room. Outside the hotel a thin, greasy drizzle was falling.

She looked quickly along the waterfront, dreading to see a reporter waiting to pounce on her, but everything was deserted as far as she could see. She hesitated. Perhaps it would have been better to stay in the hotel. It was now banned to the press, so why bother to venture out? But the fear of anyone – Jeremy in particular – finding out about her past drove her on.

There was a pleasant smell of woodsmoke, tar, kippers, bacon, and strong tea drifting from the cottages. Alice approached Constable Macbeth's house and saw him standing in his garden, feeding the chickens. He turned at the sound of her footsteps, and she smiled weakly.

'Is your third degree over?' asked the policeman.

'It wasn't so bad,' said Alice. 'I really didn't know that awful woman was a newspaper columnist, and I think they believed me.'

'I was just about to make a cup of tea. Would you like one?'

'Yes,' said Alice gratefully, thinking how very unlike a policeman Constable Macbeth looked. He was hatless and wearing an old army sweater and a faded pair of jeans. That chief detective had made it plain that the village constable would not be having anything to do with the investigation. Mr Macbeth must have riled him in some way because he had been quite unpleasant about it, Alice remembered. Blair had asked her if she had noticed or heard anything unusual that might point to the murderer, and Alice had shaken her head, but had said if she did remember anything she would tell Constable Macbeth, and that was when Blair had sourly pointed out that the village policeman was not part of the murder investigation.

Alice followed Hamish into his kitchen, which was long and narrow with a table against the window.

She looked round the kitchen curiously. It was messy in a clean sort of way. There were piles of magazines, china, bits of old farm implements, Victorian dolls, and stacks of jam jars.

'I'm a hoarder,' said Mr Macbeth. 'I aye think a thing'll fetch a good price if I just hang on to it. I have a terrible time throwing things away. Milk and sugar?'

'Yes, please,' said Alice. He gave her a cup, sat down next to her at the table, and heaped five spoonfuls of sugar into his own tea.

'Do I look like a murderer?' asked Alice intently.

'I think a murderer could look like anyone,' said the policeman placidly. 'Now this Lady Jane, it strikes me she went to a lot of work to find out about the people who were going to be at the fishing school. How did she know who was going?'

'Oh, that's easy. Heather sent us all a list of names and addresses. The idea is that we can get in touch with anyone in our area and maybe travel up with them. That's how Jeremy came to travel up with Daphne. He didn't know her before.' Alice blushed furiously and buried her nose in her cup.

'Yes, and she must have found out about me and my family after she came,' said Hamish. 'She had only to ask a few people in the village. You can't keep anything secret in the Highlands.'

'I wish she had never come,' said Alice passionately. 'She's ruined my life.'

'Indeed! And how is that?'

The rain was falling more steadily and the cluttered kitchen was peaceful and warm. Alice had a longing to unburden herself.

'If a young man was interested in a girl,' she said, not looking at him, 'would you think that young man might go off that girl if he found out she had done something . . . well, against the law, when she was a kid?'

'It depends on the young man. Now if you're talking about Mr Jeremy Blythe . . .'

'You *noticed*. He *is* rather sweet on me.' Alice removed her hat and tossed back her fluffy hair in what she fondly thought was a femme-fataleish sort of way.

'It depends on the crime,' said Hamish. 'Now if you'd poisoned your mother or . . .'

'No, nothing like that,' said Alice. 'Look, when I was about Charlie's age, I threw a brick through Mr Jenkins' window for a dare. Mr Jenkins was a nasty old man who lived in our street. The other girls egged me on. Well, he got me charged and taken to court. All I got was a warning and Mum had to pay for the window and the local paper put a couple of lines about it at the bottom of one of their pages. I mean, it was a silly little thing, really, but would a man like Jeremy mind? You see, he's awfully ambitious and . . . and . . . well, he plans to stand for Parliament, and . . . and . . . oh, do you know now I've told you, I realize I've been worrying about nothing. I should have told *him*. In fact, I'd better before anyone else does. How he'll laugh!'

'If it's that unimportant,' said Hamish, pouring himself more tea, 'then I am thinking that there is no need whateffer to tell anyone at all. In my opinion, Miss Wilson, Mr Blythe is something of a snob and would not normally be interested in you were he not on holiday . . .'

Alice leapt to her feet. '*You're* the snob,' she said. 'And rude, too. I'll show you. I'll tell Jeremy right now and when I'm Mrs Blythe, you can eat your words.'

'As you please.' Hamish shrugged. Alice rushed out of the house and slammed the kitchen door with a bang. Hamish cursed himself for being clumsy. Alice reminded him of Ann Grant, a young girl brought up in Lochdubh, only passably pretty. She had been seen around one of the flashier holiday guests two summers ago, driving with him everywhere in his car, and gossiping about the grand wedding she would have. But the holiday maker had left and Ann had gone about ill and red-eyed. She had been packed off suddenly to a relative in Glasgow. The village gossips said she had gone to have an abortion and was now walking the streets. But Hamish had heard through *his* relatives that she was working as a typist in a Glasgow office and had said she never wanted to see Lochdubh or her family again. If her family hadn't been so common, she said, then her beau would have married her.

Snobbery is a terrible thing, thought Hamish dismally. It can almost kill young girls. Would they kill because of it? That was a question well worth turning over.

Alice ran all the way back to the hotel and straight up to Jeremy's room. She pounded on the door until a muffled voice shouted, 'The door's open. I'm in the bathroom.'

She pushed open the door. Perhaps the murder had made her a little crazy or perhaps Alice had lived in a fantasy world for too long, but she justified her next action by persuading herself that they were going to be married, or would be married if she established a basis of intimacy. She strolled casually into the bathroom and sat on the edge of the bath.

'Hello, darling,' she said.

Jeremy hastily floated a large sponge over himself to act as a fig leaf and asked carefully, without looking at her, 'Have you been drinking? I know we're all shattered by this murder business but . . .'

Alice came down to reality with a bump. 'I'll wait for you in the bedroom,' she gasped. 'I've got something I *must* tell you.'

She sat nervously on the bed by the window, fidgeting with the curtain cord and wishing she hadn't been so *bold*.

Jeremy came out with a white towel knotted around his waist and drying his hair with another.

Alice turned her face away and twisted a handkerchief nervously in her hands.

'*Now* you look like your usual self,' said Jeremy. 'For a moment there I thought you were going to rape me.'

'Don't make fun of me,' said Alice, wishing he wouldn't look so amused, so *detached*. What if Macbeth should prove to be right?

But if they were married, it might come out. Better tell him now. And so Alice did, simply plunging into her story at the beginning and charging on until the end.

As she talked, she was back there in that dusty court on that hot summer's day with the tar melting on the roads outside. She could still remember her mother, crying with shame. She could remember her own sick feeling of disgrace.

When she finished, she looked at Jeremy awkwardly. He was studying her face in an intent, serious way. Jeremy was actually wondering whether to share his own guilty secret and at the same time noticing how Alice's schoolgirlish blouse was strained against her small, high

99

breasts. God, it had been ages since . . . Then there was all this fear and worry about the murder. Yes, he knew why Alice had dreaded Lady Jane printing that bit of childhood nonsense. Hadn't he himself gone through hell to try to shut her mouth? He glanced at the clock. Eight-thirty. Too early for a drink but not too early for that other tranquillizer.

He sat down beside Alice on the bed and drew her against his still-damp body. 'You don't mind?' whispered Alice.

'Of course not,' he said, stroking her hair. She smelled of nervous sweat, sharp and acrid, mixed with lavender talcum powder. He put a hand on one little breast and began to stroke it.

Alice shivered against him. She was not a virgin, having lost that through curiosity and drink two years ago in the back of a car after a party with a man whose name she could not remember. It had been a painful and degrading experience, but he had been a heavy, vulgar sort of man.

Women's Lib has a long way to go before it gets *inside* girls like Alice. As his lips began to move against her own, her one thought was, 'If I sleep with him, he'll have to marry me.'

As they lay stretched out on the bed, pressed together, as Alice's clothes were removed, she had an idiotic wish that Jeremy might have been wearing some sort of status symbol, his gold wrist watch, say. For when the all-too-brief foreplay was over and she was rammed into the bed by the panting, struggling weight of this man, it all seemed as painful and degrading as that time in the back of the car. She wished he'd hurry up and get it over with. There was that terrible tyranny of the orgasm. What *was* it? He was obviously waiting for something to happen to her. She had read about women shrieking in ecstasy, but if she shrieked, she might bring people rushing in, thinking there had been another murder.

His silence was punctuated by grunts, not words of love. At last, just when she thought she could not bear it any longer, he collapsed on top of her. She let out a long sigh of relief, and Jeremy kissed her ear and said, 'It was good for you too,' mistaking her sigh for one of satisfaction.

'I love you, Jeremy,' whispered Alice, winding her arms around him and hugging that vision of sports cars, expensive clothes, good accent, and Member of Parliament.

'Do you?' He propped himself up on one elbow. 'That's nice.' He kissed her nose and then smacked her on the bottom. 'Better get dressed. Gosh, I'm hungry.'

Alice scooped up her clothes and scuttled into the bathroom. After she had showered and dressed, she felt better. Love in the morning. How sophisticated. How deliciously decadent.

She was just putting on lipstick when Jeremy shouted through the door, 'I'll see you in the dining room. Don't be long.'

Alice's hand jerked nervously, and she smeared lipstick over her cheek. She scrubbed it off with a tissue and then ran out, hoping to catch him, but he had already left.

When she went out into the corridor, two maids were stuffing dirty sheets into a hamper and they looked at her curiously. 'Good morning,' said Alice, staring at both of them hard as if challenging them to voice their evil thoughts.

The fishing party was grouped around one large table in the far corner as if the management had decided to put them in quarantine. The Roths were there and Daphne, the major, and Jeremy. Charlie would be having breakfast with his aunt, but where were the Cartwrights?

'Don't know,' shrugged Daphne. 'I think they jolly well ought to be here handing out refunds. Pass the marmalade, Jeremy darling.'

Alice frowned. It was time to stake her claim. She slid into a chair beside Jeremy and took his hand under the table, gave it a squeeze, and smiled at him in an intimate way.

'I need both hands to eat, Alice,' said Jeremy crossly. Alice snatched her hand away and Daphne giggled.

Heather and John Cartwright were sitting in Hamish's cluttered kitchen, eating bacon baps and drinking tea. They had explained they were 'just passing'.

It was Heather who had had the impulse to talk to Hamish. Hamish was a good sounding board because he *was* the law, and although he could hardly be described as a strong arm of it, he was in a position to overhear how the investigation was proceeding.

'I just hope this won't break the fishing school,' said John gloomily.

'I should not think so,' said Hamish, turning bacon deftly in the pan. 'Provided, of course, the murderer is found. It will be in the way of being an added attraction.'

'I was shocked when Blair told me she was really that awful columnist woman.'

Hamish stood very still, his back to them as he worked at the stove. 'And you did not know this before?' he asked.

There was a little silence, and then John said, 'Of course not. Had we known then we should not have allowed her to come.'

'Aye, but did you not know after she had arrived?' asked Hamish.

Again that silence. Hamish turned round, the bacon slice in one hand.

'No, we did not,' said Heather emphatically.

Hamish carefully and slowly lifted the bacon from the pan and put it on a plate. He turned off the gas. He lifted his cup of tea from beside the stove and came and joined Heather and John at the table.

'I happen to know that you had a letter from Austria. You see, you threw it out of the window, hoping it would land in the loch. The tide was out and the boy Charlie picked it up because the stamp attracted his attention. I would not normally read anyone else's mail, but when it comes to murder, well, I don't have that many fine scruples. It was from a couple of friends of yours in Austria who ran a ski resort until Lady Jane came on holiday.'

'You have no right to read private mail,' shouted John.

Hamish looked at him stolidly.

Heather put a hand on John's arm. 'It's no use,' she said wearily. 'We did know. We were frightened. This school is our life. Years of hard work have gone into building it up. We thought she was going to take it away from us.'

'But the couple at the ski resort turned out to be married to other people, not each other,' pointed out Hamish. 'They said the publicity by Lady Jane ruined them only because Mr Bergen, the ski resort owner, had not been paying alimony for years. You are surely both not in that sort of position. When you found out, would it not have been better to try to tell the school, openly and in front of her, what she did for a living?'

'I didn't think of that,' said John wretchedly. 'You may as well know that I saw Jane on the night she was murdered. I went up to her room after dinner.'

103

'And . . . ?'

'And she just laughed at me. She said this sort of fly fishing in these waters was like grouse shooting or deer stalking – a sport for the rich. She said she was about to prove that the sort of people who went on these holidays were social climbers who deserved to be cut down to size.'

'Deary me,' said Hamish, stirring his tea, 'was she a Communist?'

'I don't think she was a member of the Communist Party, if that's what you mean,' said John. 'She seemed to want to make people writhe. She was like a black-mailer who enjoys power. In Scotland they would say she was just agin everything.'

'Did she say she was out to ruin the fishing school?'

'Not in so many words. But that's what she was setting out to do.'

'What exactly did you say?'

'I said that I had worked hard to build up this school and I begged her not to harm it. She laughed at me and told me to get out. I said . . . I said . . .'

'Yes?' prompted Hamish gently.

'You'd better tell him,' said Heather.

'I told her I would kill her,' whispered John. 'I shouted it. I'll have to tell Blair – I think Jeremy heard me.'

'Mr Blythe? Why would he hear you? Is his room next to hers?'

'No, he was out in the corridor when I left.'

'What will we do, Mr Macbeth?' pleaded Heather.

'I think you should tell Mr Blair. If there's one thing that makes a detective like Blair suspicious, or any detective for that matter, it's finding out someone's been hiding something. The pair of you have got nothing awful in your past that Lady Jane was about to expose?'

Both shook their heads.

'And apart from the short time that Mr Cartwright was with Lady Jane, you were together all night?'

'Why do you ask?' Heather had turned white.

'I ask,' said Hamish patiently, 'because any copper with a nasty mind might think that *one* of you might have sneaked off and bumped her off, if not the pair of you.'

'We had better go,' said Heather. 'Tell Mr Blair we're taking the class up to the Marag to fish. It's near enough. We must go on as if nothing had happened.'

After they left, Hamish, who already heard the sound of voices from his office at the front, ambled through with a cup of tea in one hand.

'Shouldn't you be in uniform?' growled Blair, who was seated behind Hamish's desk flanked by his two detectives.

'In a minute,' said Hamish easily.

'And I told you to keep out of this. That was the Cartwrights I saw leaving.'

'Aye.'

'Well, what did they have to say for themselves?'

'Only that they knew something they hadn't told you and now thought they should. Also that they were taking the class up to the Marag which is quite close so that you can go and see any of the members quite easily.'

'For Jesus buggering Christ's sake, don't they know this is a murder investigation?'

'Find any clues?' asked Hamish.

'Just one thing. If it had been like today, we might have found more traces. But most of the ground was baked hard. The procurator fiscal's report says she was strangled somewhere else and dragged along through the bushes and then thrown in the pool.'

'And what is this clue?'

'It's just a bit of a photograph,' said MacNab, before

Blair could stop him. 'Just a bit torn off the top corner. See.'

He held out the bit of black and white photograph on a pair of tweezers. Hamish took it gingerly.

It showed the very top of a woman's head, or what he could only guess to be a woman's head because it had some sort of sparkly ornament on top like the edge of a tiara. Behind was a poster with the part legend BUY BRIT—.

'That might have been Buy British,' said Hamish, 'which means it would have been taken in the sixties when Wilson was running that Buy British campaign and that would therefore eliminate the younger members of the fish . . .'

'Listen to the great detective,' jeered Blair. 'We all reached that conclusion in two seconds flat. Why don't you trot off and find out if anyone's been raiding the poor box in one of those churches. Damn ridiculous having so many churches in a wee place like this.'

Hamish turned to amble out. 'And get your uniform on,' shouted Blair.

'Now,' said Blair, rustling through sheafs of statements. 'According to these, they're all innocent. But one of them was so afraid that Lady Jane would print something about them that they killed her. So chase up all these people we phoned yesterday and hurry them up. And that includes background on the Roths. See if there's been a telex from the FBI. Find out if any of them have been in trouble with the police, although I think you'll have to dig deeper than that.'

Hamish changed into his uniform, admitting to his reflection in the glass that he, Hamish Macbeth, was a very angry man. In fact, he could not quite remember being so angry in all his easygoing life. He was determined to go on talking to the members of the fishing school until someone said something that gave himself away. He was not going to be frightened because it was a murder investigation. All criminals were the same whether it was a theft in the school or poaching deer on the hills. You talked, asked questions, and listened and watched and waited. The hell with Blair. He would go up to the Marag and find out what Jeremy had been doing outside Lady Jane's room. As he left by the back door, the press were entering the police station by the front. At least Lochdubh would be spared their headlines until the following morning. The newspapers were always a day late.

In any common-or-garden murder, the press would not hang about longer than a day or two. But this murderee had a title and the location was well away from their office with out-of-town expenses, so they would all try to spin it out as long as they could. Of course, Lady Jane had been one of their own, so to speak, and Hamish had learned from his relative in Fleet Street some time ago that the press were not like the police: they were notoriously uninterested in anything that happened to one of their ranks except as a subject for gossip.

The day was warm and sweaty, and although the rain had stopped, there was a thick mist everywhere and the midges were out in clouds. Hamish took a stick of repellent out of his tunic pocket and rubbed his face and neck with it.

When he reached the Marag, it was to find the fishing school diligently at work, looking like some old army-jungle movie, as each one had a mosquito net shrouding the face.

Hamish scanned the anonymous figures, picked out Heather and John by virtue of their expert casting rather than their appearance, and Charlie because of his size

107

and because his mother was sitting on a rock nearby, flapping away the mosquitoes and watching her son as if expecting him to be dragged off to prison at any moment. Hamish went to join her.

'I think this is ridiculous,' she burst out as soon as she saw him. 'It's horrible weather and the whole school should be broken up and sent home.'

'They seem quite happy,' said Hamish.

'I don't understand it,' wailed Mrs Baxter. 'Those Cartwrights suggested the school should try to go on as if nothing has happened, and they all leapt at it when just a moment before they had been threatening to ask for their money back. I told my Charlie *he* was coming straight home with me, and he *defied* me. Just like his father.' Two large tears of self-pity formed in Mrs Baxter's eyes and she dabbed at them furiously with a tissue. 'I knew I should never have let Charlie come all the way up here. The minute I got his letter, I was on the train.'

'Aye, and when did you arrive?'

'I *told* the police. I got to Lochdubh just after the terrible murder.'

'Then how is it that Mrs MacPherson down at the bakery saw you the night before.'

'It wasn't me. It must have been someone else.'

'Blair will check the buses and so on, you know,' said Hamish. 'It's always better to tell the truth. If you don't, it looks as if you might have something to hide. Did you know Lady Jane was a newspaperwoman?'

Mrs Baxter sat in silence, twisting the damp tissue in her fingers. Rain dripped from her sou-wester. 'She's been around the neighbourhood asking questions,' said Mrs Baxter at last in a low voice. 'I've never got on with my neighbours and I know they told her all about the divorce. But what's divorce? Half the population of

Britain get divorced every year. I've nothing to be ashamed of and that I told her.'

'You *told* Lady Jane?'

'Well, I phoned her before I got on the train,' said Mrs Baxter miserably, 'and I said if she wrote anything about my Charlie I would . . .'

'Kill her?'

'People say all sorts of things they don't mean when they're angry,' said Mrs Baxter defiantly. 'This is a wretched business. Do you know that detective, MacNab, was round at the house last night asking for Charlie's leader?'

'No, I did not. I'm shocked.'

'So you should be. Suspecting a mere child.'

'It is not that that shocks me but the fact that they did not immediately check all the leaders earlier in the day. Was anyone's leader missing?'

'*I* don't know. *You* should know. They fingerprinted everyone as well.'

Out of the corner of his eye, Hamish saw a white police car moving slowly round the edge of the loch.

He moved quickly out of sight behind a stand of trees and made his way silently along a rabbit track that led back down to the village. Jeremy would have to wait. Hamish went straight to the hotel and asked the manager, Mr Johnson, where the press had disappeared to, since he would have expected them to be up at the loch, photographing the school.

'There's a big Jack the Ripper sort of murder broken in London,' said Mr Johnson, 'and that's sent most of them scampering back home. The nationals anyway. This is small beer by comparison. Also, Blair got the water bailiffs to block the private road to the Marag. He hates the press. Going to solve the murder for us, Mr Macbeth?'

109

'Aye, maybe.' Hamish grinned. 'Any hope of a wee shufty at Lady Jane's room?'

'Blair had it locked, of course. No-one's to go in. Police commandment.'

'I'm the police, so there'll be no harm in letting me in.'

'I suppose. Come along then. But I think you'd better try to leave things as they are. I've a feeling that Blair doesn't like you.'

Hamish followed the manager upstairs and along the corridors of the hotel. 'They took a plan of all the hotel rooms,' said Mr Johnson over his shoulder. 'I don't know what they expect to learn from that because it's said she was strangled up on the hillside in the middle of the night, not far from where she was shoved in the pool. They've found a bittie of a photograph, and Blair got everybody down to the last chambermaid fingerprinted. No fingerprints on the photo, of course, and none on those chains that were around her legs, as if there would be anything worthwhile after that time of churning and bashing about that pool. But Mr Blair likes to throw his weight around. Here we are.'

He put the key in the lock and opened the door. Lady Jane had occupied a suite with a good view of the loch. 'I'll leave you to it,' said Mr Johnson cheerfully. 'I can't feel sad about this murder. It's turned out good for business. Every lunch and dinner is booked up solid for the next few weeks. They're coming from as far as Aberdeen, but then these oil people have more money than sense.'

Left alone, Hamish stood in the middle of the bedroom and looked around. Surely it must have dawned on Blair before anything else that Lady Jane would have brought notes of some kind. Yes, of course it had. Fingerprint dust lay like grey snow on every surface.

Well, they would hardly come back for *more* finger-prints. Hamish began his search. The suite consisted of a small entrance hall with a side table and one chair, a tiny sitting room with a writing desk, television set and two easy chairs, a bedroom with a bathroom leading off it.

There was a typewriter open on the writing desk with a pile of hotel writing paper beside it. He diligently searched the top of the desk and drawers. There was not a single piece of paper with any writing on it what-soever. Perhaps Blair had taken away what there was.

He turned his attention to the bedroom. He slid open drawers of frivolous underwear – Lady Jane's taste in that direction was rather startling – and rummaged underneath. Nothing. If she had had a handbag, then Blair must have taken it away. Two suitcases lay on a luggage rack at the foot of the bed. Locked.

He took a large ring of keys out of his tunic pocket and got to work, listening all the while in case Blair should choose that moment to return for another search. At last the first case sprang open. There was a lavender sachet, two detective stories, a box of heated rollers, and a hair dryer. No paper of any kind. The next suitcase was completely empty.

He looked under the bed, under the mattress, down the sides of the chairs, even in the toilet tank and the bathroom cupboard, but not one scrap of paper did he find.

The manager had left the keys in the door. Hamish carefully locked the room and deposited the keys in the manager's office.

He decided to go back to the Marag to see if the field was clear. But as he was making his way out of the hotel, he heard voices from the interviewing room and noticed Alice sitting nervously in the lounge outside.

111

'He's got Jeremy in there,' said Alice. 'Will this never end? He's going to see me next and then call in the others one by one. I told Jeremy about that court thing and he didn't mind, so you were wrong.'

'Is that a fact?' said Hamish, looking down at her curiously.

Alice jerked her head to one side to avoid the policeman's gaze. Jeremy had been offhand all day, to say the least.

Hamish left quickly, deciding to try to find out a bit about the background of the others. He had in his tunic a list of the names and addresses of the members of the school. Perhaps he should start by trying to find out something about the Roths. But he could not use the telephone at the police station because Blair had set up headquarters there, and although he was busy interviewing Jeremy, no doubt his team of officers would be in the office.

Hamish's car was parked outside his house. He decided to take a run up to the Halburton-Smythes. The rain had stopped falling and a light breeze had sprung up. But everything was wet and sodden and grey. Mist shrouded the mountains, and wet, long-haired sheep scampered across the road in front of the car on their spindly black legs like startled fur-coated schoolmarms.

He swung off the main road and up the narrower one which led through acres of grouse moor to the Halburton-Smythes' home. Home was a mock castle, built by a beer baron in the last century when Queen Victoria made the Highlands fashionable. It had pinnacles, turrets, and battlements and a multitude of small, cold, dark rooms.

Hamish pushed open the massive, brass-studded front door and walked into the stone-flagged gloom of the hall. He made his way through to the estates office,

112

expecting to find Mr Halburton-Smythe's secretary, Lucy Hanson, there, but the room was deserted and the bright red telephone sitting on the polished mahogany desk seemed to beg Hamish to reach out and use it.

He sat down beside the desk and after some thought phoned Rory Grant at the *Daily Recorder* in Fleet Street. Rory sounded exasperated when he came on the line. 'What's the use of having a bobby for a relative if I can't get an exclusive on a nice juicy murder? I had my bags packed and was going to set out on the road north when the Libyans decided to put a bomb in Selfridges and some Jack the Ripper started cutting up brass nails in Brixton, so I'm kept here. No-one cares about your bloody murder now, but you might have given me a buzz. I called the police station several times, and some copper told me each time to piss off.'

'It would still be news if I found the murderer, Rory,' cajoled Hamish. 'You know the people who are at the fishing school. The names have been in all the papers. See if you can find out a bit more about them than has appeared. Oh, and while I'm on the phone, if I wanted to find out about someone from New York who might have been in trouble, or someone from Augusta, Georgia, what would I do?'

'You phone the FBI, don't you, you great Highland berk.'

'I think Detective Chief Inspector Blair will have done that and I would not want to go treading on any toes.'

'You can phone the newspapers, then, but you'll need to wait until I go and get names from the foreign desk. You are a pest, Hamish.'

Hamish held the line patiently until Rory returned with the information.

He thanked the reporter and, after listening to the silence of the castle for a few moments, dialled New

113

York. He was in luck. The reporter Rory had recommended said cheerfully it was a slack day and did Hamish want him to call back. 'No, I will chust wait,' said Hamish, comfortably aware that he was not paying for the call.

After some time the reporter came back with the information on Marvin Roth. 'All old history,' he said cheerfully. 'Seems that back around 1970, he was in trouble over running sweatshops in the garment district. Employing illegal aliens and paying them peanuts. Big stink. Never got to trial. Bribed his way out of it. Wants to go into politics. Big man in town now. Donates to charities, fashionable pinko, ban the bomb and clean up the environment. No-one's going to rake up his past. Got a nasty way of hitting back. Knows all the big names and he's a buddy of my editor's, so don't say where you got the information from, for Chrissake.'

'Do you mean to tell me that you cannot print the facts?'

'Absolutely.'

'It is all very strange,' said Hamish, shaking his head. 'I have never been to New York. What is the weather like at the moment?'

They chatted amiably for five more minutes at Mr Halburton-Smythe's expense before Hamish remembered the BUY BRIT— on the section of photograph. It seemed that it must be Buy British, but could it perhaps be an American advertisement?

'Never heard of anything like it,' said the American reporter cheerfully, 'but I'll ask around.' Hamish gave him the Halburton-Smythes' phone number and told the reporter to give any information to Priscilla.

Then he phoned Augusta, Georgia. Here he was unlucky. The reporter sounded cross and harried. No, he didn't know anything about Amy Roth, née

Blanchard, off the top of his head. Yes, he would phone back, but he couldn't promise.

Hamish put down the telephone and sighed.

He heard the sound of heavy footsteps in the corridor and jumped to his feet. Colonel Halburton-Smythe erupted into the room. He was a small, thin, choleric man in his late fifties. Hamish marvelled anew that the fair Priscilla could have such an awful father.

'What are you doing here, Officer?' barked the colonel, looking suspiciously at the phone.

'I was waiting for your good self,' said Hamish. 'Miss Halburton-Smythe told me you were still having trouble with the poachers.'

'I've just been down to your wretched station. Fat chappie told me he was in the middle of a murder investigation. Told him one of my deer had been shot in the leg last night. Gave me a wall-eyed stare. Useless, the lot of you. What are you going to do about it?'

'I will look into the matter,' said Hamish soothingly.

'See that you do, and while we're on the subject of poaching, I believe you've been squiring my daughter to the local flea pit. It's got to stop.'

'It was not a den of vice,' said Hamish patiently. 'And I would say Miss Halburton-Smythe is old enough to know her own mind.'

'If I find you sniffing around my daughter again,' said the colonel rudely, 'I'll report you to your superiors.'

'You should not let yourself be getting in the bad temper,' said Hamish soothingly. 'Why, I can see the wee red veins breaking out all over your eyeballs. A terrible thing is the high blood pressure. Why, I mind . . .'

'Get out!'

'Very well.' Hamish sauntered off with maddening slowness.

115

Once out in the drive, however, he could not resist loitering and looking around for a glimpse of Priscilla.

'If you think you're going to see my daughter,' barked the colonel behind him, 'have another think. She's gone out for the day with John Harrington, Lord Harrington's son, and for your further information, she is shortly going to become engaged to him.'

Hamish realized with some amazement that hearts actually did ache. Without replying, he walked to his car, climbed in and, without once looking at the colonel again, he drove off.

When he arrived at the police station, it was to find Blair and MacNab were still at the hotel and the suspicious-eyed detective, Jimmy Anderson, was sitting behind the desk in the office.

Hamish noticed a woman's handbag on the desk. 'Would that be Lady Jane's?' he asked.

'Yes,' grunted the detective without looking up.

'And would she maybe have a diary or anything with notes?'

'No, she did not,' said Jimmy Anderson. 'Deil a piece o' paper or a note. Her money's there and her credit cards and cheque-book.'

'And it was in her room?'

'Aye, and Mr Blair still thinks someone killed her to stop her publishing something.'

'What have you got on them, just by way of a wee gossip?' Hamish reached a hand into a vase and produced a bottle of Scotch. 'You'll be having a dram, of course.'

'That's very kind of you,' said Anderson, visibly thawing. 'Don't see any harm in telling you, only don't tell Blair. Cheers. Right, now. We're waiting to hear about the Roths. Blair's keen on them all of a sudden despite that Buy British thing. He thinks there's a chance

116

Roth might have Mafia connections and Lady Jane might have been on to it. Would damage his career.'

'Would it now,' said Hamish, pouring himself a whisky. 'Mind you, it doesn't seem to have got in the way of an American politician's career before. What about Amy Roth?'

'We're trying to find a bit on her too.'

'But Lady Jane would not have had the time to find out about the Roths. I mean, if it's that difficult.'

'All these bookings were made at least eight months ago and that's when Lady Jane got the list. She's been in the States since then.'

'She certainly worked hard for her living,' said Hamish. 'A little more to warm you, Mr Anderson?'

'Thank you. Call me Jimmy. As to the rest, Jeremy Blythe's got an interest in politics as well. He was supposed to be sent down from Oxford for having an affair with the wife of one of the dons, but there's more to it than that. While he was having an affair with her, he also found time to get one of the local barmaids pregnant, and her husband raised a stink at the college. That way the don's wife found out and made a stink. Then he owed money all over the place although Daddy's rich. Wasn't studying. Sent down and finished his degree at London University. Became respectable but is still paying for the upkeep of the barmaid's kid. Her husband settled for that out of court. Daddy bought him a partnership, but he's been making rumblings of becoming the next Conservative candidate. At a party last year, old friend from Oxford started ribbing him about the barmaid and this Jeremy punched him rotten. Police called in but no charges. Filthy temper, he has.

'Alice Wilson chucked a brick through a neighbour's window when she was a kid and ended up in court. Not much there.

117

'Daphne Gore comes from a rich family. Caused a scandal by running off with a Spanish waiter who, it turned out, had no intention of marrying her but had to be bought off by Daphne's parents. Girl went into a depression and was in a psychiatric clinic for a few months. Could be a bit of insanity still around.

'Heather and John Cartwright. Very suspicious. Owned up they knew Lady Jane was out to get the school and they're both fishing mad. Not a sport with *them*, more a religion.

'Charlie Baxter. You can never tell with kids of that age, but I'm sure he's out of it. The mother, on the other hand, is a hysterical type.'

'And the major?' prompted Hamish. 'He was more humiliated by Lady Jane than any of them.'

'Oh, the fishing and all that. We heard about how he'd threatened to kill her. Don't think there's anything to worry about there. Fine old soldier. Blair likes him. But we're waiting for a full report.'

There was the crunch of wheels on the gravel outside. One minute Hamish was lounging in the chair opposite Anderson. The next he was gone – and the bottle of whisky.

Hamish ambled along the front. A pale sun was beginning to turn the mist to gold, and there was a long patch of greenish-blue sky out on the horizon where the tiny white dot of a yacht bucketed about to show the approaching wind beyond the shelter of the harbour. The tide was out, leaving an expanse of oily pebbled beach scattered with the debris of storms and flotsam and jetsam from boats.

He tried to focus his whole mind on the problem of the murder to banish the haunting picture of Priscilla languishing away the afternoon in this man Harrington's arms.

Then he saw the Roths approaching. They were an odd pair, he thought. Amy was a big, soft woman, but Marvin's six feet topped her by a few inches. Although her movements were usually slow and calm, there seemed an underlying restlessness about her. She was wearing a trouser suit of faded denim with a scarf knotted under her throat. Marvin had changed into his usual sombre black business suit, and his bald head shone in the yellow light from the sea.

'When is all this going to end?' demanded Marvin as the couple came abreast of Hamish. 'Amy isn't used to being treated the way she's been by your coppers. That Blair thinks he's hot shit.'

'I'm used to being treated like a lady,' said Amy. 'I thought all you Britishers were supposed to be gentlemen.'

'We're just like other folk,' said Hamish soothingly. 'Like sweeties. We come in all shapes and sizes and some of us are horrible.'

'Sweeties?' queried Amy, momentarily diverted.

'Candy,' translated Marvin. 'See here, Amy's like aristocracy back home. This Blair wouldn't treat your Queen like this.'

'It's to my way of thinking that he might,' said Hamish.

'Well, it's a pity Amy's folks have all passed away or they would have something to say about this.'

Hamish looked at Amy as Marvin spoke and noticed the tightening of the skin at the corners of her eyelids and the way she was obviously ferreting around in her mind for a change of subject. He had a sudden intuition that Amy had been lying about her background. Well, a lot of people did, but they didn't go around committing murder when they were found out. Or did they?

'Why doesn't Blair just arrest that major? He's the

119

only one who had it in for Lady Jane,' said Amy. 'You heard about his trick with the salmon?'

'Oh, aye, the gossip went two times around the village and back again. It is very hard to keep anything quiet in the Highlands.'

Amy muttered something like, 'Just like red hook,' and Hamish wondered whether it was something to do with fishing.

'Except murder,' said Marvin. 'This place is the asshole of the world. I don't like the country, I don't like the hick servants at the hotel. What's a FEB?'

'Nothing that would apply to you, Mr Roth. It is just an expression the barman uses.'

'Him!' said Marvin with great contempt. 'He can't even make a dry martini. One part gin to three parts warm French is his idea. Jeez, the fuckers in this dump piss me off.'

'Honey,' pleaded Amy, 'watch your language.'

Hamish's red eyebrows had vanished up under his cap with shock.

'Sorry,' said Marvin wearily. 'I guess I'm frightened. I feel trapped here. If we're going for this goddam constitutional, then we'd better get on with it.'

'Catch any fish?' asked Hamish.

'Jeremy and Heather caught a trout each,' said Marvin, 'but those salmon just can't be caught, in my opinion. They just jump about the place and keep well away from the hooks.'

'I could lend you one of my flies,' volunteered Hamish. 'I have had a bit of luck with it.'

'Say, why don't you join us for dinner tonight and bring it with you,' said Marvin. 'Everyone knows you're not on the case and we're getting a bit sick of each other. After all, one of us did it and we all sit around wondering who's going to be next.'

Hamish accepted the invitation and went on his way.

As he approached the hotel, he saw Jeremy coming down towards it from the direction of the Marag, still wearing his fishing gear.

'Got one!' he shouted as Hamish approached. He held up a fair-sized trout.

'Let's get into the hotel,' said Hamish, noticing a reporter and photographer heading in their direction.

They walked together into the little room where Jeremy placed his catch on the scales and logged the weight in the book. 'I was hearing that you were seen in the corridor outside Lady Jane's room the night she was murdered,' said Hamish.

'Nonsense,' said Jeremy, carefully lifting his fish off the scales. 'Aren't you supposed to butt out of this investigation? I don't think Blair would like to hear you had been asking questions.'

'Maybe not. But he would like to hear what you'd been up to,' said Hamish.

'Then tell him and much good it may do you,' yelled Jeremy. He rushed off, nearly bumping into Alice, who was watching them anxiously. Alice ran after Jeremy and, undeterred by the fact that he had slammed his room door in her face, she opened it and went in. He was sitting hunched on the edge of the bed. 'That blasted, nosy copper,' he said without looking up.

Alice sat down beside him and took his hand in hers. 'What's the matter, Jeremy?' she pleaded. 'You've been awful to me all day.'

'Christ, I've got enough on my mind without worrying about you,' snapped Jeremy. 'I was seen outside Lady Jane's room on the night of the murder.'

'Oh, Jeremy. What happened?'

'My father phoned me and told me about her. I got into a silly mess when I was at Oxford and I wanted to make sure she kept her mouth shut. She said if I spent the night with her, she would think about it. Can you imagine? That awful old cow.'

Alice tried to withdraw her hand. What if Jeremy had murdered Lady Jane? He looked so odd, older, grimmer, and there was a muscle jumping in his left cheek.

Jeremy turned and looked at her. 'It wouldn't have mattered so much if she had written about you,' said Alice timidly. 'I mean, it wasn't so very bad.'

'You don't know anything about it,' snapped Jeremy. In a flat voice, he told Alice of his Oxford scandals, although he omitted the fact he was still paying for the support of the barmaid's child.

'I could never have gone in for politics,' he said. He felt shaken with nerves and anger. How stupid he'd been not to have told Hamish the whole thing. He needed a drink . . . or something.

He seized Alice suddenly and pulled her down on the bed. 'Oh, Jeremy,' whispered Alice, forgetting that she had thought him a murderer a moment ago, 'do you love me?'

'Yes, yes,' mumbled Jeremy against her hair. He started to unbutton her blouse, and Alice was so thrilled and excited that he had confessed his love that she almost enjoyed the next ten minutes.

DAY SIX

Hope not for minde in women
– JOHN DONNE

Hamish was up very early. He had been unable to sleep.
It had been a miserable dinner party. Only Alice had
seemed to enjoy herself. Daphne Gore appeared to be
haunted by the spirit of Lady Jane in that she had
seemed hell-bent on ruining the evening for everyone.
Hamish could only be glad young Charlie was not
present. The boy was suffering enough from hysterical
women in the shape of his mother. Hamish had worn
the dark grey suit that he kept for his occasional visits
to church, and Daphne Gore had said he looked dressed
for a funeral. She had then started to harangue the Roths
over the American Cruise missiles, although it was
evident to all that she was merely trying to be bitchy
and didn't care much one way or the other.

They had all drunk too much, because Amy had the
nervous habit of constantly refilling their glasses without
waiting for the waiter to come around.

And then as the climax to a truly horrible evening,
Priscilla had arrived for dinner at the hotel with John
Harrington. Harrington was everything Hamish detested
in a man. He had a loud, carrying English voice,
he fussed over the wine, he criticized the food. He
had beautifully tailored clothes, a square, immaculately

123

barbered chin, a tanned, rugged face, and crinkly brown hair. And he made Priscilla laugh.

Hamish decided to take his boat out and try to catch some mackerel. He wandered down to the beach and untied the painter of his rowing boat. It was then that he saw the small figure of Charlie Baxter wistfully watching him.

'Want to go out with me?' called Hamish, and Charlie scampered down the beach.

'What are you doing out so early, laddie?' asked Hamish. 'It isn't even six o'clock yet.'

'I wanted to get out,' said Charlie. 'My mother won't mind. I often go out early for a walk. Things are pretty rough. I want to stay on with Auntie, and Mother wants me to go back.'

'Maybe I'll have a wee word with her,' said Hamish. 'Hop in and keep still.'

Charlie obeyed, sitting in the boat while Hamish pushed it out into the still waters of Lochdubh. The sun was just peeping over the horizon. The water was like glass, and the sky above was cloudless. 'Looks as if it's going to be a hot day,' said Hamish, climbing in and taking the oars. He rowed them steadily out into the loch.

'Where are we going?' asked Charlie.

'To catch mackerel. Dead easy.'

'What with?'

'A spinner. I'll stop in a bit and show you how to do it.'

'Are we going right out to sea?'

'No, just a bit further.'

Charlie relapsed into silence, hanging over the side of the boat and staring at the sunlight dancing on the water.

Hamish at last shipped the oars and picked up a reel

of stout twine with several hooks and silver spinners attached to it.

'Do we bait the hooks?' asked Charlie with interest.

'No, the spinners do the trick. Mackerel will go for nearly anything. That's why they're sometimes called the scavengers of the sea. Just unwind the line and let it trail out behind the boat,' said Hamish.

He began to row again, this time slowly and easily, shipping the oars from time to time.

Behind them, smoke began to rise from the chimneys of the village, and the twisted grotesque forms of the mountains stood out sharp against the clear sky.

'Stop the boat,' shrieked Charlie suddenly. 'I think there's something biting.'

'Pull in the line,' said Hamish, shipping the oars. Charlie wound the line in feverishly. 'There's fish on the end,' he said. 'Fish!'

'Pull them in, there's a good lad.'

Charlie jerked the line and hooks, spinners, fish, and all crashed behind him in the boat.

'There's four mackerel,' said Charlie as Hamish expertly dislodged the hooks and killed the fish. 'Can we try again?'

'Och, no,' said Hamish. 'We'll just keep to what we can eat. Ready for breakfast?'

'You mean we'll *cook* them?'

'Of course we will. It's too early to wake your mother, so we'll drop a note through the door to tell her where you are.'

Looking more childlike than Hamish had seen him before, Charlie smiled shyly and said, 'You know, everything's really so much better now that terrible woman has gone. I wish I could stay here.'

'But your auntie has just come up for the summer.'

'I overheard her say that she would stay on and put

me to the school in Strathbane if my mother would leave me.'

'And you would like that?'

'Yes, Mr Macbeth. There's that Mr Blair waiting for you on the beach,' said Charlie. 'Does that mean we can't cook our catch?'

'No, whatever happens, we'll have time to eat.'

But Hamish privately thought it must be something very important to get Mr Blair out of his bed so early.

'Well, we've got our man,' said Mr Blair after Hamish had pulled up his boat on the beach. 'While you were out enjoying yourself and playing with the weans, I got a call from Scotland Yard. Major Peter Frame was arrested two years ago for trying to strangle the secretary of the Buffers Club in Pall Mall. What d'you make of that?'

'I would say it was still not proof the man strangled Lady Jane.'

'Yes, well that's why you're a village bobby and I'm not. The man threatened her in front of witnesses.'

'Have you arrested him?'

'Not yet. He's just helping us with our inquiries.'

'I gather he's got a fine war record.'

'Not him,' sneered Blair. 'That's something else we found out about him. He looks old enough, God knows, but he's only fifty-four. He never was in the war, he never saw any action. He was a major in the Educational Corps in some unit down in Lincolnshire.'

'I am sure Lady Jane knew that,' said Hamish slowly.

'We're managing fine without your help, although instead of wasting your time fishing, you might see to your duties. That prick, Halburton-Smythe, was howling down the phone last night about some poacher.'

'I will see to it,' said Hamish, but Blair was already striding away.

126

Hamish stood looking after the detective, lost in thought. What if there had been a Lady Jane present at one of the other fishing classes? Would the same lies and petty snobberies have risen to the surface as well?

Charlie tugged his sleeve. 'I rather like Major Frame,' he said. 'He's a bit of an ass, but he's jolly kind.'

'Let's leave a note for your mother,' said Hamish, 'and then we will have our breakfast.'

But before he cooked breakfast, he phoned Angus MacGregor, a layabout who lived on the other side of the village.

'Is that yourself?' said Hamish. 'Aye, well, Angus, your sins have found you out because I am coming to arrest you after I have had my breakfast.'

Charlie listened with interest as the phone squawked.

'Nonsense,' said Hamish at last. 'Havers. You bought that new rifle and it is well known that you could not hit the barn door. I will be over soon with the handcuffs.'

Hamish put the phone down and grinned at Charlie.

'If he knows you are going to arrest him he might run away,' said the boy, round-eyed.

'That's just what he will do,' said Hamish, leading the way to the kitchen. 'We'd best hide out in here, for they'll be along with the major any moment. Yes, you see Angus has the wife and three children and it would not be right to take their useless father away from them to prison, so he will probably go to Aberdeen for a bit and he will return when he thinks I have forgotten about it. But he will not be trying to bag one of the colonel's stags again.'

After a sustaining breakfast of mackerel dipped in oatmeal and fried in butter, Hamish accompanied Charlie home and was shortly closeted with Mrs Baxter for what seemed to the anxiously awaiting Charlie a very long time indeed.

When he emerged, he merely ruffled Charlie's curls and took himself off.

He wandered along to the hotel to learn what the fishing school intended to do for the day. He found them all, with the exception of young Charlie and the major, seated in the lounge, getting a lecture on the ways of trout and salmon from John.

The Roths, Daphne, Jeremy, and Alice were in high spirits. Even John Cartwright was cracking jokes. All had heard of the major's 'arrest', and all were determined to believe him guilty.

'It seems as if Mr Blair won't be needing to grill us any more,' said John, 'so we can go back to Loch Alsh and get some good fishing.'

As they all left the hotel, Hamish noticed that Jeremy had an arm around Alice's shoulders.

Alice had spent the whole night in Jeremy's bed. She felt light-headed with debility, happiness, and relief. It was awful to have to go to the Cartwrights' station wagon with Charlie who had just joined the party and leave Jeremy with Daphne, but he had promised to spend the day with her, Alice, and now she was sure he was on the point of proposing.

The nightmare was over. The murderer had been arrested. Alice, like the rest, had not really believed that 'helping the police with their inquiries' stuff. She began to wonder if she would have to give evidence at the trial. That would be exciting since she no longer had anything to fear from the newspapers.

The countryside now looked friendly. Heather blazed purple down the flanks of the mountainsides, and a peregrine falcon soared high in the wind currents in the sky above.

And then a little cloud began to appear on the sunny horizon of Alice's mind. The clean, clear air was invigorating. Set against it, the dark, blanket-tussled writhings of the previous night seemed grimy. Then, again, he had not waited for her but had rushed off for breakfast, leaving her to make her own way down. There had been no long days of exchanged glances and holding hands. Alice shrugged and tried to feel worldly-wise. Wham bang, thank you, ma'am, was reality. All men were the same.

But her heart lifted when she climbed out of the car and Jeremy grinned and winked at her.

Her heart soared again when Daphne failed to lure Jeremy to join her in fishing at the mouth of the river. 'I'll stay here with Alice,' he said. 'She seems to be lucky.'

There it was – tantamount to an open declaration of love.

Jeremy and Alice fished amiably, if unsuccessfully, up until lunchtime. Alice had lost her fishing fever. All she wanted was Jeremy's company. But when they broke for lunch, it transpired that Jeremy was still gripped by the desire to catch a fish.

'Where's Daphne?' he said crossly. 'I haven't even had a nibble. Maybe I should have gone with her.'

'She's at the head of the loch by the river,' said Heather.

'If she's still fishing after this time, she must have got something,' said Jeremy. 'I think I'll go and look.'

Heather glanced at Alice's dismal face. 'Finish your sandwiches,' she said placidly, 'and we'll all go and look. Oh, drat, here's the village bobby. Imagine travelling all this way just to scrounge a sandwich . . .'

Hamish sauntered up, red hair and shiny uniform gleaming in the sun.

'How is Major Frame?' asked Alice. 'Have they taken him off to Strathbane?'

'No, I thought he would be here by now,' said Hamish.

'Here?' shrieked everyone.

'Aye,' said Hamish. 'They had to let him go. That business where he was said to strangle the club secretary was a bit of a storm in a teacup. The good major was drunk and the secretary objected to the fact that the major hadn't paid his membership fee and seemed to have no intention of doing so. One word led to another and the major attacked the secretary. Several members of the club pulled them apart. The police were called, but no charges pressed. You can't send a man to prison for a murder just because he got drunk and bad-tempered a wee while ago.'

'But if he isn't the murderer,' said Alice, 'who is?'

They all looked at each other in dismay.

Then a faint scream reached their ears, borne on the light breeze.

'Daphne!' said John Cartwright, lurching to his feet. They all scrambled for the loch and waded in. Hamish took off his boots, socks, and trousers and, cutting a ridiculous figure in his tunic, cap and underpants, waded into the water after them.

As they ploughed through the shallow loch towards the river, they saw Daphne. Her rod was bent, her line was taut, and she called over her shoulder, 'Keep clear! I want to get this one myself.' They all moved forward, however, watching as she battled with the leaping, plunging fish.

'She'll lose it,' said Heather. 'John, do something.'

'Not me,' said John. 'She wouldn't thank me for any help. Just look at her face!'

Daphne seemed to have aged. Her mouth was clamped tight with deep grooves of strain down either side.

Half an hour passed. Even Hamish, ridiculous in his

half dress, stayed where he was. Daphne had played her salmon – for a salmon it was – into the shallow water.

With an exclamation of rage, she suddenly threw her rod down and leapt on the salmon, falling on it in a sort of rugby tackle. Then she rose from the frothing, swirling water, clutching the salmon to her bosom.

She *ran* to the shore, stumbled up the bank, fell and cut her knee, stood up with a great tear across one wader, ran again until she collapsed on the tussocky grass with the writhing fish under her.

They all scrambled to shore. 'Let me get the hook out and kill it for you,' called John.

'Don't you dare,' said Daphne. 'That's going to be my pleasure.'

They were saved from watching Daphne kill her fish by a yell from the opposite shore. The major was standing there in full fishing rig.

He waded across to join them.

Hamish watched his approach. He would have expected the major to bluster, to scream about the disgrace of being taken along to the police station, but the major's eyes were riveted on Daphne and her salmon.

'By Jove, where did you get that?'

'Over there,' panted Daphne.

'What fly were you using?'

'A Gore Inexpressible. It's one of my father's inventions.'

'Where does he fish?'

'He's got an estate in Argyll he uses in the summer. Wouldn't even let me try, which is why I came here. I want one hundred photos to send to him.'

Heather opened her mouth to sympathize with the major over his treatment at the hands of the police, but he was already back in the water, a fanatical gleam in

131

his eye, his whole concentration bent on the foaming water.

Then she noticed the still, intent sort of look on Jeremy's face. Oh, dear, thought Heather. That remark of Daphne's about her father having an estate in Argyll really got home. Poor Alice.

'Coo-ee!'

The slim figure of Priscilla Halburton-Smythe could be seen on the opposite shore. 'Mr Macbeth,' she called.

'Better put your pants on first,' said Marvin Roth to Hamish, but Hamish was already off and wading across the loch in Priscilla's direction.

'Sheesh!' said Marvin. 'She'll scream the place down when she sees him.'

'Your Highlander is very prudish about some things,' said Heather. 'But any state of undress doesn't seem to embarrass them, and I'm sure the Halburton-Smythes have become used to it by now.'

'You're all wet,' giggled Priscilla as Hamish waded out. 'I came rushing over to tell you that Daddy's in a fearful rage. He's had collect calls from the States and from London. Lucy Hanson, the secretary, accepted the calls and messages thinking they were something to do with the estate. I asked Daddy to give them to me to pass on, but he won't.'

'Maybe if we went now we could take a look in the office when he's not around,' said Hamish, water dripping down his long, red-haired legs.

'We might be lucky. Everyone's out in the garden having tea. Haven't you got anything to dry yourself with? You look like something out of a *Carry On* movie.'

'If we open the windows of the car, I'll dry soon enough,' said Hamish. 'It is just my legs that are wet. The water did not reach my bum.'

'We'll take my car,' said Priscilla, 'then I'll drop you off back here. Anyone catch anything?'

So as they drove along, Hamish told her about Daphne's catch, and Priscilla threw back her head and laughed. She was wearing a simple pink cotton sheath, and her slim, tanned legs ended in white sandals with thin straps and very high heels. Her legs were like satin. Hamish wondered if she shaved them or whether they were naturally smooth. He wondered what it would be like to run a hand down – or up – all that silky smoothness.

'Stop dreaming,' said Priscilla. 'We're here.'

'I should have put my trousers on at a quiet bit down the road,' said Hamish. 'But there doesn't seem to be anyone about so I'll just pop them on.'

'Well, hurry up. Oh, lor!'

Hamish had got his socks on and had his trousers draped on the gravel drive preparatory to putting them on when Colonel and Mrs Halburton-Smythe and five guests including John Harrington rounded the corner of the house.

The colonel goggled at Hamish, who stood frozen, one leg in his trousers and one out. He's going to say, 'What the hell is the meaning of this?' thought Hamish.

'What the hell is the meaning of this?' screamed the colonel. Mrs Halburton-Smythe, who was younger than the colonel and had rather pretty, if faded, blond good looks, shouted, 'Come here this minute, Priscilla.'

Priscilla thought wildly of the crazy explanations about Daphne's salmon and said hurriedly, 'I'll tell you about it later. Get in the car, Mr Macbeth.'

The colonel started his watchful advance.

Hamish leapt into the car, still half in and half out of his trousers. Priscilla jumped in the other side and they fled off before the colonel could reach them.

'Now I'm for it,' said Priscilla gloomily. 'He will never listen, you know, which is why no-one ever really tells him anything.'

Hamish wriggled into his trousers. 'And what will you tell your young man? Your father told me – warned me off in fact – that you were about to become engaged.'

'I suppose I'd better get engaged to someone,' said Priscilla, concentrating on her driving and therefore missing the look of pain on her companion's face. 'After all, they did take me to London to do the Season and a fat lot of good that was. It cost them a lot of money. All the other girls seem content to marry someone suitable. My friend, Sarah, was wild about this chap, but she married someone else. She said as she walked up to the altar, she thought, "I wish it could have been so-and-so," but she's got a baby now and seems pretty happy.'

'I should think it would be hell to be married to someone you didn't love,' said Hamish, his eyes fixed on the road ahead.

'Really? One never thinks of bobbies as being romantic somehow,' said Priscilla carelessly, and the drive back continued in silence.

'Tell your father I caught his poacher,' said Hamish, 'or rather he left Lochdubh before I could arrest him, but Colonel Halburton-Smythe will not be troubled by that poacher again.'

'That might calm him down. I suppose you really have to get those messages. Look, you'd better sneak around about midnight and I'll let you in. I'll try to get them out of the desk for you.'

Hamish nodded and raised his hand in a sort of salute as she drove away. He turned his attention to the fishing party. Alice was sitting by the shore of the loch, plaiting a wreath of wild flowers, like some modern-day Ophelia, while Jeremy and Daphne could be seen out in the boat, talking eagerly. There was no sign of the Roths or the Cartwrights. Hamish took off his tunic and, using it as a pillow, stretched his long, lanky length out on the grass. He ran the whole fishing party through his brain, remembering incidents, remembering expressions, remembering what Lady Jane had said. After a time, they all became jumbled together in his head as he fell asleep.

The noise of the fishing party packing up for the day awoke him. The major had caught a salmon, not quite as big as Daphne's, but big enough to make him look as if he had just found the Holy Grail.

Charlie came rushing up. 'What did you say to my mother, Mr Macbeth?'

'There's no use me telling you now, laddie, in case things don't work out. Just say your prayers. Hop in and I'll take you home.'

So Alice travelled back with the Cartwrights, worried and lost. If only Jeremy would sleep with her that evening, then she would be sure.

Hamish found Blair waiting for him on his return. The detective was setting out for the hotel for another round of interrogation. Blair was in a fury because he had been so sure at first of the major. He took that fury out on Hamish, calling him lazy, half-witted, and useless, while Hamish stood stolidly to attention, his mind obviously elsewhere.

Blair was also at his worst with the members of the fishing party that evening. They huddled together at dinner, all now wishing they could go home. Blair *had* said that they might leave on the Sunday morning but that they could expect further calls from the police when they got home.

No-one even had the heart to raise a smile at Marvin Roth's appearance. The American had arrived at dinner

135

in full Highland dress, from plaid and kilt to skene-dhu in his stocking top.

Hamish decided to pass the evening hours by going for a long walk. There was no hope of using the phone in his office, since Blair had announced his intention of staying there himself most of the night to sift through the evidence again and make phone calls.

Alice waited in her room after dinner. And waited.

Jeremy was drinking with Daphne in the bar. At last, he escorted Daphne to her room and leaned against the door post and smiled at her. 'Are you inviting me in?' he asked.

'No,' laughed Daphne. 'Not tonight, Napoleon. I've got a headache.'

Jeremy stood frowning after she had shut the door. Anxiety gnawed at him despite the amount of gin he had drunk. He went slowly along to a room further along the corridor and rapped on the door.

'Open up, Alice,' he said. 'It's me.'

Hamish found his steps leading back to the scene of the murder. He shone his torch here and there among the bushes, not much hoping to find anything, since the police had already been over the ground very thoroughly.

He suddenly switched off his torch and stood very still. Up above the pool, in the little glade where the fishing party had sat after the discovery of the murder, a twig snapped. He began to move very silently in the direction of the glade, walking in the long grass beside the path so that his feet would make no sound. There was something ancient and eerie about the Highland silence. The night was very still. He stopped at the edge of the glade. A small moon shone down through the trees. Bars of light cut across the scene.

Moving through the flickering bars of light, crouched low like some jungle animal, was Amy Roth. Her restless hands searched the grass.

'Good evening, Mrs Roth,' said Hamish.

Amy stood up slowly and turned to face him, her face a white disc in the shadow.

'Who is it?' she whispered.

'Constable Macbeth.'

'Oh.' She gave a little laugh and brushed nervously at her clothes. 'I lost my lighter. It's gold. I thought I might have left it here.'

'A funny time and a scary place to come looking for a lighter,' said Hamish. 'Why are you *really* here?'

'It's late,' she said, moving towards him. 'I'm going back to the hotel.'

'How long is it since you have suspected your husband of the murder?' asked Hamish.

Amy put her hands to her face. 'Marvin can be so violent,' she whispered. 'But he couldn't . . . surely . . .' With a gasp, she thrust past him and fled down the path. Hamish watched her go and shook his head. He had only been guessing, but his remark seemed to have struck gold. He shone his torch around the glade and then decided to examine the ground about the pool before finishing his search. He searched and searched about the ground and the bushes when something caught his eye. He forced his way into the undergrowth and shone his torch. A strand of blue material was caught on a thorn. Strange that the forensic men had missed it.

He carefully took it off the thorn and examined it. It was of a powder blue colour and made of acrylic. He remembered Alice had been wearing a blue trouser suit on the first day of the fishing class.

He sat down thoughtfully by the pool and turned the

137

scrap of material over between finger and thumb. But someone very recently had been wearing just such a colour. His hand suddenly clenched, and he was seized with a feeling of fear and dread.

'Oh no,' he whispered.

DAY SEVEN

The test of an experienced angler is his ability to
play a good sized fish on average or light equipment.
– GILMER G. ROBINSON,
Fly Casting

At three minutes after midnight, Hamish parked his
car well away from the Halburton-Smythe castle and
finished his journey on foot. He was wondering whether
to risk trying the door and finding his own way about
when it opened and Priscilla whispered, 'Hurry up,
before we wake the whole house.'

She led the way up flights of stairs to her bedroom.
She was wearing a white cotton nightgown and negligee,
very unrevealing, but Constable Macbeth felt he had
never seen such a seductive-looking outfit in his life.

'Now,' said Priscilla, sitting down on the bed and
patting the space beside her, 'I managed to get into the
estates office when they were all jawing about your
iniquities at dinner. Mummy believed my story. She said
it was just the sort of hare-brained thing you *would* do.
There are the messages, but they're in Miss Dimwit's
shorthand.'

Hamish took the notes. 'I do shorthand myself, Miss
Halburton-Smythe. But whether I could read this. Yes,
I think . . .'

'Are you asleep, Prissie? I want to talk to you.'

'Daddy,' squeaked Priscilla. 'Into bed, quick, and under the blankets. As far over by the wall as you can get.'

Hamish was fortunately not in uniform. The night was warm so he was wearing a checked cotton shirt and an old pair of flannels.

He leapt into bed, under the blankets, and crouched down. Priscilla got in beside him and leaned against the pillows. 'Come in!' she called.

Hamish lay very still with his head under the blankets. His face was pressed against Priscilla's thigh. He tried to move it away and she slapped the top of the bedclothes as a warning to him to lie still.

Colonel Halburton-Smythe came into the room. He sat down on the edge of the bed, and Priscilla shifted to make room for him. She was jammed against Hamish, who felt like groaning.

'Look, pet, the Harringtons might leave tomorrow for the simple reason that you won't come to the point,' he heard the colonel say. 'Harrington's a fine young chap. It's not as if you're in love with anyone. You can't go on turning down one fellow after another.'

'I could get a job, Daddy.'

'Nonsense. Marriage and children's the only career for a woman. What will I tell the Harringtons?'

'Tell them anything,' yawned Priscilla. 'I'm so beastly tired, Daddy. I promise I'll be nice to John tomorrow if you'll just go away.'

'Very well,' said the colonel. 'But don't keep him waiting around too long.'

At last, to Hamish's intense relief, he heard the door close. Priscilla threw back the bedclothes and looked down at Hamish's ruffled red hair.

'You look quite sweet without that horrible uniform on,' said Priscilla. 'You must have been nearly

140

suffocated. Your face is all red and you're breathing like a grampus.'

'I'm all right,' said Hamish, sitting up with an effort. 'Let me have a look at those notes.'

Priscilla took them out from under her pillow and handed them to him. He frowned as he studied them, and then his face sharpened. 'I've got to use the phone,' he said.

'You look terrible,' said Priscilla. 'What is it? Why can't you use the phone at that police station of yours?'

'Blair's there and probably all night. Can I use the one in the estates office?'

'Yes, so long as no-one discovers you.' Priscilla felt rather sulky and wondered why. 'I wouldn't have thought you were so keen on your job.'

'Aye,' said Hamish, climbing over her to get out of bed. 'I'll just creep down the stairs. No-one will hear me.'

'Good night,' said Priscilla crossly.

Hamish smiled down at her as she lay against the pillows. 'Thank you for all you have done, Miss Halburton-Smythe.' He bent suddenly and kissed her on the cheek, turned red as fire, and fled from the room.

'Well, well,' thought Priscilla. She put a hand up to her cheek and stared in a bemused way at the closed door.

Hamish sat beside the phone in the estates office and in his head turned over the names of his many relatives. There was Rory in London, Erchie in New York, Peter in Hong Kong, Jenny in Aylesbury, which was near enough to Oxford . . .

At last, he picked up the phone and began to dial.

A pale dawn was lighting up the sky and the water as Hamish Macbeth wearily made his way along the waterfront. There was something he had to do before he went to sleep and it was something that only duty was prompting him to do. His heart felt heavy, and his lips moved in a soundless Gaelic prayer.

He turned in at a white-painted gate and went around the back of the house to the kitchen door. He rapped loud and long on the glass until he saw a light go on upstairs. He waited, hearing footsteps descending, shuffling footsteps approaching the kitchen door.

The door opened and Tina Baxter stood blinking at him nervously. She clutched a pink woollen dressing gown tightly at her neck. All colour drained from her face.

'Aye, it's me,' said Hamish heavily. 'Mind if I come in?'

She stood aside, and he walked past her into the kitchen. She followed him and sat down at the kitchen table as if her legs could no longer bear her weight.

'I was here earlier,' said Hamish, 'talking to you about young Charlie's future. You were wearing a blue dress.' He took an envelope out of his tunic pocket and extracted the piece of material he had found on the bush beside the pool. 'Is this yours?'

'Yes,' whispered Mrs Baxter. She covered her face with her hands and began to cry.

'I couldn't help it,' she sobbed. 'The disgrace. My Charlie's name in the papers. I had to shut her mouth.'

Hamish sat down opposite her. His head was beginning to clear, and his earlier fright was beginning to recede as common sense took over. The first rays of sun began to warm the kitchen.

'Mrs Baxter,' he said gently. 'Immediately after the murder all the bushes and braes and heather and trees were combed for clues by the forensic boys. It's awfy strange they didn't find this and I did.'

142

'I did it.' Tina Baxter stared at him, her face working. 'Aye, that you did. Not the murder. You cut a bit out of your dress and left it there, hoping someone would find it. So now we'll have another wee chat about Charlie. He's twelve years old. *Twelve years old*. Just think o' that. He's a strong boy but there is no way he could have overpowered a woman of Lady Jane's size. Then there's the lad's character . . .'

'It's bad blood, bad blood,' said Tina Carter, her hands clutching and unclutching the material of her dressing gown. 'His father was violent. He threatened to kill me if I didn't give him a divorce.' Her voice was rising hysterically.

'I am thinking,' said Hamish sincerely, 'that you would drive a saint to violence. I feel like striking you myself. Do you know that because of your silly clue-planting you had me thinking you knew that Charlie did it and were trying to fix the blame on yourself? You're a dangerous woman. Now, here's what you are going to do. You are going to leave Charlie here to stay with his aunt and I suggest you go back home and see one o' thae head doctors. You'll drive the bairn mad with all your hysterics.

'If you don't do what I say, I will let the newspapers know that you believed your own boy capable of murder and nearly got him accused of it by your clumsiness.'

Hamish rose to his feet. 'So think on that, Mrs Baxter. I'll bring mair scandal down on your head than you ever could have imagined.'

It was the last day of the fishing course. Unless the police requested otherwise, Blair would take their home and business addresses and allow them to leave on the Sunday morning. The river Anstey was still closed to

143

them. Heather and John had suggested they fish the Marag.

On returning to the police station, Hamish found that Blair was still asleep. He typed up his notes, studied the results, and then put them to one side. He thought long and carefully about each member of the fishing school. He decided he was being haunted by the scale of the crime. He began to read through his well-thumbed ten-volume edition of *Famous Crimes*. Motives tumbled one after another before his tired eyes. Murder for money, for passion, for revenge. Alcohol or drugs brought out the Hyde side of the character, but no-one in the fishing school case drank daily to excess and not one of them had shown any sign of being a drug user. He made one pot after another of strong tea. His dog, Towser, prowled about uneasily, stopping to lick his master's hand as if wondering what was keeping him from his bed, for Towser liked to stretch out on the bed at Hamish's feet.

'It is all a matter of a lack of conscience,' thought Hamish.

By the time the little fishing class was setting out for their last day, Hamish was sound asleep, his dog snoring at his feet, and a sheaf of notes clutched to his chest.

He was awakened by Blair shaking his shoulder. 'It's noon,' snarled Blair savagely. 'By God, I'll report you for sheer laziness. I've got a job for you. You'll come along with me to that hotel this evening and you'll take down the addresses of the whole lot of 'em. I don't just mean their home addresses, we've got those. I mean where they work and where they're likely to be visiting.'

'Get out!' said a small, shrill voice behind Blair. The large detective swung around in amazement. Charlie Baxter stood in the doorway clutching a mug of tea.

'This is Constable Macbeth's house,' he said, 'and you've got no right to bully him.'

Blair stared at the boy, who was white with anger.

Hamish, who had fallen asleep in the shirt and flannels he had worn the night before, swung his legs quickly out of bed.

'Into the kitchen with you, Charlie,' he said. 'What time will you be wanting me at the hotel, sir?'

'Six o'clock,' snapped Blair. 'And tell that kid to mind his manners.' He stomped off where he could shortly be heard haranguing MacNab and Anderson in Hamish's office.

'I've prepared breakfast for you, Mr Macbeth,' said Charlie shyly. 'It's on the table.'

'Aye, you've done very well,' said Hamish, tucking into charred bacon and rubbery egg. 'Quite the wee housewife. Aren't you going fishing?'

'I thought you might run up to the Marag with me,' said Charlie. 'You see, I have to thank you. Mother left in a rage. I don't know what you said or what Auntie said to her afterwards, but I'm to stay.'

'Isn't that the great thing,' smiled Hamish. 'Och, your ma's a decent body, but she worries overmuch about everything.'

'Perhaps we'll catch the murderer together, Mr Macbeth.'

'We might at that. Wait till I put on my uniform and we'll be off.'

There was a festival air about the fishing school. Even Daphne seemed to have stopped her bitchy behaviour. All of them had come to the conclusion at breakfast that none of them had done it and Lady Jane had probably come across a poacher or some itinerant madman. Tomorrow, they would all return home with a story they could dine out on for years.

Alice drew Hamish aside and showed him a silver and cairngorm ring she was wearing on a string around her neck. 'Jeremy gave this to me,' she said. 'He bought it at the gift shop this morning. I was going to put it on my finger, but he said to keep it secret for the moment.'

'Why?' asked Hamish curiously. 'It is not as if the man is married.'

'Oh, you men are so secretive,' laughed Alice.

'If I were to be married to the lady of my choice,' said Hamish slowly, 'I would shout it from the mountain-top.'

But Alice only giggled happily and walked away. Hamish went to sit on a rock where he could get a view of everyone in the fishing school and there he stayed for the whole of the day. At last, at five o'clock, he walked up to Heather and said, 'You are all expected in the hotel at six o'clock, Mrs Cartwright. They will want to wash and change. Mr Blair wants me to take your names and addresses, and myself will be having a bit of a word with you.'

'All right,' said Heather, looking curiously at Hamish's face. 'I'll get them together.'

'I will go on,' said Hamish, 'and make sure that no other guests are allowed in the lounge.'

At the hotel, Hamish found Blair, MacNab, and Anderson waiting for him. 'They are coming,' said Hamish, 'and will be in the lounge at six. I am just going to tell Mr Johnson to keep other guests out of the lounge. You see, I am going to find your murderer for you, Mr Blair.'

MacNab sniggered, and Jimmy Anderson said, 'You've been reading too many detective stories, Hamish. Great detective gathers suspects in the library and unmasks killer.'

'Aye, chust so,' said Hamish, walking off.

'He's mad,' growled MacNab. 'I'll tell him to go home and have some black coffee.'

'No,' said Blair. 'Let him get on with it. I want him to make a right fool of himself. I'll have him out of his cushy job in a week.'

And so Hamish found Blair surprisingly mild and cooperative when he returned. Yes. Blair grinned. MacNab would guard the door and Anderson the window.

At last, one by one, the members of the fishing party entered the lounge. Hamish stood with his back to the empty fireplace and waited until they were all seated.

'Before I take down your addresses and send you on your way tomorrow,' he said, 'there's just a few things I have to say.' MacNab stifled a laugh.

'It was a wee bit difficult for me to see at first which one of you had done the murder because you all seemed to have a motive.'

'Get on with it.' Daphne Gore yawned. 'I'm dying for a drink.'

'John and Heather Cartwright,' went on Hamish, ignoring the interruption. 'A bad press might have ruined your school, and there was no doubt that Lady Jane meant to give you a bad write-up. You had a letter from friends in Austria telling you how she had managed to ruin *them*. Mr Cartwright lives for this fishing school and Mrs Cartwright lives for her husband. Both could have committed the murder . . . or one of them.

'Marvin and Amy Roth . . .'

'I'm not going to listen to any more of this,' said Heather. She half rose from her chair, her face flushed with distress, changed her mind, and sat down again, looking not at Hamish, but at her husband.

'Marvin Roth,' said Hamish, 'was involved in a scandal some years ago when he was charged with

147

running sweatshops in the garment district of New York and employing illegal aliens. He did not want his past raked up just when he was set on entering politics, and he guessed from a remark Lady Jane made that she knew all about his past.

'Then Amy Roth. Always talking about being a Blanchard from Augusta, except you aren't a Blanchard by birth. You married Tom Blanchard ten years ago and the marriage only lasted a few weeks, but you kept his name and background. Lady Jane must have known that.'

Marvin polished the top of his bald head. 'Look here,' he said desperately. 'Amy didn't say anything about being a Blanchard by birth, now did you, hon?'

'Oh, yes, she did,' said Daphne. 'Right down to the last mint julep.'

'You misheard,' said Marvin, giving Daphne a cold, pale look.

'Then we come to Major Peter Frame,' said Hamish.

'Not again,' said the major, burying his face in his hands.

'You care very much for your reputation as an officer and a gentleman,' said Hamish. 'You have an excitable temper and you were heard to threaten Lady Jane's life. You were never in the war, nor have you a particularly upper-class background. Lady Jane gave you a rough time.

'Alice Wilson.' Alice smiled tremulously at Jeremy, who frowned and looked at the floor. 'You got into minor trouble as a child and it's plagued you ever since. There was a big reason why you did not want the matter to get out. Perhaps you might have killed because of it.'

Nobody moved, but they seemed to shrink away from Alice.

'I wouldn't,' gasped Alice. 'Jeremy, please . . .'

148

'Charlie Baxter,' went on Hamish. 'Well, you had a bad time with her ladyship, and boys of your age can do terrible things under stress.

'Jeremy Blythe. I think you are a ruthless, ambitious, selfish man. You messed up two women in your Oxford days and God knows how many more. You want to be elected a member of the Conservative party, and Lady Jane's story, had it appeared, would have meant the end of your ambitions.'

'This is cruel,' thought Alice wildly. 'He could have taken us aside one at a time. It's like some horrible game of truths, bringing all our skeletons out of the closet.' She looked angrily at Hamish, who was consulting a sheaf of notes. He raised his eyes and looked around the room. 'He doesn't know who did it!' thought Alice with a sudden flash of intuition. 'He's looking for some sign that will betray the murderer.'

'Daphne Gore. Lady Jane knew all about you. I won't go into the details of your background that landed you under psychiatric care, but I think you are unbalanced enough to kill someone, given enough stress.'

There was a shocked silence. 'If your little game is over, Macbeth,' said Blair, 'we'll get those addresses and . . .'

Hamish ignored him.

'Now we had one clue, a torn corner of a photograph with part of the legend BUY BRIT— in one corner. At first I thought it might be part of an old Buy British poster. The fragment also shows the top of a head with something sparkly on it like a tiara. I made a lot of phone calls and found out at last what the legend really read.

'It runs BUY BRITTELS BEER – a kind of beer that is sold in America.'

'Never heard of it,' said Marvin Roth.

149

'Not many people have,' said Hamish. 'It was made locally by a small firm controlled by the Mafia in the Red Hook section of Brooklyn. It was so strong the locals said it was made out of all the bodies that didn't end up in the East River. It was a bit of luck I found that out. Mrs Roth had muttered something about Red Hook, but at the time, I thought she must be talking about something to do with the fishing. It was only later I remembered Red Hook was a district in Brooklyn. I have a cousin, Erchie, who lives in Red Hook and I phoned him up. He said it was sold in small Mafia gambling clubs.

'He neffer heard of Amy Blanchard or Amy Roth, but he had heard of an Amy a whiles back who was a stripper, Amy not being a usual name in the Italian section. Now Lady Jane had been in the States, no doubt digging up what dirt she could. Lady Jane was content to wait until her column appeared to see the rest of you suffering or to imagine your suffering. But Amy caught her on the raw. She arranged to meet Mrs Roth in the woods. There she showed her a photograph of Amy the stripper, wearing very little except a spangled headdress. You, Mrs Roth, have very little in the way of a conscience. This is something I *feel* about you, rather than something I definitely know. It came on me bit by bit. The look in the back of your eyes always had a certain steady calculating hardness no matter what you were saying. So you strangled her and then you dragged the body to the pool. You wanted something to weight the body and so you went down to the beach and found some old rusty chain. As soon as you had pushed her into the pool, you felt safe. You then returned to her room and destroyed all her notes and papers. Your husband would never know you were a Brooklyn stripper who sold her favours.'

Good God, thought Heather Cartwright wildly. Do people still talk about women selling their favours?

Amy Roth sat very still, her eyes lowered.

Marvin lumbered up and sat on the arm of his wife's chair and put a hand on her shoulder and gave it a comforting squeeze.

'You're talking shit,' grated Marvin. 'I won't believe what you said about Amy. I'll tell you something else. She knows I love her. She knows that I wouldn't give a damn about her past. Mine ain't so lily white. Where's your proof?'

'She was seen,' said Hamish. 'There is this poacher, Angus MacGregor . . .'

His voice trailed away as Amy raised her eyes and looked at him. Her eyes had lost their soft, cow-like expression. They were as flat and as hard as two stones.

'You did it, didn't you?' said Hamish.

Amy Roth moistened her lips.

'Yes,' she said flatly.

'And when you said you thought your husband had done it and you were frightened he had left something incriminating behind, you were really frightened *you* had left something.'

'Yes,' said Amy again in that dreadful flat voice.

Marvin's face was white and working with emotion. Tears started to his eyes. 'You're making her say all this.' There was a long silence. 'Amy,' pleaded Marvin, 'if you did it, you did it for me. Well, the hell with politics. I wasn't ever sold on the idea anyway.'

'That was not the reason, was it, Amy?' said Hamish.

'I guess not,' she said in a dull voice. She stretched her fingers and looked at them thoughtfully. 'She messed with me, that's all. I don't like no-one messing with me.'

And as Anderson and MacNab closed in on her, she gave her husband an apologetic little smile.

Hamish leaned on the harbour wall, keeping his eyes fixed on the sea. He felt immeasurably tired. He did not want to see Amy dragged out to the police car. She would be taken to the women's prison at Strathbane.

He waited a long time while cars came and went. Then he heard Blair's voice behind him. 'That was a neat bit of work, Constable. I suppose you're laughing your head off. MacNab and Anderson have taken her to Strathbane with the rest of my men. I'm just about to follow. Fine reading it will make for my superiors. Case solved by the village bobby.'

'Och, no,' said Hamish soothingly. 'It was yourself that pointed the way. I will not be taking any credit.'

'Why did you keep this poacher witness up your sleeve? It worked the trick.'

'I chust made that up,' said Hamish, lighting a cigarette. 'It was all guesswork.'

'*What!*'

'Aye. I just took a chance. You see, Erchie told me that the only Amy he had ever heard of around the Mafia clubs away back was a young stripper. He was not sure it was the same person, at all, at all. I just thought I would chance it.'

'But what if you had been wrong?'

'Aye, well, I have no doubt you would have had me out of my job as you were hoping to do. Now Amy had been a bit of a prostitute as well. I noticed that she was always restless. That's the thing about prostitutes. They can cover up the past with a layer of ladylike veneer, but they never lose that hunted, fidgety air.'

'You having great experience of the breed,' said Blair sarcastically.

Hamish blushed. 'No, no. But there was Jessie over in Aberdeen who married that man on the council . . . Then there was how Amy behaved at dinner. I couldnae help noticing that she would pour round the wine without waiting for the waiter or the men to do it.'

'Must have been a shock for old Marvin.'

'Aye, it was that. I first started to think it might be her when I looked at her wrists. They're very strong for a woman. But it was her eyelids that clinched the matter.'

'Her *eyelids*?'

'They are strained a bit at the corners. I have always noticed that criminal-type women have this feature.'

'Mr Roth has gone with her. He's going to get some big-shot lawyer.'

'Aye, love is a terrible thing,' said Hamish mournfully.

'I think you were damn lucky,' said Blair sourly. 'I can't believe you're not going to take any credit for this.'

Hamish turned and leaned his back against the harbour wall. 'Oh, you can believe it. I have no mind to leave Lochdubh. But if you were to put a little something in your report about my hard-working, if unintelligent, help, that would be just fine.'

Blair smiled slowly and clapped Hamish on the shoulder.

'I think we've time for a drink, Hamish,' he said. 'Let's go into the bar.'

EPILOGUE

Sunday morning. All the survivors chattering and laughing over the breakfast table. Oh, the relief to have it all cleared up and be able to go home. Reporters and photographers waited outside the courtyard of the hotel. But it would be possible to drive straight past them. Only John Cartwright knew that the major had already been out to talk to them. The major was back on form, so much so that he could not bear to admit that the case had been solved by the village constable but merely paused in his bragging to say that he was jolly glad the police had cleared the matter up.

John sighed. The other guests, the new fishing school, would be arriving later in the day. Not one had cancelled. They would survive.

Alice smiled radiantly at Jeremy. He had not visited her last night, excusing himself by saying he was all washed up with all the drama of the arrest. She was wearing the ring he had given her on her engagement finger.

'Hope to see you all again,' said Major Peter Frame cheerfully. 'Better be on my way.'

'I'd better get my traps too,' said Jeremy.

'My suitcase is at the reception so I'll have another cup of coffee and wait for you here,' said Alice sunnily. Jeremy put a hand briefly on her shoulder.

'Better get mine as well,' said Daphne languidly, 'and get my fish out of the freezer. Hope it'll fit in the car.'

The Cartwrights said goodbye and went off to look at equipment for the new members of the fishing school.

Alice sat alone. It was a beautiful day and she sipped

her coffee and looked happily out at the sun sparkling on the loch. Perhaps she and Jeremy would return on their honeymoon.

All of a sudden she stiffened. Daphne had said something about hoping her fish would fit in the car. Which car? There was really only room for two in Jeremy's sports car.

She rushed out to reception and grabbed her suitcase and ran out into the courtyard. Jeremy and Daphne were laughing as they tried to find room for Daphne's enormous salmon.

'Jeremy,' cried Alice. 'I thought we were going back together.'

He strolled over to her. 'No, it's only fair I should give Daphne a lift back. After all, we did travel up together.'

'But we're engaged,' shrieked Alice. 'Look! I'm wearing your ring.'

'It was only a present,' mumbled Jeremy. 'I mean, I didn't ask you to marry me, did I?'

'You *slept* with me,' said Alice, beginning to sob. 'I might be pregnant.' She threw her arms around Jeremy's neck.

'Good God,' he said. He jerked her arms down and ran for his car. Daphne was already sitting in the passenger seat.

Jeremy climbed in and slammed the door just as Alice ran up. Her hands scrabbled at the window as he let in the clutch. The smart red sports car gave a growl and swept off.

Alice became aware of the press watching curiously from outside the courtyard and some of the hotel servants watching as well.

She picked up her case and, with her head held high, she walked back into the hotel.

* * *

Hamish and Charlie rowed slowly back to Lochdubh
after an afternoon's fishing. They had caught four
mackerel and two ling. Charlie had lost his hard,
calculating stare and was looking out at the world with
dreamy pleasure.

'There's Mr Johnson waiting for you,' he said as they
approached the shore.

Hamish was sharply reminded of the time when they
had last returned and Blair was waiting for them.

'Where have you been?' asked Mr Johnson as soon
as Hamish landed on the beach. 'I've been going out of
my wits. That girl Alice Wilson had a scene with Mr
Blythe and she's disappeared. Her case is still at the
reception and she hasn't booked in for another night.
The staff have been out searching for her.'

'You run along home,' said Hamish to the boy. 'Don't
worry, Mr Johnson. I'll find her.'

'Where would she go?' thought Hamish as he drove
up the twisting road out of Lochdubh. 'I suppose she
might just keep on walking and walking.'

He drove on through the pale Highland twilight, his
eyes searching from left to right of the road.

He was ten miles out of Lochdubh when his sharp
eyes suddenly spied what looked like a black lump on
a black rock. He drove on and parked the car around a
bend in the road. Then he began to walk back to the
rock, his shoes making no noise on the springy heather.

Alice sat on the rock, a picture of abject misery. She
was not crying, having cried all day until she could cry
no more, but she was hiccupping with dry sobs.

Hamish sat down beside her. 'Only a fool would cry
for someone who didn't really want them.'

'Go away,' said Alice, turning red-rimmed eyes to
him.

156

'No, I will not go away. You are coming with me. You have caused enough worry and trouble this day. And all over some pipsqueak you didn't even love.'

'I love him,' wailed Alice.

'No, you don't. Went to bed with him, didn't you? Aye, I thought as much. So now you've got to pretend you love him. Och, lassie, it's your pride that's hurt, not your heart. There's one silly woman charged with murder and all because of damned snobbery and here you are planning to jump in the nearest loch as soon as you get up the courage so as to make a rat like Blythe sorry.'

'I . . . I didn't . . . I wouldn't.'

'Look, I tried to tell you he was a snob. As soon as he decided Daphne was rich enough, he decided to settle for her. She'll marry him. That kind always get what they want and they'll have a dead-alive sort of marriage. You only wanted the dream, Alice. Be honest and admit it's over.'

'What if I'm pregnant?'

'Face that when it comes. When's your next period?' asked Hamish.

'Next week, I think.'

'Well, you'll maybe just be all right. Come along with me and I'll get us a drink. You're a pretty girl and you're young.'

'Do . . . do you think I'm pretty?'

'Very,' lied Hamish gallantly. 'Smashing little thing, that's what I thought when I first saw you.'

He helped her to her feet and put an arm about her shoulders and together they walked towards the road.

'It's a grand evening to be alive,' said Hamish. 'Just think about that.'

Down below them, the lights of the village twinkled in the half dark. The twilight was scented with thyme and pine and heather. A rocketing pheasant whirred up from a clump of heather at the other side of the road. Out in the loch, the fishing boats were chugging out to sea.

Hamish pulled Alice to the side of the road as he heard a car approaching. A Rolls, black and sleek, slowed. Inside sat Priscilla Halburton-Smythe. She was wearing a white evening dress and a diamond necklace sparkled against her breast. Beside her at the wheel was John Harrington. Priscilla looked at Hamish, at Hamish's arm about Alice's shoulders, shrugged, and said something to John, who looked across her at Hamish and Alice and laughed. Then the car sped away.

Alice took a deep breath of clean-scented air. She was feeling better already. Hamish's arm was comforting. She glanced up at him. He really wasn't bad-looking. His eyelashes were very long for a man and his hair was a fascinating colour of red. 'You're right,' said Alice. 'Only a fool would cry for someone who didn't really want them.'

Hamish watched the tail lights of the disappearing Rolls-Royce. 'Did I say that?' he asked, and then added in so low a voice that Alice could not hear what he was saying, 'If I said that then I am a very great fool indeed.'

He helped Alice into his car but he sat for a few moments, staring straight ahead.

'I've always wondered, Mr Macbeth,' said Alice timidly. 'What's a FEB?'

Hamish let in the clutch. 'Fucking English Bastard,' he said. And with an angry screech of tyres he swung the car around and they plunged down into the heathery darkness of the road leading to Lochdubh.

THE END

DEATH OF A CAD

CHAPTER ONE

Land of brown heath and shaggy wood,
Land of the mountain and the flood.
—SIR WALTER SCOTT

Henry Withering, playwright, slumped down in the
passenger seat of the station wagon after another
bleak look out at the forbidding landscape.

'Have we much farther to go, darling?' he asked
plaintively.

'Oh, yes,' said his fiancée, Priscilla Halburton-
Smythe, cheerfully. 'But we should be home before
dark.'

Henry wondered whether to point out that, as
they seemed to be surely approaching the land
of the midnight sun after all those weary hours of
travel, there was therefore very little hope
of reaching their destination at all. He suddenly
found himself too overpowered by the landscape
and too depressed by the change it seemed to be
creating in Priscilla to say anything, and so he
decided to go to sleep instead. But although
he determinedly closed his eyes and listened to the
hypnotic swish of the windscreen wipers, sleep
would not come. Scotland had murdered sleep.

It was not that he, an Englishman born and bred, had never visited Scotland, it was just that he had never journeyed so far north before.

'It's clearing up,' came Priscilla's cool, amused voice. 'Do look. The scenery is magnificent.'

Henry reluctantly opened his eyes.

A watery sunlight was bathing the steep barren flanks of the towering mountains on either side. As the clouds rolled back, he found himself staring up at the awesome peaks and then around at the immediate prospect of damp sheep and bleak moorland.

The sun grew stronger and a wind arose. A river meandered beside the road, shining and glittering with red and gold lights. Then the scenery was blotted from view as they drove into a cutting. A waterfall hurtled down by the side of the road on Henry's side of the car, a relentless torrent that roared in his ear as they sped past.

He glanced out of the corner of his eyes at Priscilla. There was something rather frightening about a woman who could drive so well. They had left London at dawn, and she had driven the 640 miles north, sitting back, her hands resting easily on the wheel. She was wearing beige corduroy trousers and a cream silk blouse. Her fair hair was tied back behind her ears by a tightly rolled Hermès scarf. She looked sophisticated and elegant. But it seemed to him that there was a certain buoyancy in her manner as she neared her Scottish home, an excited anticipation that had nothing to do with him. In London, he had been used to a graceful and pliant Priscilla. After they were married, he decided, he would insist he did all the driving and that she should never wear trousers again. For the first time, he wondered if she would turn out in later years to be one of those terrible county ladies who managed everyone in the neighbourhood and opened fêtes. He sulkily closed his eyes. She was not even thinking of him, of that he was sure.

In this, he was wrong.

During the journey, a great deal of Priscilla's triumph at having secured a celebrity for a future husband had begun to ebb. She had told him to wear casual clothes, but he had turned up, impeccably dressed as usual, in white collar, striped shirt, old school tie, Savile Row suit, and shoes handmade by Lobb of St James's. She wondered uneasily what he had packed in his suitcase, whether he planned to startle the Highlands of Scotland by parading the countryside attired like a tailor's dummy.

When he had asked her to marry him, all she had felt was a giddy elation at having done the right thing at last; at having finally found someone who would please her parents. Colonel and Mrs Halburton-Smythe had complained for a year because she had become a journalist, although Priscilla had tried, without success, to tell them that a job as a fashion editor's assistant hardly qualified her for the title. They had come on flying visits, always dragging some 'suitable' young man in tow. Priscilla realized uneasily she did not really know very much about Henry.

He was thirty-eight years of age, small, neat-featured, with smooth black hair and brown eyes that were almost black. His skin was sallow, and his legs were rather thin, but he had great charm and appeared to be universally popular.

Over the years, he had had various plays produced at experimental theatres, usually savage satires against the church and state. He was beloved by the Communists, Trotskyites, Marxists, and liberals. To them, he was what they wanted most, a genuine ex-Eton schoolboy, son of a landed family who had opted to join the class war. He wore faded jeans and black sweaters and rather dirty sneakers.

And then his play *Duchess Darling* had opened in London. No-one could understand what on earth had happened to Henry Withering. For it was a drawing-room comedy of the type that opens with the butler and the cockney housemaid discussing their betters. It had every cliché. Infidelity among the aristocracy, a silly-ass guardee, a gorgeous débutante, a stately duchess, and a bumbling duke. But the clothes were haute couture and it had a star-studded cast.

A clever impresario had decided that a London weary of inner-city riots, rape, and politics might be in the mood for nostalgia. The left-wing papers stoutly gave it good reviews, convinced that Henry had written a very clever satire that they could not quite understand but were afraid to say so. The right-wing press were hesitant to damn it when the cast contained so many famous names who had been brought out of moth-balls. The public loved it. It was frivolous, silly, trite, and beautifully presented. They flocked in droves. After all, it was like going to a royal wedding. No-one expected the stars to be clever, only to look very grand and rich.

Henry's success was sealed when the left wing at last found out their darling had betrayed them and the Young Communists staged a protest outside the theatre during which five policemen were sent to hospital and a member of the Royal family was seen to frown. Henry's name appeared on the front page of every major newspaper the next day.

Priscilla's work as a fashion editor's assistant had mostly been arranging fashion photographs, sitting around studios, shoving models in and out of fashions that were a cross between those of medieval page and a Japanese labourer, and wondering whether the blue-rinsed lady she worked for was ever going to allow her a chance to write. She had finally been sent to write a report on the fashions in the play. She had gone backstage and had been introduced to Henry, who had promptly invited her out for dinner. One week later he had proposed. Now, one week after that, they were on the road to Priscilla's Scottish home at the express invitation of Priscilla's rapturously delighted parents, who were organizing a house party in honour of the new fiancé. Priscilla, at the age of twenty-three, was still a virgin. Henry had kissed her five times, and that had been the sum total of his lovemaking to date. She knew what he looked like in shorts because he had been photographed in tennis whites for a society magazine. But she had never seen him in person dressed other than he was at that moment. It was odd that a man of his background should always look as if he were dressed for church, thought Priscilla, not knowing that Henry's clothes were a sort of costume to enhance his new darling-of-society image.

Beside her, Henry sat moodily listening to the rumbling of his stomach. They had stopped for a horrible lunch hours ago at a motorway café. He wanted his dinner. He wanted this nightmare journey to end.

Priscilla slowed to a stop and he looked up impatiently.

A shepherd was driving a flock of sheep down the centre of the road. He moved with an easy slow pace and did not look at the car. With an impatient grunt, Henry leaned across and honked the horn loudly. The sheep panicked and scattered.

'You awful fool,' snapped Priscilla. She rolled down the window. 'I'm very sorry, Mr Mackay,' she called. 'An accident.'

The shepherd came up and leaned in the car window. 'It's yerself, Miss Halburton-Smythe,' he said. 'Now, you should know better than to startle a man's sheep.'

'Sorry,' said Priscilla again. 'How's Mrs Mackay's leg?'

'Better, she says. We got a new doctor, Dr Brodie. He's given her the green bottle. She says it's awf'y good.'

'Are we going to sit here all day?' growled Henry.

The shepherd looked at him with mild surprise.

'My friend is tired,' said Priscilla. 'Must get on. Tell Mrs Mackay I shall call on her in a few days.'

'You mustn't hurry things in the country,' said Priscilla severely as they moved on. 'Mr Mackay was most offended.'

'Does it matter what the peasantry think?'

'They're not peasants,' said Priscilla. 'Really, Henry. I'm surprised at you.'

'Well, since you have promised to visit Mrs Mackay of the green bottle and the bad leg, I assume we must be nearly at our journey's end.'

'About another thirty miles to go.'

Henry groaned.

Lord and Lady Helmsdale sat in the back of their antique Rolls-Royce and shouted at each other, which was the way they normally conversed.

'If it weren't for this playwright-chappie, I would have turned down Mary's invitation,' said Lord Helmsdale. Mary was Mrs Halburton-Smythe.

Lord Helmsdale was small and round with thin grey hair combed carefully in strips over his bald patch. His wife was a huge woman, well over six feet tall, with a slab of a face. She was wearing an old tweed jacket and skirt and a shirt with a hard collar. On her head she sported an off-the-face blue-and-white-spotted hat. It looked remarkably like one Her Majesty had worn during her last American visit, and Lord Helmsdale had delayed their leaving by asking whether she had been ferreting around the garbage cans at Buckingham Palace again. The resultant row had been frightful. But there is nothing more cosy than a shared marital resentment, and the Helmsdales were once more drawn together by their hatred of one of the Halburton-Smythes's guests.

The target of their hatred was Captain Peter Bartlett of the Highland Dragoons.

'Why on earth did Mary ask him?' demanded Lord Helmsdale querulously.

'If you mean Bartlett, then God knows,' snapped his wife. 'But I know *why* Bartlett's going to be there. He wants to bag the first brace.' She had long chats on the phone to Mrs Halburton-Smythe and never guessed for a moment how much that lady dreaded her calls.

'Didn't think there would be any grouse shooting,' observed his lordship. 'Grouse population's declining fast, and Halburton-Smythe told me not to bring my guns.'

The previous grouse season – which begins in Britain on August 12, known as the Glorious Twelfth, and ends on December 10 – had confirmed Scottish landowners' worst fears: The grouse were dying off fast, and that could soon mean an end to Scotland's £150 million-a-year grouse 'industry.'

'My birds are disappearing as well,' grumbled Lord Helmsdale. 'Think those Animal Rights people must be poisoning them to spite me.'

'Everyone's birds are dying off,' said his wife reasonably. 'The Game Conservancy has launched a three-hundred-thousand-pound appeal to finance research. They're appealing to all landowners for cash. Didn't you get their letter?'

'Can't remember,' said Lord Helmsdale.

'Sheikh Hamdan Al Maktoum has already given them a hundred thousand.'

'Mac who?'

'He's a United Arab Emirates Cabinet Minister who has a large estate in Scotland, and you ask me the same thing every time I mention his name.'

'Well, they won't need my money if they've got that much from him,' said her husband comfortably. 'Still, we needn't let Bartlett bother us. This

168

playwright-chappie Withering's damned clever. Best play I've seen in ages.'

'I shall enjoy being rude to Bartlett,' remarked his wife. 'I shall enjoy that very much.'

'The man's an utter cad.'

Jessica Villiers and Diana Bryce were best friends – the sort of odd friendship that springs up between a pretty girl and a plain one. Diana was secretly contemptuous of the mannish, gawky, horsy Jessica, and Jessica was bitterly jealous of Diana's stunning good looks.

Both girls' parents had estates over in Caithness in the north-east. Diana and Jessica had made their come-out at the London Season at the same time. Both worked in London and had taken their holidays at the same time, not out of friendship but because August was the fashionable time to holiday in Scotland.

The Highland grapevine works for the landed gentry in the same way as it does for everyone else there, and it seemed that no sooner had Mary Halburton-Smythe hit upon the idea of a small house party to welcome the playwright Henry Withering than she was besieged by pleading phone calls from all over. Everyone wanted to come, but she had kept the guest list down, and Jessica and Diana were two of that fortunate number. As Jessica competently managed her draughty old Land-Rover along the one-lane Highland roads, Diana dreamt of snatching this famous playwright from under Priscilla's nose. Everyone knew Priscilla had about as much sex appeal as a fish. Diana had glossy black hair and a flawless

169

complexion. The fact that the men hadn't exactly all fallen at her feet during her London Season still rankled. She had not yet learned the hard lesson that women who love themselves too much are rarely loved by anyone else. She had been engaged twice and on each occasion it had been the man who had called it off.

She would have been amazed had she known that Jessica was nourishing the same dream of wooing the playwright away from Priscilla. Jessica was convinced that the fellows, in the end, preferred a girl who was 'a good chap' rather than a posturing little miss . . . like Diana, she thought, casting a brief and evil look at her best friend. Of course, there had been that distressing business two years ago, she thought, when Diana had become engaged to her, Jessica's, boyfriend. Of course, *that* engagement hadn't lasted – for how could any man enjoy the pleasures of Diana after having tasted those of Jessica?

'Who's going to be there?' asked Jessica. 'I mean apart from you and me and Priscilla and her fellow.'

'Oh, all the usual faces,' yawned Diana. 'By the time I had coerced Mrs Halburton-Smythe into inviting the both of us, I hadn't any energy left to ask who else was going to be there. There won't be any shooting with all this boring grouse problem, so I suppose the rest will be a lot of old fogies.'

Tommel Castle, home of the Halburton-Smythes, was not a real castle. It had been built by a beer baron in the nineteenth century, when Queen Victoria had made the Highlands fashionable by her visits. It had pinnacles, turrets, battlements, and a multitude of cold, dark rooms. The shallow oak stairs and corridors were guarded by fake suits of medieval armour.

Along the Highland roads heading for the castle sped the rest of the Halburton-Smythes's guests.

First to arrive was the raddled and still beautiful Mrs Vera Forbes-Grant and her banker husband, Freddy. They had a country home quite nearby. Then came Miss Prunella Smythe, a stage-struck spinster lady related to Colonel Halburton-Smythe who frequently wished she were not, and elderly Sir Humphrey Throgmorton, a collector of fine china who lived on the Scottish borders and was an old friend of the colonel.

Captain Peter Bartlett was already there, having arrived two days previously. As the first of the guests rolled up, he was lying fully dressed on his bed, admiring a silver cigarette box he had stolen from the library and wondering how much it would fetch.

Jeremy Pomfret had arrived in time for luncheon and was lolling in front of the library fire, tired from his drive up from Perth and too much food and wine.

He was a small, chubby man, and although he was nearly forty, he looked about twenty-five. He had a shock of whitish-fair hair and round blue eyes fringed with white lashes, which looked out ingenuously at the world from a cherubic face. He was very rich, and his passion was shooting anything at all that he was allowed to shoot.

He thought uneasily about the bet he had just made with Captain Peter Bartlett. Colonel

Halburton-Smythe had told them at luncheon that he was not organizing a grouse shoot this year, on account of the mysterious dearth of the game birds. So the usual retinue of beaters, made up of crofters, itinerant farm labourers, and schoolchildren on holiday, had not been hired. But anyone who wished to take his chances bagging a few brace on a walk-up was welcome to do so, the colonel had said.

Captain Bartlett had immediately turned to Jeremy.

'Brought your gun, laddie?' he asked, though everyone who was anyone knew that Jeremy Pomfret never went anywhere without a brace of shotguns.

'Yes, of course,' he replied.

'In that case, how about a bet to see which of us bags the first brace?'

And so the bet had been made, for five thousand pounds.

It had seemed perfectly reasonable and sportsmanlike at the time, especially to a mind mellowed with good claret. And five thousand pounds meant little to Jeremy. But now, sitting down by the fire and thinking it over, he began to have doubts.

Did Peter Bartlett actually have five thousand pounds to bet? He had met the captain before, briefly, at various social events in the Highlands and in London. He had always seemed a bit of a sponger, always broke. Why, then, was he so eager to bet what would be to him a large sum of money? What was Bartlett up to?

Anyway, the details were to be worked out the next night, when there was to be a buffet party held in this chap Henry Withering's honour, for Colonel Halburton-Smythe had suggested that the bet be made known to all the guests in case anyone wanted to make a side bet.

Still wondering what Bartlett could be up to, Jeremy Pomfret fell quietly asleep.

He snored gently through the noisy welcome being given to that famous playwright Henry Withering.

'This is where we turn off,' said Priscilla, slowing the car. 'We take this secondary road. The main road goes along the front of the village and stops outside the Lochdubh Hotel.'

For the first time that long and weary day, the scenery pleased Henry Withering's eye. 'Stop the car a minute,' he said. 'It's lovely.'

The village of Lochdubh lay on the shores of a sea loch of the same name. It consisted of a curve of eighteenth-century cottages, their white walls gleaming in the soft late-afternoon sun. A riot of pink and white Scottish roses tumbled over the garden fences. The waters of Lochdubh were calm and mirror-like. The air smelled of roses, salt water, seaweed, tar, and wood-smoke. A porpoise broke the glassy surface of the water, rolled lazily, and then disappeared. Henry drew a deep breath of pleasure as he watched the circle of ripples from the porpoise's dive widening and widening over the loch. A keening voice raised in a Gaelic lament arose from someone's radio.

'It makes London seem very far away – another country, a wrong world of bustle and noise and politics,' said Henry, half to himself.

Priscilla smiled at him, liking him again. She let in the clutch. 'We'll soon be home,' she said.

The car began to climb up a straight one-lane road away from the village. They reached the crest of the road and Henry twisted his head and looked back. The village nestled at the foot of two towering twisted mountains, their sides purple with heather. Then he realized they had stopped again. 'It's all right, darling,' he said. 'I'm too hungry to admire the scenery any longer.'

'It's not that. I just want to have a word with Hamish.'

Henry looked at her sharply. Her cheeks had a delicate tinge of pink. He looked ahead.

A tall, thin policeman was strolling down the road towards them. His peaked cap was pushed back on his head, and his fiery red hair glinted underneath it. He was in his shirt-sleeves, and the shine on his baggy uniform trousers above a large pair of ugly boots made it look as if he had ironed his trousers on the wrong side. He was carrying a bottle of Scotch under his arm.

What a great gangling idiot, thought Henry, amused.

But as the policeman recognized Priscilla and came up to the car, his thin face was lit up in a peculiarly sweet smile of welcome. His eyes were greenish-gold and framed with thick black lashes.

'It's yourself, Priscilla,' said the policeman in a soft, lilting accent.

Henry bristled like an angry dog. Who did this village bobby think he was, addressing Priscilla by her first name? Priscilla had rolled down the window. 'Henry,' she said, 'I would like to introduce Hamish Macbeth, our village policeman. Hamish, this is Henry Withering.'

'I heard you were coming,' said Hamish, bending down from his lanky height so that he could look in the car window on Priscilla's side. 'This place is in a fair uproar at the thought o' having a famous playwright among them.'

Henry gave a cool little smile. 'I am sure they are also excited to learn that Miss Halburton-Smythe is finally about to be married.'

One minute the policeman's face was at the car window, the next it had disappeared as he abruptly straightened up. Henry looked angrily at Priscilla, who was staring straight ahead.

Priscilla muttered something under her breath and opened the car door, nudging Hamish aside. Henry sat listening to their conversation.

'I did not know you were engaged,' he heard Hamish say softly.

'I thought you would have heard,' Priscilla whispered. 'You, of all people. You always hear the gossip first.'

'Aye, weel, I heard something to that effect, but I chust could not believe it,' said Hamish. 'Mrs Halburton-Smythe was aye saying you was to marry this one or that one.'

'Well, it's true this time.'

Henry angrily got out of the car. If he did not say something to stop this tête-à-tête, he had an awful feeling Priscilla was going to *apologise* to this village bobby for having become engaged.

'Evening, Officer,' he said, strolling around to join them.

'Why on earth are you carrying around that great bottle of whisky?' asked Priscilla.

'I won it at the clay-pigeon shooting over at Craig.' Hamish grinned.

'What an odd colour of Scotch,' said Priscilla. 'It's very pale, nearly white.'

'Weel, ye see,' said Hamish with a smile, 'the prizes was being giffen away by the laird, and his wife was alone in the tent wi' the prizes afore the presentation.'

'That explains it,' giggled Priscilla. She and Hamish smiled at each other, a smile that held a world of understanding and friendship from which Henry felt excluded.

'Explains what?' he demanded sharply.

'The laird's wife likes a drink,' said Priscilla. 'She drinks half what's in the prize bottles and then fills them up with water.'

She and Hamish burst out laughing.

'I am sure we are keeping you from your duties, Officer,' said Henry in what – he sincerely hoped – was his most patronizing tone of voice.

Hamish looked thoughtfully down at the playwright, his eyes, which a moment before had been full of laughter, suddenly blank and stupid.

'Aye, I've got to feed the hens,' he said. He touched his cap and turned away.

'Wait a minute, Hamish,' cried Priscilla, ignoring Henry's fulminating glare. 'Mummy's having a party tomorrow night in Henry's honour. Do come as well. It's drinks and buffet. Come at seven. Mummy doesn't like late affairs.'

'That's verra kind of you,' said Hamish.

'It's . . . it's black tie,' said Priscilla.

'I hae one o' those,' said Hamish equably.

'I mean dinner jacket and . . .'

'I'll find something.'

'See you then,' said Priscilla brightly.

Hamish loped off down the road. Priscilla turned slowly to face an outraged fiancé. 'Have you gone right out of your tiny mind?' demanded Henry.

'Hamish is an old friend,' said Priscilla, climbing back into the car.

Henry got in beside her and slammed the door shut with unnecessary force.

'Was that copper at any time anything more than an old friend?'

'Of course not, silly,' said Priscilla. 'You must remember, I know everyone in Lochdubh.'

'And are all the local yokels coming to this party?'

'No, Mummy's a bit of a snob and Daddy's worse and . . .'

Priscilla's voice trailed away.

She cringed inside as she thought of what her mother would say when she learned Hamish Macbeth had been invited.

Hamish – of all people!

CHAPTER TWO

cad. Since 1900, a man devoid of fine instincts or
delicate feelings.
—*The Penguin Dictionary of Historical Slang*

Jeremy Pomfret decided to have a bath before
dinner. He shared a bathroom with Peter Bartlett
and it was situated between their two bedrooms.

He threw off his clothes and wrapped his
dressing gown around him. He pushed open the
bathroom door and stood transfixed. Peter Bartlett
was standing with one foot up on the washbasin,
scrubbing his toenails. He was a very handsome
man, dark and lean, with one of those saturnine
faces portrayed on the covers of romances. He had
a hard tanned face and a hard tanned body of which
Jeremy was able to see quite a lot because the
captain had only a small towel tied about his waist.

'I say,' bleated the horrified Jeremy. 'That's my
toothbrush you're using.'

'Oh, is it?' said Peter indifferently. 'Give it a good
rinse. It's not as if I've got AIDS.'

'Don't you realize the *enormity* of what you are
doing?' demanded Jeremy in a voice squeaky with
outrage. 'You're always pinching a chap's stuff.

Yesterday it was my shaving brush. Now you're scrubbing your filthy toes with my toothbrush. Haven't you anything of your own?'

'It's all somewhere around,' said Peter vaguely. 'Met the playwright yet?'

'No, I fell asleep,' said Jeremy crossly, 'but I must say—'

'I know him.'

'How?'

'Met him in London before I rejoined the army. Awful little Commie he was then.'

'I'm sure it was just a pose,' said Jeremy, darting forward and snatching his toothbrush. He looked at it hopelessly and then threw it in the trash bucket.

'In fact,' went on Peter, easing his foot down from the handbasin, 'this damned cold dump is crawling with skeletons out of my closet. The only person going to be at this party tomorrow night who I don't know is the village bobby.'

'What's he coming for? To guard the silver?'

'No, Priscilla asked him as an honoured guest. Henry told her parents about it before the rapturous welcomes were over, and Halburton-Smythe hit the roof. He sent one of the maids down to the village with a note to the bobby to tell him not to come. Priscilla ups on her hind legs and calls him a snob, Mother joins in, and they were all at it hammer and tongs when I last saw them. But if I know Priscilla, she'll get her way in the end.'

'It's the first time I've ever stayed here,' said Jeremy. He was still smarting over the loss of his toothbrush, but he never had the courage to assert himself over anything. 'It'll be the last. I've never stayed anywhere quite so cold before. As soon as I bag my birds, I'll be off.'

'You might not win,' said Peter, leaning his broad shoulders against the bathroom wall.

Jeremy shrugged. 'Clear off, if you've finished, old man, and let me have a bath.'

'Righto,' said the captain, opening the door out of the bathroom that led to his room.

Jeremy sighed with relief and advanced on the bath. A grey ring marred its white porcelain sides.

'Dirty sod!' muttered Jeremy in a fury. 'Absolute dirty rotter. Complete and utter cad!'

Priscilla put down her hairbrush as she heard a knock at her bedroom door and went to answer it. Henry stood there, smiling apologetically.

'I am sorry, darling,' he said, taking her in his arms, and noticing again with irritation that she was several inches taller than he.

Priscilla extricated herself gently and went and sat down again at the dressing table. 'It was a bit thick,' she said. 'Did you have to tell them I'd invited Hamish as soon as we got in the door? I told you they wouldn't like it.'

'Yes, but you haven't yet told me *why* you were so bloody damned anxious to ask the bobby in the first place.'

'I like him, that's all,' said Priscilla crossly. 'He's a human being and that's more than you can say for most of the guests here. Jessica Villiers and Diana Bryce have never liked me. The Helmsdales are crashing bores. Jeremy's a twit. I don't know much about the gallant captain, but it reminds me of that rhyme about knowing two things about the

180

horse, one of them is rather coarse. Prunella and Sir Humphrey are innocent sweeties but hardly strong enough to counteract the rest. Oh, let's not quarrel about Hamish. He's not coming and that's that. Don't dress for dinner. It's informal this evening.'

'Kiss me if you don't want to quarrel.'

Priscilla smiled and turned up her face. He kissed her warmly, and although she seemed rather to enjoy it, her reaction could hardly be called passionate. But it was not sexual desire that had prompted Henry to propose. Priscilla was, to him, all that a future bride should be. He loved his new fame, he loved the money that came with it, and he loved his press image of being the darling of the upper set. The first moment he had set eyes on Priscilla, he had immediately seen her standing on the church steps beside him dressed in white satin and being photographed by every society magazine. She enhanced his image.

'Did you want to ask me something?' asked Priscilla when he had stopped kissing her.

'Yes, there doesn't seem to be a bath plug, and Mrs Halburton-Smythe told me not to ring for the servants because they don't have very many and the ones that she has might give notice if they had to run up and down the stairs too much.'

'Where is your room?'

'In the west turret, the one at the front.'

'Oh, *that* room. The plug in that bathroom was lost ages ago and we keep meaning to get another. But it's quite simple. It's a very small plug hole. You just stick your heel in it.'

'Not exactly gracious living.'

'No-one really lives very graciously these days, unless you want masses of foreigners as servants, and Daddy is suspicious of anyone from south of Calais. I must say, you have rather grand ideas for an ex-member of the comrades.'

'I never was a member of the Communist Party.'

'But what about all those early plays of yours? All that class-war stuff.'

'It's the only way you can get a play put on these days,' said Henry with a tinge of bitterness. 'The big theatres only want trash. Only the small left-wing theatres will give the newcomer a chance. You've never said anything about *Duchess Darling*. Did you like it?'

'Yes,' said Priscilla. She had not liked it at all, thinking it silly and trite, but all her other friends had loved it, and Priscilla was so used to being at odds with them in matters of taste, she had begun to distrust her own judgement.

'I'll give you some of my better stuff to read when we get back to London,' he said eagerly.

He looked down at her with affection, enjoying the cool beauty of her blonde looks. When he received his knighthood, as he was sure he would, she would look regal in the press photographs.

He bent and kissed her again. 'I shall go and put my heel in the plug hole. I hope your mama has put us together at dinner.'

'Probably not,' said Priscilla. 'But we shall survive.'

Mrs Vera Forbes-Grant, clad only in pink French knickers and transparent bra, was sitting on the end of her bed, painting her toenails scarlet.

Her husband was sitting at the dressing table trying to add some more curl to his large handlebar moustache with his wife's electric hair curler.

'Your roots are showing,' he said, studying the top of his wife's bent head in the mirror.

'Well, they'll just need to show. I once went to the hairdresser here and the girls were so busy gossiping they nearly burned my scalp off. Seen Withering yet?'

'No,' said Freddy Forbes-Grant, 'but I've seen that rotter, Bartlett.'

'Damn!' Vera's hand shook suddenly, and the bottle of nail varnish tipped over on the carpet.

'Used to be pretty thick with him, didn't you?' pursued Freddy.

'Me? Course not. For God's sake, bring over that bottle of remover and help me clear up this mess.'

'Peter's here,' said Diana Bryce, flouncing into Jessica Villiers's room and banging the door behind her.

Jessica had been busy applying blusher to her cheeks. She stopped with the brush in mid-air. 'Awkward for you,' she said with an ugly laugh.

'Poor, poor Jessica,' said Diana sweetly. 'You will maintain that fiction that Peter ditched me. Everyone knows I ditched *him*. But you were so crazy about him, poor lamb, you couldn't believe anyone would want rid of him.'

'Well, I ditched him before he got engaged to you on the rebound,' said Jessica breathlessly.

Diana eyed her with malicious amusement. 'Is that the case? I really must tease him about it.'

'And I must tease him about being given the push by you.'

Both girls glared at each other, and then Diana gave a little laugh. 'What nonsense we're talking. Who cares about him anyway? I thought we came to see the playwright.'

'Yes,' said Jessica slowly. 'I had almost forgotten.'

Henry Withering enjoyed dinner that evening immensely. He enjoyed the excellent food and the fake baronial dining room, hung with medieval banners that had been made in Birmingham twenty years before, when Colonel Halburton-Smythe had decided to redecorate the castle himself. He thought it was like a stage setting. The Halburton-Smythes did not run to footmen, but there were plenty of efficient Highland maids to serve the cold salmon hors d'oeuvres, followed by roast saddle of venison. There was a stately English butler to pour the wine. Lady Helmsdale, who was seated on Henry's right, did not once look at Captain Bartlett. Henry was rather sorry for Priscilla, who was at the other end of the table, with Lord Helmsdale on one side and old Sir Humphrey on the other. Henry had at first been wary of the good-looking captain, knowing of old his reputation with women, but in the drawing room before dinner, Priscilla had shown not the slightest flicker of interest in Peter Bartlett. Jessica and Diana had made a dead set at Henry, all very flattering and just as it should be. The fameless years of neglect were gone.

Henry was so busy being happily deafened by

Lady Helmsdale's loud and fulsome compliments that he was unaware of any other conversation at the table.

Mrs Halburton-Smythe was a faded blonde woman with quick, timid movements. She was so often dominated by her husband that she rarely voiced an opinion on anything. She would even have allowed Priscilla to invite that dreadful joke of a policeman if her husband had not been so much against it. But it could be said in Mrs Halburton-Smythe's favour that she hardly ever listened to gossip, and that was why she had seated Captain Peter Bartlett between Jessica and Diana. Jessica tried to ignore the captain by talking to Jeremy, who was on her other side, while Diana picked at her food and stared sulkily in front of her, wondering what on earth Henry Withering found so fascinating about the terrible Lady Helmsdale.

The captain, who had been drinking steadily, glanced to right and left and announced suddenly, 'Well, I must say you two girls make a lousy pair of po-faced dinner companions.'

Jessica shied like a horse and turned her head away. Diana affected not to hear. Opposite the captain, Mrs Vera Forbes-Grant leaned forward. 'I'll entertain you, darling,' she said in her husky whisky voice, 'if you don't think it rude to talk across the table.'

'I'm rather like you, old girl,' slurred the captain. 'Anything's permissible so long as it don't frighten the horses.'

'Oh, Peter.' Vera gave a nervous laugh. 'You're such a little boy when you try to shock. Do you

185

think you'll get the first brace?' Word of the bet had already gone around the guests.

'Who knows?' said Peter. 'Damned birds have been dying off like flies. 'S all a Communist plot to ruin sport.'

'What on earth have the Reds got to do with a lot of game birds?' asked Vera.

'I'll tell you,' said the captain, leaning forward and putting his elbow in the remains of some cauliflower *au gratin*. 'Acid rain.'

'Acid rain?'

'Yes, they take it up frozen, see, in planes, above the moors, and they drop out great chunks of frozen acid rain on the grouse.'

'Oh, I see. They're *stunned* to death,' mocked Vera.

'Y'know, Vera,' said the captain, roaring to make himself heard above the boom of Lady Helmsdale's voice, 'you are one very dumb blonde . . . or would be if you got your roots done. Never seen them so black.'

'There's no need to get so bloody personal,' snapped Vera.

'What's the matter?' demanded her husband, Freddy, sharply.

'Peter's had too much to drink, that's all,' whispered Vera. 'Ignore him.'

But Peter Bartlett had found a new quarry. 'Turn the volume down a bit, Agatha,' he shouted suddenly in Lady Helmsdale's direction. 'Can't hear myself think.'

'You never can,' roared Lady Helmsdale. 'Don't you know it's because you never think?'

With one of his inexplicable changes of mood,

the captain sent Lady Helmsdale an amused wink and then turned to Diana, 'You are looking very fetching tonight,' he said. 'I like that little black number. Suits you.'

Priscilla had met Peter Bartlett before but had never spent more than a few minutes in his company. She was amused to see how the obnoxious captain so easily turned on the charm. Diana was beginning to giggle and blush. Peter then said something across the table to Vera, who looked first startled, then gratified. Then he turned to Jessica and began to whisper in her ear until the frozen look of disapproval left her face and she began to look happy and excited. Priscilla then looked down the table to where Henry was laughing uproariously at something Lady Helmsdale had said.

He really is a pet, thought Priscilla. Mummy and Daddy are so pleased. It's nice to do the right thing for once. Poor Hamish. I do hope he won't feel the snub too painfully.

At that moment, Hamish was leaning on his garden gate outside the police station, enjoying the quiet evening. His slavering pet mongrel, Towser, as usual, had flopped down to sleep across his master's boots. Behind Hamish, from the back of the police station, came the mournful clucking of the hens.

The only thing that worried him was where to find a dinner jacket for the party. He had quickly recovered from the shock of Priscilla's engagement. Hamish had long ago discovered that it was easier to tuck painful things he could do nothing about at the present away into a far corner of his brain until such time as he could take some action.

He did not know the Halburton-Smythes had written to him not to come. Jessie, their dizzy housemaid, was walking out with Geordie, the baker's boy, and had met her swain only five yards from the police station. The encounter had made her forget the reason for her having been sent to the village. The housekeeper, Mrs Wilson, had told her to buy a packet of soap powder when she was down in the village, and Jessie remembered only that request. She did not find the note, undelivered, still in her apron pocket until two days later.

CHAPTER THREE

Keep your place and silent be,
Game can hear and game can see.
—MARK BEAUFOY

The members of the house party, with the exception of the guest of honour, Henry Withering, and his fiancée, Priscilla Halburton-Smythe, looked rather jaded when they gathered in the dining room of the castle on the following evening for the buffet supper.

Jeremy Pomfret appeared looking like a dissipated cherub, with blue circles under his eyes. His room and Peter's had originally been one triangular-shaped room. It had been converted into two by a wall of thin plasterboard, and the bathroom had been installed to cut across the point of the triangle. Jeremy's sleep had been disturbed by sounds of noisy love-making coming from Peter's room all night long. There had also been a lot of toing and froing, and it had sounded as if the gallant captain had been entertaining more than one lady during the night.

The beginnings of a very deep hatred for Peter Bartlett had begun to burn in Jeremy's old-fashioned, fastidious soul. That hatred had leaped into a flame that very evening, when Jeremy had gone into the bathroom to wash and shave before dinner. There were sopping-wet towels lying all over the floor, and there was a stomach-churning ring of hair round the bathtub, showing that Captain Peter Bartlett had shaved while he was having his bath.

'Filthy beast,' raged Jeremy, glowering at Peter across the room. The captain, lean, handsome, beautifully tailored, was being fawned on by Vera, Jessica, and Diana. How can any woman even tolerate being near the man? thought Jeremy. Tomorrow was the Glorious Twelfth, and Peter had still not yet said at what time he would be going out. It was not as if Jeremy could ask the servants; since it was only the pair of them, there were to be no loaders or beaters or even dogs.

Also looking the worse for wear were Lord and Lady Helmsdale. Both wore men's pyjamas in bed, and they had discovered last night that some-one had poured glue into the crotch of each pair. They had spent hours trying to get the offending mess off the embarrassing places it had stuck to. They both blamed the captain.

Sir Humphrey Throgmorton sat listlessly in a corner. He never slept very well anyway. Prunella Smythe had stayed awake most of the night in a stagestruck fever of excitement. Freddy Forbes-Grant had been awakened by his wife's getting out of bed at two in the morning, saying she was going down to the kitchens to get a glass of milk. When she had not returned by three, he became anxious and went in search of her. When he had given up the search and returned to the bedroom, it was to find Vera once more in bed and fast asleep. He wondered what she had been up to, and that wonder had kept him awake and in a nasty temper until dawn.

Colonel and Mrs Halburton-Smythe had sat up very late debating whether their daughter actually meant to marry this splendid catch or whether she would change her mind. She had resisted their best efforts and had turned down so many eligibles that they found it hard to believe she meant to meet this one at the altar. They also planned to tell the captain to leave immediately after he had bagged his brace, but as they were both frightened of Peter Bartlett's erratic bouts of vicious temper, each wanted the other to give the captain his marching orders. They had never entertained him as a house guest before and had not realized until now the full horror of the captain's behaviour. They at last settled on that well-worn ruse employed by the landed gentry for speeding the unwelcome guest on his way – placing a railway timetable beside his bed with the soonest, fastest train underlined in red, and instructing the housekeeper to pack his case and leave it in the hall.

Whatever had put the shadows under the eyes of both Diana and Jessica, they were hugging to themselves, occasionally casting triumphant looks at each other, and then turning away puzzled, each obviously wondering what the other had to look triumphant about.

As well as the members of the house party, there was a sprinkling of local notables, now clustered about Henry, asking for his autograph and laughing at his slightest joke.

Priscilla was proud of Henry. He was so good-natured, so likeable, and so much at ease that all her doubts about their engagement had been laid to rest.

He had appeared during the day in respectably worn casual clothes and was now dressed in a beautifully tailored dinner jacket, the only relic of his past reputation for bohemianism being a pink-striped frilled shirt.

And then she looked across the dining room – it was the only large room in the castle, which was why it was being used for the party – and witnessed the full glory of the arrival of PC Macbeth.

Priscilla stifled a sharp exclamation of dismay and crossed the room to join him.

'Hamish,' she hissed, 'where on earth did you get that frightful dinner jacket from?'

'It's a wee bit on the short side,' admitted Hamish ruefully, looking down at his long, lanky figure. 'But wee Archie was the only waiter at the Loch-dubh Hotel who was off duty tonight.'

The dinner jacket hung loosely on him and the sleeves only came three-quarters of the way down his arms, and his trousers were exposing a long length of woolly plaid sock.

'Come with me quickly,' urged Priscilla. 'Uncle Harry often leaves some of his gear here, and he's tall and thin. Mummy's glaring already.'

Uncle Harry was Mr Paul Halburton, Mary Halburton-Smythe's brother, an archaeologist who travelled far and wide with the minimum of baggage and who always left most of his wardrobe behind at Tommel Castle after one of his flying visits. The Halburton-Smythes had double-barrelled their name after their marriage.

Priscilla led Hamish quickly from the room before her mother could reach her.

Upstairs, in a cell-like room at the top of the castle, Priscilla rummaged through her Uncle Harry's wardrobe until she found a respectable dinner jacket and trousers. 'Put these on immediately, Hamish,' she said. 'You can hand them back tomorrow. I'll parcel up Archie's clothes and put the parcel in the hall and you can pick it up when you leave. Didn't you get my parents' message telling you not to come?'

'No,' said Hamish, removing the waiter's dinner jacket and then the abbreviated trousers. 'I would hae been most offended. I think, as it is, I should go home.'

Priscilla wrestled with her conscience. Her parents would be furious. But Hamish looked so miserable, and he did not seem to have much fun – except with some of the local ladies, Priscilla reminded herself sharply. But he saved every penny to send back to his mother and father and large brood of brothers and sisters over on the east and she was sure he never ate enough.

The door opened, and Jenkins, the Halburton-Smythe's English butler, walked in. Hamish was just about to put on Uncle Harry's trousers.

'Don't you ever knock?' snapped Priscilla.

'A good servant never knocks,' said Jenkins, his gooseberry eyes bulging with outrage. 'And what, may I ask, are you doing with this constable, and him without his trousers?'

'Don't be a silly twit, Jenkins,' said Priscilla. 'You saw Mr Macbeth arrive. He could not possibly put in an appearance in that awful dinner jacket, so I am lending him one of Uncle Harry's. What are you doing here anyway?'

'Mrs Halburton-Smythe sent me to look for you. One of the maids said she had seen you coming up here.'

Priscilla bit her lip. Somehow it had never crossed her mind even to turn her back while Hamish was changing his trousers. She had become used to the fact that the Highlander, though quite prudish and shy in some respects, was never self-conscious about appearing undressed. But Jenkins was not a Highlander. And if she pleaded with Jenkins not to tell her mother what he had seen, that might make the whole innocent business seem sinister.

'Very well, Jenkins,' said Priscilla. 'You may go.'

'And what shall I tell Mrs Halburton-Smythe?' asked Jenkins, his eyes gleaming with malice. It was not that he disliked Priscilla in any way; it was just that he was a terrible snob and he thought Hamish Macbeth had no right to be attending Tommel Castle as one of the guests.

'Chust say,' said Hamish, whose Highland accent became more marked and sibilant when he was annoyed or upset, 'that Miss Halburton-Smythe will be doon the stairs shortly, and if you add anything to that statement, ye great pudding, I'll hear o' it and I'll take ye apart bit by bit.'

Jenkins glared awfully and then he wheeled about, his arms held out as if carrying a tray, and made a ponderous, stiff-legged exit.

'He's like a butler in a fillum,' said Hamish. 'I think when he feels his act or accent is slipping, he takes the bus down tae Strathbane and sees another old movie.'

'Don't blame old Jenkins too much,' said Priscilla ruefully. 'We must have looked like a bedroom farce.'

'How do I look now?' asked Hamish anxiously, straightening down the lapels of Uncle Harry's dinner jacket.

'Splendid,' said Priscilla, thinking privately what a difference good clothes made to Hamish's appearance. He was really quite a good-looking man with his red hair and clear hazel eyes, particularly when he was out of that joke of a uniform. It would be fun to take Hamish in hand. She gave herself a mental shake.

'Well, if you're ready, let's go,' she added.

'Are you sure it is all right?' asked Hamish, hesitating.

'You *shall* go to the ball,' said Priscilla with a grin.

Hamish moved closer to her and looked down at her shyly. 'You're looking awf'y pretty tonight, Priscilla.'

Priscilla always dressed in what pleased her and never bothered about the dictates of fashion. She was wearing a leaf-green chiffon blouse with a V-necked frilled collar and a black evening skirt. Her fair hair fell in a smooth line to her shoulders. Her only jewellery was the emerald-and-diamond engagement ring Henry had bought her at Asprey's. She looked up into Hamish's eyes and felt strangely awkward and uncomfortable. Up until that precise moment, Priscilla had always been at ease in the policeman's company. With Hamish, she felt obscurely that she could be herself and that Hamish would always like her no matter what she did. It was that old feeling of undemanding intimacy that had made her stay in the room while he changed his trousers. For the moment that easiness had fled, and Priscilla felt herself beginning to blush.

She took a step backwards and mumbled, 'Let's go.' Aware of Hamish's curious eyes on her, she scooped up the waiter's clothes, draped them over her arm, and hurried from the room without looking back to see if he was following her.

When she reached the dining room, she abandoned Hamish to his fate and went to join Henry. He was happily talking to his admirers and, to her relief, had not noticed her absence from the room.

At last she looked over to see how Hamish was faring. The policeman was engaged in conversation with Jeremy Pomfret and the Helmsdales. Priscilla's parents had been thwarted in their intention of throwing Hamish out by the Helmsdales' welcome of him. For Hamish took many prizes at shooting contests and Lord Helmsdale was one of his admirers, as was Jeremy Pomfret. Lady Helmsdale did not know Hamish, but she found him a nice, pleasant man with a refreshing air of shyness – unlike that horrible Peter Bartlett, that cad, who had now drunk enough to turn nasty.

Lady Helmsdale was further pleased when Hamish turned out to have intelligent views on the decline of the grouse population. 'If the decline continues,' said Hamish, 'most of Scotland's moor owners will hae no alternative but to opt for intensive sheep farming or forestry planting, and that would mean the loss of the heather and the heather accounts for ninety per cent of the grouse. It would also lead to a verra serious loss of sporting income, rural employment, not to mention the tourist revenue.'

Jeremy, encouraged by Hamish's shy, respectful manner, found courage to air his own views. Hamish listened with half an ear, while he picked up snippets of conversation from other parts of the room. While appearing to attend closely to Jeremy and the Helmsdales, he was indulging that intense Highland curiosity of his to the hilt.

There wasn't a woman as well-dressed as Priscilla in the room, he thought. Vera was wearing last year's fashion of slim sheath with three belts. But Vera was plump, and all she had achieved was three spare tyres instead of one. Hamish knew Vera by sight. He did not know Diana, but he thought it was a pity that such a beautiful girl should be dressed in funereal black that was bunched up, Japanese-style, about her middle. The horsy girl beside her, mused Hamish, turning his gaze on Jessica, should surely never have gone in for an orange strapless gown. Every time she moved her shoulders, her bones stuck out in all sorts of odd places.

Jessica and Diana had drawn a little aside from Vera and Peter.

'I wish you would stop staring at me in that smug way and saying how tired you are,' whispered Diana. 'If you've got one of the gamekeepers into your bed, you should keep quiet about it.'

'I would hardly call Peter a gamekeeper,' giggled Jessica.

'What!' Diana almost spluttered with rage. 'He was with *me*!'

'He couldn't have been,' said Jessica. 'He was with me.'

Both girls glared at each other and then gradually the anger died out of their eyes to be replaced by a look of mutual consternation.

'He couldn't be such a bastard. Even Peter couldn't do that,' whispered Diana. 'What time did he call on you?'

'Four in the morning,' said Jessica in a small voice. 'He didn't call on me. I went to him.'

'He told me to visit him at midnight,' said Diana miserably.

Both girls held hands like children and turned and looked at Peter Bartlett. His back was to them and Vera was facing him. They saw her full, pouting lips framing a kiss.

'And guess who was with him in-between-times,' said Jessica. Her eyes filled with tears. She took a step towards the captain.

'Don't,' said Diana. 'Don't let him know we've found him out. Let's get him for this. I could kill him.'

'I wouldn't flirt so blatantly if I were you,' Peter Bartlett was saying to Vera. 'Freddy might notice.'

Vera's eyes were soft. 'After last night, Peter darling,' she said, 'he can notice what he likes. We're made for each other.'

Peter never knew quite how it happened. A few drinks and he loved the world. A few more and

198

his life seemed full of dead bores. He turned a jaundiced eye on Vera.

'I must say,' he said, 'you were certainly the best of last night's bunch. Lots to be said for middle-aged women with insatiable appetites.'

The smile slowly left Vera's face as the full implication of what he had said sank in.

'Who else was with you last night?' she demanded. 'Oh, darling, you must be joking. There can't have been anyone else.'

The captain's black eyes swivelled round to Jessica and Diana and then back to Vera. One eyelid drooped in a mocking wink.

Vera threw the contents of her glass in his face, burst into tears and ran from the room. Her husband saw her stumbling departure and ran after her.

Everyone began to talk very loudly as if nothing had happened.

Hamish had been studying the scene thoughtfully. He saw Priscilla waving to him and excused himself from the Helmsdales and Jeremy and went to join her.

'Henry's dying to speak to you again,' said Priscilla brightly. She had once more had to reassure Henry that she had no interest whatsoever in the village constable. Henry had finally noticed Hamish's presence in the room and had accused Priscilla of countermanding her parents' orders by re-inviting the constable herself. Priscilla had explained the reason for Hamish's presence, but Henry was still suspicious, although he covered his suspicions very well, and asked her to call Hamish over. He wanted to see the pair of them together again, just to put his mind at rest.

Right behind Hamish came the adoring Prunella Smythe. She was a middle-aged lady wearing a great many bits and pieces. Her hemline drooped. Bits of scarf and thin tatty necklaces hung around her neck. She had a scrappy stole around her thin shoulders with a moth-eaten fringe that had wound itself into the ends of her long dangling earrings.

Called by one and all 'Pruney', Miss Smythe's pale eyes behind her thick glasses looked out on the world with myopic wonder.

Before Henry could speak to Hamish, Pruney launched into full gush. 'I cannot tell you enough, Mr Withering, how much I adored your play.'

Peter Bartlett, who had been standing behind them mopping his face with a napkin, turned around. 'I never read anything but the *Racing Times*, Henry, but I did hear you'd got your smash hit at last. What's it about? The evil capitalists?'

'Oh, no,' said Pruney in a rush. 'Nothing like that *at all*. It's the most glorious drawing-room comedy, *quite* like the old days. None of those nasty swear words or' – her voice dropped to a stage whisper – '*sex*.'

'Sounds a bore,' said the captain.

Pruney giggled. 'It's actually quite naughty in bits. I love when the duchess says, "Marital fidelity is so yawn-making." '

Henry turned as red as fire. 'Shut up!' he said rudely. 'I hate it when people quote my play. Shut up, do you hear!'

Pruney's short-sighted eyes filled with startled tears.

'Nasty Henry,' said Peter in high good humour.

'Come along, Miss Smythe. You shall tell me all about it. I could listen to you all night.'

He led the now gratified Pruney away.

'He can't even leave Pruney alone,' said Priscilla. 'That man's a menace.'

'He minds me o' Jimmy MacNeil down in the village,' said Hamish. 'That man would lay the cat.'

Priscilla rounded on Henry. 'What on earth came over you?' she asked. 'There was no need to rip up poor old Pruney like that.'

'How would you feel if you had spent years writing good solid plays and then only been accepted and famous after you'd deliberately produced a piece of twaddle,' said Henry in a hard flat voice. 'I can't even bear a line of *Duchess Darling*.'

'Oh, darling, I didn't know you had written it like that deliberately,' said Priscilla with warm sympathy. 'And I thought there was something up with me because I didn't like it. Never mind. After this success you can write what you like. Don't glower. Look! Food. I'm starving. Lead me to it.'

She slipped her arm through Henry's and led him away. Hamish watched them go. Priscilla gave Henry's arm a squeeze and then she bent and kissed his cheek.

Hamish trailed off to where Sir Humphrey Throgmorton was sitting alone. He introduced himself and asked Sir Humphrey if he could fetch him any food.

'Later, my boy. Later,' said Sir Humphrey. 'Sit down and talk for a bit. I'm too old to circulate and the sight of that bounder Bartlett makes me ill.'

'Quite a character,' said Hamish.

'He's rotten,' said old Sir Humphrey, his little

201

grey beard waggling up and down. 'I could tell you a thing or two about that cad. The wonder is that he's never been in prison.'

Hamish looked down at him hopefully, waiting for more, but Sir Humphrey said, 'I *am* hungry after all. Could you please get me a plate of something?'

Over at the buffet, Hamish arranged a selection of cold meat and salad on a plate and took it back to Sir Humphrey.

Realizing he was hungry himself, he went back to the buffet. By the time he had picked out what he wanted, Sir Humphrey was happily talking to Lady Helmsdale. Then Hamish saw Diana waving to him. She was seated at a table in the corner with Jessica. The girls introduced themselves and Hamish merely said he was Hamish Macbeth, without adding that he was a policeman.

'Do you live near here?' asked Diana, her wide, almost purple eyes roaming over Uncle Harry's expensive suit.

'Down in the village,' said Hamish.

'Is your wife anywhere about?' asked Jessica.

'I am not married,' said Hamish.

Both girls brightened perceptibly.

'It's so nice to meet an unmarried man,' drawled Diana. 'These house parties can be a drag.'

'I'm not the only unmarried man here,' pointed out Hamish. 'I know Mr Pomfret is not married, and Mr Bartlett, I believe, is—'

'Forget about Peter,' said Jessica. 'No girl in her right mind would have anything to do with him. And Jeremy's a wet. Do eat your food . . . Hamish, is it?'

202

'Dangerous places, the Highlands, don't you think?' said Diana with a sly look at Jessica. 'All sorts of accidents can happen.'

'Like what?' asked Hamish.

'Oh, exposure, hypothermia, avalanches . . . things like that.'

'We had a murder here last year,' said Hamish.

'Yes, we all heard about that,' said Jessica. 'The murdered woman was a horrible character anyway. Don't you think it's mean when some poor person rids the earth of some obnoxious toad and then has to pay the penalty?'

'You can hardly expect me to agree with you,' said Hamish.

'Oh, why?'

'Not in my official bible,' said Hamish with a grin. 'Don't you know I'm the local bobby?'

'Oh, really?' said Diana, as if Hamish had just confessed to being the local cockroach.

'You're *that* Macbeth,' said Jessica in tones of loathing. 'I read about you in the papers.'

Hamish realized the air about him was becoming glacial and murmured something about taking his leave.

He stood up and looked about for Priscilla. She was sitting next to Henry and did not notice him. But Henry did, and put a possessive hand on Priscilla's knee.

He then thought he should grit his teeth and thank Mrs Halburton-Smythe for her hospitality, but as he approached her she gave him a horrified look and tried to hide behind a plant.

Hamish sighed and made his way to the door. Jeremy Pomfret seized his arm. 'I say,' he said, 'have you heard about this bet I've got on with Bartlett?'

'Aye, everyone's talking about it,' said Hamish. 'I hear there are a few side bets on, too.'

'Well, it's now been agreed that we go out at nine in the morning, each with a gun and cartridges, and go off in opposite directions. The first one back at the castle with a brace is the winner.'

'I wish you luck, Mr Pomfret,' said Hamish and turned to leave, but Jeremy clutched at his sleeve.

'I say, old chap,' he said urgently, 'couldn't you, well, sort of be around here at nine tomorrow morning, a sort of referee, you know?'

'What for, Mr Pomfret?'

Jeremy led Hamish into a corner.

'I don't trust the blighter,' he said in a hoarse whisper. 'You see, the bet's for five thousand pounds, and frankly, I don't believe he's got it. And he's been making some side bets, too. Unless I'm very much mistaken, that means he's certain he's going to win.'

'Maybe he's just full of confidence,' said Hamish cautiously. 'The captain's a verra good shot, I'm told. I'm sure you'll both get your brace tomorrow. The grouse may be a lot scarcer these days, but there are still plenty out there.'

'Yes, but without beaters or even a dog, it could take ages to walk up to a covey. Either of us could win. What worries me is why Bartlett is so certain it will be him, unless he's got some trick up his sleeve. Sure you won't come here at nine to see everything is aboveboard?'

'I'd like to, Mr Pomfret,' said Hamish. 'But it's like this. Unless the colonel invites me, I chust cannot put my nose into this. And the colonel is not going to invite me. In fact, he sent word to stop me coming here tonight, but the message got lost on the way. Besides, any suggestion of a referee would mean the colonel would be made to look as if he thought one of his guests was about to cheat, and he wouldn't stand for that.'

'Yes, I see what you mean,' said Jeremy, pouting like a disappointed baby. 'Sorry to have troubled you.'

Hamish continued on his way out.

He picked up the parcel containing the waiter's clothes from a chair in the hall and made his way out onto the drive.

Peter Bartlett, smoking a cigar, was pacing up and down.

'Sobering up for the big day,' he said when he saw Hamish.

'Good luck,' said Hamish politely, fishing for his car keys.

'You've heard about the bet?' asked Bartlett.

Hamish nodded. 'I hear it's for quite a bit of money,' he said.

'Yes, quite a stroke of luck that, finding old Pomfret here.' Bartlett's white teeth gleamed in a broad smile. 'And I thought I was going to have to be content with that Arab's miserly two thousand pounds.'

Hamish, who had been about to open his car door, stopped and turned around. 'And what Arab would that be, Captain?' he asked slowly.

'Just some old oil sheikh in London. He's heard stories about the honour of dining on Scottish grouse on the day of the Glorious Twelfth itself, so

I offered to get a brace for him – at a price, you understand.'

'And how will you get them to London in time for the sheikh's dinner, Captain?'

'He's paying for that. He'll have a helicopter here before nine in the morning. That'll take the birds to Inverness airport. The helicopter pilot will put them on the shuttle plane to London, and one of the sheikh's flunkeys will pick them up at London airport.'

Hamish studied the captain thoughtfully. 'And the sheikh will send you a cheque, I suppose?'

'Not likely. When I hand over the grouse, the helicopter pilot will hand me a packet – two thousand pounds in cash. I drive a hard bargain.'

'So,' said Hamish, 'if you bag a brace by noon or so, you're sure to get the two thousand?'

'Exactly,' said Peter Bartlett with a wolfish grin. 'Just can't lose.'

'So if you don't get the first brace, you'll only have to pay Mr Pomfret three thousand pounds. And, of course, those side bets you've been making.'

Peter Bartlett thrust his head forward, peering into Hamish's face in the gathering gloom. Then he threw back his head and laughed.

'Don't worry, my dear constable-chappie. I won't lose.'

'In that case,' said Hamish, opening his car door, 'I'll say good night.'

'Look here,' said the Captain, putting a hand on Hamish's shoulder, 'do you believe in that thing, you know, where you can tell what's about to happen? The second sight – that's it.'

Hamish patiently turned around. He was accustomed to weeping drunks, fighting drunks, and psychic drunks.

'And just what do you think is going to happen?' he asked politely.

'I've got this feeling someone's out to get me,' said the captain. 'I feel a lot of menace about . . . oh, it's hard to explain.'

'I think it iss very easy to explain, Captain Bartlett,' said Hamish. 'If a man puts as many backs up as you have, then it iss almost a form of suicide. I haff met people before who could not bring themselves to put an end to their lives, and so they went around goading other people into doing it for them. Good night, Captain Bartlett.'

He drove off and left Peter Bartlett staring after him.

CHAPTER FOUR

I once read the last words of a suicide, in which he
stated he hoped the jury would not return a verdict
of 'accidental death' or 'death by misadventure',
because he thoroughly understood what he was
doing when he shot himself, and did not wish it
handed down to posterity that he belonged to the
class of idiots who inadvertently would handle a
weapon in such a way as to cause risk to
themselves or others.
—CHARLES LANCASTER

Police constable Hamish Macbeth did not sleep
well. Towser lay at the end of his bed, across his
feet, snoring dreadfully. The sleepless sea-gulls
wheeled and screamed over the loch outside, an
owl hooted mournfully, and then there came the
sharp bark of a fox.

'And to think the tourists come here for the
peace and quiet,' mumbled Hamish. After another
futile hour of trying to fall asleep, he struggled out
of bed. Although it was only five in the morning,
the sky was already light. He looked out of his
bedroom window, which faced over the loch.

It had been a bad summer to date, but this

morning had all the signs of heralding a perfect day. A thin mist was rising from the glassy loch. The humped hills on the other side with their stands of larch and birch floated in the mist like a Chinese painting. He opened the window. The morning air was sweet with the smell of roses.

Hamish had succeeded in growing a splendid rambling rose over the door of the police station, and flowers rioted around the blue police sign and trailed over the steps.

The one cell in the police station had stood empty for a long time. The village drunk had joined Alcoholics Anonymous in Inverness and no more enlivened the little police station with nightly renderings of 'The Road to the Isles' and 'The Star o' Rabbie Burns.'

It was not a job for an ambitious man, but Hamish took his responsibilities seriously. He could make enough to send money home to his father and mother. His job meant he did not have to pay rent or pay for the use of the police car. It was the duty of every Celt to stay unmarried until the next in line was old enough to go out to work. But there had been a long gap between the birth of Hamish, now in his thirties, and the next Macbeth child, Murdo. And Murdo was proving to be a genius at school and would probably win a scholarship to university and so Hamish's responsibilities must go on a bit longer.

He decided to stay awake and scrambled into an old army sweater and his shiny regulation trousers. Uncle Harry's dinner jacket and trousers were hung carefully over a chair, the expensive cloth and tailoring looking out of place in Hamish's tiny shabby bedroom, like an aristocrat who has lost his way home from his club.

Towser rolled over on one side and spread himself comfortably out over the bed. Hamish looked down on the dog and sighed. There had been a time not so long ago when he had banished the dog from his bedroom – for what would, well, some girl think should she decide to share his bed?

But hope had gone. Now Hamish wondered gloomily if he was destined to share his bed with the mongrel for years to come.

He went out to the shed in the back garden to get the feed ready for the chickens and geese.

Henry had put his hand on Priscilla's knee. If only he could get that nasty little picture out of his mind.

He went about his morning chores and then went back inside and made himself a large breakfast, more for something to keep himself occupied than because he was hungry. Towser, smelling the frying bacon, slouched out of the bedroom, looking dazed and rumpled like a dissipated drunk, and placed a large yellowish paw on Hamish's knee, which was his lazy way of begging.

.Hamish picked at his breakfast and then gave up and put his plate on the floor for Towser.

He decided to go down to the harbour and look at the catch brought in by the fishing boats.

As he walked along, he kept remembering snatches of overheard conversation from the party. That Vera had been insulted by Captain Bartlett had been all too evident. So was the fact that, up until a few moments before she had thrown her drink in his face, she had been madly in love with him. Perhaps Priscilla was better off with that neat little playwright of hers, thought Hamish gloomily. She might have become engaged to someone like Peter Bartlett. How old was Henry? wondered Hamish. Certainly a lot older than Priscilla. Even older than he was himself. Probably pushing forty. It would have somehow been more understandable if Priscilla had fallen for a man as young as herself.

Lochdubh was a sea loch. The little stone harbour smelled of fish and tar and salt. He was just debating whether to mooch some herring for his dinner when his sharp ears caught the sound of heavy snoring, rather like Towser's coming from behind a pile of barrels stacked next to the sea-wall. He ambled around the barrels and stood looking down at the unlovely sight of Angus MacGregor, local layabout and poacher, lying on the ground between the barrels and the sea-wall. He smelled strongly of whisky. He was lying on his back, a shotgun cradled on his chest, and smiling beatifically.

Hamish bent down and gently removed the gun. Then he heaved the still-sleeping Angus over on his face and with experienced hands searched in the deep 'poacher's pocket' in the tail of Angus's coat. He lifted out a brace of dead grouse.

Angus had been warned off the Halburton-Smythes estate many times. The last time a gamekeeper had given him a beating, but all that had done was to make Angus swear he would continue to take every bird and beast he felt like taking off the estate. When he was crazy with whisky, he often claimed to be Colonel Halburton-Smythe's bastard son. As Angus was about the same age as the colonel, no-one even troubled to listen to the story – except Colonel Halburton-Smythe, who had been heard raging that one day he would shoot Angus and stop his lying mouth.

Hamish walked off with the brace dangling from his hand. He could not be bothered waking Angus up and charging him with theft. It was too fine a day. And taking a statement from Angus was always a wearisome business involving hours and hours of highly inventive Highland lies.

Then he remembered how Jeremy Pomfret had pressed him to 'referee' the contest for the first brace. Returning the grouse Angus had poached would give him an excuse to go to the castle and see what was happening. He might also see Priscilla.

Towser was panting for an outing when he returned to the police station, so he drove off with the large mongrel sitting up beside him on the passenger seat and the dead birds slung in the back.

The narrow road that led out of Lochdubh towards Tommel Castle wound through a chaos of tormented rocks, relics of the days when great glaciers had covered this part of the north-west of Scotland. In among the rocks, tarns filled high with water from the recent rains shone blue in the sun. These hundreds of tarns, or small pools, never failed to fascinate Hamish. On bright days, they scintillated sapphire-blue, and when the sky was heavy and grey mists twisted among the mountains, they glinted whitely or lay black and fathomless. The skies dictated the beauty of the scene, so that it was always changing, brilliant one day, weird and ghostly another.

Ahead reared up the fantastic pillared mountains

of Sutherland, with quartzite sparkling on the upper slopes and the deep purple of heather on the foothills.

As he approached the castle, he caught a glimpse of red-and-white behind a stand of larch. He stopped the car and got out. A helicopter stood on a flat piece of ground behind the trees, the pilot leaning against its side, smoking a cigarette. Hamish looked at his watch. It was eight-thirty.

'Fancy anyone wanting to eat birds that hasnae been hung,' marvelled Hamish. 'Some of thae Arabs have more money than sense.'

A few minutes later, Hamish drove up to the front door of the castle. Jenkins, the butler, had observed his approach and was standing waiting inside the open door.

'The kitchen entrance is around the back,' he said.

'I ken that fine,' said Hamish. 'Aye, it's a grand day. I just want a wee word with Miss Halburton-Smythe.'

'That will not be possible,' said Jenkins stiffly. 'Miss Halburton-Smythe and the guests are at breakfast.'

Hamish looked over Jenkins's shoulder and the butler turned round.

Red-eyed and haggard, Jeremy Pomfret was marching up to them.

'That bastard Bartlett!' he shouted.

'I assume Captain Bartlett has gone out shooting,' said Jenkins.

'I thought so,' said Jeremy bitterly. 'He's not at breakfast and he's not in his room. And his gun's gone.' He noticed Hamish for the first time. 'You see, I told you he was up to something. Sneaked out early. Well, he's been found out and the bet's off. Came to my room last night with a bottle of champers. "Have a drink, old boy," says he. Made me drink the whole bottle. Said we'd meet up at breakfast and go out together, and all the time the bastard was planning to get up early and beat me to it. God, I feel awful.'

'Aye, it's a terrible thing when they force the stuff down your throat,' said Hamish amiably.

'He didn't force it,' muttered Jeremy. 'But when a chap offers another chap champagne, a chap can't refuse.'

'True, true,' said Hamish, leaning lazily against the castle door. 'It's awf'y hard to say no to the champagne.'

'I have already told you, Mr Macbeth,' said Jenkins, 'that Miss Halburton-Smythe is not to be disturbed.'

Hamish recognized one of the maids who was crossing the hall with a tray. 'Jessie,' he said, 'be a good girl and tell Miss Halburton-Smythe I want a wee word with her.'

'Sure thing,' said Jessie, who was an American movie addict.

'Jessie,' said Jenkins sharply. 'I have informed this constable that Miss Halburton-Smythe is at breakfast.'

But Jessie either didn't hear, or pretended not to hear. Jenkins clucked with irritation and went after her.

'What are you going to do now?' asked Hamish, turning his attention back to Jeremy.

'Nothing, not with this hangover. I've a mouth

on me like a Turkish wrestler's jock strap. I'm going back to bed.'

He trailed wearily back up the stairs.

Priscilla came out of the dining room into the hall. She was wearing biscuit-coloured linen trousers, thin sandals, and a frilly Laura Ashley blouse. Her blonde hair was pinned up on top of her head. She looked as fresh as the morning.

'What did you want to see me about?' she asked Hamish.

Hamish, who had been staring at her, pulled himself together. 'I wondered if you would like me to bring over Uncle Harry's clothes or whether you would like to collect them from the police station.'

Priscilla looked amused. 'Instead of coming all the way up here to ask me what to do,' she said, 'you could have brought the clothes along with you and solved the problem.'

'Och, so I could've,' said Hamish stupidly. 'There's another thing. Angus, the poacher, was down by the harbour and—'

He broke off and cocked his head to one side. Someone was running hard up the gravel of the drive.

He went out to the front steps, with Priscilla after him.

John Sinclair, the estate's head gamekeeper, came running towards them. 'He's shot hisself,' he cried. 'Oh, what a mess!'

'Who is it?' demanded Priscilla, pushing in front of Hamish.

'It's Captain Bartlett, and he's got a great hole blown clean through him.'

Priscilla turned and clutched at Hamish's sweater

215

in a dazed way. Sinclair ran on into the castle, shouting the news.

'It's awful,' whispered Priscilla, beginning to shake. 'Oh, Hamish, we'd better go and look. He might still be alive.'

He put his arms around her and held her close. 'No, I don't think so,' he said in a flat voice.

The guests, headed by Colonel Halburton-Smythe, came tumbling out of the castle. Henry Withering stopped short at the sight of Priscilla enfolded in Hamish's arms.

'Lead the way, Sinclair,' barked the colonel. 'And you, Jenkins, call the ambulance. The ladies had better stay behind. Macbeth, what are you doing here? Oh, never mind, you'd better come with me.'

Hamish released Priscilla and set out with the colonel and the gamekeeper. Henry, Freddy Forbes-Grant, and Lord Helmsdale followed. Sir Humphrey Throgmorton returned to the castle with the ladies.

The day was becoming hot. The air was heavy with the thrum of insects and the honey-laden smell of the heather.

As they left the castle gardens, Colonel Halburton-Smythe spotted the helicopter. 'What the hell is that thing doing on my property?' he demanded. Hamish explained about the Arabs in London and the promised payoff of £2,000.

'Bartlett had no right to order helicopters to descend on my land without asking me,' said the colonel. 'Oh, well, the man's dead and he won't be needing that two thousand now.'

'Aye, that's right,' said Hamish, looking thoughtfully at the helicopter.

'Don't stand there as if you'd never seen a helicopter before,' said Colonel Halburton-Smythe impatiently.

Hamish fell into step with the others and they set out over the moors at a steady pace.

It should have been raining, thought Hamish, steady, weeping rain like they had had during the previous weeks. A tragedy in bright sunshine seemed much more frightful than one on a day when the skies were grey.

'Here we are,' said the gamekeeper, pointing ahead.

The ground sloped down. At the bottom of the slope was a wire fence. Hanging over the fence was a body, still and grotesque and unreal in the clear air.

'What a mess!' whispered Lord Helmsdale in awe as they reached the scene.

Captain Bartlett hung almost upside-down, suspended by his right leg from the top strand of the fence. The gun was on the other side of the fence, its butt in a gorse bush, the side-by-side barrels resting on the top strand of the fence, glaring wickedly like two black fathomless eyes at the group. There was no doubt the captain had been straddling the fence when he was shot.

'Don't touch anything,' said Hamish. 'The forensic boys from Strathbane will need to see everything.'

They stood around Hamish in white-faced silence.

The sun was hot. A buzzard sailed high in the clear air.

Then Lord Helmsdale cleared his throat noisily. 'You can see what happened, Macbeth,' he said, his voice once more loud and robust. 'The silly ass was using his gun as a support to balance himself as he climbed over. Everyone does it. Do it myself. Then the gun got caught in that damned bush, and when he tried to pull it clear, the triggers snagged and went off. Must have been both barrels. Look! He's blown a hole clear through his chest.'

There were violent retching noises as Freddy threw up in the heather.

'But how could that happen?' asked Henry in a shaky voice. 'There are two triggers, and besides, wouldn't he have the safety catch on?'

'He should have,' said Hamish. He stepped around the body and peered at the gun. 'But the safety catch is off. Verra careless, that. Now, those thorns are tough and springy and if the front trigger got caught, and if the captain pulled hard enough, it could pull both triggers.'

Hamish walked a few yards away and stepped easily over the fence so as not to disturb the body. He circled the gorse bush. 'It is an accident that sometimes happens,' he said. 'Even experienced sportsmen close a gun and then forget it is loaded.'

Hamish took out a clean handkerchief, took hold of the gun by the barrels, and slowly and carefully extricated it from the bush.

The gun was a Purdey, a hammerless side-lock, self-opening ejector gun. Hamish whistled softly. 'A pair o' these would set ye back around thirty-five thousand pounds,' he said.

He broke open the gun and took out two cartridges. Both were spent. He glanced at the body. 'Both barrels.' He held up the spent cartridges. 'Number six,' he said, half to himself. He laid the gun down carefully on the heather and knelt down by the fence. Carefully, he reached through the wires and felt inside the captain's jacket pockets. The others watched, fascinated, as the policeman withdrew a handful of unused cartridges. He examined them and nodded. 'Number six as well,' he said. He then stood for a long time in silence, staring at the dead man. The captain's tweed cap had fallen from his head and lay in the heather. He had been wearing a shooting jacket, corduroy knee breeches, wool socks, and thick-soled shoes when he had been shot.

Henry said sharply, 'The man's shot himself by accident. I don't see any need for the rest of us to hang about. How you can stand there, Macbeth, staring at that awful wreck of a man as if you were looking at a piece of meat on a butcher's block, beats me. And what were you doing,' he added his voice suddenly shrill, 'hugging Priscilla?'

'Policeman never did know his place,' said Colonel Halburton-Smythe.

'She was shocked and in need of comfort,' said Hamish, his eyes still fixed on the body. 'Perhaps, Mr Withering, it would be as well if you went back and looked after her. There's nothing anyone can do until the forensic team arrives from Strathbane. Would you call Strathbane police and get them to send up a forensic team as well as an ambulance?' he asked the colonel. 'I'd better stay with the body until they get here.'

'Better get Freddy away quick,' said Lord Helmsdale. 'Looks as if he's going to faint.'

'I'll be along shortly to get statements from everyone,' said Hamish.

'Why?' demanded the colonel. 'It's obviously an accident.'

'Oh, just in case,' said Hamish vaguely.

'Well, I have no doubt the matter will be taken out of your incompetent hands,' said the colonel viciously, 'as soon as the detectives from Strathbane arrive with the forensic team.'

'Just so,' said Hamish absent-mindedly.

The rest began to trail away. Henry looked back. Hamish was still standing looking down at the body.

'I think that copper's off his head,' he grumbled.

'He's cunning and lazy,' said Colonel Halburton-Smythe. 'And devoid of natural feeling. He'll probably lie down and go to sleep when we're out of sight.'

'Known Priscilla long, has he?' asked Henry.

'Priscilla knows everyone in the village,' said the colonel. 'She is too easygoing and good-natured. Macbeth takes advantage of her kindness. Priscilla doesn't know quite when to draw the line. She even went off to a film show in the village hall with Macbeth last year. I had to warn him off. Thank goodness she's marrying you, Henry.'

'Would you like me to wait with Macbeth?' asked Sinclair, the gamekeeper.

'No,' said the colonel. 'I want you to be on hand to answer questions when the police arrive from Strathbane.'

When they were out of sight, Hamish climbed

back over the fence to the side where the captain was half-hanging, half-lying. He opened the captain's game bag, which was slung around his neck, and peered inside. It was empty. He reached up to push his cap back on his head and then realized he had not put on the rest of his uniform, bar his trousers. He wished he had brought Towser with him instead of leaving the animal cooped up in the car.

He bent down and searched the springy heather near the dead man. Then, crawling along on all fours, he began to search away from the body. 'It's chust too convenient – that's what gets me,' he muttered. 'He was coming away from the moor and without his brace. Had he given up? But there's grouse available. Angus got his brace easily enough.' He thought back to the party. No-one had seemed to like the captain. The three women who had been clustered around him when he, Hamish, had arrived had turned cold and angry and bitter. And who was that girl who had suddenly begun to talk about accidents?

He searched while the sun climbed higher in the sky and its rays beat down on his head.

Then he heard the sound of voices and looked up. Walking over the crest of the hill came a familiar heavy-set figure, sweating in a double-breasted suit.

Hamish recognized Detective Chief Inspector Blair with his sidekicks, detectives Jimmy Anderson and Harry MacNab.

After them came ambulance stretcher-bearers and the forensic team and three uniformed policemen.

221

Hamish knew the investigation was about to be taken out of his hands. Although he had once solved a case and let Blair take the credit, he knew that Blair had now convinced himself that he, Hamish, had had nothing to do with it.

Walking back to stand beside the dead body, Hamish bent down and looked in the game bag again. Something caught his eye. As Blair marched up to him, Hamish slid one small grouse feather into the pocket of his trousers.

CHAPTER FIVE

*. . . nothing in his life became him
like the leaving of it . . .*
—SHAKESPEARE

Detective Chief Inspector Blair was not a Highlander. He had been brought up in Glasgow, that city which produces some of the brightest brains in the world, along with some of the biggest chips on the shoulder. Blair, as Hamish often remarked, had a chip on his shoulder so big, it was a wonder his arm didn't fall off.

Blair detested the upper classes because they made him feel inferior, and the Highlanders because they lacked any inferiority complex whatsoever.

But as he stood in front of the fireplace in the drawing room of Tommel Castle late that afternoon, he was enjoying himself. The Halburton-Smythes and their guests were grouped around him. On either side of Blair stood detectives Anderson and MacNab – like a couple of wally dugs, thought Hamish, who was standing by the window, meaning like those pairs of china dogs that not so long ago ornamented many mantelpieces in

Scotland and have now become collector's items.

Strained faces, white in the gloom of the drawing room, which had been built facing north so that the sun should not fade the carpet, turned towards Blair.

'It was a straightforward accident,' he said. Someone let out a sharp sigh of relief. There was a palpable air of slackening tension in the room.

'So,' went on Blair, enjoying their relief and glad he had kept these toffee-nosed creeps waiting so long for his verdict, 'there'll be no need for me to take any more statements from you.' He had been unable to interview the helicopter pilot, for while he was examining the scene of the crime, Hamish had returned to the helicopter, taken the pilot's statement, and had told him he could return to Inverness, a piece of high-handedness that had driven Blair wild with rage.

He cast a venomous look in Hamish's direction before going on with his lecture.

'It appears that Captain Bartlett went out very early so as to cheat on his bet and have first chance at thae birdies.' Jeremy Pomfret winced. 'But before he could use his gun to shoot them, he used it to help himself get over the wire fence. The gorse bush caught the double trigger, and boom, boom, goodbye world.'

'For heaven's sake, man, show a bit of respect for the dead,' snapped Colonel Halburton-Smythe.

Blair rounded on him. 'You should be grateful tae me for finding out so quickly it was an accident instead of suspecting you all of murder.'

'Any fool could see it was an accident,' boomed Lady Helmsdale.

'Anyway,' went on Blair in a loud, hectoring voice, 'his gun was loaded with number six shot. It went off and blew a hole through his chest. The pathologist has already confirmed that the shot found in the remains of his chest was number six. The colonel of his regiment has been informed of his death. As far as the colonel knows, Bartlett had no close relatives still alive. He'll be sending someone over this week to pick up the captain's effects just in case a relative turns up.'

'He had an aunt in London, I think,' said Diana, and then turned pink.

'Anyway,' said Blair, 'the procedure is this. In cases of fatal accident, the procurator fiscal studies the pathologist's report and the police reports. Then an inquiry is held – in camera, so you won't have to worry about the press. It may be in a week's time or a month's time, so remember, even if you've gone back home, you must be ready to go to Strathbane when you're summoned.'

The door of the drawing room opened and Jenkins came in, followed by two maids carrying tea, cakes, and scones.

Blair licked his lips and looked longingly at the teapot.

'Thank you, Mr Blair,' said Mrs Halburton-Smythe. 'If you have nothing further to add, I see no reason for you to stay.'

Blair flushed angrily. The least they could have done was to have offered him a cup of tea. He wanted to vent his anger on someone and looked about for Hamish Macbeth. But the Highland constable appeared to have vanished.

Blair crammed on his soft felt hat and signalled

to Anderson and MacNab and strutted from the room.

Hamish had not left. He had had no lunch and wanted to see if he could manage to get some tea and scones. He had slid quietly down behind a large sofa by the window and was sitting on a small footstool.

Jessie, the maid, had a soft spot for Hamish. She quietly handed him down a plate of scones and a cup of tea when Jenkins wasn't looking.

Hamish drank his tea and listened to the conversation.

'Poor Peter,' came Vera's choked voice. 'What an awful death.'

'As if you cared,' said Jessica, suddenly and loudly. 'It's a good thing it wasn't murder, considering we all saw you throwing a glass of gin over him.'

'You leave my wife alone, young lady,' said Freddy. 'Captain Bartlett was a rotter and a cad, and I'm not going to pretend he was otherwise just because he's dead.'

'I thought he . . . he was rather nice,' ventured Pruney Smythe timidly.

'Oh, he could charm anything in skirts and he didn't give a damn about age or appearance,' said Jessica with a nasty laugh. She had meant to hurt Vera, but the shaft struck home in Pruney's spinster bosom and she burst into tears.

'Now look what you've done, you horrible thing, you,' said Priscilla. 'Come with me, Pruney. You'll feel better after you've had a lie-down.'

Mrs Halburton-Smythe raised her voice. It held a note of steel. Afternoon tea in the drawing room was the one social event over which she was allowed complete control without interference from her domineering and fussy husband. 'These remarks are all in bad form,' she said. 'The man is dead and the least we can do is show some respect. We have all had a harrowing day, a lot of it unnecessarily harrowing. That man Blair is an uncouth pig. Hamish Macbeth may be a useless scrounger, but at least he's not abrasive. Now, the crofters' fair is to be held in Lochdubh in five days' time and the Mod wants us to help raise funds. And, Henry dear, it quite slipped my mind. The Crofters Commission has asked me if you will be good enough to present the prizes.'

'I'd love to,' said Henry, looking gratified. 'What on earth is the Mod?'

'It's a Gaelic festival of song,' said Priscilla, coming back into the room. 'We usually run the White Elephant stand. The crofters' sale is good fun and you can pick up some great bargains in hand-knitted woollies and thingies made out of deer horn. Oh, and the sheepskin rugs they sell are very cheap.'

Jenkins came in, looking hot and annoyed. 'It is the gentlemen of the press,' he said. 'They are all outside the front door talking to that man Blair.'

'Then clear them off the estate,' snapped the colonel. 'If that idiot Macbeth would only do his job. Phone him at the police station, Jenkins, and tell him to come here immediately. Once Blair starts pontificating to the press, he'll be here all night.'

Hamish felt himself going hot with embarrassment and wished he had not stayed to scrounge

227

tea. He knew Jessie would not betray him, but if anyone in the room walked over to the window, they would find him.

He slid to the floor and rolled his thin, lanky body under the sofa.

The voices rose and fell, becoming more animated as the shadow of sudden death rolled away. Jenkins came back to say that there was no reply from the police station, only a rude recording of a voice singing in Gaelic. Hamish groaned to himself. He never checked his answering machine, for the simple reason that since he had had a second-hand one installed two months ago, he had forgotten to play it back. The previous owner had obviously used the tape for recording his favorite Gaelic tunes.

Hamish shared the Highlander's weakness for secondhand gadgets and machinery of all kinds and, like his peers, was apt promptly to lose interest in the new toy immediately after he had got it.

The guests began to leave to spend the time before dinner in their rooms.

Hamish was about to crawl out from under the sofa and make his escape when a weight on his side told him that two people had sat down on it.

'It's been a violent introduction to the Highlands, I'm afraid,' came Priscilla's voice.

'Poor Peter,' replied Henry Withering. 'I'd hate to pop off and then sit up there hearing everyone down here being so glad I'd gone. Don't worry, Priscilla darling. I think I'm getting to like this place, despite all the dramatics. Would you like to live up here once we're married?'

'I never thought of it,' said Priscilla. 'I always

assumed you'd want to be in London. But if you think you can bear being somewhere so remote . . . well, I would love to live here. Not in the castle, I mean. Somewhere of our own.'

'We'll build our own castle,' said Henry. 'Come here. I've been longing to kiss you all day.'

Hamish sweated with embarrassment.

Henry put his arm about Priscilla's shoulders. She felt suddenly shy and looked down. Her gaze sharpened. A long bony hand crept out from under the sofa and tapped her foot. She stifled a scream.

'What's the matter?' demanded Henry.

But Priscilla had recognized that edge of navy sweater above the hand. 'I'm still shaky,' she said with a laugh. 'Come and walk with me in the garden. I've got to get some fresh air. It's stifling in here.'

Hamish waited until the sound of their voices had died away. Then he rolled out from under the sofa, opened the drawing room window, and climbed out. He made his way cautiously round the castle to the front without meeting anyone. The press had gone. His car was hidden behind the vast bulk of the Helmsdales' antique Rolls-Royce. Towser gave him a sad, reproachful look.

'Aye, it's like an oven in here,' said Hamish. 'I'll just take you home and give you a drink of water.'

The sunlight was now soft and golden as Hamish drove along the waterfront. Fishing boats were lined up at the pier, bobbing gently in a slow oily swell that was rolling in from the Atlantic. I hope it disnae rain, thought Hamish. I still have things to look for.

When he had fed and watered Towser and

229

turned the dog loose in the garden, he poked around his small kitchen looking for something to eat. There was nothing in his refrigerator but an old piece of haggis and some black pudding. He opened the food cupboard and found a can of beans. Then he went out to the hen-house and collected five eggs.

He was settling down to a dinner of fried egg and beans and strong tea when he heard Towser yipping an ecstatic welcome.

'Come in,' he shouted, 'the door's open.'

Thinking it would be one of the villagers, he got to his feet to look for another cup.

'And what were you doing, hiding under the sofa, Hamish?' said a cool, amused voice.

Hamish put the heavy pottery cup he had just lifted out back in the cupboard and brought down a delicate china cup and saucer instead.

'It's yourself, Priscilla,' he said. 'Sit down and have a cup of tea.'

'Is that your dinner?' asked Priscilla.

Hamish looked thoughtfully at his half-eaten eggs and beans.

'Well, to my way of thinking, it is more like the high tea,' he said eventually. 'I would not be distinguishing it with the title of dinner. Do you want some?'

'No, I have to get home soon. Dinner is at eight and I've got to change. But I'll have a cup of tea. Now, Hamish . . .'

'I was searching for clues,' said Hamish, looking at her hopefully.

Priscilla slowly shook her head. 'The truth, Hamish.'

Hamish gave a sigh. 'I was that thirsty and I wanted some tea. Jessie saw me sitting down behind the sofa and gave me some when no-one was looking. Then I felt guilty and I thought your father would have a fit if he saw me, so I slid under the sofa. I couldnae bear the idea of you courting and me listening,' said Hamish, blushing and averting his eyes, 'so I had to attract your attention.'

'You are the most terrible scrounger I have ever met,' giggled Priscilla. 'Still, it can't have been nice for you having to deal with Blair again. What a brute of a man! Thank goodness it was an accident. Can you imagine if someone had bumped off the terrible captain what it would be like? All our faces splashed over the tabloids.'

Hamish buried his nose in his cup. 'Does it no' surprise you,' he said at last, 'that it wasn't a murder?'

'Not really,' said Priscilla, after a pause. 'The world's full of hateful people, but no-one bumps them off. Too often the people murdered are innocent kids going home from school or old-age pensioners. Things are getting worse in the South, you know. Sutherland must be the last place on God's earth where you don't have to lock your door at night.'

'I wouldn't be too sure o' that,' said Hamish. 'I'm troubled in my mind. I keep seeing him with his chest shot to hell, hanging over that wire fence like a bunch o' rags. I knew of him afore this – the wild Captain Bartlett. Never to speak to, mind. I mean, I knew him by sight. He was full of life and not so bad when he hadn't the drink taken. The fence wasn't all that high. He had long legs on him. The

231

way I see it, he would normally have pushed the wire down and stepped over.'

'It's an accident that's happened before, even to good marksmen, Hamish.'

'Aye, maybe.'

'You're not eating your food.'

'I hate baked beans,' said Hamish, loudly and forcibly. What he really meant was that he hated Priscilla's being engaged to Henry Withering, and felt he must vent his feelings somehow.

'Oh, wait a minute. I'll be back soon,' said Priscilla, exasperated.

She returned five minutes later carrying a small parcel. 'I knocked at the back door of the butcher's. Mr MacPherson was still there and I got you two lamb chops. Go and get some potatoes out of the garden and I'll fix you dinner.'

Soon Hamish was sitting down to a meal of grilled lamb chops, fried potatoes, and lettuce from the garden.

'It's very kind of you, Priscilla,' he said. 'I don't want to keep you. I thought you would be wanting to run back to Henry.'

'I'll see him at dinner,' said Priscilla vaguely.

Priscilla was filled with a sudden reluctance to leave the narrow, cluttered kitchen at the back of the police station. The back door was open, and homely smells of wood-smoke, kippers, and strong tea drifted in as the villagers of Lochdubh settled down for the evening. It was six-thirty, but very few people, apart from the Halburton-Smythes, ate as late as eight in the evening.

Henry had kissed her very passionately and said he would join her in her bed that night. At the time,

232

Priscilla had said nothing to put him off, feeling it ridiculous in this modern day and age to hang on to a virginity she was soon to lose anyway. But Hamish emitted an aura of an old-fashioned world of courting, walking home in the evening, and holding hands; a world where it was all right to remain a virgin until your wedding night.

What would it be like, mused Priscilla, to be a policeman's wife? Perhaps the sheer boredom of living in a tiny remote place like Lochdubh would make her nervous and restless. And yet she had said she would live there with Henry.

'I had better go home,' she said, collecting her handbag.

'Aye,' said Hamish sadly.

They stood looking at each other for a long moment and then Priscilla gave an odd, jerky nod of her head and turned and left.

Hamish sat for a long time staring into space. Then he got out the car, called Towser, and drove off in the direction of the Halburton-Smythes' estate. He had driven halfway there when he saw the poacher, Angus MacGregor, walking along. He was not carrying his gun and had the dazed look of a man who has been asleep all day long.

Stopping the car, Hamish called him over. 'I should book you, Angus,' he said.

'Whit fur?' demanded the poacher, his bloodshot eyes raised to the sky as if calling on heaven to witness this persecution at the hands of the law.

'I found you dead-drunk down at the harbour this morning,' said Hamish, 'and in your back pocket was a brace o' grouse. You'd been poaching on the Halburton-Smythes' estate again, ye daft auld fool.'

'Me!' screeched Angus, beating his breast. He began to rock to and fro, keening in Gaelic, 'Ochone, ochone.'

'Shut up and listen to me. I'll not be taking you down to the police station. I hae something in mind for you,' said Hamish, staring ahead, drumming his long fingers on the steering wheel.

Then he said, 'I want to see you the morn's morn with that dog o' yours, Angus. I've a bit o' work for you.'

'And what iss a man to get paid?'

'A man gets nothing. A man does not get his fat head punched. Be at the police station at six, or I'll come looking for you.'

Hamish drove off. He drew to a halt again where he had seen the helicopter and got out with Towser at his heels.

He walked until he had reached the scene of the captain's death and then he said to Towser, 'Fetch!'

Towser was an indiscriminate fetcher. He brought everything he could find if asked. Hamish sat down on a clump of heather to wait.

He looked up at the sky. Little feathery clouds, gold and tinged with pink, spread a broad band of beauty over the westering sun. The colour of the heather deepened to dark purple. The fantastic mountains stood out sharply against the sky. As every Highlander knows, the ghosts and fairies come out at dusk. The huge boulders scattered over the moorland took on weird, dark, hunched shapes, like an army of trolls on the march.

Hamish lay back in the heather, his hands behind

his head, as Towser fetched and fetched. At last he sat up.

There was a small stack of items at his feet. Five old rusty tin cans, a sock, an old boot, one of those cheap digital watches people throw away when the battery runs out, the charred remains of a travelling blanket, an old thermos, and a broken piece of fishing rod.

Towser emerged, panting through the heather, dragging a piece of old tyre.

'Enough, boy,' said Hamish. 'We'll be back tomorrow. Maybe we're searching too near.'

'Not tonight, Henry,' said Priscilla Halburton-Smythe. 'It's this terrible death. I think I'm feeling shocked. I simply don't feel romantic. I'm awfully sorry.'

'All right,' said Henry sulkily. 'If that's the way you feel . . . Where did you vanish to early this evening?'

'Just out. I felt I had to get out. Good night, darling. I'll be back to normal tomorrow.'

She gently closed her bedroom door in his face.

Jenkins marched into the breakfast room in the morning and stood to attention before his master. 'Sinclair has just been to report that Hamish Macbeth, that poacher MacGregor, and their dogs are out on our moors, sir.'

'The devil they are,' said the colonel, turning red. 'Didn't he tell them to hop it?'

'Sinclair did, sir, but Macbeth said he was within his rights. He said he was looking for clues.'

'The insolence of that man is beyond anything,'

said the colonel. 'Phone Strathbane and tell Blair to come over here and give Macbeth the dressing down of his life, and if he doesn't get over here sharpish, I shall report him to his superiors.'

'Certainly, sir,' said Jenkins with a satisfied smile.

The guests looked at each other uneasily.

'What is he doing?' asked Diana. 'I mean, it was an accident.'

'He's probably poaching,' said Colonel Halburton-Smythe. 'I know that man poaches. He's only using this looking-for-clues nonsense to cover up the fact he's a poacher himself. And what is he doing with that rascal MacGregor, if he's not poaching?'

Jenkins came back into the room. 'Strathbane says that Mr Blair is already on his way here. He wanted to assure you personally that the procurator fiscal's report tallied with his own. In fact, he should be here now.'

'Good,' said the colonel. There was the sound of an arriving car scrunching on the gravel outside. 'That'll be him,' said the colonel. 'Show him in.'

Blair could easily have phoned in the news, but he was still smarting over what he considered the Halburton-Smythes' rudeness in not offering him tea and, like most thin-skinned people who have been snubbed, he could not leave the snubbers alone.

His fury on learning that Hamish was supposedly looking for clues was tinged with satisfaction. He was in a vile temper and giving Hamish a bawling out appealed to him immensely.

'I'll go out and see him now,' said Blair.

Priscilla looked up and saw Hamish, with Angus

236

MacGregor behind him, standing at the entrance to the breakfast room. She signalled wildly to him to escape, but Hamish stayed where he was, his face unusually set and grim.

'Good morning, Chief Inspector,' said Hamish.

Blair swung about, his piggy eyes gleaming. He opened his mouth to yell.

'It was murder,' said Hamish Macbeth. 'Captain Peter Bartlett was murdered. And I hae the proof o' it right here.'

Blair's mouth dropped open and he stared stupidly. A heavy shocked silence fell on the room.

Into that silence came again the soft Highland voice of PC Macbeth.

'Och, aye,' he said. 'It was nearly the perfect murder.'

CHAPTER SIX

You may kill or you may miss,
But at all times think of this—
'All the pheasants ever bred
Won't repay for one man dead.'
—MARK BEAUFOY

Hamish walked into the room and placed a red-and-white plastic shopping bag on a small table by the window. He rummaged in the bag, then turned around, holding up to the stunned gathering two spent shotgun cartridges.

'These,' he said, 'are number seven shot, not number six.'

There was a puzzled silence, finally broken by Blair. 'What the devil are you talking about, you great gowk?' he cried furiously. 'What has all this nonsense got to do with murder?'

'I think these belonged to Captain Bartlett, and I think he used them yesterday,' said Hamish, unperturbed.

'Nonsense,' said Blair. 'Anyone could have fired them.'

'But the captain was the only one out shooting,' replied Hamish, inwardly sending an apology up to heaven for the lie when he thought of Angus the poacher's brace of grouse. But Angus had just assured him they had been shot miles from where the captain died, although still on the estate, and Hamish had years of experience of knowing when the poacher was telling the truth and when he was lying. 'Besides, the season just began yesterday.'

'Then they were from last season,' said Blair with a pitying smile.

'Och, no,' said Hamish. 'The last season's shooting ended in December, eight months ago. They haven't been lying out on the moor all that time, in all that rain and snow.'

Lord Helmsdale nodded in agreement. Blair saw that nod and felt his lovely neat accident verdict beginning to slip away. 'Get on with it, then,' he snarled.

Hamish turned back to the plastic bag and produced two grouse. He held them up.

'I found these hidden in the heather, not very far from where the captain was murdered. Angus's dog found them. I think we shall find that they were killed with number seven shot, with these' – he held up the two spent cartridges – 'and that the captain had bagged them before he was killed.'

'Oh, aye?' sneered Blair. 'Your poacher friend found them, did he? Maybe that was because *he* bagged them and *he* hid them away.'

'Well, he was up on the moor on the morning of the murder,' admitted Hamish.

'And what number of shot does *he* use?'

'Number six,' said Hamish.

'Bartlett was shot with number six, so, if it was murder, then, you great pillock, your friend did it!'

239

'Och, but he couldn't have . . .' Hamish began, but Blair started to interrupt. He was silenced by Lord Helmsdale.

'Let Macbeth speak,' said Lord Helmsdale crossly. 'When it comes to guns and shooting, he knows what he's talking about.'

Blair looked about to protest, but then he nodded to Hamish to continue.

'The time of the shooting was put at around seven in the morning,' said Hamish. 'I was down at the harbour at seven and there was Angus, sleeping like a pig. So he didn't murder the captain.'

There was a restless stirring among the small audience. I didn't know Hamish could look so cold and hard, thought Priscilla illogically. She glanced round at the others. All were staring fixedly at Blair, as if willing the detective to prove Hamish wrong.

'How did you come to this ridiculous conclusion?' scoffed Colonel Halburton-Smythe. 'Murder, indeed! Those grouse and cartridges don't mean a thing.'

'Well,' said Hamish, 'you remember when we found the captain, he had been climbing over the fence when he was shot.'

'Yes, yes,' said the colonel testily.

Hamish glanced quickly at the others who had come with them to the scene of the shooting – Henry, Freddy, and Lord Helmsdale. They all nodded.

'Good,' said Hamish. 'We're all agreed. Now, it is obvious Bartlett was coming in this direction, away from the moor. So, that could only mean, as his game bag was empty and his gun was still loaded, that he had been unable to bag his brace and was giving up and heading back here. He should have unloaded the gun, but people are careless sometimes, and that's how they shoot themselves accidentally.'

'Just like Bartlett did,' said Blair, looking triumphantly around the room, but Hamish continued as if he had not heard him.

'But I stepped easily over that fence, and the captain's legs are – were – as long as mine, so there was no need for him to use the gun to help himself over. That's what made me suspicious in the first place.

'So I checked the game bag again and it wasn't empty.' There was a sharp intake of breath from someone in the room. Hamish turned and dipped again into the plastic bag. From it, he produced a small box for carrying fishing hooks. He took something out and held it up. They craned forward to see. It was a tiny feather, a greyish feather with a brown tip. 'A breast feather from a grouse,' said Hamish. 'And there was another one.' He held it up. 'It was lying on the ground near the body.

'It looked to me as if the captain *had* bagged his brace before he died. So that would mean he was on his way back here. And it would also mean he would not have needed to reload the gun. It meant, too, that someone had removed the grouse from the bag, and that someone' – he looked slowly round the room – 'is the one who murdered him.'

'Look, laddie,' said Blair heavily, 'say Bartlett was going to cheat and get his grouse before the agreed time, then why wouldn't he have been the one who hid them in the heather, ready to be picked up quickly and get them first to the castle to win the bet, and then to the helicopter to ship them to London?' Everyone knew by this time what the helicopter had been doing there.

Hamish's soft voice went inexorably on. 'The captain was too experienced on the moors. He would know there would be a great likelihood of a fox picking them up. And if not, the crows would have found them. There was already a crow picking at this pair when we got to them. They wouldn't have been in any fit state to go to London.'

'This is all very well,' said Diana in a strained voice. 'But I don't quite understand what you're getting at. How did the murderer go about it?'

'This is how I think it happened,' said Hamish. 'I believe that the murderer intended to kill the captain sometime during their stay here. If the captain had gone out at nine o'clock as agreed, he couldn't have managed it, what with people up and awake. He would have waited for another opportunity.

'But the captain decided to cheat and left at dawn. The murderer must have seen him, realized what he was up to, and saw his opportunity to kill him without a witness. He followed him out to the moor, taking a gun and cartridges with him.

'It wouldn't have been easy to find him in the poor light, but when the captain got his brace, the murderer followed the sound of the shots. He met the captain on his way back here to the castle and they came face to face as the captain stepped over that fence.

'The murderer fired both barrels at point-blank

range. What he did next shows he is a very clever man indeed. He opened the captain's gun and found it unloaded. He checked the game bag and found the grouse, so he knew the gun had been fired. He took the spent cartridges from his own gun, the ones that had killed the captain, and put them in the captain's gun, closed it again, then carefully tangled it in the gorse bush. Now it looked like an accident.

'But our murderer was more than just clever. He examined the captain's pockets and came across a handful of unused cartridges. They were number seven shot, and the captain was killed with number six shot. So the murderer took the number sevens and replaced them with the number sixes he had brought with him.

'Then he had to get rid of the grouse, otherwise the police would wonder why his gun was still loaded *after* the captain had got his brace. He took them from the bag and hid them in the heather. He should have hidden them farther away, but maybe he wanted to rush back and get into his bed before the household was awake.

'What the police found was a dead man full of number six shot, two spent number six cartridges in his gun, and more number sixes in his pocket. The murderer was sure everyone would think it was accidental death. It should have been the perfect murder.' He glanced sharply at the faces turned towards him, faces that were no longer looking to Blair for help. They all looked shocked and strained.

'But the fence and the feather in the game bag made me suspicious, so I arranged with Angus and

243

our dogs to do a bit of tracking this morning. We backtracked over the captain's trail, in the direction away from the castle and, sure enough, we found the freshly used cartridges, number sevens. It took us a couple of hours, tracking in increasing circles away from the spot where the body was found, to find the grouse.

'I think that when the birds are examined, it'll be found they were shot around the morning of the twelfth and that they were killed with number seven shot.'

'It's still all speculation,' said Blair furiously.

'I should suppose,' said Hamish, 'that his gear is still in his room and his car is still out front. I suggest we search both and see if he had any more cartridges with him.'

'Go and have a look, Jenkins,' barked the colonel.

'This is all a muddle, you village idiot,' said Blair, turning a dangerous colour of puce. 'You keep calling the murderer a "he." How do you know it was a man?'

'I don't,' said Hamish. 'It could just as easily have been a woman.'

Voices rose in a furious buzz. 'He's a better fiction writer than I am,' came Henry's sharp tones. And Mrs Halburton-Smythe's voice, shaky with tears: 'This is a nightmare. You must stop Macbeth making up these lies, Priscilla.'

Jenkins came back into the room, carrying a small box. He handed it to Colonel Halburton-Smythe. The colonel opened it and looked gloomily down at the contents. 'Number seven,' he said in a hollow voice.

Everyone looked at Blair again as if he were their last hope. Hamish studied their faces. They were all, even Priscilla, willing Blair to say that Hamish Macbeth had made a mistake.

But Blair's heavy head was down on his chest. 'I'll need to call the boys in,' he mumbled.

'Speak up!' demanded Lord Helmsdale.

'I'll need tae get statements from ye,' roared Blair suddenly, making them all jump. 'This is a bad business. And you'll all need tae stay here until your rooms are searched. Come wi' me, sir,' he said to the colonel.

The colonel followed him out. The rest stayed where they were, stricken, looking accusingly at Hamish, and listening to the mumble of voices from the hall.

Blair was in a quandary. He sweated to think what his superiors would say if they learned he had been made to look a fool by the local bobby. But if he could get Hamish out of the investigation before anyone from Strathbane arrived, then he could make it look as if he, as a diligent officer, had been unsatisfied with the accident verdict and had returned to the scene of the crime.

'Look here, sir,' he said in oily, wheedling tones. 'This is going to take a wee bit of time. Now I am sure you don't want the television and press to harass your wife, daughter, or guests. If you would let me set up headquarters here with MacNab and Anderson, we'll soon get to the bottom of this.'

'You'll find this dreadful murder had nothing to do with me or my guests,' said Colonel Halburton-Smythe.

'Exactly,' cried Blair. 'And you won't want your

245

family or guests troubled with a lot of haranguing, which they would get if they allowed that Macbeth to stay around.'

The colonel hesitated. In all fairness, he could hardly bring himself to agree with the detective inspector's description of Macbeth's possible line of questioning. It was Blair who was notorious for his bullying mánner. But Blair now seemed conciliatory and was behaving in a servile manner – which was more the way the man ought to behave, thought the colonel. He knew Hamish Macbeth would suspect each and every one of the guests. And Hamish, never as overawed by the local gentry as the colonel thought he ought to be, would not dream of taking the heat away from the castle by questioning the locals first. Then there was Priscilla to consider. The colonel, deep down, had always feared that one day Priscilla might horrify them by upping and saying she wished to marry the village policemañ. It was only a half-formulated idea, never openly admitted, for the colonel was too much of a snob to bring that thought up into the open and look at it. But it niggled away at the back of his mind. Then there was the final clincher. If it hadn't been for Macbeth's interference, this sordid death would still be considered a respectable and gentlemanly accident – which Colonel Halburton-Smythe was still convinced it was. He found himself saying that Blair could stay at Tommel Castle, provided he agreed to keep the press at bay.

'But don't go upsetting the servants, mind,' said the colonel. 'No ringing the bells and making them fetch and carry. It's hard enough to get good servants these days. I don't want them handing in their notice because some copper decides to behave like a lord of the manor.'

Blair bit back an angry retort and bared his teeth in a horrible fawning smile instead.

In his new cringing manner, he thanked the colonel profusely and then went back to the breakfast room and jerked his head at Hamish as a signal that the policeman was to follow him out into the hall.

'Not here,' said Hamish, seeing Jenkins lurking in a corner of the hall. 'You're chust dying to have a go at me. Let's go outside.'

He walked ahead out of the castle, and with a muttered curse, Blair followed him.

Hamish walked up to his car and then turned and faced the detective inspector. 'Out wi' it, man,' he said laconically.

Blair took a deep breath.

'In the first place, Officer,' he snarled, 'You are incorrectly dressed. I shall put in a report about that.'

Hamish was wearing a worn checked shirt and an old pair of flannel trousers.

'Secondly, I am still convinced that this was an accident. You had no right to crawl about the moors looking for clues wi'out phoning me and telling me what you were doing. Thirdly, you should not have sent that helicopter pilot off before I saw him. You're standing there, you big scunner, thinking you're cleverer than me because you think you solved that last case. Well, it was a fluke, see. It's all going in ma report, and I'll see you in front of a police committee yet, you cheeky bugger.'

'Aye, well,' said Hamish amiably, 'that would be

the terrible thing. I can see it now,' he went on dreamily, 'telling all the bigwigs how Detective Chief Inspector Blair wanted to let a murder pass as an accident. I'm wearing my old clothes because that uniform of mine can't stand much more—'

'Whit?' roared Blair. 'Listen, laddie, I happen to know you had the money for a new uniform last year.'

Hamish bit his lip. He had not spent the money on a new uniform, but had sent it home to his family.

'Anyway,' said Hamish airily with a wave of his hand, 'to get to the matter of the helicopter pilot. His name's Billy Simpson and I typed out his statement and you can have it today. In any case, his statement doesn't matter now, for the pathologist's report says the captain died before the helicopter arrived. But I can tell all this to that police committee you were threatening me with.'

'Maybe I was a bit hasty,' said Blair. 'We'll forget about the pilot. Just you run along and look after all those interesting cases like kiddies nicking sweets from the local shop and leave the big stuff to the experts.'

'I was at a party here the night before the shooting,' said Hamish. 'I could describe what the guests were like and how they behaved to the captain.'

Blair clapped him on the shoulder. 'Maybe I'll drop down to the station and get it from ye later.'

'So I'm not to have the honour of putting you up?' said Hamish.

Blair puffed out his chest. 'I'll be staying here at the castle. The colonel's invitation.'

Hamish looked amused.

'So just run along and keep out of it,' said Blair.

'Aye, wi' an expert like yourself around,' sighed Hamish, 'you won't be needing me.'

He opened the car door. 'Don't forget to get the grouse examined,' he said.

Blair grunted and turned to walk away.

'And don't forget the gun room,' said Hamish sweetly.

Blair swung about.

'What?'

'The gun room . . . in the castle,' said Hamish patiently. 'Someone shot the captain, and unless they were silly enough to have the gun lying about their bedroom, you'll probably find a gun has been borrowed from the gun room, cleaned, and put back.'

Police Constable Macbeth drove sedately out of the estate and along the road to Lochdubh. He pulled to the side of the road at the top of the hill overlooking the village, switched off the engine, and climbed out of the car.

A mist was rising from the loch below, lifting and falling. One minute the village lay in its neat two rows, and the next was blotted from view.

'I hate that man!' cried Hamish loudly. A startled sheep skittered off on its black legs.

He took a great gulp of fresh air. Hamish hardly ever lost his temper, but Blair's dismissal of him from the case was infuriating. Hamish, in that brief moment, hated not only Blair but Priscilla Halburton-Smythe as well. She was nothing but a silly girl who had become engaged to a man simply because he was famous. She was not worth a single moment's heartbreak. And let Blair solve the case if he could!

Hamish reminded himself fiercely that he had settled for a quiet life. He had had chances of promotion and had sidestepped them all, for he knew he would find life in a large town unpleasant. He would need to obey his superiors who might turn out to be like Blair. He loved his easy, lazy life and the beauty of the countryside. Apart from his hens and geese, he rented a piece of croft land behind the police station where he kept sheep. There was enough to be made on the side in Lochdubh, what with the egg money, the sale of lambs, and the money prizes he won at the various Highland games. Why should he throw it all away out of hurt pride – because a detective had insulted him and the daughter of the castle had made it obvious she enjoyed money and fame, even if that fame was only reflected glory?

His anger went as quickly as it had come, leaving him feeling tired and sad.

He climbed back in his car, stopping outside Lochdubh to give a lift to a sticky urchin who had wandered too far from home.

Once inside the police station, which had an office on one side, with one cell, and the living quarters on the other, he hung a notice on the door referring all enquiries to Strathbane police, and then went inside and firmly locked and bolted it.

The newspapers and television would be along soon, and Hamish knew that ordinary constables were not supposed to give statements to the press. It was easier to pretend he was not at home instead of having to open the door every five minutes to say, 'No comment.'

He ate a late breakfast, and then, taking Towser, decided to walk about the village and make sure all was quiet. Murder at the castle should not distract him from more petty crimes. The crimes committed in the village were usually drunkenness, petty shoplifting, and wife-beating – or husband-beating. Drugs had not yet reached this remote part of north-west Scotland.

He went on his rounds, dropping into various cottages for cups of tea. Then he ambled along to the Lochdubh Hotel to pass the time of day with Mr Johnson, the hotel manager.

'What's this I'm hearing?' said Mr Johnson, ushering Hamish into the gloom of the hotel office. 'They're saying it's a murder up at Tommel.'

'You get the news quickly,' said Hamish.

'It was that Jessie. Does she ever do any work? She's always down in the village, mooning over that boyfriend of hers. She says the Mafia wasted Captain Bartlett – there was another American movie showing at the village hall the other night. *The Godfather*, I think it was.'

'No, it wisnae the Mafia,' said Hamish with a grin. 'I won't be having anything to do with the case. It's that scunner Blair from Strathbane. He told me to push off.'

'Blair doesn't know his arse from his elbow,' said Mr Johnson roundly. The bell rang on the reception desk outside. He hurried to answer it. Hamish listened, amused, to the sudden horrible refinement of the hotel manager's accent. 'Oh, yes, Major Finlayson, sir,' twittered Mr Johnson. 'We have a very good cellar, and Monsieur Pierre, our maître d', will be delighted to discuss our wine list with you. Is modom well? Good, good. Grand day for the fishing, ha, ha.'

'Silly old fart,' said the manager, walking into the office and shutting the door. 'I hate wine snobs.'

'Who in the name o' the wee man is Monsieur Pierre?' asked Hamish.

'Och, it's Jimmy Cathcart from Glasgow. He thought it would look better if he pretended to be French. Mind you, when we get the French tourists, he says he's American. Now, what about this murder, Hamish?'

Hamish looked hopefully towards the coffee machine in the corner.

Mr Johnson took the hint and poured him out a cup.

Hamish sat down, nursing his cup of coffee, and described his findings.

'But you can't just leave it there!' exclaimed Mr Johnson when Hamish had finished.

'It is not my murder. It is Blair's.'

'Good heavens! That man couldn't find his own hands if they weren't attached to his arms. Are you going to let a murderer roam around on the loose? He might murder again.'

'It's not my case,' said Hamish stubbornly. He drank his coffee in one gulp and put the cup down on the desk. 'To tell you the truth, I no longer care if the whole damn lot of them up at that castle drop dead tomorrow.'

CHAPTER SEVEN

... one of those people who would be enormously
improved by death.
—SAKI

By early evening, the mist had thickened. Hamish
was able to make out some figures clustered around
the outside of the police station. He quietly made
his way around to the back door so as to avoid the
gentlemen of the press.

The thick mist had blotted out all sound. Hamish
fried a couple of herring for his dinner and gave
Towser a bowl of Marvel Dog, a new dog food
given to him free by the local shop to try out.
Towser ate a mouthful and then tottered around
the kitchen, making dismal retching sounds.

'What a clown you are,' said Hamish. 'You
know I brought home some liver just in case
you didn't like Marvel Dog. Sit yourself down until
it's cooked.'

He had been feeling calm and peaceful just
before his return home, but as he lifted down the
heavy frying pan – Towser liked his liver medium
rare – he was overcome by another wave of
sadness. Was this what the future held for him?

253

Chatting away in the evenings to a spoilt mongrel?

There came a sharp, impatient knocking on the front door. Hamish hesitated. He began to wonder if his relative, Rory Grant, who worked in London for the *Daily Chronicle*, had perhaps been sent up to cover the murder. He should have phoned Rory, he thought. It was too early perhaps for the Fleet Street boys to have arrived, unless Blair had released the news very quickly and some of them had managed to fly up from London.

He put the pan on the stove and dumped the liver into it and then cautiously tiptoed his way to the front door. He pulled aside the lace curtain at the window at the side of the door. In the misty half-light, he could just make out the sharp features of Detective Jimmy Anderson, Blair's underling.

Cursing his own curiosity, he unlocked the door. 'Come in quickly,' said Hamish. 'I've been avoiding the press.'

'They've had short shrift from Blair,' said Anderson. 'But headquarters in Strathbane phoned the news of the murder to the local paper after Blair told them about it. They'll have phoned Fleet Street. The Scottish television stations are here and all the Scottish papers from Dumfries to John o'Groat's. You'd think they'd never had a murder in Scotland before.'

'It's a rich-folks' murder,' said Hamish, 'and that makes a world o'difference. Come ben.'

Anderson followed Hamish into the kitchen and stood watching as Hamish seized the frying pan and turned the liver over.

'That smells good,' said Anderson. 'Sorry to interrupt your dinner.'

'It's no' for me,' said Hamish, blushing. 'It's fur ma dog.'

'I bet ye buy it presents for its birthday,' jeered Anderson.

'Don't be daft,' said Hamish furiously, remembering with shame that he had bought Towser a new basket for his birthday just last month. 'What brings you here?'

'The fact is,' said Anderson, 'I could do with a dram.'

'Oh, aye? And you staying in splendour at Tommel Castle.'

'I rang the bell to ask for a drink,' said Anderson, his sharp blue eyes roaming about the kitchen as if searching for a whisky bottle, 'and that berk, Jenkins, answered. "Police are not to ring bells for the servants," he says. "I'll remember that, mac," says I. "Just fetch me a drink." "Colonel Halburton-Smythe's instructions," says he, "but the officers of the law are not to imbibe intoxicating liquor while on duty and will take their meals in the servants' hall." I told thon old ponce where he could put his servants' meals and he told the colonel, who told Blair, and Blair's gone all creepy and told me I'd better take a walk until he calmed the colonel down.'

'I might have something,' said Hamish, piling the liver into Towser's bowl. 'Then again, I might not.'

'I thought,' said Anderson, staring at the ceiling, 'that perhaps you might like to get a run-down on all the statements.'

'I'm not on the case,' said Hamish, 'but come through to the living room and I'll see what I can do.'

Hamish's living room was not often used. It did not even boast a television set. Bookshelves lined the walls, and the mantelpiece was crammed with various trophies, which Anderson examined. 'You seem to have won everything,' he commented. 'Hill running, clay-pigeon shooting, angling competition, even chess! Bring in much money?'

'The hill running does, and the angling,' said Hamish, 'and sometimes the shooting if it's at a big game fair. But often the prize is something like a salmon or a bottle of whisky.'

He took out a glass and began to fill it with whisky.

'Steady on,' said Anderson. 'I'll need some water in that.'

'It's watered already,' said Hamish, 'and don't ask me why, for I cannae be bothered telling you.' For although Hamish did not mind discussing the laird's wife's penchant for topping up the prize bottles of whisky with water with the locals or Priscilla, he had no intention of running down the good lady's reputation to an outsider.

'Here's to you,' said Anderson. 'Round the wallies, round the gums, look out, stomach, here it comes.'

'Chust so,' said Hamish stolidly. He studied Anderson covertly. Anderson was a thin, restless man with oily fair hair and a discontented foxy face. Of the three, Blair, McNab, and Anderson, Hamish had, in the past, found Anderson the most approachable.

'The last thing', said Anderson, 'that I heard before I left was that forensic had taken a gun out of the gun room. It was a John Rigby. They've taken it back to Strathbane to double-check, but they're sure as anything it was cleaned right after the murder. Could the murderer have switched cartridges, seeing as how Bartlett had a Purdey and he had a John Rigby?'

'The Rigby's a twelve-bore, isn't it?' asked Hamish.

Anderson nodded.

'Any twelve-bore cartridge goes into any twelve-bore gun.'

'How long would it take to clean a shotgun?'

'About five minutes,' said Hamish. 'You put a little gun-cleaning fluid into each barrel and then you scrub the inside of each barrel with a phosphor-bronze brush. Then you put a patch on the jag – that's a wee piece of flannelette on a rod sort of thing – and you push that through the barrels. If you're doing the job properly, you finish it off with gun oil on a lamb's-wool mop, go over the extractors with a toothbrush to remove any powder that may have got caught, and then go over the metal parts of the gun with an oily cloth. I suppose they've dusted the guncleaning equipment for prints?'

'A set of gun-cleaning thingumajigs has gone, says the colonel. And it'll not surprise you to learn there were no prints on the gun.'

'Checked everyone's clothes for oil?'

'Not a sign of it. Even Pomfret's clothes are clean, and you'd expect his shooting clothes would have some oil on them.'

'I think our murderer must have been used to shooting,' said Hamish cautiously.

'Why? It doesn't take much expertise to go right

257

up to someone and blow a hole in his chest.'

'Well,' sighed Hamish, 'here's what I'm thinking. I don't believe the murderer could have counted on the captain being conveniently at that fence and in the perfect position to fake a suicide. An amateur might just have loaded two cartridges into the gun before going out. A man used to shooting would automatically fill his pockets with cartridges. The murderer had enough cartridges with him to change his for the captain's – I mean not only in the gun, but in the captain's pockets as well. Anyway, we know how it was done. The question is – why? How well did they all know him?'

'Oh, they all knew him, all right. Seems they've run into him at various house parties. Everyone very vague. Miss Smythe is the only one who's definite in her statement. She said she met him two years ago when she and some of her friends went to the Highland Dragoons' annual rifle shoot. She is also the only one who seems to have liked him.

'Jessica Villiers and Diana Bryce came in to see Blair together. He told Jessica to go and Diana to stay. The girls exchanged sort of conspiratorial, warning looks. Diana starts patronizing Blair. "One meets the same people over and over again in our set, but I don't suppose someone like you is aware of that" type of thing. Jessica called in and says the same thing. Blair blows his top and starts bullying them and everyone else. Everyone clams up on the spot. Captain Bartlett could be offensive, they say, but not as offensive as *some* – meaning Blair, of course. Blair is also high-handed with the servants. Servants who might be the gossipy type clam up on the spot and play the old retainer bit.'

'And who is the chief suspect?' asked Hamish, rising and filling up Anderson's glass.

'Thanks. Well, the chief suspect is Jeremy Pomfret. He's the one who had the bet with Bartlett.'

'Dearie me,' said Hamish. 'Mr Pomfret has pots of money, and five thousand pounds to him would be like a five-pound note to me.'

'OK, Sherlock, who would you pick?'

'I think there's a lot of them with motives,' said Hamish. 'I was at a party at the castle the night before the shooting. One minute Vera Forbes-Grant was drooling over Bartlett, and the next, she'd flung her drink in his face. Jessica and Diana had their heads together and they were staring at the captain in hate and horror, as if they'd just learned something awful. Diana started to yak to me about how easy it is to die from an accident in the Highlands, and when I said I was the local bobby, she clammed up. I think Freddy Forbes-Grant knows his wife had an affair with Bartlett. I think Sir Humphrey Throgmorton has reason to hate Bartlett as well. The Helmsdales didn't like him either. Henry Withering knew him. How well, I don't know.

'As for Jeremy Pomfret, he wanted me to come up to the castle and referee the shoot, but I had to tell him the colonel wouldnae stand for that. He didn't trust Bartlett and he didn't like him.'

'What I don't understand,' said Anderson, 'is that this house party is supposed to be so that the chosen few can meet the famous playwright. But most of them seem to have a grudge against Bartlett, and all seem to have known him. Weird that they should all end up at the same house party.'

'Not really,' said Hamish. 'Diana was right about meeting the same people. These landed gentry only visit each other, you know, and there's not that many folk this far north, so it stands to reason you'd end up running into the same people over and over again. I thought you would have known that.'

'Not me,' grinned Anderson. 'You don't often get crime in such elevated circles. The only highfalutin one I was ever on was that fishing one last year, but they were all visitors. I'm a town man, and there's usually plenty in Strathbane to keep us busy, what with keeping an eye on thae Russians from the Eastern Bloc fleet and trying to smash the poaching gangs. We've got those big council estates and most of the folks are unemployed and as tight as ticks with booze from one week's end to the other.'

'What about the paraffin test?' asked Hamish suddenly.

'Oh, to see if anyone had fired a gun recently? They don't use the paraffin test any more. They took swabs from everyone's hands and they've taken them back to the lab for tests. But they're pretty sure the murderer was wearing gloves.'

'So you're looking for the gloves?'

'Everyone's going to be up at dawn, combing the grounds,' yawned Anderson. 'Then we're checking up on all the guests. We'll soon be getting reports from all over. They're a cagey lot. They must know we'll find out all about them sooner or later, so you'd think they'd come clean.'

'With someone like Chief Inspector Blair, it's a

260

pleasure not to help him in anything,' said Hamish.

'He's not bad when you get to know him. He's awf'y good at routine work. This is a bit out of his league.'

Hamish picked up the whisky bottle and put it away in a cupboard. Anderson cast a longing look after it before getting to his feet. 'Will I pass on to Blair what you said about the motives?' he asked.

Hamish thought of Blair, and then reminded himself severely there was a murderer at large. He shrugged. 'Why not?' he said.

'I'll drop along tomorrow evening,' said Anderson, 'and let you know how things are going.'

'Aye, well, that would be grand,' said Hamish reluctantly. He had a very human longing to leave Blair to his own devices and watch him make a muck of the case.

After Anderson had left, Hamish began to wonder if he would be any better than Blair at finding out who the murderer was. And the more he wondered, the more his curiosity took over from his hurt at Blair's snub.

He went into his office. There would be no harm in making a few calls to various friends and relatives. Like many Highlanders, Hamish had relatives scattered all over the world, and he was thankful he had still a good few of the less ambitious ones in different parts of Scotland.

He walked over to the wall where there was a large faded map of the north of Scotland and gazed at the county of Caithness, finally pinpointing the Bryces' and Villierses' estates.

The nearest town to both was Lybster. He sat

down at his desk and phoned his fourth cousin, Diarmuid Grant, who had a croft outside Lybster. The conversation took over an hour. Things could not be hurried. There was the weather to be discussed, the decline in the grouse population, the vagaries of tourists, the price of sheep at the Lairg sales, the welfare of Diarmuid's large brood of children, before the backgrounds of Jessica Villiers and Diana Bryce could be gone into.

By the time he put down the phone, Hamish was conscious of a feeling of excitement. He may as well, he thought, put through a few more calls and find out what he could about the other members of the house party.

By eleven o'clock, he had only gone half-way down the list.

He decided to leave the rest until the morning.

The next day was calm and quiet, 'a nice soft day' as they say in Scotland, which means a warm and weeping drizzle.

There was no news from the castle. Even Jessie failed to appear in the village. Hamish politely dealt with any members of the press who turned up. He considered 'No comment' too rude a form of dismissal for his Highland taste, served anyone who arrived at the police station with strong tea and biscuits, and sent them on their way to Tommel Castle, turning a deaf ear to their complaints that they had already been there and had been turned away at the gates.

He called in at the grocers-cum-hardware-cum-post-office-cum-off-licence for a bottle of good whisky in anticipation of Anderson's promised evening visit. He made various phone calls to friends and relatives around Scotland and then to Rory Grant on the *Daily Chronicle* in London. Satisfied he had collected enough to open up several new angles in the case, he settled down to wait for Anderson.

But the long quiet day dripped its way into darkness and there was no sign of the detective.

Again, Hamish felt anger rising up inside him. A proper superior officer would at least have had him out searching the moors for clues instead of leaving him in such isolation.

He tried to forget about the case, but his mind kept turning over what he had heard on the phone and what he had overheard at the party.

Hamish usually preferred warm bottled beer as a drink, but that evening he found himself opening up the bottle he had bought to entertain Anderson and pouring himself a hefty measure.

Soothed at last by the spirit, he was able to convince himself he was better off out of the case. Surely Blair, with the whole forensic team and two detectives to help him, would produce something.

But the next morning he awoke to a day of wind and glitter. A warm gale was blowing in from the Gulf Stream, carrying snatches of voices and strains of radio music from the nearby houses. The sun sparkled on the choppy waters of Lochdubh, hurting Hamish's eyes as he struggled out to feed the hens and geese. A sea-gull floated with insolent ease near his head, eyeing the buckets of feed with one prehistoric eye. In the field behind the police station, rabbits scampered for shelter, and up against the blinding blue of the sky, rooks were being tossed by buffets of wind like bundles of black rags. It was a day of false spring, a day of anticipation, a day when you felt if something did not happen soon, you would burst. Streams of peat-smoke rushed down from the chimney, to be shredded by the minor gales blowing around the corner of the station. Hamish, like most of the villagers, kept the kitchen fire going winter and summer because the hot water was supplied from a boiler at the back of the hearth.

The one nagging fact that there was a murderer on the loose and that he was not being allowed to do anything about it returned to plague him.

Hamish collected the eggs from the hen-house and returned to the kitchen. Someone was knocking loudly on the door of the police station.

Expecting a hung-over member of the press, Hamish went to open it.

Anderson stood on the step, a wide grin on his face.

'You're to come with me, Macbeth,' he said.

'Where?' asked Hamish.

'To the castle. Blair's been deposed.'

'Come in and wait till I put my uniform on,' said Hamish. 'What happened?'

Anderson followed him into the bedroom.

'Well, you ken how Blair's been oiling and creeping around the colonel . . .'

'I didn't,' said Hamish. 'You just said he'd turned creepy.'

'Aye, well, he's been touching his forelock to the colonel while snapping and bullying the guests. I told him what you had said, and he lost his temper and insisted on keeping them all up half the night. Turns out the colonel roused the Chief Constable out of his bed and read the riot act and the Chief roused the Super at Strathbane out of *his* bed and read the riot act, so at dawn Chief Superintendent John Chalmers arrives and rouses *us* up out of our beds. Why had Blair subjected possibly innocent people to such a grilling? Because, says Blair, of vital new evidence. Where did said evidence come from? From the local bobby, chips in I. Where is said local bobby? Dismissed from the case, says Miss Priscilla Halburton-Smythe, appearing in a dressing gown, because Hamish Macbeth is too highly intelligent a man for Inspector Blair, she says nastily, and if you ask her opinion, Blair wants said Macbeth off said murder in case said Macbeth solves it. Get Macbeth, says the Super, and sends Blair out to join the common bobbies who are plowing through the heather still looking for that gun-cleaning outfit. So here I am.'

Hamish laughed. 'I'd love to see Blair's face. But will he no' make life a misery for you when this case is over?'

'No,' said Anderson. 'I'm a bigger creep than Blair, and I'll toady so much, he'll forget about the whole thing.'

'Nearly ready,' said Hamish, buttoning his tunic.

'What about a bit o' breakfast?' wheedled Anderson. 'They're not going to give us time to have any when we get to the castle.'

Hamish made bacon-and-egg baps and tea, eating his own breakfast in record time and then standing impatiently over Anderson until the detective had finished.

He agreed to go in Anderson's car, leaving Towser to roam the garden.

'Find out anything more?' asked Anderson.

'Aye,' said Hamish. 'A lot more. I tell you this, Jimmy Anderson, it's a fair wonder someone waited this long to murder Bartlett!'

CHAPTER EIGHT

Boundless intemperance
In nature is a tyranny, it hath been
The untimely emptying of the happy throne,
And the fall of many kings.
—SHAKESPEARE

Superintendent John Chalmers looked like an age-ing bank clerk. He was tall and thin, with grey hair and watery blue eyes that peered warily out at the world as if expecting another onslaught of the slings and arrows of outrageous fortune. He had a small black moustache like a postage stamp above a rabbity mouth. His ears stuck out like jug handles, as if God had specially made them that way to support his bowler hat.

He had been out in the grounds somewhere and was returning to the castle when Hamish and the detective arrived.

He greeted Hamish courteously and asked him to accompany him into the castle.

The colonel had given up his study to the police. It was a dim little room filled with the clutter of a man who had lost interest in field sports some years ago. Dusty game bags were thrown in one corner

267

under shelves of Badminton Library books on hunting, shooting, and fishing. A pair of green wellington boots held a selection of fishing rods.

There was an unusual stuffed fox in a glass case. It was lying down on its side, looking as if it had been sleeping peacefully at the time it was shot. The superintendent looked down at it sadly for several moments before taking off his bowler hat, polishing it with his sleeve and hanging it on one of the fishing rods.

He sat down behind a battered wooden desk, waved Hamish into a chair opposite, and said to Anderson, who was hovering in the doorway, 'Go down to the kitchens and question the servants again. See if you can get them to like you. People will not talk if you put their backs up.'

When Anderson had gone, he turned to Macbeth. 'Now, Constable,' he said, 'it looks as if we'll need to start over from the beginning. The people at this house party are very upset and claim they have been treated badly. I do not know if that is true or not, but we'll soon find out. I gather from Anderson that you know a little about the guests?'

'I know quite a lot more now,' said Hamish. 'I made various phone calls to find out about their backgrounds.'

'We now have several reports coming in from different police stations. Ah, here is PC Macpherson, who will take the shorthand notes. Now, the first one who's agreed to be interviewed all over again is Colonel Halburton-Smythe. Having dragged me into the case, he is naturally now anxious to be as helpful as possible. You listen closely to my line of questioning, and if there's something you know that we don't know, I shall expect you to step in and put in your own questions. Take that chair over by the window and look as unobtrusive as possible.'

Macpherson went to fetch the colonel, who soon came bustling in. He looked taken aback to see Hamish there, but after a little hesitation he sat down and faced the superintendent.

The colonel appeared pleased to answer the series of polite and simple questions. He said the party had gone on much later than they had expected – until two in the morning. No-one had therefore been up and about around the time the captain was supposed to have gone out on the moors. Yes, he had known about the bet with Pomfret, but not about Bartlett's deal with the Arabs. The guns in the gun room had not been used since last season. This August, Bartlett and Pomfret had brought their own guns.

Hamish remained quietly in his chair, looking out of the window, which faced on to the front of the castle.

The colonel ended by saying that Henry Withering and his daughter wanted to be interviewed next, as they were going out for the day.

The colonel went out and Henry Withering came in. He was wearing a lovat green sweater over a checked shirt and cavalry-twill trousers. He seemed composed and anxious to be helpful.

No, he said, he hadn't a clue who would want to bump off poor Peter. Mind you, he went on, there was no denying Peter was a terror with the ladies and had a way of putting people's backs up.

269

'And do you have a gun yourself, Mr Withering?' asked Chalmers.

There was a slight pause while Henry studied his nails. 'I've got one somewhere,' he said eventually. 'Probably at home at my parents' place in Sussex.'

'Are you a good shot?'

'Never was much good,' said Henry. 'Can I go now?'

'Just a little longer,' said Chalmers soothingly. 'How well did you know Captain Bartlett?'

'Well, I used to run into him a lot. He spent a little time in London before he rejoined his regiment. One meets the same people at parties and that sort of thing.'

'By parties, I assume you mean social parties?'

'Yes.'

'But it appears that, until recently, you did not go to social events. You are on record as saying you despised them.'

Henry laughed. 'Very possibly,' he said. 'I usually tell the press what they want to hear. But one went just the same.'

'I don't know,' said Chalmers cautiously, 'that I would say it was the press exactly, meaning the mass media. No-one had heard of you until recently. But I believe you wrote an article once for *The Liberated Workers' World*.'

'One says silly things in one's youth.'

'This was three years ago.'

'Look,' said Henry with an engaging smile, 'I'm afraid I'm a bit of a fraud. I had to go along with all that left-wing stuff simply because you have to be left-wing to get your plays put on. The big theatres only take trash. You've no idea what it's like to sweat your guts out on a play and then find no-one wants to put it on.'

'So you only knew Captain Bartlett as someone you bumped into at parties?'

'Absolutely.'

'You must, on the other hand,' said Hamish Macbeth softly, 'haff seen a good bit of the captain when you were both sharing that flat off Sloane Square. That would be two years ago.'

'Not really,' said Henry, not looking at Hamish, but continuing to smile at the superintendent. 'I said he could share my digs when he was up in London, that sort of thing. I was away in the provinces most of the time. I came back to find the place a mess and that he'd been using my phone to call someone in the States. I left his suitcase with the porter at the block of flats and changed the locks.'

'Nonetheless, Mr Withering,' said the superintendent severely, 'you said nothing in your earlier statement about having known Captain Bartlett particularly well.'

'I didn't,' said Henry. 'Casual acquaintance, that's all.'

Chalmers took him slowly and carefully over all the things Henry had said in his earlier statement, congratulated him politely on his forthcoming marriage, and told him to tell Miss Halburton-Smythe to step along.

'You've been busy, Constable,' said Chalmers when Henry had left the room. 'How did you find out Bartlett had been staying with him?'

'I have a relative who works for the *Daily Chronicle*,' said Hamish. 'He asked the man who runs the social column about Bartlett. Seems this social editor has a memory like an elephant and he had written an article on Captain Bartlett, calling him the everlasting debs' delight. It appears that part of doing the Season was to have an affair with Peter Bartlett. He had been an indefatigable, deb-chaser since he was a young man. A merry life o' broken hearts and paternity suits.'

'Was he attractive?'

'Aye, he was a fine-looking man, a bit like a fillum star. I suppose you've had the forensic results of the swabs taken from everyone's hands?'

'Yes, they're all as clean as a whistle. We had a bit of excitement over the results of Pomfret's swabs, but he turns out to be a heavy smoker and it can often turn up almost the same results. I understand it was you who discovered it was murder, not accident.'

'Did Mr Blair tell you that?'

'No, it was Colonel Halburton-Smythe. Much as he dislikes Blair, he is confident that an expert like myself will soon prove Blair was right and you were wrong.'

Hamish grinned. 'And if it hadnae been for my interference, they could all have been feeling comfy?'

'Something like that.'

Priscilla Halburton-Smythe walked into the room. She was wearing a dark red silk blouse with a cream pleated skirt. Her smooth blonde hair was curled in at the ends.

Superintendent John Chalmers looked at her with approval.

He took her through her statement, ticking off

each point. Then he half-turned and looked expect-
antly at Hamish.

And for the first time, the superintendent began
to have serious doubts about Hamish's intelligence.
The constable was sitting staring vacantly into
space, a half-smile curling his lips.

Chalmers frowned. The minute he had heard of
this village constable and of how competently he
had outlined how the murder had been done,
he had lost no time in sending Anderson to fetch
him. Unlike Blair, Chalmers was only interested in
results. The fact that this trait had elevated him to
the rank of superintendent should have told Blair
something.

Hamish was in the grip of a powerful fantasy.
He could see it all as clear as day. He was accusing Henry Withering of the murder, and
Priscilla was throwing herself into Hamish's arms
for protection. Henry's face was distorted in a
villainous sneer.

'Macbeth!'

Hamish came back to reality with a bump.

'Have you any questions to ask?'

Hamish shifted uncomfortably. 'Well, Miss
Halburton-Smythe,' he said, not meeting Priscilla's
clear gaze, 'I wass, as you know, at the party afore
the morning the murder took place. I am surprised
you have not mentioned in your statement that Mrs
Forbes-Grant threw her drink at the captain.'

Priscilla flushed and looked uncomfortable. 'You
must admit, when it came to women Peter was
enough to try the patience of a saint,' she said. 'I
assumed at the time he had made one of his off
remarks. Earlier in the day, he told me my home

273

was the most pretentious, uncomfortable slum he had ever had the ill luck to be billeted in. I nearly slapped his face. I suppose you could describe him, on the face of it, as a man who could hold his drink in that he never fell over or was sick over your shoes or anything like that. But when he'd had a couple, he would turn immediately from being a very charming and attractive man to a downright nasty one.'

'Had you known him particularly well before this visit?' asked the superintendent.

'If you mean, was I ever one of his victims, the answer is no. As I said in my earlier statement, I had met him from time to time during the shooting season at other people's houses.'

'And do you know how to handle a gun?'

'A shotgun? Yes.'

'And would you describe yourself as a good shot, Miss Halburton-Smythe?'

'Oh, no, Superintendent.' Priscilla suddenly smiled at Hamish. 'I'm certainly not in Hamish's class.'

'Hamish being . . . ?'

'Police Constable Macbeth.'

One watery blue eye swivelled curiously in Hamish's direction. Hamish folded his arms and looked at the ceiling.

'That will be all for the moment,' said Chalmers, turning back to Priscilla. 'Do you know who's volunteered to be next?'

'Pruney . . . I mean Miss Prunella Smythe. She wants to get it over with so that she can go down to the village and buy some things.'

'Very well. Send her in.'

'I suppose you're looking for a pair of gloves?' asked Hamish.

'Yes, we can't eliminate the guests simply because they passed the forensic test. There is evidence that our murderer was wearing gloves,' said Chalmers.

Pruney fluttered in and sat down, crouched in the chair in front of the superintendent, and stared at her shoes – which were of the Minnie Mouse variety – as if she had never really seen them before.

'Miss Smythe,' began the superintendent.

Pruney started violently, her handbag slid off her lap, she bent to retrieve it, and her thick glasses fell off her nose and landed with a clatter on the floor.

Hamish went to help her, but she brushed him away. She snatched at her handbag, which was upended on the floor, and all the contents spilled out. There were a small medicine bottle, a bunch of keys, eight hairpins, an old-fashioned powder compact, a romance entitled *Desert Passion*, and a tube of wine gums.

'Now, now,' said Hamish, gently taking hold of her frantically scrabbling hands, 'this is not the Gestapo. Chust sit yourself down and let me get these things.' Pruney retreated to the chair while Hamish carefully replaced all the items in her handbag and then popped her glasses back on her nose. 'Now, what about a cup of tea?' he asked.

Pruney gave him a watery smile. 'So kind,' she said. 'Really, it has all been too much for me. Poor Captain Bartlett. Such a fine man. Such a loss. No,

275

'I shall do very well now, thank you, Officer. Tea will not be necessary.'

Hamish retreated to his post by the window.

'I've been reading over your statement, Miss Smythe,' said Chalmers, 'and it is very clear and straightforward. I see no reason to keep you very long.'

He took her carefully back over her first meeting with the captain at the regimental rifle shoot, and then asked her gently if she had specifically come to the house party to meet him again.

'Oh, no,' exclaimed Pruney. 'It was Mr Withering I wanted to meet. I had seen his play in London, you know, and adored every word. The minute I heard Mary – that's Mrs Halburton-Smythe – was having him as a guest, I simply pleaded with her to ask me.'

'You appear to be the only person who has a good word to say for Captain Bartlett,' observed the superintendent.

'Indeed?' Pruney's round, ingenuous eyes looked at the superintendent and then at Hamish. 'I found him such a kind man. Mr Withering was unnecessarily sharp with me when I was only trying to be pleasant, and Captain Bartlett was most comforting. That horrible man, Blair, accused me of having an affair with him. Me!' exclaimed Pruney, although she looked highly gratified.

'You strike me, Miss Smythe,' came Hamish's soft voice, 'as being the kind of lady who sees only the best in people.'

'I think that is surely a better attitude to life than always finding fault,' said Pruney, who was beginning to evince signs of enjoying herself.

'Aye, but that may mean you might have noticed a lot of useful clues without *knowing* they were useful,' said Hamish. 'What did you think, for example, of that incident at the party when Mrs Forbes-Grant threw her drink at the captain?'

'I thought she must be drunk,' said Pruney. 'Mrs Forbes-Grant loves sweet things. She is always eating cakes and chocolates, and when she drinks alcohol, she drinks awful things like rum and Coke or *crème de menthe* or sweet champagne, and I read a most fascinating article the other day which said that all that sugar puts the alcohol into the bloodstream quicker. It is not like the old days, you know. Ladies do drink an awful lot at house parties. I was at a party on the borders last year and a lady of my age lifted up her skirt and *snapped her garter*.'

'That's verra curious,' said Hamish with great interest, while the superintendent glared at him impatiently. 'I was not aware that ladies wore garters any more.'

'That's what I thought!' cried Pruney. 'But a most obliging gentleman at the party told me they sold them in naughty shops.' Her eyes gleamed behind her thick spectacles. 'I find gentlemen's attitudes to the changing fashions in ladies' underwear most interesting. Only the other week—'

'Quite,' said the superintendent repressively. 'To get back to that point the constable was making, can you tell us anything you might have overheard that struck you as curious?'

Pruney giggled and put her hands to her face. 'It's rather like gossiping in the dorm,' she said. 'Still, it *is* a murder investigation. There was just one little thing. I could not sleep and I went downstairs to look for a copy of *The Times* to do the crossword. I find *The Times* crossword quite soporific. As I was passing Captain Bartlett's room, I saw a light under the door.' Pruney blushed. 'I was about to knock, thinking he could not sleep either and might be glad of company, when I heard Mrs Forbes-Grant's voice very clearly. She said, "You can't have. Not you of all people. I don't believe a word of it."'

'And what did the captain reply to that?' asked Hamish.

'I could not hear. The doors are very thick,' said Pruney regretfully. 'He said something because there was a sort of masculine rumble. Then I saw Miss Bryce walking along the passage towards me. She gave me a nasty look, as if I had been eaves-dropping, which of course I hadn't, so I went on downstairs. When I came back up about ten minutes later, the light under the captain's door was out.'

'Did you hear anything else?' asked the super-intendent. Pruney wrinkled her brow. 'No,' she said at last.

'Perhaps you might remember something more,' said Hamish. 'You strike me as a highly observant lady.' Pruney preened. 'If anything comes to mind, tell me or the superintendent here.'

'I most certainly shall,' said Pruney, gathering up her handbag. 'I wouldn't tell that nasty man, Blair, anything. He is not a silly man, but overambitious. I am glad he has been toppled.' She smiled at them warmly and scurried out.

'We had better have Mrs Forbes-Grant in,' said the superintendent. 'See if you can find her, Macpherson. The minute that woman comes in here, I shall accuse her of having an affair with Captain Bartlett.'

'Do you think that's a good idea?' asked Hamish cautiously. 'People are no' ashamed o' infidelity these days. If you're kind and sympathetic, she may tell you herself.'

The superintendent shuffled his papers. Then he said mildly, 'You may be right.'

Hamish let out a slow sigh of relief. He sometimes wondered how many murderers escaped justice because of power struggles in the police department.

There was an altercation outside the door. It appeared that Freddy Forbes-Grant was insisting on being present while his wife was interviewed, and PC Macpherson was firmly refusing permission.

The superintendent was just rising from his seat to go to his constable's aid when Macpherson ushered Vera in.

She was the only member of the house party to have donned mourning. She was wearing a plain black suit with a necklace of seed pearls. Her thick dyed-blonde hair was simply styled and the severe cut of the suit flattered her figure.

There was a loose pouch of flesh under her chin, and a disappointed droop to her full mouth, but she was still, thought Hamish, a very sexy woman. Her large blue eyes looked pleadingly at the superintendent.

'I don't think I can take much more of this,' she said in her husky voice. 'The murder's bad enough without having to be dragged over and over every little bit of it.'

'We won't keep you long,' said Chalmers soothingly. He took her through her statement, and then said mildly he was surprised she had not told Mr Blair about throwing her drink at the captain.

'I lied to him,' said Vera defiantly. 'He kept shouting and shouting at me, so I thought it better to say nothing.'

'I apologize on behalf of the Strathbane police,' said Chalmers. 'No-one is going to shout at you. You are a valuable witness. Now, what caused that scene?'

'Where I threw the drink at him?'

'Yes.'

Vera bit her full bottom lip. 'Look,' she said, 'he made a nasty remark about my hair. He said my roots were black. I was feeling tired and over-wrought. My nerves are not very strong. The minute I had tossed the drink at him, I was so ashamed of having made a scene that I burst into tears and left the room.'

'And did he also make a remark about Miss Bryce and Miss Villiers?' asked Hamish.

'What?'

'Just before you threw your drink at him,' said Hamish, 'you were looking up at him and your lips were framing a kiss. He said something. You looked horrified. He turned and looked pointedly at Miss Bryce and Miss Villiers, then he turned back and gave you a knowing look, and he winked. *That* was when you threw your drink at him.'

'I don't know what you are talking about,' cried Vera, an ugly tide of red beginning to crawl up her neck.

'Mrs Forbes-Grant,' said Hamish in a soft voice.

'We are from the police department and not the Moral Rearmament. It would be quite easy, I think, to prove that you had an affair with Captain Bartlett. Now, that is your own business. You are a very beautiful woman and must often be plagued with men chasing you.'

Vera gulped and looked at Hamish, who gave her a charming smile.

'Freddy doesn't know,' she said. 'Freddy mustn't ever know.'

'And he won't,' said Hamish, 'unless it has a direct bearing on the murder. But it would be nice to get it out of the way. The only thing that's suspicious about it is your refusal to talk. You must see that.'

There was a long silence while Vera looked down at her plump hands on her lap.

'All right,' she said at last. 'I did have an affair with him a few years ago. I didn't know he was going to be here. He made me think he still loved me. I visited his room, the night before the party. He said . . . he said I couldn't stay the rest of the night or Freddy would find out. I thought he loved me. I was prepared to run away with him. He said . . . at the party . . . I hadn't been the only woman who had been in his room. I told him he was lying. And then he turned and looked at Diana and Jessica, and turned back to me and winked. I knew all in that moment – he'd used me as he'd used me before. I saw red. I must have been mad, because I can't afford to leave Freddy anyway.'

There was a long silence.

Chalmers said, 'How long have you been married to Mr Forbes-Grant?'

'Twenty years.'

'And he knew nothing of your affair with Captain Bartlett?'

'Oh, no. Freddy's quite stupid. But he can make money. That merchant bank of his is one of the most powerful in the country. He's more or less retired. He wanted to come and live up here and start afresh. The simple life,' said Vera with a harsh laugh. 'But he runs the bank by phone.'

'Where did your affair with Captain Bartlett take place?' asked Hamish.

'In London. Freddy was abroad. We keep a flat in Knightsbridge.'

'And did Captain Bartlett at any time suggest you leave your husband?'

'No. We were two of a kind. I used to give him money out of my allowance. It sounds awful now. Peter used to say I loved money more than men.'

'And is that true?' asked Hamish, genuinely curious.

'It's all men are good for in the long run,' said Vera. 'Oh, you occasionally meet some fellow and think it's springtime all over again. But nothing lasts . . . except money.'

Chalmers cleared his throat. 'Can you use a shotgun, Mrs Forbes-Grant?'

Vera laughed. Hamish thought she looked like someone leaving the confessional. She had told the worst and now she could relax.

'No, I can't,' she said. 'But it doesn't take any expertise to blow a hole in someone at point-blank range. I could have done that.'

Chalmers patiently took her over the rest of her statement.

'You'd better see Freddy now,' said Vera, rising and smoothing down her skirt. 'You won't tell him . . . ?'

Chalmers shook his head. 'Not unless it becomes necessary.'

'You mean, not unless one of us did the murder? Don't worry, Freddy couldn't kill a fly.'

She drifted out, leaving a heavy aroma of Arpège in the room behind her.

Freddy Forbes-Grant entered the room about a minute later.

It took ages to calm him down in order to get him to say anything coherent at all. But when he finally decided to talk reasonably, his statement had very little to add to what he had already said. Captain Bartlett had insulted his wife on the evening before the murder and had upset her terribly. She was not the only one Bartlett had upset. No, said Freddy, he did not believe in blood sports and never used a gun. They had more or less invited themselves to the Halburton-Smythes when they heard about Henry Withering. Both he and his wife had seen the play in London and thought it a rattling good show. He had written personally to the Secretary of State for Scotland to complain about Blair's harassment, and would complain again if Chalmers wasn't more careful and courteous. He, Freddy Forbes-Grant, considered all policemen some lower form of life anyway.

'He knows about his wife's affair,' said Hamish, after Freddy had crashed out.

'How do you make that out?' asked Chalmers.

'Thon is one very frightened man,' said Hamish.

'Something's terrifying him. I could smell him from here – fear-sweat. Angry, blustering, ranting people are usually frightened.'

'Like Colonel Halburton-Smythe?'

'Och, no. That one was born a scunner.'

Macpherson, who had left to find another victim, returned to say that no-one else was available until the afternoon. They had either gone out or had sent messages via the servants to say they were not to be disturbed. Dr Brodie was with Sir Humphrey Throgmorton, who was in need of a sedative.

Chalmers turned to Hamish. 'In that case, you may as well tell me what you've discovered about the others.'

Hamish prised a small notebook out of his tunic pocket.

'Captain Bartlett,' he said, 'was having an affair with Jessica Villiers four years ago. He met her friend, Diana, and dropped Jessica. He actually became engaged to Diana Bryce for two whole weeks before jilting her. The Helmsdales have reason to hate the captain. He turned up at a ball they were giving in their home near Dornoch with some other army officers. They got drunk and took the place apart. He painted a moustache on a portrait of a Helmsdale ancestor. The portrait was by Joshua Reynolds. The captain refused to pay for any of the damages. He went to sleep drunk with a cigarette burning in his hand and set his bedroom on fire. With the luck of the drunk, he jumped from his window on to the lawn and fell asleep again without warning anyone. The fire spread and burnt down most of the guest wing. It did not become a police matter, because Helmsdale inexplicably refused to prosecute. It came out later in county gossip that Helmsdale had fired a shotgun at the captain and missed. Captain Bartlett said if Helmsdale sued him, then he would sue Helmsdale for attempted manslaughter. It was at that point that Lady Helmsdale, beside herself with rage, punched Captain Bartlett and broke his jaw.'

'Golly!' said Chalmers. 'Don't tell me old Sir Humphrey has a reason to kill the captain as well?'

'He might have. He's a fanatical collector of rare china. He had some people to afternoon tea awhiles back and they brought along their houseguest, Captain Peter Bartlett. The poor old boy had the tea served in a very rare set. He went on bragging about the value and beauty of it. Captain Bartlett dropped his teacup and saucer on the hearth, smashing it and ruining the set.'

Chalmers sat for a long time deep in thought. Then he said, 'It's very curious that so many people with reason to hate Bartlett should be gathered together under one roof.'

'The British Isles is full of other people wi' mair reason to bump Bartlett off than any of the folks here,' said Hamish. 'I wass checking up all around. I am telling you this so's you will not be surprised when you get my phone bill. If we begin to think the murder was committed by someone outside the castle, then we are going to have a terrible job. There was a wee lassie in London killed herself with an overdose of sleeping pills when the captain jilted her, and then there's a lot of husbands as well who've threatened to kill him at one time or another.'

'Where did he get the stamina?' asked Chalmers

in awe. 'Look at the evidence we've got from old Vera – three women in the one night.'

'He was supposed to have been one of those people who only need about four hours sleep a night,' said Hamish. 'And Captain Bartlett was always known as a Don Juan. Aye, it's an unfair world when you think of it. If that man had been a woman, he'd have been called a harlot!'

'Let's get back to Jeremy Pomfret,' said Chalmers, shuffling his papers. 'Did you unearth anything about him?'

'Nothing sinister,' said Hamish. 'He's rich, got an estate in Perthshire, met Bartlett from time to time on various shoots. Never a friend of the captain's. He was sure Bartlett was going to try to cheat over this bet they had. He was very hung over when I saw him on the morning of the murder, but he could have been putting that on for my benefit. He had asked me to be at the castle to referee the shooting, but I refused and told him the colonel would probably take it as a personal insult. Still, his very asking me to be there could have been a smoke-screen, for the murder, as we know, took place much earlier.'

'He appears to have told Blair he loathed Bartlett,' said Chalmers. 'The reasons he gave were that Bartlett had pinched his toothbrush and used it to scrub his toes, and evidently the captain had a disgusting habit of shaving in the bath. Makes you wonder what the ladies saw in a man like that.'

'Och, women are funny,' said Hamish. 'Take the case of Heather Macdonald, her that was married to a fisherman. She kept that cottage of theirs so clean, it wasnae human. You had to take off your boots and leave them outside when you went visiting. She wouldn't allow him to smoke and she starched the poor man's shirts so stiff, it was a wonder he could sit down in the boat. But she ups and offs last year wi' a tinker from the side-shows at the Highland games, and he was a dirty gypsy who didn't have a bath from the one year's end to the other. I don't think,' added Hamish sadly, thinking of Priscilla, 'that the ladies are romantic at all.'

CHAPTER NINE

The wild vicissitudes of taste.
—SAMUEL JOHNSON

Priscilla had decided to visit Mrs Mackay, she of
the green bottle and the bad leg. Henry had readily
agreed to go with her. Putting thirty miles between
himself and Tommel Castle seemed an excellent
idea.

Despite the police investigation, Henry was in a
high good humour. He had received a visit from
several members of the local Crofters Commission
who had formally asked him if he could still be
counted on to hand out the prizes at the fair on the
following day. They had been courteous and highly
flattering. Henry had been made to feel like a local
squire.

As Priscilla drove competently along the Highland roads, he looked out across the glittering
windy landscape and thought it might be quite
a good idea to buy a castle. There seemed to
be castles all over Scotland for sale. It would be
wonderful publicity. Somehow, he must manage to
get himself a coat of arms. If he sold the film rights
of *Duchess Darling*, they could film the whole thing

in his castle. He had more than enough money to decorate it in style. Then, after his marriage, he would invite journalists from the Sunday newspaper colour supplements. Yes, a castle was a definite possibility.

Priscilla looked beautiful and happy. Just getting away from the gloomy atmosphere of death was enough to make both of them feel like schoolchildren at the beginning of the holidays.

Henry told her to stop when they were on a deserted stretch of road and then took her in his arms. She was passionate and responsive, and he felt a heady feeling of triumph as his hand slid up under her skirt for the first time. But his searching hand stopped short of its goal. He had a sudden prickling feeling at the back of his neck, a feeling he was being watched.

He released Priscilla and turned around. An elderly man was peering in the car at Henry's side.

'What the hell do you think you're doing?' shouted Henry.

'I wass passing,' said the old man in a quavery voice, 'and I thought to myself, thought I, Those people are having the bad trouble with the steering. I saw you both fumbling away.'

'Mr McPhee,' said Priscilla, who had recognized the old man, 'we were not having trouble with anything at all. Thank you for your concern.'

Mr McPhee smiled. 'It is not any trouble at all, at all. Are you sure it is not your clutch that is wrong?'

'No, not *my* clutch,' said Priscilla, and giggled, and that giggle of hers made Henry even more furious.

'Drive on,' he said.

'I haven't introduced you,' said Priscilla. 'Mr McPhee, this is my fiancé, Henry Withering. Henry, Mr McPhee.'

'Oh, of course, you are that playwright that everyone iss talking about,' said Mr McPhee. 'It iss a grand thing to have a way with the words. I mind my daughter Elsie's youngest boy, David, was a fair hand with the words when he wass at the school.'

'Priscilla, will you drive on or do I have to get out and walk?' snapped Henry.

'Goodbye, Mr McPhee,' said Priscilla politely. 'I am sorry we have to rush. Give my regards to the family.'

'How on earth could you bear to be civil to that dirty old peeping Tom!' raged Henry, as soon as they had started moving.

'He is *not* a peeping Tom,' said Priscilla. 'His eyesight is bad. He is very old, but very kind and charming. Furthermore, that grandson of his, David, is now the drama correspondent of the *Glasgow Bulletin*. You ought to be nice to people while you're on the way up, darling. You might meet them on the way down.'

'I'm no longer "on the way up," ' said Henry crossly. 'I've already arrived!'

Priscilla drove on in a grim silence until they turned off the road and bumped up a heathery track to the Mackays' little white croft house, which was perched on the side of a hill.

'Now, do be nice,' cautioned Priscilla.

'Of course,' said Henry sulkily, wondering whether to remind Priscilla that a leading London columnist had described him as 'the most charming man in London.'

Henry brightened perceptibly as soon as they were inside the croft house. He was always on the look-out for things to add to his store of witty after-dinner conversation. He took one look around the Mackays' living room and treasured up each bit of bad taste. The carpet was virulent green and ornamented with sugar-pink cabbage roses. The wallpaper was in an orange-and-black abstract pattern. There were horrible china ornaments everywhere: cats, dogs, little girls holding up their skirts. The tea-cosy was a doll in a crinoline gown. There was an enormous china wall-plaque above the fireplace depicting a cottage in shrieking reds and yellows and decorated with a dusting of tinsel, bearing the legend 'My Grannie's Hielan' Home.'

He set himself to please. He described famous people he had met and exotic countries he had been to. He punctuated his conversation with many 'Of-course-this-will-come-as-a-surprise-to-you-buts,' until gradually he began to wonder if he had said something wrong.

Priscilla was very still and silent. The Mackays, at first courteous and animated, began to look at him stolidly.

Henry could not bear unpopularity. He began to ask them questions about themselves, which they answered in polite monosyllables.

When Priscilla stood up and said they must leave, it was a relief.

They drove off in silence, and then Priscilla said in a small voice, 'Did you have to be so patronizing, Henry?'

'I behaved very well,' said Henry stiffly. 'Good God, Priscilla, they're not the easiest of people to talk to. They're as thick as pig shit.'

'They are not! They are very intelligent and very sensitive and they knew immediately you thought the things in their house were a hoot. You kept looking round at everything with a sort of unholy glee.'

'You'll be saying next I should admire their taste,' scoffed Henry. 'All those ghastly ornaments. And that carpet screaming at the wallpaper.'

'It's cosy,' said Priscilla. 'Look, if you've been brought up among old, old things that have been used for generations, you have a longing for things that are bright and new. The government grants have made a difference. They have some money for the first time in their lives. It's only people who've been used to comfort who find domestic antiques beautiful. Mr Mackay's son has an arts degree from Glasgow University. These people are *different*. And they often know what you're thinking. What's this big thing about good taste anyway? We went for dinner with those friends of yours before we left London, you know, those two raving queens in Pont Street. Everything was exquisite and the cooking was cordon bleu, but they were screeching and vulgar and petty. And in my opinion, anyone who puts funny junk in the loo is the absolute end.'

In the bathroom of Henry's London flat was a framed series of mildly pornographic Victorian photographs.

'Don't preach to me!' said Henry. 'What about the glorious load of fakes in that home of yours?

Fake armour, fake panelling – your father's probably a fake colonel.'

Priscilla tightened her lips. If Henry had been a woman, he would have been damned as a bitch, she thought.

'It's no use talking to you,' said Henry. 'Look this murder has put us all on edge.'

'I am *not* on edge!' Priscilla's angry voice seemed to fill the car. 'You did not have to talk about countries you had been to and then carefully explain where they were on the world map. When you were talking about Lawrence Olivier, you might have called him by his proper name instead of talking about "dear Larry". And I can only assume "darling Maggie" is Princess Margaret, since, in your case, it could hardly have been Margaret Thatcher. I wonder the comrades ever put up with you. They must have loved being patronized. Were you one of those slobs who titillated the Left with cosy stories of sodomy and beatings at Eton?'

'Shut up!' shouted Henry, because what Priscilla had said was true.

'No, I won't,' said Priscilla. 'It's almost as if you had unlearned how to be a gentleman, and now you've started being a gentleman again, you've forgotten how to go about it. You even hold your knife and fork as if you're holding a couple of pencils. People like Mr Mackay and yes, even old Mr McPhee, are gentlemen.'

'What do you know about anything, you bloodless little Sloane Ranger?' howled Henry. 'You with your "Not tonight, Henry" and your prissy little disinfected mind.'

'We are definitely *not* suited,' said Priscilla in a quiet voice.

'You're overwrought and talking rubbish,' said Henry in a conciliatory tone. 'Didn't I get on well with those people from the Crofters Commission? Honestly, darling, I am a very popular fellow, or had you forgotten?'

'That's in London,' said Priscilla darkly. 'Everything's different in London.'

Henry shrugged and fell silent. She was in a bad mood. He would talk her round when they got back to the castle.

The day had changed. Great black, ragged clouds were rushing in from the east, a reminder that autumn comes early in the Scottish Highlands. Small wizened trees creaked and swayed beside the road, and the tarns on the moors gleamed black under the looming shadows of the mountains. The Two Sisters, the mountains above Lochdubh, stood up against the sky, as sharply silhouetted as if they had been made out of black cardboard.

Priscilla drove straight past the castle gates, where a group of shivering journalists and cameramen were huddled. She stopped about a mile along the road at a disused lodge.

'It's only a little walk,' she said, 'and it will bring you out in front of the castle.'

'And where are you going?'

'Somewhere,' said Priscilla, tight-lipped.

Henry muttered something under his breath and climbed out.

After Priscilla had roared off, he turned about to walk back to the main gates of the castle. Why should he let the chance of a lot of glorious free publicity slip past? And he had seen a London television unit when they had driven past. When he arrived, the press hailed him with delight.

Hamish was back at the police station in Lochdubh. Detective Chief Superintendent Chalmers was staying at the Lochdubh Hotel. Blair, Anderson, and MacNab had been transferred to a boarding-house at the other end of the waterfront.

He was interrupted during his evening chores by two American tourists whose car battery had gone dead. Hamish jump-started it and then invited the tourists in for tea. They were a pleasant couple from Michigan. Hamish, like most Highlanders, felt more at home with Americans than he did with the English. He chatted away happily for an hour and then sent them on their way, telling them to call at the garage when it opened at nine the following morning, and promising to see them at the crofters' fair.

He had noticed while he was entertaining them that the kitchen floor was sorely in need of a scrub. He changed out of his uniform into his old clothes, got a pail of soapy water and a scrubbing brush, and got to work, fending off Towser, who thought it was some sort of game.

He was aware of being watched, and looked up. The evening was growing dark and he had not yet switched on the electric light in the kitchen, but he recognized the slim figure lurking in the doorway.

'Come in, Priscilla,' he said. 'I've just finished.'

'You'd better put down newspapers, Hamish, until the floor dries,' said Priscilla, 'or Towser will ruin your good work.'

'There's a pile on the chair over there,' said Hamish. 'Pass them over.'

'I'll put them down for you,' said Priscilla, switching on the light.

Hamish looked sharply at her, but she quickly bent her head, her thick hair falling forward to shield her face.

'I was just about to have my supper,' said Hamish. 'I would ask you to join me, but I suppose you'll soon be getting back to the castle for your dinner.'

'I would like to stay,' said Priscilla in an uncharacteristically small voice.

'Aye, well, you'd better go ben to the office and call your parents and tell them where you are or they'll be worried.'

'I don't want to tell them I'm here,' said Priscilla.

'No, well, chust tell them you are going round to the Church of Scotland to discuss the arrangements for the White Elephant stall. We'll go along afterwards and that'll make it all right.'

'All right, Hamish,' said Priscilla meekly. She left the kitchen and he looked curiously after her.

He thought gloomily of the two mutton pies he had bought at the bakery on his road home. Then he shouted, 'I'm stepping out. Back in a minute.'

He ran into his back garden and cleared the fence with one lanky leap. He knocked on his neighbour's door.

Mrs Cunningham, a faded English lady who ran a bed-and-breakfast, answered the back door.

'I hae a guest for supper,' said Hamish breathlessly, 'and I've only got mutton pies and I cannae be offering her those.'

Mrs Cunningham folded her thin arms over her scrawny bosom.

'Constable Macbeth,' she said severely, 'you promised to unstop that drain-pipe of mine.'

'Tomorrow,' said Hamish. 'I'll be round in the morn wi' ma ladder.'

'Promise?'

'Aye, cross ma heart and hope to die.'

'Well, Mrs Wellington, her up at the church, gave me a venison casserole because I promised to help her out, baking the cakes and scones for the fair. I can't stand venison. You can have it.'

'Thanks,' said Hamish.

Soon he was back in his kitchen. The sound of running water came from the bathroom. Priscilla had decided to wash her face and put on fresh make-up.

Hamish put the casserole in the oven and pulled the cork on a bottle of red Bulgarian wine that one of the fishermen had bought in Ullapool from a member of the Eastern Bloc fishing fleet and had passed on to Hamish.

When Priscilla appeared, he suggested they should go into the living room and have a drink until dinner was ready. Hamish felt that venison casserole merited the title of dinner.

'Have a dram,' he said, producing the bottle he had bought to entertain Anderson.

'Going in for the hard stuff?' asked Priscilla. 'I thought you always drank beer.'

'So I do, but I can tell you this, Priscilla – sometimes there are things that happen that call for a good stiff belt o' the cratur.'

'Yes,' said Priscilla gloomily. 'I'll have a stiff one.'

'Now, what's the matter?' asked Hamish, when they were both seated.

'I don't want to talk about it,' said Priscilla. 'Tell me about the case.'

'We had a rough afternoon,' said Hamish, settling back in his chair. 'Sir Humphrey received us in his bedroom, muttered about two sentences, and fell asleep. Then that Diana was flouncing and bitching all over the place. You didnae tell me she had been engaged to Bartlett?'

'I thought you knew.'

'I know now. But she says she ditched Bartlett, not the other way round. She was seen approaching Bartlett's bedroom on the night of the murder. She said she was on her way down to the kitchens. Screamed she hadn't slept with him, and when we said we knew the brave captain had had Vera, Jessica, and Diana all on the same night, she broke down and yelled that Vera had done it . . . the murder, I mean. Jessica was worse. She said Diana was an expert shot . . .'

'You mean Peter slept with all three of them? That man is disgusting.'

'Maybe. Maybe the ladies are chust as disgusting. Then came the Helmsdales. We couldn't separate them. Bartlett had nearly burnt down their home and Helmsdale had tried to shoot him and Lady Helmsdale had broken his jaw. When taxed with it, they told us we were lying. We couldnae get a bit o' sense out the pair of them. It was like trying to get a statement from Tweedledum and Tweedledee.'

'Don't you think it might have been someone outside the castle?'

'It could well be, but something in my bones tells me it's one of them up at Tommel. Where did you go today?'

'Henry and I went to call on the Mackays.'

'How's her leg?'

'It's better. But she needs an operation on her varicose veins.'

'If she needs an operation, why is Brodie giving her medicine?'

'Because he knows and she knows what the matter is. But she's frightened of hospitals and she belongs to the old school and expects the doctor to give her some medicine when he calls. I shouldn't think there's much in her green bottle of medicine but coloured water.'

'Aye, he's terrible against the pills and bottles, is Dr Brodie. I was surprised he gave Sir Humphrey tranquillizers.'

'Probably nothing more than Milk of Magnesia. He says if people think they're getting tranquillizers, they calm down amazingly.'

'Captain Bartlett once broke a valuable piece of china at Sir Humphrey's.'

'That was terrible,' said Priscilla. 'He's a fanatical collector.'

They drank more whisky and then moved through to the kitchen for dinner. The venison casserole was excellent, and Hamish accepted Priscilla's compliments on his cooking without a blush. They giggled over the nastiness of the Bulgarian wine, and then, after supper, went along to the Church of Scotland manse.

Priscilla had drunk so much, she was a little unsteady on her feet, and Hamish took her arm.

The sky had cleared, the weather making another of its mercurial changes. The cold wind had dropped, although angry little waves smacked against the shingle of the beach.

'I had two American tourists in for tea,' said Hamish.

'That'll be the Goldfingers from Michigan,' said Priscilla. 'They're staying at the Lochdubh Hotel.'

'And how did you learn that?'

'I saw Jessie in the village when I was coming to see you. She told me all about them. She was on her way to see if she could catch a glimpse of them.'

'But why? There's nothing odd about them.'

'It's the name, silly. She thinks they're out of a James Bond movie.'

Priscilla reached the manse just in time. She had only been in the door two minutes before the phone rang and it was her father, his voice sharp with anxiety, demanding to know when she would be home.

'I won't be much longer, Daddy,' said Priscilla.

'Well, leave your car at the police station and get that useless copper, Macbeth, to run you back. I don't like the idea of you being out on your own with a murderer on the loose.'

'So you've decided at last it *was* murder,' said Priscilla.

'Never mind what I've decided,' grumbled her father. 'I'll expect you here in half an hour.'

Priscilla was glad of an excuse to cut short her visit, for she did not like Mrs Wellington, the minister's wife, a bossy, tweedy woman who bullied her husband.

When they took their leave, Priscilla told Hamish he was expected to drive her home.

'I would have done that anyway,' said Hamish seriously. 'And I want you to lock your bedroom door.'

Priscilla shivered.

'It's funny,' mused Hamish, as they drove up the winding hill that led to the castle, 'Captain Bartlett had a word wi' me when I left the party. He was outside on the drive. He had a premonition something was about to happen to him. There was something took place at that party to give him the feeling he was in danger.'

'I wish it were all over,' sighed Priscilla.

'Henry will look after you,' said Hamish, flashing her a quick sideways look.

'Yes,' said Priscilla with a brittle laugh. 'Aren't I lucky?'

Hamish drove up through the side road to the castle, although he was sure the gentlemen of the press would have packed it in for the night.

He pulled up outside the looming dark bulk of the castle, got out, and held open the door for Priscilla.

'Are you coming in?' she asked.

Hamish shook his head.

'I enjoyed this evening,' said Hamish politely. 'It is a pity you are engaged, for I had it in mind to try that new hotel up the Crask road tomorrow night.'

'The Laughing Trout? I haven't heard very good reports of it, Hamish, but it's only been open a few weeks. Do you mean you thought of taking me there for dinner?'

'Yes. I aye hae a wee bit o' a celebration after the crofters' fair.'

Priscilla turned and looked at the castle. Henry would be wondering what had happened to her. Tomorrow would be a long day. The press would turn up at the fair, and Henry would expect her to pose for photographs.

'It seems a bit odd, but we're old friends, Hamish, and, yes, I would like to go for dinner with you.'

'I am most honoured,' said Hamish courteously. As she turned away, he added sharply, 'Be careful, Priscilla.'

She gave a choked little sob and flung herself into his arms.

He patted her clumsily on the back, murmuring, 'There, there. It iss all right. Hamish will look after you.'

She finally drew back and dried her eyes. 'Sorry, Hamish,' she mumbled. 'See you tomorrow.'

Hamish watched until she had gone inside the castle. He drove sedately to the gates and out on to the road. Then he turned on the police siren full blast and raced down to Lochdubh.

'That policeman's drunk,' said Mrs Cunningham, peeping through her lace curtains. Two of her boarders joined her at her window. 'Did you ever?' said Mrs Cunningham. 'Blasting that police siren when there's no need at all and now he's doing cart-wheels up the side of the house to his back door.'

CHAPTER TEN

A crofter's son once defined a croft as a small area
of land entirely surrounded by regulations.
—KATHARINE STEWART

Summer returned for the day of the crofters'
fair. Hamish rose early and unstopped Mrs
Cunningham's drainpipe. He was interrupted by
the superintendent, demanding to know why
PC Macbeth had been sounding his police siren.
Hamish said he had been testing it out, as he did
periodically, because you never knew when it
would come in handy, to which Chalmers replied,
'Well, go easy on the booze, son.'

As all the members of the house party were to
attend the crofters' fair, Chalmers said he had got
Colonel Halburton-Smythe to agree to a further
search of all the rooms in the castle. He ordered
Hamish to attend the fair and to see if he could
elicit any further information from the guests.

Hamish tactfully did not point out that he had
promised to attend anyway and that the police
car was being used to transport cakes and scones
to the fair.

The school kitchens were being used for

last-minute baking. When Hamish arrived there shortly after nine o'clock, it was to find all the members of the house party helping out. Even old Sir Humphrey Throgmorton appeared to be completely recovered and was beating batter in a bowl with a gingham apron tied round his waist.

Lady Helmsdale advanced on Hamish with a bowlful of raisin-spotted batter. 'Be a good man,' she boomed, 'and give that a stir while I get on with something else.'

'I'm surprised to see you all here so early,' said Hamish. 'I thought you wouldn't turn up until this afternoon.'

'Got to keep these people on the move,' said Lady Helmsdale. 'Can't have them moping around the castle being badgered by those scribe-chappies and nosy coppers and dosing themselves with tranquillizers. Tranquillizers, pah! Lot of muck, if you ask me. In my mother's day, a good dose of castor oil put an end to stupid fancies. People are getting murdered every day. Can't take this one too seriously. Fact is, the world's a better place without that cad.'

'You cannae expect me to approve of people taking the law into their own hands,' said Hamish.

'Why not?'

'That's anarchy.'

'Nonsense, Bartlett was a cockroach. Someone stepped on him. Jolly good for someone, is all I can say.'

She moved off to make sure everyone was working.

Hamish noticed Priscilla and Henry were working together at a table over in the corner. They seemed to be enjoying themselves. Hamish thought they might have had some sort of reconciliation after a quarrel. They were being playful and giggling a lot, rather like a couple trying to show the world how really happy they were, reflected Hamish, feeling sour with jealousy.

Carrying the bowl, he moved over to join Diana and Jessica.

'Can't we ever get away from the police?' said Diana nastily.

'I'm not policing at the moment,' said Hamish mildly. 'I'm beating cake mixture.'

'I don't mind you joining us,' said Jessica. 'Unlike Diana, I don't have a guilty conscience.'

'I'm tired of your bitching, Jessica,' said Diana. 'Some friend you've turned out to be. You're so jealous of me, you can't resist making a crack at every opportunity.'

'Why on earth should I be jealous of you?' demanded Jessica.

Diana ticked off the items on her fingers. 'I have looks, and you don't. I attract men, and you don't. Peter was wild about me and he thought you were a joke. He said it was rather like screwing the old grey mare who ain't what she used to be.'

Jessica picked up a bowl of batter and slammed it full into Diana's face.

'Now, now,' bleated the Reverend Tobias Wellington, bustling forward. 'Christian charity, girls! Christian charity!'

'Oh, piss off, you old fruit,' said Diana, clawing batter from her face.

Mrs Wellington brushed her husband aside and strong-armed both the girls out of the kitchen into

305

the school-yard where her voice could subsequently be heard berating both with magnificent force and energy.

'I do wish she wouldn't go on and on,' said Pruney Smythe, appearing at Hamish's elbow. 'It reminds me of my school-days.'

'Serves them both right,' said Vera Forbes-Grant, with her mouth full of freshly baked cake. 'This stuff's delicious.'

'Leave some of it for the fair,' said Lady Helmsdale. 'You've eaten half a chocolate sponge cake already.'

Diana and Jessica came back, looking chastened. Now that they were both under attack, their odd friendship had resurfaced.

'Ghastly old trout,' muttered Diana. 'I bet she wears tweed knickers.'

'I've a good mind to put a dose of rat poison in her bloody cake,' said Jessica. 'Let's clear off and find a pub. Thank God, they don't have licensing hours in Scotland.'

'Exit Goneril and Regan,' murmured Sir Humphrey.

'Goodness, did someone say something about gonorrhoea?' asked Lady Helmsdale.

Sir Humphrey flushed. 'No, no, dear lady. I was referring to the daughters in *King Lear*. Shakespeare, you know.'

'Oh, *him*!' sniffed Lady Helmsdale. 'Can't stand the man. Awful bore.'

With the absence of Diana and Jessica, the cooking party became very merry. Even Freddy Forbes-Grant, who had been mooning around his wife, suddenly brightened up and began to help with the preparations. Jeremy Pomfret, who had been in the grip of an almost perpetual hangover since the murder, drank a glass of Alka Seltzer and began to look almost human again.

Hamish waited around even after the first batch of cakes was ready, hoping Priscilla would look at him or smile at him, or show in some way she had not forgotten their dinner date. But Mrs Wellington sharply ordered him to get a move on, and so he set out with the police car loaded up with boxes of cakes, pies, and scones for the fair, which was to be held on a sloping field at the back of the village.

Colonel Halburton-Smythe and his wife had gone on ahead and were already there, loading up a mass of junk on to a table that constituted the White Elephant stand. It was a sort of recycling of junk. People bought it one year and then handed it back the next. Fat little ponies cropped the grass, their tiny owners strutting about, brandishing large riding crops.

Some gypsies were setting up side-shows. Hamish wandered over. 'I'll be keeping an eye on you lot,' he said. 'No bent rifle sights this year, no glued-down coconuts, and no brick-hard dartboards which no dart could possibly stick in.'

'We've got to make a living,' whined one.

'But you've begun to cheat all the time,' complained Hamish. 'It fair breaks my heart to see the children wasting their pocket money and not even winning a goldfish for their pains.' He picked up a rifle from the rifle range and held it up to his eye. 'Deary me,' he said mildly. 'Bent again. Fix those sights, or get out.'

He wandered off, followed by a volley of Romany curses.

On the other side of the field, Mrs Mackay was setting up her spinning wheel, preparatory to giving her annual demonstration. 'This is the last time ever, Hamish,' she said. 'I feel such an old phoney, me that buys all my clothes from Marks and Spencer.'

'Aye, well, the tourists like it,' said Hamish. 'How's your leg?'

'Better. As long as I don't walk about too much, I'll be all right.'

'I hear you had the royal visit?'

'Oh, Miss Halburton-Smythe and her fellow. Aye. Talk the hind leg off a donkey, he would.'

'I'd better be getting back for the next load,' said Hamish. 'There's the stuff to collect from St Mary's after I've done with the Church of Scotland.'

Like most Highland fairs, the crofters' one dithered along in a chaotic mess until two in the afternoon, when everything suddenly took shape. Henry Withering was right there in the swing of things, buying a sheepskin rug, a Fair Isle sweater, and a bottle opener with a deer-horn handle.

The sun was high in a cloudless sky, and the field where the fair was being held commanded a good view of the loch. The village of Lochdubh looked down at its mirrored reflection. Surprised and delighted children were winning prizes at the fair-ground stands. The cakes, scones, and home-made jam were disappearing fast.

Priscilla had spoken courteously to the press about the murder, about her forthcoming marriage, about her ideas on modern womanhood.

Hamish thought she was doing very well. She was wearing a simple blue cotton shirtwaister and she looked cool and fresh.

Hamish did not know that Priscilla was hating every moment of it. The morning had started well with all the fun in the school kitchen. She had promised to be nice to the press for Henry's sake, but after she had given serveral very lengthy interviews, she told Henry she had talked enough. Taking her arm, he silently piloted her straight into another press interview, this time with a raddled female columnist who smelled of whisky and whose perpetually angry eyes were always on the look-out for another victim to tear to pieces. Normally, she specialized in savagely criticizing Princess Diana's clothes or Prince Charles's speeches, that ruse of the inferior woman journalist who tries to put herself on a par with the famous by putting them down.

Between interviews, Henry had found time to tell Priscilla of his dream of buying a castle and entertaining all the trendy Chelsea set, along with magazine writers and journalists from the Sunday colour supplements. Priscilla felt a lump rising in her throat. Life was beginning to stretch out in front of her in a series of exhausting press interviews. Henry found the Lochdubh community funny and quaint, something to exhibit to his London friends. Priscilla looked around the pleasant, old-fashioned scene, the purple mountains, the tranquil loch, the friendly, innocent faces of the crofters and felt Henry was turning her into a stranger in her own community.

But when it came to the prize-giving, Henry was

superb. He made a warm, funny, amusing speech. He presented the first prize – pony racing – to a small child in jodhpurs. He picked her up in his arms and beamed at the cameras. 'He's going to kiss her,' thought Priscilla wildly, and Henry did.

He presented the prize for the best home-made jam and insisted on tasting it, rolling his eyes ecstatically. The crofters were delighted with him. They appreciated hard work, and Henry *was* working hard to make every prize recipient feel special.

'I suppose our date is off,' said a gloomy voice in Priscilla's ear.

She swung about and looked up into the hazel eyes of PC Macbeth.

'Why?'

Hamish shuffled his feet. 'Well, the pair of you seem to be doing just grand. And it now seems odd to have asked out another man's girl.'

'Yes,' said Priscilla bleakly.

'I thought you would be up there with him.'

'I felt I'd had enough exposure to the press for one day,' said Priscilla. 'And it's Henry's show.'

'It is that,' said Hamish admiringly. 'If his plays ever flop again, he'd make his fortune as an actor.'

'I doubt it,' said Priscilla. 'Ham actors are out of fashion.' She blushed hotly. 'I didn't mean that. It's the heat.'

'So we are not going out for dinner?'

'I think I could still manage to go,' said Priscilla, not looking at him. 'I mean, it's not as if I can drop in on you any more once I am married. I'll make some excuse and meet you at the police station at seven.'

Hamish looked over her head, his eyes

310

sharpening. The crowd were laughing at one of Henry's jokes. At the back of the crowd loomed the bowler-hatted head of Detective Chief Superintendent Chalmers. Behind him came Blair, Anderson, MacNab, and six uniformed officers.

'Something's up,' said Hamish.

Chalmers and the rest shouldered their way through the crowd to where Freddy Forbes-Grant was standing.

'Excuse me,' muttered Hamish, making off in the same direction. He arrived in time to hear Chalmers saying softly, 'We would like you to come with us, Mr Forbes-Grant.'

'What?' demanded Freddy, turning red with anger. 'Push off. You're spoiling the fun.'

'We do not want to make a public scene,' said Chalmers. 'Think of your wife.'

'What *is* all this?' demanded Vera.

A silence had fallen on the crowd. Henry's voice from the platform tailed off. Old Mr Lewis, who had won the prize for the best marrow, stood with the huge vegetable in his arms and stared open-mouthed.

'Come along,' said Chalmers, taking Freddy by the arm.

'Keep your hands to yourself,' shouted Freddy, jerking his arm free.

Chalmers sighed. 'You leave me no alternative. Frederick Forbes-Grant, I hereby charge you with the wilful murder of Captain Peter Bartlett and would like to caution you that anything you say may be taken down and used in evidence against you.'

'You're mad,' said Freddy, tugging at his handlebar moustache.

A great silence had fallen on the crowd.

Then Vera whispered, 'Oh, no. Look, there's something I've got to tell you . . .'

'Oh, what's the use. I did it,' said Freddy loudly. 'Put on the manacles.'

'Just come along quietly,' said Chalmers.

The police crowded around Freddy and they all began to move away towards the cars.

Hamish caught up with Chalmers. 'Are you sure?' he asked.

'Pretty sure. A pair of thick gloves was found stuffed down the side of a chair in his bedroom. We can't say anything definite until the lab has a look at them, but it certainly appears as if they've been used in the murder. There's a smear of oil on them.'

'But the rooms were searched thoroughly by Blair!'

'Oh, Blair.' The superintendent shrugged.

'He may not be all that bright,' said Hamish, 'but I'm sure when it comes to routine police work, he's pretty thorough.'

'Meaning someone else put them there? But Mr Forbes-Grant has just admitted to the murder.'

'Aye.' Hamish pushed back his cap and scratched his head. 'Do you want me to come along?'

'I don't think there's any need. You stick to your duties here. I'll telephone you when we get a statement and let you know what he said.'

Vera Forbes-Grant was being ushered into a car behind the one that was taking her husband to Strathbane. She looked shocked and excited at the same time.

A buzz of voices rose as the police cars drove

away. The press were tumbling out of the beer tent, the less experienced rushing for their cars, the older hacks staying to collect eyewitness accounts of the arrest.

Henry's voice, coming over the loudspeaker system, startled them all. 'I think, for the sake of all the people of Lochdubh who have worked to make this fair a success,' he said, 'we should go on and not let this terrible murder spoil our day. There is nothing we can do. If Mr Lewis will bring that splendid marrow of his back up to the platform, he will receive his prize. Now, Mr Lewis, tell the folks how you managed to achieve this giant.'

'What happened?' Priscilla found Jessica and Diana standing beside her. 'We've just arrived,' said Jessica, 'and someone said someone has been arrested.'

'Freddy,' said Priscilla. 'They've arrested Freddy for the murder.'

Both girls exchanged startled glances. Then Jessica let out a slow breath of relief. 'Of course, it must have been him,' she said. 'He must have found out about Vera and Peter. That old bag, Vera, will be swanning all over the place now, saying Freddy killed for her sake.'

'I am very sorry for Vera,' said Priscilla. 'It came as a terrible shock.'

'She'll get over it.' Diana shrugged. 'She'll be drooping around the castle by tonight, trying to queen it over the rest of us as if she's some sort of *femme fatale*, instead of the worn-out old trollop she really is.'

'The pair of you make me sick,' said Priscilla, shaken out of her normal calm. 'If Mummy doesn't

313

tell you to pack and leave, then I shall.'

'Don't get so uppity,' said Diana, with a drunken giggle. 'We weren't going to stay anyway. That dump of a castle is enough to make anyone commit murder. Come on, Jessica. Let's have a beer.'

They ambled off, arm in arm.

Priscilla began to feel the beginnings of a headache behind her eyes. The whole scene took on an air of unreality. Flags and striped awnings fluttered in the bright sunshine, the music from the carousel blared out, almost drowning Henry's voice. Henry. That was the only bright spot in this horrible day, thought Priscilla, with a sudden rush of affection for her fiancé. Although he looked as shocked and strained as the rest of them, he was manfully standing out in the glare of the sun, taking time over each presentation, compèring the Highland dancing, accepting the judges' reports for the piping competition, and making the children laugh by pretending a set of bagpipes had come to life and was trying to strangle him.

I'll tell Hamish I can't make it tonight, thought Priscilla, and looked about for the tall figure of the policeman. But there was no sign of Hamish Macbeth.

Hamish was sitting in the beer tent with Diana and Jessica. They had already told him that they had both known all along it was Freddy, although, said Diana, 'At one time I thought it might be Priscilla.'

'Now why on earth would Miss Halburton-Smythe want to murder Captain Bartlett?' asked Hamish.

'There's always been something creepy about

Priscilla,' said Diana. 'These repressed virgins can be dangerous.'

'How do you know she's a virgin?' asked Hamish curiously.

'You can always tell,' hiccupped Jessica. 'That frozen touch-me-not look always gives them away.'

'And is there something so terrible in being a virgin in your early twenties?'

'It's weird, that's what it is,' said Diana. 'I think Henry's waking up to the fact she's a cold fish. Anytime he calls at her bedroom door, she keeps him standing outside.'

'You're getting away from the murder,' said Hamish.

'No, I'm not. I've seen Priscilla out on the moors with a gun and she handles it like a man.'

'She's all right,' said Hamish, 'but by no means an expert.'

'Known her a long time?' asked Diana slyly.

'Yes.'

'And you're sweet on her,' teased Jessica.

'Aye, I am that, me and the rest of the folk in Lochdubh. We haff always known Miss Halburton-Smythe to be decent and kind, qualities that are as admired in the Highlands as they are anywhere else. It makes a nice change when you think of the silly bitches you sometimes find yourself stuck with. Good day to you, ladies.'

'What's got into him?' asked Jessica, staring after his retreating back.

'Who cares? We'd better put our heads together and find some way to bring Vera down a peg. It's not as if she ever cared a rap for old Freddy . . .'

315

Hamish walked out of the beer tent. He had a sudden feeling as he made his way through the crowd that Priscilla was looking for him to cancel their dinner date. He did not look round but hurried as fast as he could to his car. Perhaps if he avoided her, she might change her mind.

Jeremy Pomfret was leaning up against his Volvo in the car-park. He was smoking a cigarette and beaming drunkenly about him. He hailed Hamish like an old friend.

'Tremendous news about Freddy, hey?'

'I seem to be the only person who's sorry for the man,' said Hamish. 'Why are you so delighted, Mr Pomfret?'

'It's all been hanging over us. I mean, I always knew it must have been one of us. Blair thought I was the prime suspect because of the bet. It's great to know we can all go home now and forget about it.'

'I don't think he did it,' said Hamish abruptly.

'Here, you can't go around saying things like that!' exclaimed Jeremy, turning pale. 'The police said he did it, Freddy said he did it, so it's all wrapped up nice and tight.'

'In my opinion,' said Hamish, 'the murderer's still on the loose.'

'You'd better be careful,' said Jeremy. 'You'd better be very careful, Macbeth. Halburton-Smythe don't like you. He's already had Blair in trouble with the Chief Constable. Blair's a detective. He can stand a bit of aggro. But you're nothing but the village bobby.' Jeremy's normally pleasant expression had changed to one of dislike and suspicion.

Hamish touched his cap and turned away.

'Keep out of it,' Jeremy shouted after him. 'Just keep out of it! D'you hear?'

Hamish got in his car and drove down to the police station. Priscilla's car was still parked outside. Her parents must have run her down to the village in the morning.

He went into his office, sat down at his desk, and called police headquarters at Strathbane. He was told Chalmers was busy and could not come to the phone.

Hamish sighed and took out his notebook, where he had jotted down odd fragments of information about the house guests. He read them over and over again, and then put his large regulation boots up on the desk and thought hard.

The sharp ringing of the phone a half hour later startled him. He snatched it, expecting the call to be from Chalmers, but it was only Mrs Wellington, the minister's wife, demanding his help in carrying tables and chairs back to the church hall.

Hamish was just leaving when the phone rang again. But before he picked it up, he had a feeling that the caller was Priscilla, still trying to cancel the dinner date.

He put on his cap and left the police station, leaving the phone ringing.

'Where have you been?' asked Henry Withering as Priscilla walked up to him.

'I've just been to the phone box down the road to call someone in the village,' said Priscilla. 'It's someone I promised to visit this evening and I wanted to tell . . . her I couldn't make it.'

'I should think not,' said Henry with a grin. 'You've got me to look after.'

'You don't seem to need much looking after,' said Priscilla. 'You've been marvellous today, Henry. The fair would have been a disaster without you.'

'I think I've done enough,' said Henry. 'Let's get back to the castle and have a nice cool drink. Where's your car?'

'It's down in the village, but anyone in the car-park will give us a lift.'

'OK, I'll just say my goodbyes to the Crofters Commission people and join you in a minute.'

Priscilla waited until he had gone and then took a notebook out of her handbag and scribbled a message to Hamish on a sheet of paper. She could pop it through the letter-box of the police station when she got there. She finished the note and looked for Henry. He was talking earnestly to her father about something. Colonel Halburton-Smythe laughed and clapped him on the shoulder.

Daddy's so pleased with him, thought Priscilla. I *have* done the right thing.

Henry and Priscilla were dropped outside the police station by Mrs Wellington. They had passed Hamish on the road. Mrs Wellington had signalled to him to stop, but the policeman had either not seen her, or had pretended not to.

'What on earth is your car doing at the police station?' demanded Henry.

'Didn't I tell you?' said Priscilla. 'Daddy phoned when I was calling on Mrs Wellington last night and told me to get Hamish to run me home.'

'I thought he didn't like him.'

'He doesn't. But Daddy was concerned about my safety. I just have to leave a note for Hamish about some church arrangements.' She pushed open the garden gate of the police station and Towser treated her to a slavering welcome.

'Don't be long, darling,' called Henry. 'I need that drink before the press conference.'

Priscilla turned back and leaned on the garden gate. 'What press conference?'

'This is big news. They'll all be back at the castle tonight. I've got your father to agree to let me hold a press conference and deal with the media for him.'

'But Daddy's way of dealing with the media is to lock them outside the estate,' said Priscilla, 'and a bloody good idea, too. I've talked and talked and talked today on your behalf, Henry. I've had cameras poked in my face and I've had to parry some pretty personal questions. There's been an arrest. Vera's going to be in need of some looking after.'

'Oh, Vera.' Henry shrugged. 'That one will be enjoying every minute of the drama.'

'Vera's all right,' said Priscilla. 'For all her nonsense, she really does care for Freddy. Can't you keep the press away?'

'Until I see a contract for the film rights and make sure a secondary company has taken *Duchess Darling* on the road, I won't feel secure,' said Henry. 'OK, I know this murder's dreadful. But it's a windfall for me. No publicity is bad publicity, and you'd better get used to that. So just deliver that note and let's get going.'

Priscilla looked at the note in her hand. She walked up to the front of the police station. She stared at the letter-box. Then she raised the flap and let it bang and walked back to the car with the note still crumpled up in her hand.

'Ready to go?' said Henry.

'Yes, ready,' said Priscilla evenly.

Hamish returned to the police station at six. He switched on his answering machine. A Gaelic voice wailed out the beauties of Lochnagar. He switched it off. He must really find out how it worked one day.

He phoned Strathbane again and this time got through to Chalmers.

'He's given us a full confession,' said Chalmers. 'Seems quite cocky about it all now. Says he knew Bartlett had had an affair with Vera and so bumped him off. The lab's still working on the gloves. They were the ones used in the murder, all right.'

'But can't they tell from the swabs they originally took from Freddy's hands and the inside of the gloves whether he actually wore them?'

'Don't know. One of the boffins has come up with a theory that Freddy actually used fine surgical gloves under the heavy leather ones.'

'And what does Mr Forbes-Grant say to that?'

'Says he can't remember. Says we've got our murderer, so why are we wasting time with a lot of damn-fool questions.'

'And Vera Forbes-Grant – she was about to tell you something at the fair. What was it?' asked Hamish.

'She says she just wanted to tell us that her

husband couldn't have harmed anyone. But she seems to have changed her tune. She's actually *proud* of him. Can you credit that?'

'Aye, in a way,' said Hamish cautiously. 'I'm no' easy in my mind about this. I cannae think Freddy would have been cold-blooded enough. The murder may have been done on the spur of the moment, but it was done by someone who didn't lose his head and thought of everything. I don't like those gloves turning up conveniently like that.'

'I'm under a lot of pressure,' said Chalmers. 'I *want* the murderer to be Forbes-Grant. I want the Chief Constable off my back. I want the press off my back. What's up with the news these days? Why don't the Libyans bomb Harrods or something? Why doesn't another Russian reactor blow up?'

'Now, now,' said Hamish soothingly. 'It is of no use wishing a section of the population to die a terrible death just to get the press off your back.'

'Everyone will be on my back tomorrow,' sighed Chalmers. 'I'm going back to that castle and I'm going to take them all through their statements again, and I'm going to have as many men as can be spared combing the moors for more clues.'

'Have you told the colonel yet?'

'That's my next call,' said Chalmers gloomily. 'I'll expect you at Tommel Castle at nine in the morning. Where will you be if anything crops up?'

'The Laughing Trout.'

'Dear God.'

'It's a new restaurant, up on the Crask road.'

'Personally, I wouldn't go near any place with a twee name like that. Enjoy yourself.'

Chalmers rang off.

Hamish rushed to wash and change. It looked as if Priscilla was going to keep the date after all.

CHAPTER ELEVEN

I maintain that though you would often in the
fifteenth century have heard the snobbish Roman
say, in a would-be off-hand tone, 'I am dining with
the Borgias tonight,' no Roman ever was able to say,
'I dined last night with the Borgias.'
—MAX BEERBOHM

'No, Hamish,' said Priscilla Halburton-Smythe
severely. 'You cannot keep Uncle Harry's clothes.'

Hamish stood sheepishly in front of her in all
the splendour of Uncle Harry's dinner jacket and
trousers.

'I'll take them off,' he said. 'You are only
wearing a sweater and trousers, so I'll look a bit
odd.'

'Keep it on for the evening,' said Priscilla. 'I've
got a dress and high heels in this plastic bag. I had
to climb out the back way.'

'I suppose the press were all there,' said Hamish
sympathetically.

'They were all inside, being entertained by
Henry. He felt it would be better to get it all over
with rather than being pestered by them when we
tried to go out of the castle gates. But I'm afraid I

couldn't face them myself. You know how it is. Mummy would never even begin to understand why I wanted to go out for dinner, so I climbed out of the window of that little upstairs drawing room that nobody ever uses and slid down the roof. No-one saw me leave, not even the servants. I'd left my car down the side road.'

'Won't Henry be upset when he finds you missing?'

'He won't. I'll climb back in the way I climbed out. I told him I was going to bed and I locked my door on the outside when I left. I'll only be a minute changing.'

She disappeared into the bathroom and Hamish sat down to wait. This must be what it's like when you have an affair with a married woman, he thought. I wish Henry didn't exist. I wish we could go out for an evening without all this secrecy.

Priscilla emerged in record time wearing a filmy red chiffon dress and high-heeled black patent leather sandals.

'You'd better hide your car in the garage and we'll take the police car,' said Hamish.

While she put her car away, he locked up the police station and then stood holding open the door of his car for Priscilla. She got in with a flurry of chiffon skirts and black-nyloned leg just as Mrs Wellington walked past.

'Evening,' said Mrs Wellington, her eyes bulging with curiosity.

Hamish slammed the car door before Priscilla could say anything, jumped into the driving seat and drove off with a roar.

'That's torn it,' said Priscilla. 'She'll tell Daddy.'

'He would be bound to hear sooner or later,' said Hamish. 'You cannae keep anything quiet around here.'

'I know that,' said Priscilla. 'I was just hoping it would be later rather than sooner.'

The Laughing Trout, previously called The Caledonian Arms, had reopened under the new name only recently. The first sinister sign of a possibly indifferent kitchen to meet Hamish's eye was a row of painted cart-wheels against the fence of the parking area. People who went in for painted cart-wheels, reflected Hamish gloomily, often had peculiar ideas about food.

A harassed woman answered the bell in the small reception and told them they were lucky there was a table free, and to go and wait in the bar.

Hamish ushered Priscilla into the bar and they sat down in two mock leather armchairs in front of an electric log fire.

The harassed woman handed them enormous menus and rushed off.

'What would you like to drink?' asked Hamish.

'Campari and soda.'

'I'll have the same.'

'I've never seen you drink Campari and soda before,' said Priscilla.

'And never will again,' said Hamish. 'But I've a feeling that this is the sort of place where they'll be better able to cope with two of the same kind of drinks.'

'Do you think they come and serve you, or do you have to go to the bar?'

'I think I'll need to go and get them,' said Hamish.

The bearded barman was demonstrating back casts to a balding gentleman who was wearing a double-breasted blazer with an improbable crest.

He ignored Hamish and continued talking.

'I'm telling you, that was a twenty-pounder at the end of my line, and I knew it,' he was saying.

An unhealthy-looking girl came into the bar behind the counter, fiddled with the till, and went out again.

Hamish sighed. He had come across this sort of situation before. In some mysterious way, various cockney families seemed able to find out when a new hotel was about to open up and they descended on it en masse, offering their services – uncle behind the bar, mother at reception, daughter and auntie in the kitchen. They ruined the trade with bad manners and worse food before flying off, like locusts, to descend on yet another Highland hotel.

Hamish took a step back. Then, with a flying leap, he vaulted the bar and, ignoring the barman's cries of outrage, proceeded to pour two campari and sodas.

'I'll call the police,' shrieked the barman.

'I am the police,' said Hamish. 'If you do not behave yourself, I shall take time off and check that gantry to make sure all your measures comply with government regulations.'

'No need for that,' said the barman. 'I didn't see you waiting. You only had to ask.'

'And a fat lot of good that would have done me,' said Hamish. 'Lift the flap, put these on my bill, and shut up.'

He carried the drinks back to Priscilla.

'I've a feeling we should leave,' she said.

'Oh, let's stick it out,' said Hamish. 'Cheers. What's on the menu?'

'Very little, especially when you consider the enormous size of the thing. I'll read it out. First course is a choice of Rabbie Burns Broth, Mary, Queen of Scots Sizzling Scallops, and the Laughing Trout's Pheasant Pâté.'

'I'll try the broth.'

'So will I. Next comes Truite à la Flora Macdonald, Poulet Écossais, and Gaelic Steak. What on earth is a Gaelic Steak?'

'A herring.'

'Seriously.'

'I havenae the faintest idea.'

'The menu,' said Priscilla, 'has been approved by The Wee Touch O' Scotia Society. Never heard of them.'

A pallid-faced waiter drifted up to them. 'Are yiz ready?' he said.

'What's a Gaelic steak?' asked Hamish.

'It's fillet steak flambéed in whisky.'

Hamish looked across at Priscilla, who nodded. 'Well done,' she said. 'Mine'll be the same,' said Hamish, 'and we'll have two broths to start. Where's the wine list?'

'Back o' the menu,' said the waiter.

Hamish turned over the menu. All the wines were from a place called the Clachan Winery. 'Have you not got any French wine?' asked Hamish.

'No,' said the waiter. ' 'S all Sco'ish.'

'You from Glasgow?'

'Aye, ah'm working in ma holidays. Ah'm at the Polytechnic.'

327

'Well, here goes. We'll try a bottle of the fine fruity burgundy of Cromarty.'

' 'S your funeral,' said the waiter, taking the menus and slouching off.

He poked his head back round the door a moment later to summon them to a dining room that smelled overwhelmingly of new paint. Various diners were sitting about talking about fishing in high, strangulated voices.

A grey mess of soup was put in front of each of them along with two half rolls.

'To take my mind off this,' said Hamish, 'how's Vera Forbes-Grant?'

'She came back just before I left and Mummy was looking after her. She's awfully proud of Freddy. She even was prepared to see the press, but Henry . . . Henry thought it would be best if he saw them alone.'

'Chust so,' said Hamish, bending over his soup.

Priscilla flushed. 'It's not as if Henry's *hogging* the press, it's just he thought Vera might say something she shouldn't and that wouldn't help Freddy at his trial.'

'When are you thinking of getting married?'

'I don't know,' said Priscilla miserably. 'I suppose Mummy'll organize all that.'

'Are yiz finished?' asked the waiter at Hamish's elbow.

'Aye,' sighed Hamish, 'you can take mine away.'

'And mine,' said Priscilla.

'Who's going to be the first to taste the wine?' said Hamish.

'I notice he didn't have the courage to let you try it first,' said Priscilla. 'Let's both drink at the same time. A toast! No more murder.'

'No more murder,' echoed Hamish, raising his glass.

Priscilla took a sip and wrinkled her nose. 'Tastes a bit like turpentine.'

'I hope the steak's all right. You can't do much to ruin a fillet steak. I'm surprised you like yours well done as well. I thought everyone ate them rare these days.'

'Not any more.'

The waiter placed two plates of steak and vegetables down in front of them.

'Considering the prices they charge,' said Hamish, 'you would think they'd put the vegetables on separate dishes.'

Priscilla sank her knife into her steak. Blood gushed out on to the plate.

'Here, laddie!' called Hamish. The waiter slouched up.

'We said well done,' protested Hamish. 'These are raw.'

'Aye, weel, that's the way a Gaelic steak's cooked.'

'And what way is that supposed to be?'

The waiter drew himself up to his full height of five feet four inches, puffed out his chest, and declaimed, 'It is put in the pan and the whisky is poured over it and then it is flambéed.'

'But it's supposed to be cooked a bit before you set it on fire,' complained Hamish. 'Take it away and cook it properly.'

'But you ordered a Gaelic steak and that's what you got,' said the waiter.

'There is no such thing as a Gaelic steak,' said

Hamish, exasperated. 'It is a figment o' your overheated brain.'

Hamish picked up both plates and stalked off to the kitchen.

'Won't do him any good,' said the waiter gloomily.

The barman, the cook, the receptionist, the bookkeeper, and a maid were all sitting round a table in the kitchen eating fish and chips. They all shared a startling family likeness.

Hamish took one look at their pinched cockney faces and headed for the stove. 'Don't ask me what I'm doing,' he said, over his shoulder, 'for if I hear one more word about Gaelic steaks, I might forget myself and tell ye what to do with them.'

'He's the police,' said the barman gloomily. They all stared stolidly as Hamish melted butter in a pan and proceeded to fry the steaks.

'Just go on eating as if he wasn't here,' said the barman.

'What's this?' demanded Hamish suddenly, looking at a rack of good French claret.

'We keep that for special customers,' said the cook.

Hamish finished frying the steaks in grim silence. He put them back on the plates, tucked a bottle of claret under his arm, and made his way back to the dining room.

'I would hae been better to have cooked you a meal back at the police station,' he said to Priscilla. 'It makes me sick the way the Scottish Tourist Board moans on and on about the decline o' tourists. If they checked up on places like this, they might get them to come back.'

'Never mind, Hamish. It tastes lovely now and you've got us some decent wine.'

'I was silly to bring you here,' said Hamish. 'We could have gone to the Lochdubh Hotel. The only reason I didn't want to go there was because your father would have heard all about it before we'd even sat down. I thought if we came here, he might not find out until tomorrow.'

'As it is, it's a wonder he hasn't phoned already,' said Priscilla. 'Mrs Wellington will surely have told him by now.'

'But not where we've gone,' pointed out Hamish.

The other guests had left. They were alone in the dining room.

'Who do you think murdered Bartlett?' asked Hamish after a brief silence. 'You must have thought about it.'

'I didn't really. I was pretty sure it must have been someone from outside. I know Mummy's guests are pretty obnoxious, but . . .'

'Yes, why are they obnoxious? I mean, why ask those particular people?'

'A lot of people were pressing for invitations to meet Henry. Mummy just chose the first and most pressing requests. We owed the Helmsdales and Sir Humphrey hospitality. Pruney's all right. Mummy thought, for some hare-brained reason, that Diana and Jessica were friends of mine. Jeremy had already been invited anyway. It just happened, that's all.'

'What were the Helmsdales like when you stayed with them?'

'I never really thought about it. Their place is comfortable, the food is appalling, and the guests usually entertain themselves. We stayed there for a week last October. I travelled up from London. I've known both of them since I was a child. Lady Helmsdale is always so massive and booming that one never thinks of her as a woman with normal jealousies and weaknesses and that sort of thing. Helmsdale himself is a caricature of the Scottish landed aristocracy. I don't really believe he thinks deeply on any subject.'

'Odd, when you think of it,' said Hamish. 'They, the Helmsdales, I mean, must have been in love at one time.'

'Oh, I shouldn't think so,' said Priscilla, surprised. 'One always marries someone suitable, you know, if one is like them. She was a Tarrison, you know, the big flour company, and he had a title and needed money. That's the way it's done.'

'And what about your case? You wouldn't marry someone just to please your parents?'

'It's not so strange. I mean the whole idea of having a Season is to meet the right sort of bloke.'

'But the Season's finished. You don't get presented to the Queen any more or anything like that.'

'No, the court presentations went out a long time ago. They tried to replace the ritual by having the debs curtsy to a cake at the Grosvenor House Hotel, but that began to seem pretty damned silly after a bit. But it still goes on – quieter, maybe. One's parents throw a cocktail party to tell people one's Out, and then bung one into secretarial college while one lives in squalid digs with a lot of other debs. But one still goes to Ascot, Henley, and Goodwood and all that. The pas and mas are very much in the background but they ferret out who has money and who hasn't, and who's pretending to be one of the upper set, but isn't.'

'Amazing,' said Hamish. 'Here we are, rushing towards the end of the twentieth century, and here am I, a respectable bobby who has to take you out in secret, just as if I were the footman in Victorian times.'

'It's all my fault,' said Priscilla miserably. 'I should stand up for myself. I'm all Daddy and Mummy have got and I can't bear to disappoint them.'

'By going about with someone like me? You're awf'y young, Priscilla.'

'I'm old enough to know my own mind and to know that I should not be creeping around having dinner with you at some tatty restaurant when I'm newly engaged.'

'Yes, why *did* you come out this evening?'

'I forget,' said Priscilla, tears standing out in her eyes.

'I shouldnae be grilling you,' said Hamish gently. 'It's all none o' my business, after all. Did you hear what happened to Peter Fisher, him that went down to Ullapool to see if he could defect to Russia?'

Priscilla shook her head and Hamish leaned back in his chair and proceeded to tell a long and extremely Highland story about the adventures of Peter Fisher until Priscilla began to laugh.

Then he got Priscilla to tell him some of her adventures as a fashion editor's assistant.

It was beginning to get dark outside, and suddenly Hamish became aware that they had been sitting in the deserted dining room for some time.

'I'd better get the bill,' he said regretfully. He crossed to the wall and pressed a bell.

After some time, the waiter appeared, minus his white jacket.

'Ah thocht ye'd be awa' hame tae yer beds,' he said.

'I could hardly do that without paying the bill,' said Hamish.

The waiter jerked his thumb in the direction of the kitchen. 'He says it's on the house.'

'If by "he" you mean the barman who's probably the manager as well, go and tell him from me that I know this place is owned by the Belmont Catering Company, and there is no reason to cheat them further. Get my bill.'

The waiter went off and eventually slouched back with the bill. Hamish noticed he had not been charged for the bottle of claret, but felt he could not bear any more argument. He paid the bill, and when the waiter had left, he looked sadly at Priscilla.

'In a way, this is goodbye, Priscilla,' he said. 'As you say, you will not be able to drop in at the police station when you're a married woman.'

He held out his hand, and Priscilla slipped her own into it. She looked into his eyes, wanting to tell him all her worries about Henry, about the engagement, and yet feeling it would be disloyal to Henry to discuss him with another man.

'Sorry to interrupt,' came a sarcastic voice from the dining-room door.

Hamish dropped Priscilla's hand as if it were a hot brick and turned about.

Anderson was standing in the doorway.

334

'Chalmers sent me to get you,' he said. 'There's been another murder.'

'There *can't* be,' gasped Priscilla. 'Did Freddy escape?'

'It wasn't Freddy,' said Anderson heavily. 'Mr Forbes-Grant's secure in prison in Strathbane. His wife's been murdered.'

'Vera!' cried Priscilla, hanging on to the table. 'How?'

'Poison. Someone poisoned her.'

CHAPTER TWELVE

Thou shalt not kill, but needs not strive
Officiously to keep alive.
—Arthur Clough

'This gets more like a Hammer horror movie every day,' grumbled Henry Withering.

No-one answered him. They were all huddled in the drawing room, listening to the footsteps of the police moving about upstairs in Vera's bedroom.

'How do they know it's poison?' whispered Priscilla in Henry's ear.

'Don't ask me. Suppose you've only got to look at her. The whole thing's awful. There was a body hanging in the room as well.'

'A body!' squeaked Priscilla.

'Not a real one. Someone had made a pretty lifelike dummy and even embellished it with a handlebar moustache and strung it up over Vera's bed.'

Pruney, who had been crying off and on since Priscilla's return home, started to sob again, an irritating snuffly sound.

'Let's go outside,' said Henry. 'They can fetch us for statements when they need us.'

Outside the castle, a wind was rushing through the rhododendrons that bordered the drive. A small moon sailed high above through black ragged clouds.

'I have to ask you this,' said Henry. 'I know there's been another murder, and we're all shocked and all that . . . but what the hell were you doing dining out with that copper and all dolled up in heels and a party gown?'

'I had to get away,' said Priscilla. 'You don't understand, Henry. I said I would meet Hamish for dinner because he's, well, an old friend and comfortable to be with. I knew it wasn't the thing to do and I was going to cancel the evening, but then you came out with this press-conference business, and I couldn't *bear* it. I just wanted to run away. Henry, how *can* you go on forcing me on the press, just to see a few more grainy photos of yourself and me on the front page?'

Henry sighed. 'You're very young, Priscilla,' he said, unconsciously echoing Hamish. How could she know, he wondered, about the long years of wanting to be recognized, of knowing you could write and seeing the fame go to lesser people? She treated his experiences with the Communists with tolerant amusement, as if his interest in them had been some sort of fashionable fad. But they had cared for him and they had believed in his work, thought Henry, with a sudden longing for the old days of cold rehearsals and chipped teacups in draughty halls. He was famous now, but he missed the camaraderie of the experimental theatre groups and the occasional mothering laced with unselfish love from intense young girls who were prepared to die on the barricades to change the world.

He sighed again. Sometimes it was hard to know what *was* the real world. For a moment at the crofters' fair, he had felt sure he had found his niche in life at last. He had felt he belonged. Now, it all seemed as if he had been taking part in some brightly coloured sort of *Brigadoon.*

Instead he said, 'You've got to stop running around with that copper, Priscilla. Do you want to break our engagement?'

'Yes. No. I don't know,' said Priscilla wretchedly. 'Mummy and Daddy were so pleased.'

'Do you mean to say you only got engaged to me because you thought I was suitable? You'll be wearing a crinoline next.'

'I can't explain, Henry,' said Priscilla. 'Right at this moment I don't know what I think. Who on earth killed Vera?'

'She might have done it herself.'

'It doesn't seem possible. She was actually proud of what she thought Freddy had done.'

'Meaning you don't think Freddy did it?'

'Well, Hamish doesn't.'

Henry drew a deep breath.

'Until you make up your mind to break the engagement, do me a favour and keep that man's name out of our conversation.'

'It happened quite early on in the evening,' Chalmers was saying to Hamish at that moment as they both stood in Vera's bedroom. The body had been taken off to Strathbane.

'It seems she went up to her room about seven and started screaming the place down. Everyone

338

rushed up. Vera was gabbling and pointing at that dummy strung up over the bed. She rounded on the others and accused them all of playing a nasty trick, ordered them out, and locked herself in. About eight o'clock, that Diana went up to her room and passed Vera's on the way. She said she heard scrabblings and choking noises. Asked why she didn't call for help, she said she just thought Vera was carrying on to get attention.

'The guests and the Halburton-Smythes are now convinced she took her own life. I can't look at it that way. I think we've got the wrong man in prison in Strathbane, and that someone else killed Bartlett and then killed Vera because she knew something.'

'Maybe she did,' said Hamish. 'She liked money. Maybe she was blackmailing the murderer. What was she eating or drinking?'

'Tea and cakes. There was nothing left on the cake plate but crumbs, and those and the dregs from the teapot have been taken away for analysis.'

'She had a terrible sweet tooth,' said Hamish. 'If anyone wanted to poison some cakes – well, we were all down in the school kitchens baking like mad and passing round bowls of stuff to be beaten and putting trays in the ovens.'

'We'd better get down there and have a look and hope they've left the cleaning up until the morning.'

Hamish and Chalmers hurried out to the police cars. Henry was just coming in with Priscilla. He had an arm about her waist. Priscilla avoided looking at Hamish.

The headmistress of the primary school refused to open her door, claiming they were only masquerading as policemen and she had read about thugs like them.

'It's me, Mrs Mackenzie,' called Hamish. 'Macbeth! Take a look through the letter-box.'

The letter-box was cautiously poked open. Chalmers flicked a lighter under Hamish's face.

There was a squeak of alarm and the metal flap of the letter-box dropped. 'Hamish Macbeth,' came Mrs Mackenzie's shaky voice, 'does not own a dinner jacket.'

'Mrs Wellington's got a spare key,' said Hamish. 'We'll try the manse.'

Mrs Wellington was wearing a voluminous flannel nightgown when she answered the door. Hamish was glad Mr Wellington had found God, because it certainly looked as if he would need to wait until he got to heaven to get his reward. She went back in and emerged wrapped in a large tweed coat, produced the key, and insisted on accompanying them.

One look at the school kitchen was enough to tell both Chalmers and Hamish that they would be lucky if they found one fingerprint. Tables were scrubbed and counters were shining.

Hamish fished in the pocket of Uncle Harry's dinner jacket and took out his notebook, glad he had transferred it into the pocket with his other bits and pieces before he went out for dinner.

He licked the end of his pencil and then began to write in meticulous shorthand as Chalmers asked Mrs Wellington to remember where everyone was standing and what they were doing.

But Mrs Wellington was one of those bossy women to whom the very rapping out of orders is an end in itself. She had barked at people to do various things and then had moved on to bully someone else without waiting to see whether her orders were carried out or not.

Nonetheless, Chalmers persisted with his questions as the night wore on and a rising wind soughed about the schoolhouse with a lost, wailing sound.

When Chalmers had at last finished, Hamish asked, 'Do you mind if we see the cupboards where you keep your cleaning materials and things like that?'

'I am very tired,' said Mrs Wellington, 'and I see no reason . . . oh, very well. They're over here, underneath the sinks.'

Mindful of Uncle Harry's trousers, Hamish took out a clean handkerchief, spread it on the floor, knelt down and poked his red head into the cupboards. Then he suddenly stiffened and appeared to point like a dog.

He eased the handkerchief out from under his knees and draped it over one hand. He reached into the cupboard and brought out a cylindrical cardboard container with the label Buggo. He read the list of ingredients carefully and then opened the lid.

'Empty,' he said. 'This is roach powder. I haff never heard of the cockroaches being in Lochdubh.'

'It was that American lady, Mrs Fitzgerald, who left it,' said Mrs Wellington. 'You remember her, Mr Macbeth, the one who turned up at the Lochdubh Hotel for her holidays two years ago with a suitcaseful of mosquito repellent, disinfectant, flea powder, ant spray – the works. She gave that roach powder to Mrs Mackenzie for the school kitchen.'

'And did she use it?' asked Hamish, sitting back on his heels.

'I don't know. Ask her.'

'You'd better come along with us. She thinks we're muggers pretending to be policemen.'

'What are you getting at?' said Chalmers.

'Mrs Forbes-Grant loved cakes,' said Hamish. 'Everyone knew that. She was eating all she could in the kitchen this morning. Someone may have made a special batch of cakes, just for her, and put something like this roach powder in them. This powder contains, or did contain when the box was full, sodium fluoride. There were cake crumbs found in her room.'

'We'd better get a box and take everything,' said Chalmers heavily, 'disinfectants, cleaners, the lot.'

Mrs Wellington persuaded Mrs Mackenzie to open her door. Mrs Mackenzie blinked at the packet of roach powder.

'I mind that American lady giving it to me,' she said. 'I didnae like to disappoint her by saying we didn't have any roaches. I just put it under the sink with the other stuff.'

'And you never used it?' asked Chalmers.

'No. I did not have any reason to.'

Carrying the box with the contents of the school-kitchen cupboards, Chalmers and Macbeth made their way back to their cars.

'That murderer must be laughing at us,' said Chalmers bitterly. 'Not content with poisoning

Vera Forbes-Grant, he, or she, put that grisly dummy up above the bed first.'

'Och, no, that was done for different reasons.'

'Who did it?'

'I should think that terrible pair, Jessica and Diana. It's funny, when I first saw them I thought they were a typical couple of country girls. Now I think they're silly and vicious. I'm sure they strung up that dummy.'

'Why? the woman had just seen her husband accused of murder.'

'Because Vera had an affair with Bartlett, and they're still jealous of her. Because Vera probably milked the last little bit o' drama out of our accusing her husband.

'Or maybe you'll find we were meant to discover it was them who played the dirty trick on her. That way, we might not suspect them of the murder.'

Priscilla Halburton-Smythe thought the night would never end. One by one they were called into the colonel's study to make their statements, and each person seemed to be gone an hour. By the time it was Priscilla's turn, she was too exhausted to think clearly. She felt she was living in a nightmare where she was doomed to sit in this study, making statements to the police over and over again. Hamish, still in evening dress, was sitting over by the window. He looked elegant and remote. She wished he were wearing his usual scruffy old clothes or worn uniform. He did not look like the Hamish she knew.

At last she was dismissed. Henry was waiting for her at the foot of the stairs.

'How did it go?' he asked sympathetically.

'As usual,' said Priscilla bitterly. 'I'm an old hand at making statements.'

'Well, I've made mine, and dawn is breaking. Let's go to bed.'

Priscilla looked at him warily. 'Look, darling,' he said, 'surely this is not the night to play the prude.'

'Henry, the last thing on my mind at this moment is sex. I don't believe for a moment that Freddy shot Peter. I think the murderer is one of us – or the murderess. The only thing I'm taking to bed tonight is a hot-water bottle.'

'Very well,' he said coldly. 'But it's beginning to appear to me as if there's every possibility of this rubbish going on after marriage. You may be lousy in bed for all I know. In a way, you're asking me to buy the goods before I see them.'

Priscilla clutched hold of the banister. 'Perhaps you're right,' she said wearily. 'But I am still going to my room alone and I am locking the door behind me.' She turned and went up the stairs.

'I suppose if that village bobby comes knocking, you'll open your door, and your legs, soon enough,' he shouted after her.

Priscilla put her head down and ran up the remaining stairs. She collided with the solid bulk of Lady Helmsdale.

'What were you doing in my room?' cried Priscilla.

'I was looking for an aspirin,' said Lady Helmsdale.

Although Priscilla was tall, Lady Helmsdale seemed to loom over her in the darkness of the corridor.

Lady Helmsdale had pale eyes and they were fixed on Priscilla's face in an unnerving stare.

Fear gripped Priscilla. She realized she had never really known Lady Helmsdale. In fact, what did she know of any of the guests, even Henry?

She gave a choked sob, pushed past Lady Helmsdale into her room, and slammed and locked the door.

But although she undressed, got into bed and clutched the hot-water bottle, she could not seem to get warm.

A timid knock at the door made her heart leap into her mouth.

'Who is it?' she called.

'It is I – Pruney.'

'Pruney, I'm exhausted. Is it very important?'

'Yes.'

Priscilla sighed. She climbed out of bed and opened the door.

Pruney stood blinking at her behind her enormous glasses.

'I've got to talk to someone,' she whispered.

'Come in,' said Priscilla. 'I'm too cold to sleep anyway.' She left the door unlocked, hoping Pruney only intended to stay a couple of minutes.

She sat down on the edge of the bed and Pruney sat next to her, twisting a handkerchief in her nervous fingers.

'What is it?' asked Priscilla gently.

'He loved *me*.'

'Who?'

'Captain Bartlett. He loved me,' said Pruney, striking her bosom, which was covered by the embroidered yoke of her old-fashioned nightgown.

'Did he actually say so?' asked Priscilla.

'Not in so many words, but his *actions* . . . He was so kind to me at that party, and . . . and . . . later when I went upstairs, I saw him. He said he was going to talk to Vera. I said, "Won't Freddy object to that?" He laughed and said, "Freddy won't know. I just rap once on the door and walk quickly away. She knows that's the signal to come to my room." '

'But didn't that tell you that Peter was a philanderer?' said Priscilla awkwardly.

'No, no,' said Pruney eagerly. 'He *explained*. He said, "You must think me an awful flirt, but those days are over. I just have to see her on a matter of business. I'm thinking of mending my ways and settling down." And then he raised my hand to his lips and he kissed it,' said Pruney, holding her right hand against her cheek. 'I looked into his eyes and saw a decent love and concern there, and knew I had been instrumental in making him decide to reform. I have had to listen to rubbish from Jessica and Diana, implying they both had affairs with him. It cannot be true. He wouldn't look at *them*. And Vera! That gross, horrible woman. She has a husband . . .'

'Had,' said Priscilla. 'Vera's dead. Remember?'

'And good riddance,' said Pruney with sudden venom. 'She was probably bumped off by one of the servants. She's the sort of woman who has affairs with servants and milkmen and people of that class. Vera was a murderee.'

She clutched Priscilla's arm in a powerful grip. 'Peter loved *me*,' she cried. 'You do believe me, don't you? Someone has *got* to believe me.'

'Is everything all right, Miss Halburton-Smythe?' came a cool voice from the doorway.

Pruney gasped and jumped to her feet.

Hamish Macbeth stood on the threshold.

'I'm just going,' she squeaked, and scurried out past him.

Hamish came in and closed the door.

'What was all that about?' he asked.

'Oh, Peter couldn't leave anything in a skirt alone. He kissed her hand and made poor Pruney think he'd fallen for her. Why are you here?'

Hamish sat down on the bed, and then yawned and lay down and stretched out. 'I'm going away,' he said. 'I chust wanted to make sure you were all right. I had a feeling you'd still be awake.'

'Henry might have been in here.'

'So he might,' said Hamish equably. 'But it wasn't Henry's voice I heard.'

'Where are you going?' said Priscilla, lying down beside him and clasping her hands behind her head.

'Chalmers has decided to try a long shot. He's got the address of that aunt of Bartlett's in London and wants me to go and see her.'

'But the police down there could do that, surely?'

'Aye, but he thinks my famous charm might unearth something. We're getting no farther with the case up here, and things are verra serious. Now, Bartlett got engaged to Diana in London, he ditched Jessica in London. There might be something there, or, failing that, this aunt might know of a further connection between Bartlett and the rest of the guests.'

'How long will you be away?'

'I'm going down on the night train. I cannae get

a sleeper in the second class and the police don't run to first-class fares. I'll spend the day in London and then come straight back up.'

'I wish you weren't going,' said Priscilla in a small voice. 'I'm beginning to be frightened of everyone, except Mummy and Daddy, and they never were the sort of parents one could talk to, you know. Earlier this evening, Mummy said with tears in her eyes that the only good thing in this whole mess was my engagement to Henry.'

'Well, that is something,' said Hamish, staring at the ceiling.

'But it's all going wrong, Hamish,' wailed Priscilla. 'I think I'm frigid!'

Hamish slid a comforting arm about her shoulders. 'Now, now,' he said, 'I am thinking that a couple o' murders are enough to freeze anyone.'

Priscilla responded with a choked sob. She buried her head on his chest and began to cry.

'There, now,' said Hamish, pulling her into his arms and stroking her hair. 'Once these murders are solved, you'll be able to see things a bit more clearly.'

Hamish had a sudden pang of sympathy for Henry. Priscilla was wearing a short scanty nightdress and was pressing against him for comfort. He realized she had absolutely no idea of the effect she was having on him.

He grimly tried to keep his thoughts on something else as he rocked her like a child and murmured soothing nonsense in her ear.

'I might have guessed,' said Henry Withering, walking into the room and glaring at the couple on the bed. 'Give me back my ring, Priscilla.'

Priscilla started to say something, but Hamish tightened his grip and looked blandly at Henry. Priscilla took off her ring. Hamish took it from her and held it out to Henry, who walked up to the bed and snatched it.

'You'd better think up something to tell your father in the morning,' said Henry, 'because he's going to hear all about this.'

Priscilla struggled free from Hamish's embrace. 'Henry!' she called desperately. But the slamming of the door was the only answer.

'Now, don't start crying again,' said Hamish. 'You wanted out of that engagement. Didn't you?'

Priscilla hung her head. 'But Daddy's going to be furious.'

Hamish swung his long legs off the bed. 'If you don't start thinking for yourself,' he said, 'you're going to end up in another mess. I'm sick to death of hearing what Daddy and Mummy would think. You're a nice girl, Priscilla, but they've kept you ower young for your own good. Take my advice and go and wake your father and give him your version. And make sure you put it plainly enough. Henry had every reason to think the worst. What a frustrated man he must be! You're enough to try the patience of a saint. I am your old friend Hamish. But a village copper has feelings – and eyes – and you're parading about with practically nothing on.'

Priscilla snatched up her dressing gown and wrapped it around her. 'I'm sorry, Hamish,' she mumbled.

'Aye, well, God knows you're safe enough with me. Chust make sure you cover up when there's anyone else around. I'll be back from London as fast as I can. In the meantime, don't trust anyone. If you're that worried, you might try talking to your mother or father as adult to adult and not like a child.'

'Stop patronizing me, Hamish,' said Priscilla.

'You get back from the world the way you treat the world. You treat me like a big brother. What else do you expect?'

'I expect a little sympathy and understanding. You're as bad as Henry.'

'Poor Henry. There are times when I think you need a good slap on the bum to bring you to your senses.'

'Oh, get out,' said Priscilla wearily, 'and take your so-called charm with you.'

CHAPTER THIRTEEN

But, Sir, let me tell you, the noblest prospect which
a Scotchman ever sees, is the high road that leads
him to England!
—SAMUEL JOHNSON

The crowded train from Inverness to London gave
Hamish ample time to reflect on the stoicism of
the British. As they chugged their way through the
Grampians, the air-conditioning was blasting into
the carriage. People rose and put on their coats and
sat down again.

Hamish complained to the guard.

'You're the only person that's complaining,' said
the guard sourly. 'If I were you, I'd gang doon the
train and find a compartment with the heat on.'

'But there's ground frost tonight,' said Hamish
plaintively. 'Why is the air-conditioning on?'

'Fur the American tourists.'

'Oh, the Americans, is it?' said Hamish. 'And
here's me thinking you maybe had the Laplanders
or the Eskimos on board.'

'It's folk like you that make British Rail a
failure,' said the guard obscurely, moving away.

Hamish sighed and took down his overnight bag

and made his way along the train. He was glad he was not in uniform. The last time he had worn his uniform on the London train, the passengers had treated him like a walking tourist office.

What on earth *did* the American tourists make of all this? thought Hamish, as he eventually settled into a vacant seat farther down the train. No buffet car and eleven hours to make the journey to London.

'Hullo!' piped a small voice.

Hamish looked up.

A boy with a pinched white face was sitting opposite him, clutching a comic. Hamish looked about and then looked back at the child.

'Are you travelling on your own?' he asked.

'Naw, I'm with them,' said the boy, jerking his thumb across the aisle where four men were drinking beer and playing poker.

'Which of them's your dad?'

'None of them,' said the boy.

'Uncle, then?'

'Don't know 'em from Adam.'

Hamish surveyed the white little face and the knowing eyes of the child.

'What's your name?'

'Wee Alec. Alec MacQueen.'

'Well, Alec, what are you doing travelling on this train with four men you don't know?'

'It's my maw's idea,' said Alec. 'Man, I'm fair sick of the trains.'

'Oh, they're friends of your mother?'

'Naw.' Alec put his pointed elbows on the table between them and leaned forward. 'It's like this. If you've got a Family Rail card and you take a child

352

along, you get a third knocked off the price o' the fare. Disnae need to be your own child. Anyone's child'll do. So my maw tells one who tells the other that if anyone wants to borrow me, they can. She charges five pounds a head for my services,' said Alec proudly. 'Then when we get to London, they turn me over to some other blokes who are coming back up. Then I pick up another lot at Inverness and come back down, so's I can go back up with them ones what I came down with.'

'Are you on your school holidays?'

'Aye, but it disnae matter one way or the other. If she's got a good fare, my maw takes me off the school.'

'And do you like it?'

'Naw, I hate it,' said Alec. 'I want to be in the school with my friends.'

Hamish looked wildly round the compartment. There were a lot of children on the train. Were they all for hire?

'Would you like me to do something to stop it?' he asked.

'I would like that fine,' said Alec. 'But I don't want my maw to get in trouble with the police.'

Hamish opened his mouth to say he was a policeman, and then thought the better of it.

Nobody seemed to care about education these days. He couldn't remember the last time he had seen a truant officer. He could call on Alec's mother or report her to the Royal Society for the Prevention of Cruelty to Children, but they were surely overloaded with more dramatic cases of child cruelty.

He chatted idly to Alec until the child fell asleep,

his narrow head and greasy, lank hair rolling with the motion of the train.

When they arrived in Edinburgh, Hamish left the train and went in search of a phone. He put through a reverse-charge call to Rory Grant on the *Daily Chronicle*, forgetting it was the middle of the night. But he was in luck. Rory was on night shift.

'What do you want, you great Highland berk?' came Rory's voice over the crackling of a bad line.

'I have often wondered how this word "berk" came about,' said Hamish.

'It's rhyming slang. Berkeley Hunt.'

'Tut, tut, that's no' very nice,' said Hamish, shocked.

'Did you put through this expensive long-distance call just to ask me the meaning of rude words?'

'No, I have a wee story for you.'

Hamish told him about Alec, and then finished by saying, 'I would like to do something to help the boy. He is a kind of Scottish Flying Dutchman, if you take my meaning.'

'It's a nice human-interest one. Whether they'll send me to meet the train is another thing. I'm out of favour these days. Didn't even get sent up on that murder of yours – or murders, I gather, from the stuff coming over on the tapes. But I tell you what I'll do. I'll phone the story round for you – there's that big Scottish Sunday's got an office in London – and in return I want you to fill me in on some background on the murders.'

'I will do my best,' said Hamish. 'I have an appointment later in the morning. If you can

354

meet the train, maybe we can have breakfast somewhere.'

'I'll try. If not, phone me at home during the day.'

Hamish ran back to the train and found his seat had been taken by a hot and cross-looking woman. Alec was still asleep. Once more, Hamish collected his overnight bag and went in search of a free seat.

The only one to be found was back in the freezing compartment. With a sigh of resignation, he pulled another sweater out of his bag, put it on, and settled down and tried to sleep.

Somewhere after Carlisle, the air-conditioning went off and the heating came on. He arrived in London eyes gritty with sleep and sweating profusely.

As he got off the train, he looked along the platform and smiled in satisfaction. Rory had done his work well. There were five reporters and three photographers clustered around Wee Alec, who was proudly holding forth, although there was no sign of Rory.

Hamish went to the Gents and changed into a clean shirt, shaved with an electric razor, parked his bag in a station locker, and went in search of breakfast.

At ten o'clock, he took the District Line to Chelsea and walked along the Kings Road to Flood Street, where Captain Bartlett's aunt, a Mrs Frobisher, had a house.

The air felt very warm, and a brassy sun was shining through a thin haze of cloud.

Chalmers had promised to phone and warn Mrs Frobisher of his arrival.

The door to Mrs Frobisher's home was opened by a dumpy, suet-faced girl dressed in a black off-the-shoulder T-shirt, black ballet tights, and scuffed shoes.

'Good morning,' said Hamish politely. 'I am Police Constable Hamish Macbeth of Lochdubh, and I am here to speak to Mrs Frobisher.'

'Get lost, pig,' said the girl. The door began to close.

Hamish put his foot in it. 'Now, what is a beautiful creature like yourself doing using such ugly words?' he marvelled.

'She don't want to see you.'

'Miranda!' interrupted a sharp voice. 'Who is it?'

'It's that copper you don't want to see,' the girl roared over her shoulder.

A door in the hallway opened behind her and an elderly lady emerged, leaning on a cane. Her hair was white, and her face criss-crossed with wrinkles.

She peered around Miranda's bulk. 'You don't look like a policeman,' she said doubtfully. 'I received a call from Scotland, saying an officer would call on me and I told whoever it was that I had no wish to see the police again.'

'I can well understand that,' said Hamish. 'I'll try not to take up too much of your time.'

'You seem harmless enough,' said Mrs Frobisher. 'Come in. Bring us some coffee, Miranda.'

The girl sulked off, crashing her fat shoulders off either wall of a narrow passage at the back of the hall.

'Your daughter?' asked Hamish politely.

'Good heavens, no,' said Mrs Frobisher, leading

356

the way into a small sitting room on the ground floor. 'I am much too old to have a daughter of Miranda's age. Miranda is my maid. I got her from an agency. They send me very strange girls. But then, I don't suppose anyone in their right mind wants to be a maid these days. Now, what on earth do you want? I've talked and talked to policemen about Peter. I don't think I can add any more.'

'There's been another development,' said Hamish, and told her about the murder of Vera.

'Gosh,' said Mrs Frobisher, sitting down abruptly. 'What a frightful thing to happen. Are you sure it wasn't suicide? I always thought that woman was unstable.'

'I think she was killed by someone baking cakes for her with roach powder,' said Hamish. 'It's too nasty and complicated a death for suicide.'

'I met her once,' said Mrs Frobisher. 'Peter brought her here. A greedy woman. Greedy for sex, greedy for money. But I think I know who it is who has been committing these murders. It must be Diana Bryce.'

'And why is that?'

Miranda clumped in with a tray with a pot of coffee and cups, thumped it down, and banged her way out.

'I wasn't sure when I heard about the shooting. But poison! I could well see Diana doing that. She threw every kind of fit when Peter broke off the engagement. She followed him to a night-club and made the most awful scene. He told me about it. The poor boy was worried, I could see that.'

'You were fond of your nephew,' said Hamish gently.

357

Mrs Frobisher's old wrinkled face crumpled like a baby's, and for a moment Hamish thought she was going to cry. But she eased herself to her feet and poured two cups of coffee.

'Yes, very fond,' she said. 'He was not always so wild, so irrational. He was quite bright at Sandhurst, and seemed set for a good military career. He was always taking up hobbies and then dropping them. I always told him he was turning my home into a graveyard for his abandoned hobbies. There's his stamp collection, his model airplanes, his computer, his wood carvings, his . . . oh, so many things.'

'I would like to see them, if I may,' said Hamish.

'His parents died when he was still at school,' said Mrs Frobisher, her eyes staring past Hamish to days of long ago. 'I took care of him. I don't have any children of my own. But after he left Sandhurst, I couldn't really have him staying here. I'm too old-fashioned and he always brought girls home.'

'Jessica Villiers?'

'No, he hasn't stayed here since he was a young man. I haven't heard of her.'

'The Helmsdales? Did he talk of them?'

She shook her head.

Patiently, he took her through the names of all the members of the house party. Diana Bryce and Vera were the only names familiar to her.

Hamish then led the conversation off on to more general subjects, hoping that when he guided her back to Peter Bartlett, she might remember something to give him just one clue.

She became animated as she talked, and he guessed she was lonely. She asked him to stay to lunch, much to Miranda's obvious fury.

They were just finishing a miserable little lunch of cold quiche and limp salad when Mrs Frobisher suddenly said, 'I've just remembered. You mentioned the name of Throgmorton. Sir Humphrey Throgmorton?'

Hamish nodded.

'I've just remembered something about him. He hurt Peter's feelings very much. Peter called around to his home. Tea, I think it was. Wait a bit. It's coming back to me. Well, poor Peter broke a cup and saucer by accident, and not only did this Sir Humphrey throw a terrible scene, but he wrote to Peter's colonel-in-chief and complained. The colonel never liked Peter and this was jam to him. Peter said the old man used it as an excuse to give him the dressing down of a lifetime. Peter said Sir Humphrey was a closet homosexual and as vengeful as sin. Can you imagine anyone making such a fuss over some old china?'

'No,' said Hamish, although he privately thought that any collector would see red, given the same set of circumstances.

Mrs Frobisher looked at him almost shyly. 'I have two tickets to *Duchess Darling* – for the matinée this afternoon. I did not feel like asking someone to go with me because of Peter's death. But if you have the time . . . ?'

Hamish groaned inwardly. Seeing Henry's play would remind him of Henry and that would lead to thoughts of Priscilla. He had been able to put her out of his mind while he concentrated on the case, and he did not want thoughts of her to muddle up his brain.

But the longer he spent with Mrs Frobisher, the more chance there was of her remembering more.

'I would be delighted to go,' he said. 'May I telephone someone first?'

'Of course. There's a phone over on that desk by the window. I'll go and change while you make your call.'

Hamish phoned Rory Grant at home and listened patiently while the reporter grumbled about being woken up.

'When do you start work?' asked Hamish, when he could get a word in.

'Seven o'clock this evening.'

'I might go round to the office with you. I want to look at some of the library cuttings.'

'Oh, you do, do you? They aren't cuttings any more. Everything's on computer. What's in it for me?'

'Background on these murders.'

'OK. Do you want to come to the office, or call round here first?'

'I don't know how I'll be placed for time. If I haven't turned up at your place by six, I'll meet you at the office.'

Hamish found it hard to concentrate on the play. He was gloomily sure that Henry had somehow managed to persuade Priscilla to become re-engaged. He decided at the end of the play to go back with Mrs Frobisher and see if he could winkle any further information out of her.

The old lady was tired and leaned heavily on her cane, but there was a faint flush on her old cheeks. She had obviously enjoyed the outing.

When they got to Flood Street, Hamish said tentatively, 'I won't keep you much longer, Mrs Frobisher. I have another call to make. Could I just see some of Captain Bartlett's things?'

'I have them all in a room upstairs. The police have been through them already, of course.'

She led the way upstairs and pushed open a bedroom door. The room was, as Mrs Frobisher had said, a graveyard of hobbies. The model airplanes swung from the ceiling, a collection of rocks and fossils lay on a table, albums of stamps were piled on a chair.

'What's this?' asked Hamish, crossing the room to a little china cabinet in the corner. It contained several dainty porcelain figurines. 'Was this one of his hobbies?'

'Yes, he started collecting bits of china from the salerooms after he had been to Sir Humphrey's. Funny I should have forgotten all about Sir Humphrey until today. Peter had a sort of magpie mind. His hobbies were all other people's enthusiasms. He would take something up for a bit, throw himself into it, then he would get bored and cart the lot around to me for safekeeping.'

'Isn't it a wee bit odd,' said Hamish, studying the pieces of china, 'to think that the captain would become a collector of porcelain and yet everyone seems to think he deliberately broke a rare cup and saucer?'

'If he *did* do it deliberately,' said Mrs Frobisher loyally. 'But it's hard to explain. I do not think he had the soul of a collector, unless you call collecting other people's hobbies collecting. The china phase did not last long. What's that you've got?' she said, seeing Hamish had a ragged bunch of manuscript in his hand.

'Seem to be regimental reminiscences,' said Hamish. 'Another of his enthusiasms?'

'I suppose so,' said Mrs Frobisher. 'He scribbled from time to time.'

'Is that a fact?' said Hamish slowly. He carefully went through the room, checking any papers, reading letters, until he heard Mrs Frobisher stifle a yawn.

'I'd better be on my way,' said Hamish. He thanked her for lunch and the theatre outing and took his leave, promising to visit her the next time he was in London.

He walked back to Sloane Square and took the District Line to Blackfriars and walked along to Fleet Street. He stood for a moment at the corner of Ludgate Circus and looked up towards the great bulk of St Paul's Cathedral.

Images of the different people connected with the murder whirled around and around in his brain, facts jostled against facts, and then the kaleidoscope of bits and pieces slowly stopped revolving and settled down into a pattern.

But he had to be sure.

He set off for the *Daily Chronicle* offices ·at a run.

'You been drinking?' asked Rory impatiently, as he led Hamish upstairs to the reporters' desk. For Hamish was walking like a blind man, bumping into walls, his eyes fixed in an odd inward-looking stare.

'No,' said Hamish slowly. 'Look, I haff to make a call.'

'And if the night news editor comes up, how do I explain why I am letting you use the phone?'

'Tell him it is because I know who murdered Bartlett and Vera Forbes-Grant, and I can take you with me to be in at the kill.'

'You're sure?'

Hamish rubbed the damp palms of his hands against his trousers.

'Very sure. I need one more bit of proof, and it's a long shot.'

'Go ahead and phone, and if the news editor says OK, I'll book us both on a flight.'

Hamish phoned Tommel Castle and told Jenkins to fetch Mr Chalmers.

The superintendent came on the line. 'You were right about the roach powder,' he said. 'But we're no further with solving the case.'

'This is who did it,' said Hamish.

Chalmers listened in growing amazement. 'But that's guesswork!' he exclaimed. 'Proof, laddie. Where's the proof? It's only in books that the criminal breaks down and confesses.'

'I want the name of every journalist who was there just after the first murder and who did not stay on,' said Hamish. 'I'm at the offices of the *Daily Chronicle* at the reporters' desk. I'll wait for your call.'

'You think one of *them* was an accomplice?'

'An unwitting one,' said Hamish. 'I'm making a wild guess that our criminal handed one of them a package to either keep until called for, or to take to a certain address.'

'But no journalist would be naive enough to do that?'

'Oh yes, they would, if it meant getting a bit of background and the person seemed innocent enough.'

'I've a funny feeling you're out on a limb there, Macbeth. But stay where you are until I call. It might take all night, and if it's a London journalist you're after, then I'll need to ask the Yard for help.'

Rory came back looking excited. 'By God, Hamish,' he cried, 'if you can pull this one off, I'll be able to get drunk for a fortnight. What do we do now?'

'We wait,' said Hamish.

'And pray.'

CHAPTER FOURTEEN

Methought I heard a voice cry, 'Sleep no more!
Macbeth does murder sleep.'
—SHAKESPEARE

Summer lay dying outside Tommel Castle. A chill wind blew across the moors and rattled the windows and sent puffs of smoke from the fire belching out into the drawing room.

They were all gathered for afternoon tea, even Freddy Forbes-Grant, who had been released from prison. He had stoutly maintained he had confessed to the murder only because he thought his wife had committed it. There was not enough hard evidence to hold him. Blair swore the gloves had not been in Freddy's room when it was first searched, and Anderson and MacNab backed him up. Freddy's moustache drooped, and he looked thoroughly miserable. Mary Halburton-Smythe poured tea with a steady hand and tried not to think it would have been more decent of Freddy to have mourned in his room instead of crawling about downstairs like the skeleton at the feast.

Priscilla felt the nightmare would never end. Henry had apologized. He had said his jealousy had got the better of him and he should have realized Hamish had only a brotherly interest in her. Colonel Halburton-Smythe had taken him aside and explained everything. So much for the adult talk with her father, thought Priscilla bitterly. She was once more wearing her engagement ring. How Hamish would despise her! She felt trapped, and yet did not feel she could summon up enough courage to deal with Henry until the shadow of murder had lifted. It would be easier to cope with him in London where everything was lighter and more fickle.

The guests had been told they could leave for their respective homes on the following day, provided they did not travel anywhere else or leave the country.

'Cake?' said Mrs Halburton-Smythe brightly, holding out a plate of sliced seed cake to Pruney.

Pruney turned pale and shook her head. Everyone was drinking tea with cautious little sips, eyeing the others warily.

There came the clump of official boots and voices from the hall.

'Not again,' groaned Lady Helmsdale. 'I've made so many statements, I've given fingerprints, I've watched coppers searching my undies – I feel like shooting the lot of them.'

The door opened, and Chalmers came in. Behind him came Blair, Anderson, and MacNab, who took up positions round the room. Then came Hamish Macbeth, followed by what looked like a shorter, squatter version of himself – Rory Grant.

Priscilla wondered if Hamish was ill. A thin

sheen of sweat filmed his face, and his eyes were hard and fixed.

'Go ahead, Macbeth,' said Chalmers quietly.

Hamish knows the identity of the murderer, thought Priscilla hysterically. 'He hasn't once looked at the teapot.'

'It's been a difficult case,' said Hamish quietly. 'So many of you had reason to want Bartlett dead. But only one of you had the nerve, the lack of morals, and the sheer cunning to kill not only Bartlett but Mrs Forbes-Grant as well. And one of you had exceptional luck. These crimes were the work of a gifted amateur.'

He fumbled in a pocket of his tweed sports jacket and brought out a notebook and glanced down at one of the pages.

Priscilla looked around the room. Every face was tense and strained. Who did it?

'I was not absolutely sure of the identity of the killer until last night,' said Hamish.

Diana's voice rang out, high and sharp. 'You don't know at all! You haven't a clue. You're watching us to see if anyone looks guilty. You've been watching too many films, just like that stupid maid.'

'No,' said Hamish. 'I know who did it. It was you . . . Henry Withering.'

There was a stunned silence.

Then Henry said in an amused voice, 'This is better than the theatre. Do go on. Why on earth should I kill Bartlett?'

'Because Captain Peter Bartlett wrote *Duchess Darling*. Not you.'

'Rubbish,' said Henry calmly. 'It's had reviews

367

in all the papers. It's a box-office smash. He would have said something.'

'You probably changed the title. Captain Bartlett said he only read the racing papers. He knew you had a success. He'd heard that. He did not know it was his play until the night of the party I attended. Miss Smythe quoted a line from the play. Captain Bartlett looked highly amused. You were very angry and told Miss Smythe to shut up. This is how I think it happened.

'Captain Bartlett's aunt, Mrs Frobisher, said the captain had a magpie mind. He was always adopting other people's enthusiasms and hobbies. He even started collecting china after he had been to Sir Humphrey Throgmorton's.'

'What!' exclaimed Sir Humphrey, evidently more shocked by this revelation than by the identity of the murderer.

'He was living with you, Henry Withering, for a short while. You wrote plays. He decided to write one. You made out you had "written down" when you wrote *Duchess Darling*. You said you had produced something silly and trite because that was what the West End theatres wanted. I saw the play in London. I didn't think much about it until afterwards. Whoever wrote that play believed in every silly line. If I looked at it another way round and thought of the personality of Captain Bartlett, then it all made sense.'

'You're talking rot,' said Henry. No-one shrank from him, not even Priscilla. It was obvious that everyone in the room thought Hamish was talking rubbish as well.

'Captain Bartlett left the play behind when he

quit your flat and you found it. After a time, it dawned on you that this might just be what the public wanted. You must have enjoyed tricking them. Anyway, I think Captain Bartlett, who was a notorious gambler and sponger, confronted you with it after the party. I think he would have exposed you at the party in front of everyone – and thereby saved his life – if he had wanted to take the credit. I suggest he told you you could keep the fame so long as you passed all the money over to him. There was something about you, all the same, that made even the bold captain worried. He told me he was sure someone was out to get him. So, as insurance, he told Vera Forbes-Grant. Miss Smythe overheard Vera saying "You can't have. I don't believe it. Not you of all people." '

Hamish turned to Freddy. 'Did your wife have any money of her own, Mr Forbes-Grant?'

'No,' said Freddy dismally. 'Not a penny. I gave her a generous allowance. But not too much. She would have left me if I had given her more. She thought I was stupid, that I didn't know she'd had an affair with Bartlett. I didn't want to lose her. I loved her.' He began to cry in a helpless, dreary way.

'Your wife may have had a soft spot for the captain,' said Hamish, 'but she loved money more than anything or anybody. She knew now what the captain had known.

'Henry was awake that night after the party, watching and waiting. Perhaps he planned to follow Bartlett when the captain went out as planned with Mr Pomfret, wait until they separated, shoot Bartlett, and throw the blame on Mr Pomfret. But he happened to see the captain going out long before the appointed time. Having rigged it to look like suicide, he returned and went to bed, confident he would never be found out. Luck had been on his side. No-one else had been awake when the captain went out.

'Then Vera told him she knew Bartlett was the author of the play. I think Henry agreed to pay her while waiting his chance. As in the first murder, he waited for the right opportunity and seized it. He took a can of roach powder from the cupboard under the sink in the school kitchen, poured it into a bowl of cake mix, and then baked that batch of cakes himself. It was easily done. Everyone was milling about, beating up cake mix and putting cakes in the oven.'

'But Vera couldn't have suspected Henry,' cried Priscilla. 'She believed Freddy had done it. She was proud of him.'

'She wanted to think Freddy had done it. It made her into the *femme fatale* she'd always wanted to be. It removed any fear of Henry. Henry must have denied he murdered Bartlett. He wouldn't have wanted Vera to know that as well. She would have asked for double the money. Henry put the gloves into Freddy's room, a clumsy trick, but it paid off. Freddy thought Vera had murdered Bartlett, and so he confessed.

'I took a lot of the baking to the fair myself. But other people were going up and carrying stuff as well. Henry and Priscilla arrived with Mr and Mrs Wellington. They had boxes of cakes in the car. All Henry had to do was extract his box and put it with all the things he'd bought at the fair.

'I don't think he even needed to give Vera the cakes. He knew her passion for sweet stuff. All he had to do was put them in her room. He had nothing to do with that dummy strung up over her bed. The Chief Superintendent here already knows that was a particularly nasty trick played by Jessica Villiers and Diana Bryce.'

Jessica began to cry, but Diana looked defiantly round the room.

'You can't arrest us for a trick,' she said. '*We* didn't murder Peter.'

'But Henry Withering did,' said Hamish flatly.

Henry leaned his head against the back of his chair. He appeared very relaxed and amused.

'You're guessing and you know it,' he said. 'You haven't a shred of proof.'

Hamish went out to the hall and came back in carrying a large box.

'After the supposed suicide of Bartlett had been discovered to be murder, you gave this parcel to Charles French of London Television News. You told him it was some clothes you didnae want and he was to leave it at their reception desk in London and you would pick it up when you went back south. French didn't think anything about it. You are a famous playwright. Perhaps you gave him some exclusive background.'

Hamish opened the box. 'In here,' he said, 'we have cleaning equipment from the gun room, and a pair of thin plastic gloves like the kind women wear when they're bleaching their hair. In the bathroom cabinet in your room, there was a clutter of stuff left by previous occupants, including a hairdressing product for bleaching the hair. There is also a raincoat stained with gun oil. It was clever of you. The post office would have told us if anyone from the castle had posted a parcel.' He nodded to Anderson and MacNab.

'Wait a bit,' said Colonel Halburton-Smythe. 'You cannot arrest Mr Withering. He's my daughter's fiancé!'

'All right,' said Henry. 'Now you've got that parcel, there's no point in me pretending any longer. But why couldn't it have been anyone other than you, Macbeth? To be found out by the local yokel!' He gave a harsh laugh. 'But it was the way you described it. Peter was sharing my flat. You're right about him adopting other people's enthusiasms. I was working on a play, *Animal Firm*, and he said he never went to the theatre because you couldn't see jolly plays any more. Then he said he would write one. God, how I laughed. But he had tremendous energy and could do without sleep and he worked day and night. Before he could send it to anyone, he started pursuing some girl, I forget her name. He forgot all about the play. Anyway, he wasn't paying any rent, and I told him to leave.

'I came across his stupid play one evening after *Animal Firm*, the best thing I'd ever written, had been rejected by the National Theatre. Peter's play was so awful, it was priceless. I was about to throw it away when I thought suddenly that if I polished it up a bit and changed the title, it might appeal to all the Peter Bartletts of this world who wanted something that wouldn't strain their brains. I gave it to an impresario who thought up the idea of having it expensively dressed and bringing back some of the famous lords and dames of the theatre.

When it took off, I thought I'd better square Peter, but I couldn't find him. I didn't know he'd gone back to the army. When all the publicity began to appear and Peter didn't get in touch with me, I thought I was safe. The title was different and a good lot of the lines were mine – or rather, I'd polished up Peter's lines.

'When I saw him here, I felt sick. But it dawned on me very quickly he hadn't a clue I'd used his play. I didn't think he'd be likely to see it. It was ages since he'd been to the theatre. Then Pruney started quoting from it. He came to my room that night. I told him he had no way of proving it was his play, but he said he could dig up some old friends he had told at the time about it, and that he would make enough of a stink to cast doubts on the authorship. Then he said I could have the fame if he could have the money – all of it. I agreed, but I knew I'd have to kill him. Sooner or later, he'd tell someone. He was proud it had been put on and thought it a famous joke. He wouldn't have kept it secret long, not with the way he drank.' Henry fell silent. Anderson and MacNab moved towards him, but stopped as he began to speak again.

'I didn't think of shooting him. Not at first. I stayed up all night, keeping a watch on his door. I saw Vera go in and Pruney listening, but I couldn't get nearer to hear what was said. I thought if he came out to go on the prowl, I'd push him down the stairs or something like that. I nearly fell asleep, nearly *was* asleep when he came out with his shooting togs on. The rest was as you described. I put the cleaning stuff and a raincoat in that box and hid it in a bush behind one of those pillars at the gates. I knew I had to move the box because sooner or later the police would find it. Funny, if I'd just wiped my fingerprints off everything and dumped it . . . Still, I can't think of everything,' said Henry with a ghastly social smile. 'I gave the parcel to that journalist. He never thought anything odd about it. I was lucky all along. Yes, Vera black-mailed me. I had to make love to her to convince her I was a gentle, caring soul and not a murderer. I promised to pay her to keep quiet about the play. But I knew I'd have to get rid of her as well.' He turned in his chair towards Priscilla, who shrank away from him. 'No publicity is bad publicity. Isn't that right, darling?' As Anderson and MacNab came up on either side of him, he rose to his feet. 'You should see your stupid faces,' he said. And then he began to laugh. He was still laughing as they led him from the room.

The trial of Henry Withering, with all its attendant publicity, was over at last. Priscilla Halburton-Smythe, who had vague thoughts of returning to her job, stayed on at Tommel Castle instead. Winter was settling down on the Sutherland mountains.

Colonel and Mrs Halburton-Smythe had been shocked and shaken over Henry Withering's arrest. Their shock had not improved their attitude to their daughter. Fear of what might have happened to her made them treat her more like a fragile blossom than ever. They kept begging her not to return to London, to stay in Sutherland where it was 'safe' from doubtful suitors such as Henry.

It was when they said they had invited Jeremy

Pomfret to dinner and made it obvious they had begun to look on him in the light of a possible son-in-law that Priscilla decided to make her escape back to London.

Jeremy, who had sworn not to stay at Tommel Castle again, had nonetheless accepted the invitation. He had enjoyed all the publicity surrounding the murder trial and seeing his picture in the newspapers, and so the cold castle had become endowed with a certain glamour in his eyes. It was small comfort to Priscilla that that glamour obviously did not extend to herself. She had not seen Hamish since the day Henry had been accused of murder. Her parents were, irrationally, furious with Hamish, blaming him obscurely for all the notoriety that had descended on their home.

Priscilla thought Hamish might have gone to Strathbane, for surely the solving of two murders would be enough to give a village constable instant promotion. She was surprised one morning to hear Jenkins complaining that Hamish Macbeth was becoming lazier and ruder every day.

All at once Priscilla wanted to see Hamish, to talk about the murder, to talk as much of it out of her brain as possible. It was a forbidden subject at Tommel Castle.

She drove down to Lochdubh, hearing her car tyres crackle over puddles of ice in the road, seeing the snow-capped mountains glittering against a pale blue sky.

The police station looked deserted and, for a moment, she thought Jenkins might have been mistaken and Hamish had left.

She made her way round the back of the station.

Hamish was just climbing over the fence into his garden from the croft at the back, two empty feed pails in his hands. His red hair flamed in the sunlight and his tall, lanky figure looked safe and reassuring.

He stood for a moment watching Priscilla, and then he walked forward.

'I didn't think you were going to speak to me again,' he said.

Priscilla smiled. 'I've been upset and shocked, Hamish. But I've got over it now. I'm thinking of leaving for London next week.'

'Aye, going back to the same job?'

'No, I've lost that. It was a silly little job anyway with a miserable pay. I think I might train for something – computers or something.'

'Come into the kitchen and I'll make us some tea.'

Priscilla followed Hamish into the kitchen and sat down at the table. Towser put his head in her lap and gazed up at her soulfully.

'I thought you would have been promoted,' said Priscilla, stroking Towser's head and watching Hamish as he got the tea-things out of the cupboard.

'Didn't you hear?' said Hamish. 'Poor Mr Chalmers. He died of a heart attack. Blair took the credit for everything. Didn't you read about it in the reports of the trial?'

'I wasn't called as a witness,' said Priscilla, 'and Mummy and Daddy told the servants to stop delivery of the newspapers.'

'I thought Jeremy Pomfret might have told you,' said Hamish, giving her a sidelong look.

'Jessie's been gossiping,' said Priscilla.

'Sounded to me like you were going to be Mrs Pomfret.'

'Let's not talk about Jeremy. Didn't either of those two detectives tell anyone it was you who was responsible for solving the murder?'

'No, they have to work with Blair.'

'But Rory Grant wrote a dramatic exclusive about how you solved the murder.'

'It *was* an exclusive. The other papers, and some of them with much bigger circulations, carried Blair's version. Nobody could write anything until after the trial. *Sub judice.* By that time Chalmers was dead. I'm glad in a way. I like it here.'

'Yes,' said Priscilla, wondering not for the first time why Hamish's homely, cluttered police station always seemed a safer, cosier, and more welcome place than Tommel Castle.

He put a cup of tea in front of her. 'Bring it through to the living room,' he said. 'I've been making some improvements.'

Priscilla obediently walked through to the living room and then stood and looked around. There was a new carpet on the floor, a warm red shaggy carpet. The walls had been newly papered and two pretty chintz-covered armchairs were placed in front of the fire.

'This is lovely, Hamish,' said Priscilla. 'How on earth could you afford all this? I know you send every penny home.'

Hamish grinned. 'I kept a wee bit o' the grouse money back for myself.'

'The grouse money?'

'Aye, it was the morning of the murder. I found

377

Angus, the poacher, dead-drunk down at the harbour with a brace o' grouse in his back pocket. I was going to return them to your father. Well, there was the murder and all. That helicopter was standing by, and after I had taken down the pilot's statement, I remembered Captain Bartlett telling me the pilot had instructions to hand over two thousand pounds for the first brace. So I went to my car where I'd left Angus's birds and took them and handed them over.'

He beamed at her proudly.

Priscilla carefully put down her cup and got to her feet. 'A man had been shot, his chest blown away,' she said in a thin voice, 'and all you could think of, you great moocher, was how to turn it to your advantage!'

She turned and ran from the house.

Hamish stood for a moment, staring at the spot where she had been.

Then he sprinted out of the room, out of the house and into the garden.

Priscilla was standing by her car, leaning her head on the roof. Her shoulders were shaking.

He came cautiously up behind her. 'Dinnae take it so hard,' he pleaded. 'It iss not me who's the murderer.'

She turned round and buried her face on his shoulder.

'Priscilla,' said Hamish suspiciously, 'I have a feeling you're laughing.' He tilted up her head.

'Oh, Hamish,' giggled Priscilla, 'you are the most shocking man I know.'

Hamish rolled his eyes. 'Do you hear?' he cried to a passing sea-gull. 'Here's her that gets engaged tae criminals telling the force of law and order on Lochdubh that he's shocking. Come along ben, Priscilla, and I'll get us something to eat.'

'What? Grouse?' demanded Priscilla, still giggling.

'Aye, I just might hae a wee bit.'

With a companionable arm about her shoulders, he led her towards the police station, pushed her gently inside, followed her in, and closed the door firmly behind them on the cold outside world.

THE END

DEATH OF A HUSSY
by M. C. Beaton

The scenic Highland town of Lochdubh has been shaken up by the arrival Maggie Baird, a hefty and tweed-loving Englishwoman who is determined to become the town's leading lady. But Police Constable Hamish Macbeth – renowned for his sleepy style of policing – is not fooled by her matronly facade, and his intuition proves correct when she mysteriously disappears, and then returns a few months later newly svelte, sleek, and ready to start entertaining a stream of seedy suitors. But before her transformation pays off with a marriage proposal, Maggie is murdered and crime has indeed hit Lochdubh, leading Hamish on a trail marked with passion and greed as he works to discover the truth behind the death of a hussy.

A Bantam Paperback
0 553 40967 0

DEATH OF A GLUTTON
by M. C. Beaton

Peta Gore is the bane of her partner's otherwise successful life. Trying to work with Peta on a matchmaking business that Peta uses mostly for her own purposes, Maria Worth has come to hate her old friend, a noisy, vulgar glutton. But this time Maria is determined to keep her latest singles' event a secret from Peta. The gathering is to be at Tommel Castle Hotel in the remote Scottish village of Lochdubh, the perfect setting for a particularly difficult group. Nothing can go wrong. Except that somehow Peta finds out about the gathering and shows up, thoroughly disgusting everyone. Guests and staff band together in mutual loathing. But does someone hate her enough to kill her?

A Bantam Paperback
0 553 40972 7

DEATH OF A PRANKSTER
by M. C. Beaton

When Police Constable Hamish Macbeth receives the news that there has been a murder at Arrat House, home of the relentless practical joker Arthur Trent, previous experience leads him to suspect that this is no more than another prank. But when he arrives, he finds that Trent is most decidedly dead, having been stabbed and stuffed in a closet. For suspects, there is a houseful of greedy relations, all of whom are more interested in the contents of the will than in the crime at hand. To complicate matters further, Chief Inspector Blair, Hamish's old nemesis, arrives on the scene as determined as ever to stand in the way of Macbeth's investigation. When his former flame, Priscilla Halburton-Smythe, gets involved as well, Hamish quite nearly has his hands full. Accordingly, the charming constable must enliven his sleepy style of detecting – and M. C. Beaton once again offers up a witty and well-crafted mystery peopled with quirky characters and a most endearing sleuth.

A Bantam Paperback
0 553 40967 9

DEATH OF AN OUTSIDER
by M. C. Beaton

Nobody in the Scottish town of Cnothan had liked the abrasive Englishman, and now that he has been murdered – in a most original fashion – nobody much minds. Constable Hamish Macbeth's hard luck is that he happens to be on temporary duty in this cloistered Highlands village when the killer strikes. And he has his work cut out for him, dragging from Mainwaring's close-mouthed neighbours enough facts to start solving this peculiar case. But Hamish is crafty, and with practised aplomb he slowly extracts from the locals a scandalous tale of illicit romance, secret vices, real-estate wheeling and dealing, even witchcraft – all so unbelievable that it can only be true.

A Bantam Paperback
0 553 407937

DEATH OF A PERFECT WIFE
by M. C. Beaton

He has his home, his cattle, hens and geese, his friends and neighbours, and soon, he hopes, he'll have lovely Priscilla Halburton-Smythe as well. God's in his heaven and all's right with the world . . . until someone poisons village newcomer Trixie Thomas.

Being english and unemployed, Paul and Trixie Thomas have two strikes against them from the beginning. But Trixie isn't one to notice when people don't like her and soon she has the whole village involved in her Anti-Smoking League, vegetarian cooking, and birdwatching society. She even wheedles a few bits and pieces of old furniture and china from her frugal Scots neighbours. So when she's murdered, not everyone is devastated. Truth to tell, there is even some quiet rejoicing, and as for motives . . . Hamish is up to his elbows in them.

A Bantam Paperback
0 553 40794 5

DEATH OF A SNOB
by M. C. Beaton

When Jane Wetherby offers Police Constable Hamish Macbeth a 'holiday' at her 'Happy Wanderer' health farm on the isle of Eileencraig, his flagging spirits begin to rise. Thinking that he has finally found the source of some tender, loving care, Hamish is tempted away from his sleepy Highland town of Lochdubh, and his beloved dog Towser. Unfortunately, the visit doesn't prove to be the holiday Hamish had hoped for. Windswept Eileencraig is inhabited by hostile islanders, more than a few of whom would gladly be rid of 'The Happy Wanderer' and its proprietor. The company at the health farm is hardly better, for Jane's volatile party includes an ex-husband, an illicit lover, and Heather Todd, an unadulterated snob who criticizes just about everyone and everything. And when Heather is found lying at the foot of a cliff with a broken neck, no one is too broken-up – and Hamish must enliven his distinctively sleepy style of policing in order to solve the death of a snob.

A Bantam Paperback
0 553 40968 9

A SELECTION OF NOVELS
AVAILABLE FROM BANTAM BOOKS

THE PRICES SHOWN BELOW WERE CORRECT AT THE TIME OF GOING TO PRESS.
HOWEVER TRANSWORLD PUBLISHERS RESERVE THE RIGHT TO SHOW NEW RETAIL
PRICES ON COVERS WHICH MAY DIFFER FROM THOSE PREVIOUSLY ADVERTISED IN
THE TEXT OR ELSEWHERE.

☐	40793 7	**Death of an Outsider**	M C Beaton	£3.99
☐	40794 5	**Death of a Perfect Wife**	M C Beaton	£3.99
☐	40967 0	**Death of a Hussy**	M C Beaton	£3.99
☐	40968 9	**Death of a Snob**	M C Beaton	£3.99
☐	40967 9	**Death of a Prankster**	M C Beaton	£3.99
☐	40972 7	**Death of a Glutton**	M C Beaton	£3.99
☐	50329 4	**Danger Zones**	Sally Beauman	£5.99
☐	40727 9	**Lovers and Liars**	Sally Beauman	£5.99
☐	50326 X	**Sextet**	Sally Beauman	£5.99
☐	50540 8	**Killing Floor**	Lee Child	£5.99
☐	40922 0	**The Juror**	George Dawes Green	£5.99
☐	50475 4	**The Monkey House**	John Fullerton	£5.99
☐	40846 1	**In the Presence of the Enemy**	Elizabeth George	£5.99
☐	40238 2	**Missing Joseph**	Elizabeth George	£5.99
☐	17511 4	**Payment in Blood**	Elizabeth George	£5.99
☐	40845 3	**Playing for the Ashes**	Elizabeth George	£5.99
☐	50385 5	**A Drink Before the War**	Dennis Lehane	£5.99
☐	50584 X	**Darkness, Take My Hand**	Dennis Lehane	£5.99
☐	40884 4	**Fast Forward**	Judy Mercer	£5.99
☐	50619 6	**Dark Skies**	Stan Nicholls	£4.99
☐	50586 6	**Farewell to the Flesh**	Gemma O'Connor	£5.99
☐	50438 X	**Mount Dragon**	Lincoln Preston	£5.99
☐	50496 7	**The Relic**	Lincoln Preston	£5.99
☐	50542 2	**The Poison Tree**	Tony Strong	£5.99

All Transworld titles are available by post from:

Book Service By Post, P.O. Box 29, Douglas, Isle of Man IM99 1BQ

Credit cards accepted. Please telephone 01624 675137,
fax 01624 670923 or Internet http://www.bookpost.co.uk or
e-mail: bookshop@enterprise.net for details.

**Free postage and packing in the UK. Overseas customers allow
£1 per book (paperbacks) and £3 per book (hardbacks).**